"Oh . . . I know you," Diana said, surprised at herself for thinking that he was actually delicious-looking even though everyone else thought so, too. "You're the famous Henry Schoonmaker." She bravely held his gaze. "The one who can't sit still and breaks hearts all over the place. Well, that's what they say, isn't it?"

"Why do you girls always love gossip so much?" he asked in reply. "Do you think all the stories about me are true?"

"If they are true, then you are a very interesting person." She smiled, tucking her lower lip under her teeth.

"Well, I deny them all categorically." He shrugged before continuing: "Except the one about me liking pretty girls, which is more or less true. But how old are you? You can't have been out very long at all. Look at you, you've probably never even been kissed, and you're—"

"I have too been kissed," she interrupted, the way a child would. She felt her cheeks flush, but was too thrilled to be right where she was to really mind.

"Not very well, I'd bet," Henry replied with an arch of his eyebrow.

BOOKS BY ANNA GODBERSEN

The Luxe

Rumors

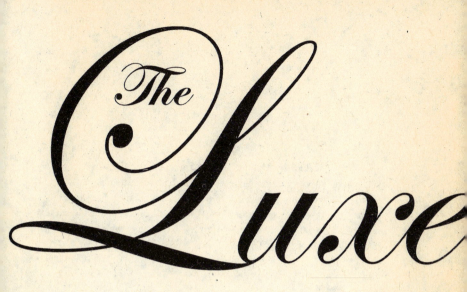

The Luxe

ANNA GODBERSEN

HarperCollins*Publishers*

The Luxe

Copyright © 2007 by Alloy Entertainment and Anna Godbersen

All rights reserved. Printed in the United States of America.

No part of this book may be used or reproduced in any manner whatsoever
without written permission except in the case of brief quotations embodied in critical
articles and reviews. For information address HarperCollins Children's Books, a division
of HarperCollins Publishers, 1350 Avenue of the Americas, New York, NY 10019.

www.harpercollins.com

Produced by Alloy Entertainment
151 West 26th Street, New York, NY 10001

ON THE COVER: Dress by Justin Alexander

Library of Congress Cataloging-in-Publication Data

Godbersen, Anna.

The luxe / Anna Godbersen. — 1st ed.

p.   cm.

Summary: In Manhattan in 1899, five teens of different social classes lead dangerously scandalous lives, despite the strict rules of society and the best-laid plans of parents
and others.

ISBN 978-0-06-134568-5

[1. Conduct of life—Fiction.   2. Social classes—Fiction.   3. Wealth—Fiction.
4. Love—Fiction. 5. Manhattan (New York, N.Y.)—History—19th century—
Fiction.] I. Title.

PZ7.G53888Lux   2007   2007020876
[Fic]—dc22   CIP
                                                                                      AC

Design by Andrea C. Uva
❖
First paperback edition, 2008

For Suzanne and Gordon

It was the old New York way . . . the way of people who dreaded scandal more than disease, who placed decency above courage, and who considered that nothing was more ill-bred than "scenes," except the behaviour of those who gave rise to them.

—Edith Wharton, *The Age of Innocence*

The Luxe

Prologue

On the morning of October 4, 1899, Elizabeth
Adora Holland—the eldest daughter of the
late Mr. Edward Holland and his widow,
Louisa Gansevoort Holland—passed into the
kingdom of heaven. Services will be held
tomorrow, Sunday the eighth, at 10 a.m., at the
Grace Episcopal Church at No. 800 Broadway
in Manhattan.

—FROM THE OBITUARY PAGE OF THE *NEW-YORK NEWS OF
THE WORLD GAZETTE*, SATURDAY, OCTOBER 7, 1899

*I*N LIFE, ELIZABETH ADORA HOLLAND WAS KNOWN not only for her loveliness but also for her moral character, so it was fair to assume that in the afterlife she would occupy a lofty seat with an especially good view. If Elizabeth had looked down from that heavenly perch one particular October morning on the proceedings of her own funeral, she would have been honored to see that all of New York's best families had turned out to say good-bye.

They crowded Broadway with their black horse-drawn carriages, proceeding gravely toward the corner of East Tenth Street, where the Grace Church stood. Even though there was currently no sun or rain, their servants sheltered them with great black umbrellas, hiding their faces—etched with shock and sadness—from the public's prying eyes. Elizabeth would have approved of their somberness and also of their indifferent attitude to the curious workaday people pressed up to the police barricades. The crowds had come to wonder at the passing of that perfect eighteen-year-old girl whose glittering evenings had been recounted in the morning papers to brighten their days.

A cold snap had greeted all of New York that morning, rendering the sky above an unfathomable gray. It was, Reverend Needlehouse murmured as his carriage pulled up to the church, as if God could no longer imagine beauty now that Elizabeth Holland no longer walked his earth. The pallbearers nodded in agreement as they followed the reverend onto the street and into the shadow of the Gothic-style church.

They were Liz's peers, the young men she had danced quadrilles with at countless balls. They had disappeared to St. Paul's and Exeter at some point and then returned with grown-up ideas and a fierce will to flirt. And here they were now, in black frock coats and mourning bands, looking grave for perhaps the first time ever.

First was Teddy Cutting, who was known for being so lighthearted and who had proposed marriage to Elizabeth twice without anyone taking him seriously. He looked as elegant as always, although Liz would have noted the fair stubble on his chin—a telltale sign of deep sorrow, as Teddy was shaved by his valet every morning and was never seen in public without a smooth face. After him came the dashing James Hazen Hyde, who had just that May inherited a majority share of the Equitable Life Assurance Society. He'd once let his face linger near Elizabeth's gardenia-scented neck and told her she smelled better than any of the mademoiselles in the Faubourg Saint-Germain. After James came Brody Parker Fish, whose family's town house neighbored the Hollands' on Gramercy Park, and then Nicholas Livingston and Amos Vreewold, who had often competed to be Elizabeth's partner on the dance floor.

They stood still with downcast eyes, waiting for Henry Schoonmaker, who emerged last. The refined mourners could not help a little gasp at the sight of him, and not only because he was usually so wickedly bright-eyed and so regularly with a drink in hand. The tragic irony of Henry appearing as a pallbearer on the very day when he was to have wed Elizabeth seemed deeply unfair.

The horses drawing the hearse were shiny black, but the coffin was decorated with an enormous white satin bow, for Elizabeth had died a virgin. What a shame, they all whispered, blowing ghostly gusts of air into one another's ears, that an early death was visited on such a very *good* girl.

Henry, his thin lips set in a hard line, moved toward the hearse with the other pallbearers close behind. They lifted the unusually light coffin and stepped toward the church door. A few audible sobs were muffled into handkerchiefs as all of New York realized they would never again look on Liz's beauty, on her porcelain skin or sincere smile. There was, in fact, no Liz, for her body had not yet been recovered from the

Hudson River, despite two days of dragging it, and despite the handsome reward offered by Mayor Van Wyck.

The whole ceremony had come on rather quickly, in fact, although everyone seemed too shocked to consider this.

Next in the funeral cortege was Elizabeth's mother, wearing a dress and a veil in her favorite color. Mrs. Edward Holland, née Louisa Gansevoort, had always seemed fearsome and remote—even to her own children—and she had only become harder and more intractable since her husband's passing last winter. Edward Holland had been odd, and his oddness had only grown in the years before his death. He had, however, been the eldest son of an eldest son of a Holland—a family that had prospered on the little island of Manhattan since the days when it was called New Amsterdam—and so society had always forgiven him his quirks. But in the weeks before her own death, Elizabeth had noticed something new and pitiable in her mother as well. Louisa leaned a little to the left now, as though remembering her late husband's presence.

In her footsteps was Elizabeth's aunt Edith, the younger sister of her late father. Edith Holland was one of the first women to move prominently in society after a divorce; it was understood, though not very much discussed, that her early marriage to a titled Spaniard had exposed her to enough bad humor and drunken debauchery for a whole lifetime. She went by her maiden name now, and looked as aggrieved by the loss of her niece as if Elizabeth had been her own child.

There followed an odd gap, which everyone was too polite to comment on, and then came Agnes Jones, who was sniffling loudly.

Agnes was not a tall girl, and though she appeared well dressed enough to the mourners still pressing against the police line for a better look, the black dress she wore would have been sadly familiar to the deceased. Elizabeth had worn the dress only once—to her father's funeral—and then passed it down. It had since been let out at the waist and shortened at the hem. As Elizabeth knew too well, Agnes's father had met with financial ruin when she was only eleven and had subsequently thrown himself off the Brooklyn Bridge. Agnes liked to tell people that Elizabeth was the only person who had offered her friend-ship in those dark times. Elizabeth had been her *best* friend, Agnes had often said, and though Elizabeth would have been embarrassed by such exaggerated statements, she wouldn't have dreamed of correcting the poor girl.

After Agnes came Penelope Hayes, who was usually said to be Elizabeth's *true* best friend. Elizabeth would indeed have recognized the distinct look of impatience she wore now. Penelope never liked waiting, especially out of doors. One of the lesser Mrs. Vanderbilts standing nearby recognized that look as well, and made a virtually inaudible cluck. Penelope, with her gleaming black feathers, Egyptian profile, and wide, heavily lashed eyes, was much admired but not very generally trusted.

And then there was the fact—uncomfortable to all assembled—that Penelope had been with Elizabeth when her body disappeared into the cold waters of the Hudson. She had, everybody knew by now, been the last person to see Elizabeth alive. Not that they suspected her of anything, of course. But then, she did not look nearly haunted enough. She wore a cluster of diamonds at her throat, and on her arm, the formidable Isaac Phillips Buck.

Isaac was a distant relation of the old Buck clan—so distant that his lineage could never be proved or disproved—but he was still formidable in size, two heads taller than Penelope and robust at the middle. Liz had never cared for him; she had always harbored a secret preference for doing what was practical and right over what was clever and fine. Isaac had never seemed to her like anything more than a taste-monger, and indeed, the gold cap now on his left canine tooth matched the watch chain that extended from under his coat to his pants pocket. If that lesser Mrs. Vanderbilt standing nearby had said aloud what she was thinking—that he looked more flashy than aggrieved—he likely would have taken it as a compliment.

Once Penelope and Isaac passed, the rest of the crowd

followed them into the church, flooding the aisle with their black garb on the way to their familiar pews. Reverend Needle-house stood quietly at the pulpit as the best families of New York—the Schermerhorns and Van Peysers, the Harrimans and Bucks, the McBreys and Astors—took their seats. Those who could no longer stop themselves, even under that lofty ceiling, began to whisper about the shocking absence.

Finally, Mrs. Holland gave the reverend a brusque nod.

"It is with heavy hearts—" Reverend Needlehouse began. It was all he managed to say before the arched door to the church went flying open, hitting the stone wall with a resounding bang. The ladies of New York's polite class itched to turn and look, but of course decorum forbade it. They kept their elaborately coiffured heads facing forward and their eyes on Reverend Needlehouse, whose expression was not making that effort any easier.

Hurrying down the aisle was Diana Holland, the dearly departed's little sister, with a few shining curls coming loose from under her hat and her cheeks pink from exertion. Only Elizabeth, if indeed she could look down from heaven, would have known what to make of the smile disappearing from Diana's face as she took a seat in the first pew.

THE RICHMOND HAYES FAMILY

REQUESTS THE PLEASURE OF YOUR COMPANY

AT A BALL IN HONOR OF THE ARCHITECT

WEBSTER YOUNGHAM

ON THE EVENING OF SATURDAY

THE SIXTEENTH OF SEPTEMBER

AT NINE O'CLOCK AT THEIR NEW RESIDENCE

NO. 670 FIFTH AVENUE

IN THE CITY OF NEW YORK

COSTUMES ARE REQUIRED

"THEY HAVE ALL BEEN ASKING FOR YOU," LOUISA Holland told Elizabeth, quietly but firmly.

Elizabeth had spent eighteen years being groomed as her mother's prized asset and had become, among other things, an expert interpreter of her tones. This one meant Elizabeth was to return to the main ballroom and dance with a partner of her mother's choosing at once, most likely a young man of enviable, if slightly inbred, lineage. Elizabeth smiled apologetically at the girls she had been sitting with—Annemarie D'Alembert and Eva Barbey, whom she had met that spring in France and who were both dressed as courtesans from the Louis XIV era. Elizabeth had just been telling them how very far away Paris seemed to her now, though she had only stepped off the transatlantic steamer and back onto New York soil early that morning. Her old friend Agnes Jones had been perched on the ivory-and-gold striped damask love seat as well, but Elizabeth's younger sister, Diana, was nowhere to be seen. Most likely because she suspected that her behavior was being monitored, which, of course, it was. Elizabeth's irritation at the persistent childishness of her younger sister flared up, but she quickly banished the feeling.

After all, Diana hadn't enjoyed the formal cotillion debut that Elizabeth had two years ago, just after her sixteenth birthday. For the elder Holland sister there had been a year with a finishing governess—she and Penelope Hayes had shared her, along with various tutors—and lessons in comportment, dance, and the modern languages. Diana had turned sixteen last April with no fanfare during Elizabeth's time abroad. The family had still been in mourning for their father, and a big to-do had not seemed appropriate. She had simply started attending balls with Aunt Edith in Saratoga during their summer stay there, so she could hardly be held responsible for seeming a little rough.

"I'm sure you are sorry to leave your friends," Mrs. Holland said, steering her daughter from the feminine hush of the parlor and into the main ballroom. Elizabeth, in her shepherdess's costume of white brocade, looked especially bright and especially tall next to her mother, who was still wearing her widow's black. Edward Holland had passed away at the beginning of that year, and her mother would be in formal mourning for another year at least. "But you seem to be the young lady most in demand for waltzes tonight."

Elizabeth had a heart-shaped face with delicate features

and an alabaster complexion. As a boy who would not enter the Richmond Hayeses' ballroom that evening once told her, she had a mouth the size and shape of a plum. She tried to make that mouth smile appreciatively now, even though she was concerned by her mother's tone. There was a new, unsettling urgency in Mrs. Holland's famously steely presence that Elizabeth had noticed almost as soon as she'd departed from that great ship. She had been gone since her father's burial nine months ago, and had spent all of spring and summer learning wit in the salons and how to dress on the Rue de la Paix and allowing herself to be distracted from her grief.

"I've already danced so many dances tonight," Elizabeth offered her mother.

"Perhaps," she replied. "But you know how very happy it would make me if one of your partners were to propose marriage to you."

Elizabeth tried to laugh to disguise the despair that comment raised in her. "Well, you are lucky I'm still so young, and we have years before I even have to begin picking one of them."

"Oh, no." Mrs. Holland's eyes darted around the main ballroom. It was dizzying, with its frosted glass dome ceiling, frescoed walls, and gilt mirrors, situated as it was at the center of a warren of smaller but equally busy and decadent rooms. Great potted palm trees were set up in a ring close to the walls, shielding the ladies at the room's edge from the frenetic dancers gliding across the tessellated marble floor. There appeared to be four servants to every guest, which seemed ostentatious even to a girl who had spent the last two seasons learning to be a lady in the City of Light. "The one thing we do not have is time," Mrs. Holland finished.

Elizabeth felt a nerve tingle up her spine, but before she could prod her mother about what *that* meant, they were at the perimeter of the ballroom, close to where their friends and acquaintances waltzed, nodding hello to the lavishly outfitted couples gliding across the dance floor.

They were the Hollands' peers, only seventy or so families, only four hundred or so souls, dancing as though there would be no tomorrow. And indeed, tomorrow would probably pass them by while they slept under silken canopies, waking only to accept pitchers of ice water and shoo away the maid. There would be church, of course, but after an evening so glittering and epic, the worshipers would surely be few. They were a society whose chief vocations were to entertain and be entertained, punctuated occasionally by the reinvestment of their vast fortunes in new and ever more lucrative prospects.

"The last man to ask for you was Percival Coddington," Mrs. Holland told Elizabeth as she positioned her daughter next to a gigantic rose-colored marble column. There were several such columns in the room, and Elizabeth felt sure that they were meant to impress as much as to support. The Hayes family, in building their new home, seemed to have seized on every little architectural feature as an opportunity for grandeur. "Mr. Coddington inherited his father's entire estate this past summer," her mother went on, "as you well know."

Elizabeth sighed. The warm thought of the one boy she knew would not be at the Hayeses' costume ball that evening could not have made the looming prospect of Percival Coddington any less appealing. She had known Percival since they were children, when he was the kind of boy who avoided human contact in favor of intentionally harming small animals. He had grown into a man of welling pores and frequent snorts and was known as an obsessive collector of anthropological artifacts, although he himself was too weak-stomached ever to travel on an explorer's ship.

"Stop," scolded her mother. Elizabeth blinked. She hadn't thought she'd betrayed any emotion. "You would not be so complaining if your father were here."

The mention of Mr. Holland caused Elizabeth's eyes to well, and she felt herself softening to her mother's cause.

"I'm sorry," Elizabeth answered, trying to keep her voice level. She felt the dryness in her throat that always preceded tears and willed them away. "It's just that I wonder if the accomplished Mr. Coddington will even remember me when

I have been so long away."

Mrs. Holland sniffed as the Misses Wetmore, who were one and three years older than Elizabeth, passed. "Of course he remembers you. Especially when the alternative is girls like *them*. They look as if they were dressed by the circus," Mrs. Holland commented coldly.

Elizabeth was trying to think of something nice to say about Percival Coddington, and missed what her mother said next. Something about someone being vulgar. Just as her mother pronounced the word, Elizabeth noticed her friend Penelope Hayes on the second-floor mezzanine. Penelope was wearing a ruffled, poppy-colored gown with a low bodice, and Elizabeth couldn't help but feel a little proud to see her friend looking so stunning.

"I shouldn't even have dignified this ball with my presence," Mrs. Holland went on. There was a time when she would not have so much as called on the upstart Hayes women, despite her husband's having accepted a hunting invitation from Jackson Pelham Hayes once or twice, but society's opinion had moved on without her and she had recently begun acknowledging them. "The papers will report that I condone this sort of tacky display, and you know what a headache that will give me."

"But you know it would have been a bigger scandal if we hadn't come." Elizabeth extended her long, slender neck and gave her friend up above a subtle, knowing smile. How she wished she were with her instead, laughing at the poor girl whose bad luck had forced her to dance with Percival Coddington. Penelope, gazing down, let one darkly made-up eyelid fall—her signature slow, smoldering wink—and Elizabeth knew that she was understood. "And anyway," Elizabeth added, turning back to her mother, "you know you never read the papers."

"Right," her mother agreed. "I don't." Then she jutted the one feature she shared with her daughter—a small, dimpled nub of a chin—as Elizabeth offered the subtlest shrug to her best friend on the mezzanine.

They had become friends during that period in her early teens when Elizabeth was most interested in what it meant to be a young lady of fashion. Penelope had shared that interest, though she was ignorant of the rules of the society she so deeply wished to be a part of. Elizabeth, who was only just beginning to care about all those rules, had cultivated her as a friend anyway. She had quickly discovered that she liked being around Penelope—everything seemed sharper and fizzier in the company of the young Miss Hayes. And soon enough Penelope had become a deft player of society's games; Elizabeth could think of no one better to have at her side during an evening's entertainment.

"Oh, look!" Mrs. Holland's voice rang out sharply, bringing Elizabeth's focus back to the ballroom floor. "Here is Mr. Coddington!"

Elizabeth put on a smile and turned to the inevitable fact of Percival Coddington. He attempted a bowlike gesture, his glance darting across the low-cut square of her bodice. Her heart sank as she realized that he was dressed as a shepherd, in green jodhpurs, rustic boots, and colorful suspenders. They *matched*. His hair was slicked back and long at the neck, and he breathed audibly through his mouth as Elizabeth waited for him to ask her to dance.

A moment passed, and then her mother singsonged, "Well, Mr. Coddington, I have brought her to you."

"Thank you," he coughed out. Elizabeth could feel his eyes lingering on her uncomfortably, but she kept herself upright and smiling. She was, by training, a lady. "Miss Holland, will you dance?"

"Of course, Mr. Coddington." She raised her hand so that he could take it. As his damp palm pulled her through the crowd of costumed dancers, she looked back to smile reassuringly at her mother. She could at least have the gratification of seeing her pleased.

Instead, she saw her mother greeting two men. Elizabeth recognized the slender figure of Stanley Brennan first, who had been her father's accountant, and then the imposing figure of William Sackhouse Schoonmaker, patriarch of the old Schoonmaker clan, who had made a second fortune in railroads. His only son, Henry, had dropped out of Harvard back in the spring, and since then the daughters of New York's elite families had talked of nothing else. At least, the letters Elizabeth received from Agnes while she was in Paris were full of his name, and how all the girls were aching for him. He had a younger sister, Prudie, who was a year or two younger than Diana, though she wore only black and was rarely seen because she disliked crowds. Elizabeth's impression of Henry Schoonmaker was still vague, though she had seen him and heard his name spoken often enough in their younger years, usually attached to some prank or other.

Elizabeth's partner must have sensed her thoughts going elsewhere, because he brought her attention back with a pointed comment. "Maybe you *wanted* to stay in the drawing room with the ladies," Percival said, bitterness surfacing in his voice.

Elizabeth tried not to stumble on her partner's poor footwork. "No, Mr. Coddington, I am just a little tired is all," she told him, not entirely falsely. Her ship had missed its arrival date by three days; she had been home for less than twenty-four hours. She barely had her land legs yet, and here she was dancing. Her mother had insisted by letter that she not retain the services of her French maid, so she had been left to do her own hair and care for her clothing all by herself during the entire journey. Penelope had stopped by in the afternoon to teach her the new dance steps and to tell her how furious she would have been had the ship been any later and caused her best friend to be a no-show on one of the most important nights of her life. Then she'd gone on about some new secret beau, whose identity she would reveal to Elizabeth later, as soon as they had a moment alone. There were simply too many servants hovering during those pre-ball hours for the naming of names to be prudent. Penelope had seemed even more competitive about her looks and dress than usual—because of the boy and because the ball was the debut of her family's new home, Elizabeth assumed. Also adding to Elizabeth's strain, of course, was her mother's odd behavior.

Plus there had already been quadrilles, and dinner, and polite talk with several of her aunts and uncles. She had had to give the same account of her rocky transatlantic passage several times already. And just when Elizabeth had finally sat down with friends for a glass of champagne and a little talk about how absolutely stunning everything was, she had been forced back into the center of activity. To dance with Percival Coddington, of all people. But she kept smiling, of course. It was her habit.

"Well, what are you thinking about, then?" Percival frowned and pressed his hand into her lower back. Elizabeth couldn't think of anyone she would trust less to move her backward across a floor of exuberant, slightly tipsy people.

"Uh . . ." Elizabeth started, realizing that she had been

thinking that even the drawing room was not a total respite. Truthfully, she had been just a little bit relieved to leave Agnes, even though Agnes was such a loyal friend, because the leather-fringed dress she wore was ill-fitting and unflatteringly tight. Elizabeth had been distracted with pity during their entire conversation. Agnes seemed, especially next to her new glamorous Parisian friends, like an embarrassing remnant of childhood.

She focused again on Percival's animated, ugly face and tried to keep her feet going *one, two, three* across the floor. She thought about the evening thus far—all the hours of mindless chatter and carefully accepted compliments, all the studious attention to appearances. She recalled the calculated luxury of her time in Paris. What had she been doing, *really doing*, all this time? What had *he*—that boy she had been trying so hard to forget, indeed believed she *had* forgotten—been doing all that time she was away? She wondered if he had stopped caring for her. Already she could feel the stunning weight of a lifetime of regret for letting him go, and she knew that it was enough to bury her alive.

All at once the room turned mute and violently bright. She closed her eyes and felt Percival Coddington's hot breath on her ear asking if she felt all right. Her corset, which her maid, Lina, had practically sewed her into hours earlier, felt suddenly, horribly constricting. Her life, she realized, had all the charm of a steel trap.

Then, as quickly as the panic had come, it went. Elizabeth opened her eyes. The sounds of joy and giddy indulgence came rushing back. She glanced up at the great domed ceiling glowing above them and reassured herself that it had not fallen.

"Yes, Mr. Coddington, thank you for asking," Elizabeth finally responded. "I'm not sure what came over me."

Two

Cloakroom, one o'clock.

Bring ciggies.

—DH

$\mathcal{D}$IANA HOLLAND SAW HER MOTHER ASCEND THE twisting marble staircase on the far side of the ballroom, supported by some big older fellow whom she felt sure she knew. Their family friend and accountant, Stanley Brennan, trailed behind. Just before they moved out of view and toward some surely lavish second-story smoking room, Mrs. Holland looked back, caught Diana's eye, and gave her an admonishing glance. Diana cursed herself for being spotted and then briefly considered staying in the great central ball-room to wait patiently for one of her cousins to ask her to dance. But patience was not in Diana Holland's nature.

Besides, she had been so proud of her cunning in writing the little invitation during a freshening-up in the ladies' dressing room earlier in the evening. She'd then slipped it to the architect Webster Youngham's assistant, who was stationed near the arched entryway in order to explain the many architectural references that had been incorporated into the Hayes family's new home. She had pushed her way through the crowd, curtsied, clasped his hand, and palmed him the note. "You truly are an artist, Mr. Youngham," she'd said, knowing full well that Mr. Youngham was already drunk on Madeira and lounging in one of the card rooms upstairs.

"But I'm not Mr. Youngham," he told her, looking adorably confused. As soon as she saw that look, Diana knew she'd hooked him. "I'm James Haverton, his assistant."

"Nevertheless." She winked before disappearing back into the crowd. Haverton had broad shoulders and dreamy gray eyes, and even if he was just an assistant, he seemed like somebody who had gone places and done things. She hadn't seen anyone nearly so nice-looking in the intervening hour.

So Diana picked up her skirt and moved quickly between the enormous planters and the wall. She looked behind her once before leaving the ballroom to make sure no one was watching and then slipped into the cloakroom. It was massive and overly ornamented, Diana thought, especially for a room that was chiefly occupied by coats. It didn't matter to *them* that the room was Moorish-themed, with a colorful mosaic floor and antiquities displayed in the turret-shaped alcoves carved from the walls.

Diana looked around her, trying to locate her French lieutenant's coat. She had come dressed as the heroine of her favorite novel, *Trilby*, who appears for the first time on a break from her job as an artist's model in a petticoat and slippers and a soldier's coat. Diana had not been allowed to wear a petticoat without a skirt, but she felt the thrill of having gotten away with something just wearing the rest of the costume at all. Her mother had even had a shepherdess costume made for her so that she would match her older sister, Elizabeth, which would have been hideous in addition to humiliating. Instead, here she was in a satisfyingly bohemian red-and-white striped skirt and a simple cotton bodice that she had ripped in a few places on the sly. No one got it, of course—all the other girls Diana's age were conformists at heart and seemed to have dressed up as themselves, only with more powder and artificially narrowed waists.

She was just beginning to wonder if one of the servants hadn't mistaken her perfectly shabby gray coat for her own, when she was startled by one single clang from the clock in the corner. She gasped, surprised, and stepped backward—a little unsteadily after all the champagne she'd been sneaking—and when she did, she felt the chest of a man and a pair of hands on her hips. Her whole body flushed with adrenaline.

"Oh, hello." She tried to make her voice flat and indifferent, even though this was by far the most exciting thing that had happened to her all evening.

"Hello," Haverton's mouth was very close to her ear.

Diana turned slowly and met his eyes. "I hope you brought cigarettes," she said, trying not to smile too much.

Haverton had short, straight eyebrows set far apart, which made his eyes look open and earnest. "I didn't think ladies of your class were allowed to smoke."

Diana affected a pout. "So you didn't bring ciggies?"

He paused, his eyes lingering on her in a way that made her feel not at all like a lady. "Oh no, I brought them. It's just that I'm not sure whether I should give you one or not. . . ." Diana noticed a little mischief shining in his eye, and concluded that it must be the glimmer of a kindred spirit.

"What do I have to do to convince you?" she asked, turning her head jauntily.

"This is serious, what you are asking me to do," he replied with an air of put-on gravity. Then he laughed. Diana liked the sound of it. "You're pretty," he told her, smiling unabashedly now.

Diana and her sister could not have shared more physical characteristics and looked less alike. Like Elizabeth, she had the small features and round mouth of the Holland women, although she still had the softness of her baby fat. She liked to think that her dark hair added a certain mystery, although it was in truth a sort of medium brown, and untamable. Her eyes were always being described as *vivid*. And of course she and her sister had the same chin—their mother's. She hated her chin. "Oh, I'm all right," she answered him, glowing with false modesty.

"Much better than all right." He continued to observe her as he pulled a cigarette case out of his breast pocket. He lit one and handed it to her.

Diana took a drag and tried not to cough. She loved smoking—or at least the idea of smoking—but it was hard to practice doing it right with her mother and the staff always watching her. She was pulling it off, though—at least she thought she was—exhaling little puffs into the air. It felt right, especially with all the metallic and turquoise detail in the room suggesting some hazy, far-off locale. She raised an eyebrow, wondering how Haverton was going to make his move. "So, if you're an architect, does that make you an artist?"

"Depends whom you ask," he replied lightly. "Some of us like to think that we make the most monumental and lasting kind of art."

"That's very nice," Diana said blithely. "Because you see, I have been trying to find a real artist all night."

"Whatever for?" he asked, leaning into the coats and putting his cigarette to his mouth.

"Well, to kiss, of course." Diana drew her breath in after she spoke. Even she was occasionally surprised by the audacious things that came out of her mouth.

Haverton exhaled thoughtfully, the smoky sweet smell of tobacco surrounding them. For a moment, Diana felt like she could have been a million miles off in a tent hidden away in some souk in Tunis or Marrakech, arranging for secret deals in magic powders.

"It occurs to me," Haverton started, the hard edges of his American voice reminding her that she was still in New York, on a street as familiar as Fifth Avenue, no less, "that you are being a very naughty girl."

"You think so?" Diana asked, dragging on her cigarette amusedly. She, too, sank into the soft wall of coats, moving a little closer to Haverton.

"Well, how often do young ladies of your class meet strange older men in oversize closets, with all of society a few heartbeats away?"

"What makes you think there is any comparison between me and the girls of *my class*?" Diana pronounced the last two words in disgust. The girls of her class were slaves to rules, going about life—if you could call it that—like bloodless mannequins. "I told you I was looking for an artist," she went on impatiently. "So if you're going to go on thinking conventionally and just like everybody else, I may as well leave."

Haverton smiled and dropped his cigarette onto the black-and-white marble-tiled floor. He stepped on it before shooing it to the corner with his toe. He looked very old to Diana all of a sudden, even though he couldn't have been more than twenty. Then he was moving toward her fast. As soon as their lips touched, she knew there wasn't going to be any magic. This was not the heart-stopping touch that she had been waiting for all evening, and it didn't help especially that his style of kissing was akin to mashing one face against another. Her whole body went slack with the disappointment.

Diana kissed him back, just to make sure her instinct was correct, but she had been kissed before, and she knew what it felt like when it was good. Haverton ranked far below Amos Vreewold, whom she had kissed several times in Saratoga over the summer, and only slightly better than her first kiss, at age thirteen, which had been so acrid an affair that she had banished the boy's identity from even her own memory. Diana was finally accepting the fact that James Haverton, architect's assistant, was not the kind of artist she was looking for when the door creaked and a foot sounded at the threshold.

"Miss Diana—?" said a male voice, more hurt than shocked.

Diana felt Haverton's grip tighten momentarily as they turned toward the door. Diana recognized Stanley Brennan's long, tired face immediately. He was only twenty-six—he had taken over from his father as Mr. Holland's accountant—but his constant anxiety gave him a prematurely aged appearance.

"Your mother. She sent me to check on you . . ." he said haltingly. "To make sure you weren't getting into trouble."

Haverton let go of Diana's waist and stepped back. He didn't look especially pleased by Brennan's entrance, but he kept quiet. Diana felt freer almost instantly, rejoicing as she was in having Haverton's rough chin off her face.

"Thank you, Brennan," she said. "Would you like to accompany me back to the ballroom?"

Brennan stepped forward cautiously, reaching toward the rips that Diana had put in her costume. They had widened during the poor excuse for a tryst.

"Oh, stop, it's fine." She lifted her arm for him to take. Then she turned to Haverton. "Thank you for explaining the Islamic references in the Richmond Hayeses' coatroom to me. I will remember it always."

She looked back once, and imagined that the grimace on Haverton's face was the beginning of his life as a lonely man broken by disappointments. It was her fate to leave such casualties in her wake, she thought as she and Brennan exited and walked in the direction of the main ballroom.

"I won't tell your mother," Brennan whispered as their shoes shuffled along the gleaming marble corridor. "Though I feel, as your late father's friend, that I should remind you that that kind of behavior could be your ruin."

"I'm not afraid," Diana said gaily.

"You're like my little sister almost, and it is my responsibility to look after you. Your mother thinks so, anyway." He stopped walking, as if to convey his seriousness. "If she found out what you had been up to and that I knew about it, that would be the end of both of us."

"Well, that is very true." Diana paused next to him. They could already hear the shouting and music from the ballroom, and in a moment they would be swept back under the bright lights. Diana turned the corners of her mouth down in a fake pout, even while her eyes shone with flirtation. "But would that really be so bad?"

Then she laughed, grabbed Brennan's hand, and pulled him back into the center of things. She was searching for an inexpressible *something*, and she wasn't about to let one sour little kiss slow her down.

Three

Not sure if I can make it
to your party tonight.
My apologies, if this is the case.

—HS

"LITTLE BO PEEP. THAT'S TOO PERFECT FOR LIZ,"
Penelope Hayes said, as she said nearly everything, with a quarter ounce of venom.

"Well, at least she didn't forget her humble American origins while she was swanning about with the Frenchies," her friend Isaac Phillips Buck replied. "And at least she didn't go bland marquis et marquise like everybody else," he added with a sniff.

Penelope gave a careless shrug. If he wanted to praise Elizabeth Holland, whom she had long ago singled out as her principal rival and thus her only possible best friend, and who was now circling the polo-field-size dance floor with that toad Percival Coddington, it was fine with her. She was feeling entirely better now that she had seen how very impressed everyone was by her family's new house and hosting style. And, of course, by her.

There had been a dark moment earlier, when the messenger arrived with the note. She had just returned from the

Hollands', where she had gone to welcome Elizabeth back and chastise her for nearly missing the party. Her heart had clenched, reading the careless missive, and then she had flown into a rage that—she could admit this now—had not been especially fair to the maids attending to her before the party. It was not so much that she feared the writer of the note would not come to love her—how long could any boy hold out, really?—but that this particular boy might miss this particular party. After all, what better place for him to realize she was truly the center of the universe, and that keeping their relationship secret was a colossal waste?

Now, observing her family's ballroom from the mezzanine, her torso cinched beneath her flamenco dancer's red flounces to a perfect eighteen inches, she felt supremely confident that he would come. It was the evening of the Richmond Hayeses' ball, the evening when they reached their apotheosis as a top-drawer family—there was simply no place else to be. She was certain he would arrive shortly. Well, almost certain. Penelope rested a confident hand on her hip even as she clenched and unclenched her fist around the note in her other hand.

"Would you look at Elizabeth, holding herself so high and mighty," Penelope said. The dozens of delicate yellow-gold bangles lining her forearms jangled.

Isaac drew himself up to his full height and rested his

hands on his rotund belly, which went undisguised by his jester outfit. "I think she is trying to keep out of the way of Percival's breath."

Then they laughed, as they always laughed: mouths closed and through their noses. Penelope and Elizabeth hadn't really become friends until they shared a French tutor in their early teens. (Later Penelope had overheard that this arrangement had been thought up by Mr. Holland to perturb Mrs. Holland, and had never forgotten the slight.) He had been an adorable and lanky fellow whom Elizabeth used to enjoy making blush by asking him, for instance, to explain the difference between *décolletage* and *décolleté*. It was comical what lengths Elizabeth seemed to go to these days to prove what a proper little miss she was. Penelope never worried so much over anything, especially not whether she was perceived as a lady.

Which was all well and good, since Penelope *was* something less than a lady, at least from the point of view of members of the old Dutch families like Elizabeth's mother, who nonetheless had been enjoying the lavishness of the Hayeses' ballroom all evening. A ballroom, Penelope couldn't help but thinking, far more vast and sparkling than the Holland ballroom. The Hollands lived in an old and really rather plain sort of mansion in Gramercy Park with a staid brown face and the rooms all in neat rows. And that wasn't even a fashionable part of town anymore.

Penelope might have felt bad for Liz that she still lived in such a backwater while the Hayes family had moved on to Fifth Avenue uptown, with its strip of grand new residences, except that she knew very well Liz's mother was always talking about the Hayeses and how they were a made-up family. Which was a rather harsh way of looking at it. It was true that the Hayes fortune had begun when Penelope's grandfather, Ogden Hazmat Jr., gave up his modest tailoring business in Maryland and began selling cotton blankets to the Union army for the price of wool. But ever since Granddad had moved to New York, changed his name, and bought a Washington Square town house from a bankrupt branch of the Rhinelander family, the Hayes clan had been entrenched in New York society.

Now they'd left Washington Square behind forever, and resituated themselves in the only private home in New York with three elevator banks and a basement swimming pool. They had arrived, and they had the mansion to prove it. Or a *palazzo*, as her mother consistently and irritatingly referred to it.

"Good work tonight, Buck," Penelope said, her full lips breaking into a smile of enormous pride. In parlor chatter, Penelope's beauty was occasionally derided as being all lips, but the jabbering hens who said so were certainly in error: Penelope's lips were no more striking than her eyes, which were wide and blue and capable of welling with innocence or scorn in equal measure.

"Only for you," he replied in his nasally faux-British accent. Isaac had something of a case of Anglomania, and it had lately spread to his diction.

Since Isaac was only half-acknowledged by the Buck clan as one of their own, he was obliged to work for a living, and had made himself indispensable to hostesses like Mrs. Hayes. He always knew where to get the freshest flowers, and where to find handsome young men who were willing to dance and fun to dance with, even if they weren't exactly marriageable. He knew how to shriek at the cooks so that the meats would come out just done enough. Isaac's shriek was not pretty, but his parties always were.

"I have to say," Isaac went on drolly, "everyone does look their best this evening. It wasn't *all* in vain. I mean, the jewels alone. You could buy Manhattan with those jewels."

"Yes," Penelope agreed. "Though it never fails to shock me how people can dump a trainload of baubles over some piece of hide."

"Oh, that's just Agnes you're talking about, and she barely has any baubles. Anyway, I think she's supposed to be Annie Oakley, and I believe if you queried her dressmaker, he would say the getup was *suede*."

"Hah. You know very well that Agnes doesn't have a

dressmaker, Buckie." Penelope smirked. "And Amos Vree-wold as a matador? Please." She turned to her friend, one dark eyebrow high.

"Now, now. It's not every man who can look dignified in tights."

"Oh, look—there's Teddy Cutting!" Penelope inter-rupted the survey of costumes. Teddy, with his blond hair and sparkly blue eyes and inherited shipping fortune, was just the sort of boy Penelope had been flirting with at balls since she'd come into society two years ago. Teddy had a crush on Eliza-beth Holland, which was the real reason Penelope always made a point of dancing with him. She watched as the young women, with their great starched skirts and puffed sleeves, flocked to Teddy, who bowed gallantly and went about kissing each of their gloved hands.

"Teddy looks yummy." Isaac let one hand float up to his chin. "He chose French courtier like everybody else, but he did do it well."

"Well enough," Penelope replied nonchalantly, for wherever Teddy went, there was usually a certain someone even bet-ter just behind. She snapped her fingers at one of the passing waiters, balled up the note she had received earlier in the day, and dropped it into her empty champagne glass. She placed her glass on his tray without meeting his eyes and then helped herself to two more flutes.

That was when Henry Schoonmaker strode through the arched entryway at the far end of the ballroom and the whole world seemed to faint just a little bit. Penelope kept herself upright, even as her heart began to beat triumphantly and her face tingle in anticipation. Even among the dashing and rich, Henry Schoonmaker stood out for being so beautiful and so slippery at once. He came to his friend Teddy's side, and Penelope rolled her eyes as he began kissing the flurry of gloved hands as well.

Henry always looked in good humor and good health—which was due in part to his penchant for outdoor sports and in part to the drink that was his constant accessory—and even from across the largest private ballroom in New York City, the tanned perfection of his skin was evident. He had the shoulders of a general and the cheekbones of a born aristocrat, and his mouth was most often fixed in an expression of mild mockery. Like Elizabeth Holland, Henry was the descendant of one of New York's great families, but he was much, much less concerned with being *good*.

"Those girls are embarrassing themselves," Penelope remarked of her cousins and friends below. She ran her fingers over her slick dark hair, which was parted sharply along the middle of her scalp and drawn down to the nape of her neck, framing the perfect oval of her face. Intricate silver filigreed combs fanned out behind her head. "I think I'm going to go save our friend," she added, as though the thought had just occurred to her.

Then she gathered up the yards of red crepe de chine covering her legs and began to glide toward the curving marble staircase.

"Buckie," she called, a few steps down the stairway. She turned to meet his eyes with a look of particular intensity. "That's the man I'm going to marry."

Isaac raised his champagne flute, and Penelope beamed with her declaration. How could she fail when she had somebody as wily as IPB on her side? Penelope turned back down the stairs and in a few moments she was standing on the main floor of her ballroom. A reverential hush settled on the room as the faces in the crowd turned toward her in a wave. Amongst all the white satin and powdered wigs, her red dress made her stand out even more than usual. She cut through the group of girls she had just pronounced fools and reached Henry Schoonmaker in a few breathless moments.

"Who let you in?" She greeted him without a smile. She placed her fist on her hip, causing the gold, gypsy-style bracelets to clatter down her wrist. "*You're* not wearing a costume. And it said very clearly on your invitation that this was to be a costume ball."

Henry turned to her with a face of casual amusement, not even bothering with a faux self-conscious examination of his black tails and trousers. "Have I done wrong, Miss Hayes? See, I don't have time to read my mail anymore, but a little bird told me you would be having a party tonight. . . ."

It was whispered among the women of New York that Henry always had the band paid off in advance, because they frequently struck up a waltz just precisely when he needed to end a conversation. The band began playing now, and Henry gave a gentle nod in Penelope's direction. She could not stop the corner of her mouth from twitching, smile-like, for a moment. He kept his intense gaze fixed on her as he began walking her backward into the room until they were waltzing.

For a moment the crowd just watched, dazzled by the lightness of the couple moving across the floor. But Penelope was very good at arousing jealousy, and her cousins and friends were not very good at standing still when they were jealous. Soon other, less bright couples began dancing, too, so that the gleaming pattern of the marble floor was blotted out by the bright swinging skirts of the girls and the nimble black feet of their partners.

There were plenty of eyes still on the flamenco dancer and the dandy in tails; Penelope knew how much she was watched, so she spoke quietly as they moved. "Why did you send me that note?" she asked, tilting her head slightly as they turned.

"I like teasing you," he answered. "This way, I knew you'd be especially grateful to see me."

Penelope considered this for a moment, but there was something in his lively, deep brown eyes that told her he was lying, just a little bit. "You were someplace else before you came here, weren't you?"

"Now, what would make you think a thing like that?" he replied with unwavering amusement. "I've been looking forward to this precise moment all day."

"You lie very well," she told him. "But I knew you wouldn't stay away."

Henry stared at her carelessly and did not answer. He just pressed his hand into her skirt, somewhat lower than the small of her back, and kept moving her through the crowd. She felt in that moment as though they were a known item, and that all those lesser girls were already crying into their hankies at the thought of Henry William Schoonmaker being married. The music seemed to be playing triumphantly and just for her. She could have gone on like this forever. She might have, too, had not the large, whiskery figure of Henry's father appeared over his shoulder and pulled him out of the dance.

"Pardon me, Miss Hayes," the elder Mr. Schoonmaker said in a voice that was level but devoid of apology. The rest of the dancers kept moving, but Penelope found herself horribly stalled in the center of everything, her great performance curtailed by this large, odious parental presence. She felt a fit coming on but somehow managed to contain it. The other dancers were pretending not to notice what was going on, but they were all terrible fakers. Penelope wondered if Elizabeth was out there watching. She had wanted to reveal her secret relationship to her friend with maximum drama, and this exchange wasn't helping anything. "I am going to have to borrow Henry for the rest of the night. It's quite urgent, and we must leave immediately, I'm afraid."

Instinct made Penelope smile even through her misery, and she tipped her head. "Of course," she answered. Then she watched, alone, from the middle of that epic room, as her future husband disappeared amongst all those ordinary bodies. Penelope knew, despite the still-dancing masses, that for her the party was over.

THIS IS TO CERTIFY THAT I,

WILLIAM SACKHOUSE SCHOONMAKER,

DO LEAVE ALL MY WORLDLY POSSESSIONS,

AS ITEMIZED BELOW, INCLUDING ALL

HOLDINGS RELATING TO BUSINESS,

REAL ESTATE, AND PERSONAL PROPERTY,

TO _____.

*H*ENRY SCHOONMAKER PRETENDED TO STUDY THE piece of paper for another moment, and then he did what he always did when he found something too serious or too boring to bother trying to comprehend. He spread his long thin lips back from his perfectly white teeth and laughed.

"Awful morbid, Dad," he said. "We left a party for this?"

His father stared back at him, large and unsmiling in his black suit and thick, dark muttonchops. William Schoonmaker had small eyes skilled in intimidation and dyed his hair an inky black out of vanity. Because of his frequent turns to rage, his skin was a patchy red, and his mustache curled down around his pink chin. But one could see, under all that, the fine, aristocratic features that he had bequeathed to his son.

"*Everything* is a party to you," his father finally said in reply. Henry saw the father he knew best emerge now—the full, unpleasant personality Mr. Schoonmaker reserved for when he was in his own home or office. Henry had been raised by his governesses, and so his father had always seemed a distant and awesome figure, charging about the house while a fleet of underlings made awkward, obsequious gestures in the vain attempt to please him.

Henry pushed the sheet of paper back across the polished walnut pedestal table toward his father and stepmother, Isabelle, and hoped he wouldn't be bothered about it again for the rest of the evening. Isabelle smiled apologetically at him and gave a surreptitious little roll of her eyes. She was twenty-five—only five years older than Henry himself, and they had often been dance partners before her marriage last year to the richest and most powerful of the Schoonmaker men. It was almost strange to see her in his own house; she still looked like Isabelle De Ford, who was always good for a flirt and a laugh. It might have been all about money, but Henry still felt secret respect toward the old man for winning her.

"You shouldn't be so hard on Henry," she said in a high, girlish voice and brushed a golden curl away from her face.

"Shut up," his father replied in his deep rasp, without so much as turning to look at her. Isabelle made a frowning face and continued playing with her hair. "Get those silly looks off your faces, both of you. Henry, pour yourself a drink."

Henry did not like to appear overly obedient to his father, and they avoided each other enough that indeed he rarely had the opportunity. But there was about his father the rangy, discriminating air of all extraordinarily powerful men, and there was a part of Henry that craved his attention, that longed for the man to notice his actions and approve. At this particular moment, however, he chose to listen to his father because what he most wanted in all the world was a drink. He crossed the room and poured himself a Scotch from one of the cut-glass decanters on the side table.

The room was dark and heavy with the cigar smoke that attended all his father's dealings. The walls and ceilings were of ornate carved wood—the virtuoso Italian craftsmanship so familiar to Henry that he barely noticed it anymore. So this was the sort of place where business got done, Henry mused with a touch of wonder. His life was so absolutely crammed with play that the serious mood of this room felt like a foreign territory. Earlier, he had dined at Delmonico's on Forty-fourth Street, and then there had been an interlude at one of those downtown saloons where one could hear rags and dance with working girls, and then off to Penelope's grand fete. He got a little perverse thrill from being slightly tipsy in the midst of his father's serious decor.

The elder Schoonmaker shifted in his seat. His young bride yawned. "So tell me about you and Miss Hayes," Henry's father said abruptly.

Henry sniffed his drink and studied himself in the mirror

over the bar. He had the smooth chin and slender features of a man of leisure, and his dark hair was pomaded to the right. "Penelope?" he repeated thoughtfully. Though he had little or no desire to discuss his romantic entanglements with his father, it was a subject mildly preferable to family wills.

"Yes," his father urged him on.

"Everyone thinks she is one of the great beauties of her generation." Henry thought of Penelope, with her gigantic eyes and dramatic red dress, which seemed calculated to frighten people as much as to seduce them. He knew from personal experience that Penelope was not frightening—but then, he knew how to enjoy her. He wished he were back at the party, moving her exquisite body across the dance floor.

"And you?" his father went on. "What do you think?"

"I very much enjoy her company." Henry took a sip of Scotch and savored the burning tingle against his lips.

"So you want to . . . marry her?" his father asked, leadingly.

Henry couldn't help a little snort at that. He caught Isabelle staring at him, and he knew that she was now thinking not like a stepmother, but like all the other girls of New York, obsessing over how and when Henry Schoonmaker would marry. He lit a cigarette and shook his head. "I haven't met a girl I could think about so seriously, sir. As you have often pointed out, I am not serious about much."

"Then Penelope is not someone you could see as your wife," his father confirmed, leveling his fierce eyes at Henry.

Henry shrugged, remembering last April when Penelope had been staying in the Fifth Avenue Hotel. Her family had left their old house on Washington Square, and the new one wasn't yet completed. Even though he hardly knew her, she'd invited him up to the suite she'd had all to herself and welcomed him in nothing more than stockings and a shirtwaist. "No, Dad. I don't think so."

"But the way you were dancing . . ." He paused. "Never mind. If you don't want to marry her, that's good. Very good." He clapped, stood, and came around the table to tower over Henry. "Now, who do you think would make a good wife?"

"For me?" Henry asked, managing to keep his face straight.

"Yes, you good-for-nothing boulevardier," his father spat out, his momentary good humor quickly evaporating. The famous Schoonmaker rage was one parental touch that Henry had not been deprived of in his childhood, and it had arisen at everything from broken toys to bad manners. William Schoonmaker sat down noisily in the baby-soft leather club chair next to Henry. "You don't think I'm just idly curious about your paramours, do you?"

"No, sir," Henry replied, blinking his dark lashes at his father. "I do not."

"Then you're smarter than I give you credit for."

"Thank you, sir," Henry said, meaning it. He wished his voice wouldn't get so small at times like these.

"Henry, I find your louche lifestyle personally offensive." His father stood again, pushing the club chair backward across the parquet floor, and began circling the table. "And I am not the only one."

"I'm sorry for that, Dad, but it's my lifestyle, not yours," Henry replied. He had regained his voice and was forcing himself to keep his gaze steady in his father's direction. "Or anybody else's."

"Possible, but doubtful," his father went on, "since it is my money—inherited, yes, but multiplied many times over by my hard work—that has allowed your lifestyle."

"Are you threatening me with poverty?" Henry asked, glancing at the will as he lit a new cigarette with the old one. He tried to look careless as he exhaled, but even saying the word *poverty* gave him an unpleasant feeling in his stomach. The word had a sick lilt to it, he had always thought. His first semester at Harvard he had shared a suite with a scholarship boy named Timothy Marfield—his father's idea of character-building, Henry later discovered. Timothy's father clerked twelve-hour days at a Boston bank to pay his son's tuition, and Henry liked Tim, who knew all the best watering holes in Cambridge. But it was the first time Henry had ever really thought about someone doing that soul-crushing thing called working, and the realization still haunted him.

"Not exactly. Poverty does not become a Schoonmaker," his father finally answered. "I am here to suggest an alternative course. One I think you will find far more palatable than an empty bank account," he went on, lowering his head and staring into his son's eyes. "Marriage."

"You want me to *marry*?" Henry asked, fighting back a laugh. There was no one less marriageable in all of New York, and even those sycophantic, underpaid society columnists knew *that*. He tried to picture a girl with whom he would actually want to trip across the lawns of Newport or the decks of European luxury liners forever—but his powers of imagination failed him. "You can't be serious."

"I certainly am." His father glowered at him.

"Oh." Henry shook his head slowly, hoping to appear to be considering his father's proposal. "There would have to be a long search, of course, to find a girl worthy of becoming a Mrs. Schoonmaker . . ." he offered.

"Shut up, Henry." His father wheeled back around the room and put his large hands on his young wife's shoulders. She smiled uncomfortably. "You see, I already have someone in mind."

"*What?*" Henry said, his cool beginning to evaporate.

"Someone with class and sophistication and good family

breeding. Someone whom the press likes and will embrace as your bride. As a *Mrs. Schoonmaker*, Henry. Someone who will come across as a conduit of civility and culture. I am thinking of—"

"Why do you care?" Henry interrupted. He was fully mad now and standing. Isabelle made a little gasping noise when she saw the two Schoonmaker men facing each other down.

"Why do I care?" his father roared, pacing around the table. "Why do I care? Because I have ambitions, Henry, unlike you. You don't seem to understand that every move you make is reported in the society pages. And the people I care about read those pages—however silly they are—and they talk. You make us all look ridiculous, Henry. With your dropping out of college and running around town . . . Every time you open your mouth, you tarnish the family name."

"Doesn't answer my question," Henry shot back. His father, with his explosive temper and famous love of money, would seem to have satisfied quite a few ambitions already. He had built a railroad company from scratch and made it hugely profitable, had treated the tenements built on his family's ancestral lands like his own personal mint, and had married two society beauties and buried one. "I really don't get it, Dad," Henry said. "What do you *want?*"

Isabelle's small, pointed elbows came excitedly to the table. "William wants to run for office!" she blurted.

"What?" Henry's face puckered. He was unable to disguise his incredulity. "What office?"

His father looked almost embarrassed by the revelation, and it quieted the tension in the room. "I've been talking to my friend from Albany, and he wagered me that . . ." Mr. Schoonmaker trailed off and then shrugged his shoulders. Henry knew that his father was a longtime friend and rival of Governor Roosevelt's, and he nodded at him to continue. "I admire the man's call to public service," William enunciated, his voice growing warm and stately. "Who says the noble class should not be involved in politics? It is our noblesse oblige. Man is nothing if he cannot rule his world in his time and leave it better off when he departs for—"

"You don't have to give *me* the speech," Henry interrupted, rolling his eyes. He was infuriated by this stroke of bad luck. "What office do you want, anyway?"

"Mayor first, and then—" his father started.

"And then who knows!" Isabelle broke in. "If he becomes president, *I* will be the first lady."

"Well, congratulations, sir." Henry sat back down dejectedly.

"So there will be no embarrassing me anymore. No more tales of your wildness in the papers. No more bad publicity," the elder Schoonmaker pronounced. "Now you see why you must marry a lady. Not a Penelope. A girl with morals, whom the voters like. A girl who will make you look respectable.

A girl . . ." Henry watched as his father leaned a hip against the table and pretended to have an idea. He raised his eyebrows at Isabelle. "A girl like Elizabeth Holland, say."

"What?" Henry snapped. He knew the older Holland girl, of course, although he hadn't had a conversation with her since before he went to Harvard, and she had been very young and gangly then. She was impeccably beautiful, it was true, with her ash blond hair and small, rounded mouth, but she was so obviously one of *them*. She was a rule-follower, a tea-sipper, a sender of embossed thank-you cards. "Elizabeth Holland is all manners."

"Exactly." His father pounded his fist on the table, which caused the golden liquid in Henry's snifter to slosh back and forth.

Henry couldn't speak, but he knew his face was twisted with outrage and disbelief. His father could not have suggested a poorer match. What he had prescribed for his son was nothing short of a prison sentence. He could feel the life of quiet gentility already rolling out before him, like the endless manicured lawns on which so many narcoleptic garden parties had been held by the matrons of his class, in Tuxedo Park and Newport, Rhode Island, and all those other places.

"Henry," his father said warningly. He snatched up the piece of paper and waved it in the air. "I know what you're thinking, and you should stop it. Now. I want you married and respectable. You will have to do away with Penelope. I am giving you an opportunity here, Henry." He paused. "But God help me, if you cross me, I'll see that every damn picture frame goes to Isabelle. I will throw you out and it will be very swift, and very, *very* public."

The thought of a brown future of threadbare clothing and rotting teeth made Henry feel suddenly, horribly sober, and his eyes drifted to the bottles crowded together on the sideboard. For a moment, he wished he could go back to Harvard—all the readings and lectures had seemed so pointless when he was there, but he saw now how college might have been a way for him to carve his own path, to guard against these threats of pennilessness. It was too late for that now.

His bad behavior and pathetic marks ensured that, without his father's intervention, he would never have a place there again. Henry stared into the silent amber bottles and knew that the only route to independence left to him was through the quiet, deathlike boredom of a life with Elizabeth Holland.

Five

The ideal ladies' maid will be awake before her mistress, with warm water for washing the face, and will not go to sleep until she has undressed her mistress for bed. She may require a nap during the day, when her mistress does not need her.

—*VAN KAMP'S GUIDE TO HOUSEKEEPING FOR LADIES OF HIGH SOCIETY*, 1899 EDITION

$\mathcal{L}$INA BROUD REARRANGED HER ELBOWS ON THE SILL and stared out into the tranquil darkness surrounding Gramercy Park. She had been sitting this way for many hours, in the bedroom where she had dressed the elder of the Misses Holland in layers of chemise, poplin, whalebone, and steel earlier that evening. Miss Holland—no longer Lizzie, as she had been called in childhood, or Liz, as she let her sister call her, but Miss Holland, the junior lady of the house. Lina was not looking forward to her return. Elizabeth had been away for so many months that her personal maid had almost forgotten what it felt like to serve. But from the very moment that morning when Elizabeth had reentered the house, she had gone about reminding Lina precisely what was expected of her.

She scrunched up her shoulders and sighed as she dropped them. She was not like her older sister, Claire, an altogether softer person, content to read the latest *Cité Chatter* in the narrow attic bedroom that they shared, gazing at drawings of the Worth gowns she herself would never wear. Claire was twenty-one, only four years older than her sister, but acted as though she were Lina's mother. Since their real mother had been dead for years, in many ways she was. But Claire was also childlike in her gratitude for every little trinket the Hollands bestowed upon her. Lina could not bring herself to feel the same way.

She shifted in her simple black linen dress, with its boat neck and low, dowdy waist, taking in the luxury of Elizabeth's bedroom: the robin's-egg-blue wallpaper, the wide mahogany sleigh bed, the shiny silver bathtub with heated water piped through the walls, the perfume of peonies erupting from porcelain pitchers. Since Elizabeth had come out, she had begun to fancy herself an expert on the decoration of interiors, and if asked, she likely would have said that the Holland rooms were really rather modest. Well, compared with the ridiculous mansions of Fifth Avenue millionaires, perhaps they were. It seemed to Lina, sitting under the small Dutch painting of the quaint domestic scene in the big gold frame, that Elizabeth had become blind to her own extraordinary privilege.

But Lina did not hate Elizabeth. Could not hate her, no matter how much she distanced herself with elaborate clothing and fine manners. Elizabeth had always been Lina's model for how to act and be, a glimmer of hope that she would not always live a life so simple and plain. And it was Elizabeth who had convinced her, one night ten years ago, that they must go downstairs—all the way to the carriage house—to find out who was wailing in the middle of the night. Lina had been scared, but Elizabeth had insisted. That was when Lina had first come to love Will Keller, who was beautiful even then.

Will had been orphaned at the age of eight by one of those fires that blew through the tenements like they were kindling, trapping men and babies in dark closets. Will, who had been taken in by his father's former employers with the understanding that he would serve, even at that tender age, had wailed when he dreamed of fires. Though it didn't matter very long after that, because he stopped dreaming of those things when Lina and Elizabeth became his friends.

There was a difference between them even then, of course, but they were all children and as such equally banned from the Hollands' grown-up world of dinner parties and card games. During the day they were all under the care of Lina's mother, Marie Broud, who had been the Holland girls' nurse, and she never made any distinction among her charges. She had often scolded Will and Elizabeth equally for their many schemes. Claire was too timid to join in these pranks, and Diana too young. But Lina had always hurried along with them, desperate to play a part. At night they would crawl about the darkened house, giggling at those great portraits of Elizabeth's forefathers, sneaking sugar from the kitchen and silver buttons from the morning room. They stole old Mr. Holland's playing cards with the pictures of ladies in undergarments on the backs and wrinkled their noses at them. They really were friends back then, before Elizabeth's sense of self-importance swelled and she stopped having time for her old playmates.

Lina wasn't sure when things changed. Maybe around the time that her mother died and Elizabeth began her lessons with Mrs. Bertrand, the finishing governess. Lina had been almost eleven then, awkward of body and eager to find fault in everything. She didn't often like to think back on those years. Elizabeth, a little less than a year older than she, had become suddenly absorbed in her lessons in civility, in how to hold a teacup and when the proper time to return a call from a married female acquaintance was. Her every gesture seemed intended to convey to Lina that they were not of the same cloth, that they were no longer friends. And now Elizabeth was the sort of girl Claire read about in her magazines.

For years Lina had existed quietly, and practically alone, despite attending to Elizabeth all day and night and sharing sleeping quarters with her sister and the other young women on the Holland staff. She'd been too shy to maintain her childhood friendship with Will without the buffer of Elizabeth. So she had watched him grow taller and finer looking from afar. There had been dark years for him, too—she had heard stories of his drinking and fighting from the housekeeper,

Mrs. Faber, and had wondered what dissatisfaction lived in his heart. It was only that summer—when, with Elizabeth gone, she was temporarily and gloriously freed from her regular duties—that she and Will had become friends again. They shared cigarettes after his long days were done and jokes at the expense of Mrs. Faber. They imagined aloud what their lives would be like if they were free to do as they wished. Before, she always wondered where he used to disappear to. Now she knew that he wasn't dangerous at all, that he spent nearly every moment he wasn't working with a book. Books about the excesses of the leisure class, and the theory of democracy, about politics and literature, but most of all about the West and how anybody with drive could make his way there. Now the summer was almost over, and she still hadn't found a way to tell him that she wanted to go out West, too. With him. That she was in love with him.

Lina was brought back from her thoughts of Will by the actual sight of him. One of the Hollands' broughams came to a stop in front of the house, and Will leaped down from his perch to hush the horses and open the door for the ladies. She looked at his back, wide at the shoulders and long at the torso, with the poignant *X* of black suspenders across it. Elizabeth came first, holding up her arm for Diana, who, for all her big talk, was looking rather fatigued. And then Will put his arm up for Mrs. Holland, whose small black figure came quickly to the ground. Then the women walked one after the other through the still night and up to the door. Lina could hear Claire welcoming them as Will walked the horses around to the carriage house.

She knew Elizabeth would soon be advancing up the main stairs, and she felt a rebellious instinct rise up in her. Once she arrived, Lina would have to undress her young mistress, and wouldn't be in bed herself until after morning's light. Just imagining the very task she had performed thousands of times, but escaped for months, caused her body to flush with resentment. She pushed herself up from the sill and shuffled hurriedly out of Elizabeth's room and down the long carpeted hall. She reached the back servants' stairs in a few moments, and then hustled down two steps at a time.

As Lina moved toward the kitchen, she could hear the Holland women on the main stairs, going up. She paused and considered whether she would be punished, and how, for abandoning her duties on Miss Holland's first night back in New York. But she wanted to tell Will about all the French airs her mistress had acquired. She wanted to see him laugh and know she had caused it. And maybe . . . maybe she would find a way to tell him how she felt. So she gave herself a little nod and dashed through the kitchen and out the rear pantry door, which Elizabeth had installed last fall to facilitate deliveries from the grocer.

Then she stepped lightly onto the hay-covered ground of the carriage house. Will had been removing the equipment from the horses. It lay there on the ground in neat rows so that he could clean it before putting it away. The threadbare cotton of his blue collared shirt clung to his skin from working with those gleaming black animals. His sleeves were rolled above his elbows, and his hair was damp where it hung beneath his ears.

He took a step forward and met her eyes, then stopped as though he had realized something.

"Hey," he greeted her quietly. He looked over her shoulder, toward the door, and then smiled tightly as he refocused his eyes on her. "Shouldn't you be upstairs, helping the Misses Holland?"

Lina stood still near the door and smiled uncontrollably. She hugged herself and waited for him to invite her in like usual, but then he turned his gaze away and spoke in a very different tone from the one she had grown used to over the summer. "You know you're testing your luck, sneaking around at night. Now that Miss Liz . . . I mean, Miss Elizabeth is back. You shouldn't. You . . . can't."

Lina's heart was startled in her chest, and time stretched slowly in front of her. She was so confused by the way he was acting. It was as though all the closeness that had grown between them over the summer had disappeared in an instant, or had only ever existed in her imagination. She blinked, wishing that he would just look at her for a moment.

Then he did finally bring his gaze to meet hers. His face was frozen and his mouth was set and his eyes were blank. The horse nearest him shifted, prancing in place and shaking its head. A moment passed, and then Will reached up and quieted the large animal.

"Will," she said, her voice rising with an unpleasant pleading quality that she could not control. She desperately wanted him to say something familiar and encouraging, to make some joke that would eclipse the awkwardness she was feeling now. "Why can't I visit with you like usual? The ladies do it during the day, with tea, but because we're who we are, we have to do it at odd hours and in—"

"Lina," Will interrupted. She was jarred by the name, which he rarely used. Over the summer he had always used her childhood nickname, Liney, to address her. He looked to the ground and sighed. Then, without meeting her eyes, he moved toward her. He gently took both of her hands, and for a second Lina thought her heart might stop. But then he pushed her back toward the kitchen. "I'm sorry, Lina," he said softly as he moved her up those four wooden steps and into the house. "Not tonight. You can't be here tonight."

"But why not?" she whispered.

Will stared at her. His brow was tensed and his eyes

seemed very blue and very serious. He just shook his head, like whatever he was thinking was something she wouldn't understand. "Just not tonight, all right?"

And then she was in the kitchen and the door had closed in her face. Lina reached out for a wall in the darkness. She slid down to the floor, which smelled of cooked onions and dirt, and there she remained. She sat like that for a long time, feeling lonelier than perhaps ever. Outside, the sky began to turn from black to the darkest purple.

She was still there when the door to the servants' stairs opened, and a figure in a white silk wrap hurried across the floor. The girl was as darting and iridescent as a ghost, and she kept her head down as she moved.

She had already pushed through the door to the carriage house when Lina realized that the girl was Miss Elizabeth Holland.

Six

Paris, August 1899

The summer is almost over, and I now understand my role more clearly—what it is to be a young lady of the Holland family, and all that is expected of me. I must not always be so indulgent and careless—although I find it difficult to regret anything I have done.

—FROM THE DIARY OF ELIZABETH HOLLAND

ELIZABETH, WRAPPED IN THE WHITE SILK KIMONO her father had bought on a trip to Japan and given to her for her sixteenth birthday, hurried through the kitchen and out the back door. She was moving with the trembling determination of a desire that had been building in her all night. She kept her head down as she stepped onto the first of four steps made of old pliant wood and then onto the stable floor.

She stood there on the soft ground, the air all around her heavy with late-summer heat and motes of hay. She listened to the sounds of horses gently shifting in their stables and felt fully awake for the first time all night. These things—the sound of the animals, the crisp and quiet night, the sweetness of the hay—they were everything she had tried so hard not to think about while she was gone. She stepped lightly in her satin slippers, trying to keep her kimono from catching any incriminating bits of hay.

"You came," Will stated, though it sounded more like a

question. His legs dangled off the loft where he slept, and his hair was greasy from humidity and work. He had the habit, when he was nervous or annoyed, of pushing it repeatedly behind his ears. Will, unlike the boys her friends lusted for, had a hooked nose from the time it was broken in a brawl, and thick, expressive lips. His eyes were a bright, wounded blue, and he was sitting in a familiar position—it was the position of waiting. "I'd nearly given up on you," he added, the cautiousness of his phrasing masking the fear in his voice.

Looking up at Will, Elizabeth felt elated and weary at once, and she realized what a very long night it had been. The whole ball—all that shrieking laughter, all those elaborate gowns—seemed like the stuff of a bright, absurd dream that had passed with the coming of morning. There had been dances with enough bachelors to make her mother happy, some of them less eligible and more charming than Percival Coddington. She had found time to catch up with Penelope, and they'd clasped hands and whispered appreciatively back and forth about each other's dresses. She'd forgotten to needle Penelope about the secret affair—she was a bad friend, she realized now, but she would make a big show of begging Penelope to tell her who the unnamed beau was later. They'd agreed that the terrine was delicious, though they had both been too excited to really eat any of it, and that they'd drunk more champagne than they had meant to. But champagne, they agreed, as they always had before, was not to be resisted. It had been a very long night, but it seemed to her now that it could have ended nowhere but here.

"I'm sorry . . . but you know you shouldn't always be waiting," Elizabeth finally answered, even though she might as easily have told him that she'd thought of him every day and that their separation had been excruciating. She wanted to tell him about the far-off places that she had seen, how the broad avenues of Paris curved and opened onto grand vistas unimaginable in straight-up-and-down New York. There were many things she wanted to say, but instead she mumbled: "I wouldn't want you to count on my coming even when I might not be able—" She stopped herself when he looked away. "Please, Will," Elizabeth said then, a little desperately, her chest aching at the sight of Will's downcast eyes. *"Please . . ."*

It was remarkable how quickly she adjusted from her big comfortable room upstairs to down here in the carriage house, how quickly all the rules that governed her daily life became useless and silly-seeming. Of course, she had long told herself to reverse this course. In Paris, she was sometimes sure that she could, that she had outgrown Will, that she was now fully the lady her social position called for. But when she came off the ship and down the plank that morning, she saw him waiting with the family carriage and realized that he, too, had grown up. He was somehow even handsomer than he had

ANNA GODBERSEN

been before, and she knew from the way he carried himself that he was no longer the sort of boy to get in useless fights. There was purpose in his every gesture. And here she was now, stuttering and stammering, near *begging* him to adore her again, the way a girl in love would. That's what she was, after all: a girl in love.

But all that could not stop a few stray thoughts from returning to the words that her mother had uttered just before Elizabeth had set out on the dance floor with Percival Coddington. *The one thing we do not have is time.* Her words hovered like an augury over Elizabeth's head, even now, as she stood on the stable floor.

"You were gone so long," Will said quietly, and shook his head in a show of despondency. Elizabeth looked up at him and tried to banish those words still looming like storm clouds. "And then tonight, standing out on the street, waiting for the ball to be over, not knowing what you were doing in there, who's touching you, who's—" He looked straight at her then, which made any further words unnecessary. One of the horses shifted, hooves against the hay, and neighed softly.

"Will, I couldn't *not* go to the ball." She widened her eyes helplessly, wondering why he had to fight with her over things she couldn't change, especially on her first night home. After all, wasn't she the one risking everything she had ever known, creeping around the house at night? Couldn't he just

70

love her in the time they had? "I'm here now, Will. Look at me, I'm *here*," she said softly, stepping forward. "I love you." She almost laughed because she meant it so much.

"I kept picturing you inside, dancing with those other men." Will fixed his grip on the wooden edge of the loft, and then went on. "Those Henry Schoonmaker types with their hundred-dollar suits and their country houses even bigger than what they have in town . . ."

Elizabeth reached the ladder and took two steps up. The wood was rough on her soft, unblemished hands, but she hardly thought of that now. She kept her eyes on Will's and a crescent smile on her lips. "Henry Schoonmaker? That cad? You must be joking." She couldn't help laughing her high, fine laugh outright now.

She didn't know where it came from, this urge to comfort and hold Will, but it was as deep in her as fate. She didn't even know when their childhood adoration had turned into adult love, but whatever it was that pulled her to Will had always been there. She'd never met anyone so true, so stubbornly good. Sometimes he verged on righteous, but Elizabeth knew how to calm him down. She looked up at Will, all worn out with feeling, and knew he was ready to not be angry anymore.

Will lowered his eyes and pushed his hair behind his ears once again. Then he raised his face slightly and peeked at Elizabeth. "Are you laughing at me, Lizzie?"

"I would never," she said seriously, rising another step on the wooden ladder.

Then he swung his legs upward and stood, his worn leather boots making the loft shake. When he reached the ladder, he bent and swooped Elizabeth up, so that she was folded into his arms. He smelled like horses and sweat and plain soap—it was a smell she knew and adored. "I'm so happy you're back," he whispered into her neck.

Elizabeth closed her eyes and said nothing. It was so rare and so good, this being touched. She hadn't known how much she'd missed it until now.

"So what kind of evening was it?" he asked, speaking low, directly into her ear as he set her down on the loft's plank wood floor. "Elegant or wild?"

She pressed her face into his chest and tried to recall the party, but all she could remember were her mother's ominous words and the strange looks she kept shooting at her daughter. Elizabeth considered her reply, and finally said, "Boring." Then she looked up at his big, handsome face and wished she could forget the evening and who she was and what her obligations were. She had come down here because what she wanted—against all her upbringing—was to be close to him for a few hours. "I thought about you the whole time. Now can we never talk about fancy-dress parties again?"

He smiled and gently laid her down on the spring

mattress he kept in the corner of the loft, under the wood beams where he hung his clothes to dry. Elizabeth untied her silk kimono. He hovered over her, holding her face in his big hands and kissing her lightly again and again. A natural smile spread, unbidden, across her face. "I think you do love me, Miss Holland," he whispered.

The light of an already advanced morning streamed through one small window. A certain feeling of agitated ecstasy coursed through Elizabeth's comfortable body, reminding her that comfortable was not how she was supposed to be feeling at all. It was her second morning back in New York, but she had not yet slept in her own bed.

"What are you thinking about?" Will whispered, propping himself up on his elbow.

"I hate that question," she said, because she was again thinking about her mother's warning, and how waking up in the warm crook of Will's arm was the opposite of heeding her. She sat up and looked out the window onto the vegetable garden in the back. "I should go." She could hear the lack of conviction in her own voice.

"Why?" Will slid his hand inside her kimono and rested it above her heart. The touch made her conscious of how quickly it was beating, and that every moment she spent there made her more nervous about the goings-on in the house. Lina, despite her strange absence the night before, would likely be arriving soon with hot chocolate and ice water to find an empty bed. Elizabeth forced herself to give Will a quick kiss on his soft lips and then push herself out of his grasp.

"You know why." She stood, wrapping her robe around her. Elizabeth looked down at the horses stirring in their stables below and tried to look like she was doing what she thought was right. "If my mother found out that I come here—if anyone found out—it would be the end."

"But if we moved out to Montana . . . or California . . . nobody would care what we did. We could lie in bed all morning," he said, his voice growing warm and persuasive. "And then, when we did get up, we could go for horse rides, or whatever we wanted, and . . ."

Elizabeth had heard all this before, but she could tell that he'd thought about it much more in her absence. She liked it when he talked this way. He was the only boy she knew who looked into the future and tried to imagine how it would be better than the present. Will was the most frightening and beautiful and exacting person she had ever known. Being somewhere far away from New York, where they could be just any boy and any girl, was the prettiest idea she could think of. There would be no more hurtful misunderstandings, because she wouldn't have to sneak around and visit him only when she knew the rest of the house was too exhausted to notice.

She turned back, half-ready to entertain the fantasy, but she was silenced by what she saw: Will, wearing only his faded black long johns, his chest slender and strong and naked with a few errant hairs, raising himself up from the bed and onto one knee. Elizabeth had seen this position before. She knew what it meant.

"Maybe you should be thinking about a new kind of life . . ." he said softly, and then reached for her hand. Elizabeth snatched it away instinctively as her heartbeat regained its rapid, nervous pace. She looked down at her palm and wished that her sense of propriety didn't make her do things like that.

"I'll be back when I can, all right?" She forced herself not to look into Will's face, which she knew would be twisted with confusion. If she did, she might realize how afraid she was of losing him. She might become neglectful of all the things a good girl like her must do.

She climbed the familiar wooden steps into the kitchen, readying herself to scale the servant's stairs to her bedroom, where she could do what the rest of the girls of her set were doing: sleeping off the first ball of the season, content in the knowledge that they could doze into the afternoon, dreaming all the while of the dresses they would wear and the boys they would dance with in the coming months.

"Morning, Miss Holland."

Elizabeth turned to see Lina, sitting in her constant black dress at the heavy, uneven table in the kitchen where the cook took her breaks. While Elizabeth was in Paris, her maid had grown longer and skinnier, and the freckles splattered across her nose had increased in number. The sight of her, looking plain and a little sullen in the early morning, caused Elizabeth to gasp. She could feel sweat collecting in the small of her back, and closed her robe around her to disguise the flush that was spreading to her throat. Elizabeth was surely beginning to panic, so she was shocked by the calmness in her voice: "I have been looking for you everywhere. I am ready for my bowl of chocolate now. And bring water also. I have been all night without it."

Then Elizabeth turned for the stair. "Where were you last night, anyway?" she added as she hurried out of the kitchen. She tried to tell herself that she had pulled it off—Lina was too sulky a girl to pay attention to Elizabeth's doings. And anyway, how long could she really have been sitting there?

Seven

At the Richmond Hayeses' ball, on the evening
of September the sixteenth, the young lady of
the house was seen dancing quite amorously with
a certain young man whom we shall refer to by
the initials HS. They were a pair so obviously
pleased by each other's company that members
of society are whispering that an engagement is
not far off, though an announcement had yet to
be made by press time. . . .

—FROM THE SOCIETY PAGE OF THE *NEW-YORK NEWS OF
THE WORLD GAZETTE*, SUNDAY, SEPTEMBER 17, 1899

"THE PAPERS WERE JUST FANTASTIC," ISAAC PHILLIPS Buck put in, extending his pinkie as he sipped from his porcelain teacup. "Most fun I've had since Remington Astor was caught kissing one of the kitchen boys. *That* was a good scandal."

"Oh, they were ridiculous." Penelope drew her long, ringed fingers over the head of her Boston terrier, Robber, and smiled absently. She wore a dress of black faille with a low, square neck, tight waist, and tiered skirt and was looking especially slight next to Buck, who was sweating in the late summer heat. They were the only people in the large parlor room, with its twenty-five-foot ceilings and many pieces of French furniture upholstered in matching blue-and-white striped silk. "I don't know why you bring them to me," she added with a yawn. She had been resting all day, and her body still had that pleasant, lazy feeling she associated with the day's first waking moments.

"Oh, what's that old adage . . . heart-stopping envy is the

sincerest form of flattery? You should learn to view the papers as I do."

"I do *try*, Buck, but all of this God-this, God-that, God disapproves of your mansion . . ." Penelope tried to seem more dismissive than amused, but she couldn't help a little giggle. There was so much bombast out there. "I mean really, the man *must* have something better to do with his time."

"He does have all eternity to use it up." Buck laughed, and Penelope rolled her eyes. "Well, at least the papers seem to agree with you about a certain Schoonmaker. They're predicting you and Henry will be engaged by the end of the season," Buck told her, his eyes bulging with this news coup. "They even brought in an astrologer to confirm it."

Penelope felt a delirious surge of confidence in her chest, but restrained herself from actually clapping in triumph.

"But really, they could have saved the astrologer and just asked the Misses Wetmore," Buck went on. "They looked like they'd been slapped when they saw you on the floor with him last night. *They* knew instantly."

"Adelaide Wetmore needs to be slapped," Penelope said quickly, before she became visibly giddy. The thought of her and Henry being linked in the papers was positively thrilling. He was so careful to always keep them a secret, but now all of New York would be obsessing over whether it was true or not. Soon even Elizabeth would have to acknowledge that the only perfect boy in New York belonged to Penelope. She forced away her smile. "All the same. It's so pompous, all this spilled ink over a little party. Next time you shouldn't let them come."

She couldn't complain, though. Not really. Some of the coverage was Bible-thumping about exposed shoulders, but the vast majority were long and faithful renderings of the extravagant evening. And Buck was right: There was no pleasure like being envied on a mass scale. Not to mention the paper's assistance in pushing her affair along. It had now been confirmed by the press and by the stars: Henry was going to be hers, really and truly, for all to see.

Outside, the bells of St. Patrick's rang three o'clock. It was time. "Buckie," Penelope said, standing, "you have to go now."

Buck sighed. "But Penny, we haven't even dished about the gowns yet. . . ."

"I know, Buckie, but there's all week," she told him firmly, walking over to the chaise that he was sitting on. She extended her arm and he took it, albeit a little sadly. The only time Buck irritated her was when he acted like a sullen puppy.

Bernadine, the Hayeses' head servant, stood at the front door with Buck's hat in her hands. He thanked her and then she swept open the door to the glowing sight of Henry Schoonmaker, standing by himself on the steps. Penelope clenched her fists with delight that he was here right on time, for once. Henry was dressed in his usual fitted black coat and his face was as handsome and uncreased as ever, but there was something unusual in his features. Penelope was used to a serenely playful Henry, but right now he just looked a little bit . . . confused.

"Schoonmaker," said Buck, extending his hand. "What are you doing here?"

"Hello, Buck." Henry shook the other man's pudgy hand resignedly. Penelope tried to place his strange expression, but all she could think was that he looked like he had been caught. "Just paying a visit here and there, wanted to drop this off with Miss Hayes," Henry continued tightly as he reached into his pocket and brought out a folded piece of card stock sealed with wax.

Penelope's heart instantly constricted in anger. Leaving a *card*? What about their usual Sunday tryst? He could not breathe into her ear how unbelievably ravishing she looked with a *card*. It might be good news, she tried to tell herself, but then, Henry never took the time to write formal letters, and he was not in the least the shy sort who might put in a note what he could not say aloud.

"Won't you come in, and tell me what it's about?" Penelope said slowly, taking the odious envelope out of his hand. She fixed her burning, determined eyes on him.

"Go in," Buck said. "I'm leaving, anyway." He turned to kiss Penelope good-bye on either cheek. "Be good," he told her as he kissed her right side. "But not too good," he whispered into her left ear.

Henry put a leather-gloved hand over his mouth, coughed, and nodded good-bye to Buck. He followed Penelope into the grand entry hallway as the door closed; she had managed to get him inside. Unlike those of the old houses, the Hayeses' entryway was bright and shiny, with its black-and-white-checked marble floors and mirrored ceilings. Sometimes Penelope felt like a mere speck amongst the architecture, but she did like that her reflection could be found almost everywhere.

"Bernadine, you can go back to your sewing," Penelope told her servant.

The older woman nodded, her weighty chin creasing several times as she did. "Mrs. Hayes wanted me to tell you that Reverend Needlehouse has decided to join the family for dinner this evening, and she insists you be ready to receive him at five o'clock."

Penelope rolled her eyes as Bernadine disappeared behind a door disguised by rich wall ornamentation. She could feel her temper rising. There were irritations everywhere: So Henry thought he could just slip away? So her mother wanted to curtail her afternoon? What was next? When the maid was gone, Penelope took a breath to calm herself. Then, without turning to face Henry, she said, "I get the feeling you were trying to leave me a note and skip away. You *know* Sunday is our day."

After a moment he replied in a stiff tone, "You have not even read my card, so how could you begin to guess at its intention?"

Penelope did not ask herself what he was thinking. Instead, she turned her head and let him gaze at her striking profile and impossibly tiny waist. She could hear his soft breathing, and she waited. She heard him shift on his feet and pull at his watch chain.

"As long as I'm here," he said at last, "I might as well have an iced tea or a Scotch or whatever you're serving."

"We have whatever you'd like, Mr. Schoonmaker." She was still facing away from him, fully aware of what Henry thought of her figure. She wanted him to watch and wonder whether she were really angry or not. "But you see I've just sent my maid away, so I will have to prepare it myself."

"All right, then, if you can do it in a hurry," Henry replied. "I can't stay long."

Penelope shot him a crisp smile and then gave him one long, suggestive wink. She began walking down the shimmering, reflective hallways, her heels clicking against the marble, listening for Henry's steps behind her.

The kitchen was dark but clean, with its rows of iron

pots and pans hanging from the ceiling. There was a fire going in the corner, but no sign of any of the cooks or servants. Penelope looked at Henry's card and then back at him. "I wonder what it says?" she asked with an arched eyebrow.

Henry pursed his lips. Penelope noted the sheen on his perfect, lightly bronzed face and the twinkle in his dark eyes as he took a step forward. "You like me, don't you?" he asked, ignoring her question.

There was a touch of irony in his voice, but his tone was more serious than she had ever known it to be before. Penelope nodded. "I suppose I do." She held her breath as she waited to see where this was going.

"Why?" Henry's eyes were gazing steadily at hers. If she hadn't known better, she would have mistaken his expression for earnestness. She wondered, for a brief moment, how close to a proposal they might be.

"*Why?*" she repeated, and then let out a loud, flat laugh. "Because in romance—as in all things—I choose only the best for myself. I am the best of the girls of my set, Henry, and you are the best of the men. The richest, the brightest." She took a step toward him. "The most fun. Because I want everyone to look at us and just dry up with envy that two people so superior in every respect have found each other. That's *why*."

Henry lifted an eyebrow and looked down at his polished shoes. "The richest, the brightest, the most fun . . . Sounds about right." He nodded again at his shoes before looking up and giving Penelope one of those full, glowing smiles. "Anyway, as I was saying, I'm surprised that a house of this size and status—the best, as you say—would not have a kitchen staffed at all daylight hours," he said, watching her.

"In a house this new and grand, we have more than one kitchen, naturally. And I told the staff they wouldn't be needing this one today." Penelope brought his note to her face and drew it along under her nose as though smelling it might give her some indication of its contents. She pretended to consider a moment before tossing it into the fire, where she watched it flare up with a self-satisfied smile. Then she turned and surveyed the various surfaces that filled the large room. She chose a high, narrow table and arranged herself on it. Her back pressed against the wall; her legs dangled over the edge.

"I guess you'll have to tell me what that card said yourself," Penelope said flirtatiously. She moved her hands over the bodice of her dress to smooth it, discreetly revealing more skin than she would have shown to the general public, and then pulled a small cigarette from the folds of her skirt. She smiled at Henry, lit her cigarette, and exhaled. She recognized that in the moment, despite being one of the richest girls in all New York, she looked rather cheap. She had known Henry a little while now, and she was well aware that he liked these contradictions.

The right side of Henry's mouth spread in a smile, and she knew she had his attention.

"Did you enjoy yourself last night, Mr. Schoonmaker?" she asked. "If I remember correctly, our conversation was cut short."

"Why, I did enjoy myself, Miss Hayes." His golden brown eyes darted around the room as he unbuttoned his coat and laid it across a chopping block. "I cannot imagine how a ball could possibly have been *more* enjoyable."

"We certainly tried to do everything to please our guests," Penelope replied. "Most especially you, Mr. Schoonmaker. If there was anything amiss, I hope you will tell me now."

Henry paused, and then, as though an idea were slowly coming to him, he took a step in Penelope's direction. She felt the full weight of the movement. "Now that you mention it, it seems that I saw much too little of *you*."

"You didn't see enough of *me*?" she asked.

"No." Henry let his mouth hang just open, as though he was waiting for the punch line. "I did not."

Penelope smiled and pulled at her bodice so that her décolletage seemed suddenly at a very great risk of being fully on display. "Better?"

"Much." Henry took the remaining steps necessary to reach his hostess and put both arms around her waist.

"You danced *excellently* last night," Penelope went on as

Henry began putting airy kisses on her neck. She was pleased that he did not stop to reply. "In fact, I think we danced excellently *together*." Penelope paused as Henry put his lips on the small depression at the center of her clavicle and moved on to the other side of her neck. "And, since you know me to be *very* modest, I shall have to add that it was not my opinion alone."

"No?" Henry pulled away from her neck, and his eyes met hers. She saw that they were filled with some far-off amusement.

"No. In fact, I heard from Buckie that the general opinion of the room was that we were *such* a good pair on the dance floor that *vows* should be made on it." Penelope could not help but gasp, for Henry had somehow managed, all of a sudden, to have his hands under her skirts and on the backs of her knees. The touch sent a ticklish shudder up her legs. But Penelope was not about to let her insinuation pass unheeded; she flashed her blue eyes, creased the left corner of her mouth upward, and said, "Tell me, Mr. Schoonmaker, what do you make of that?"

But Henry, who considered himself a true gentleman and so never made promises he could not keep, and whose hands were now somewhere around the middle backs of her thighs, stopped Penelope's inquiry with a kiss full on the mouth.

"Henry," she whispered, low and smoky after the kiss, looking over his shoulder to the still-crackling fire. "What did it say?"

"The letter?" Henry's mouth moved on to her ear. "Nothing, Penelope. It didn't say anything."

"Tell me, Henry."

He pulled away, just far enough to look her straight in the eyes. It was then that Penelope saw something new and profound in his gaze. Something that looked, if she was not mistaken, like the stirrings of love. "You will know soon enough," he finally told her, before kissing her gently on her perfect pink lips.

The kiss flushed Penelope with confidence, and then she gave herself entirely to the pleasure of having Henry Schoon-maker all to herself in the kitchen on a Sunday afternoon. She couldn't wait to be official, and, in his words, *she would know soon enough*. Sweet satisfaction spread through her as she began to think just how soon that would be.

Eight

One young lady in particular rose above prideful pulchritude: Miss Elizabeth Holland, daughter of the late Edward Holland, was like a diadem amidst garish rubies, glowing with poise and subtle beauty in a brocade shepherdess costume made uniquely for her by a famed Paris dress-maker. We predict her impact on society will be great and good.

—FROM THE "GAMESOME GALLANT" COLUMN IN THE *NEW YORK IMPERIAL*, SUNDAY, SEPTEMBER 17, 1899

$\mathcal{S}$UNDAY WAS ELIZABETH HOLLAND'S SORT OF DAY, which was one of the reasons that Diana had first come to despise it. She hated Sundays because they usually started with church and ended with informal visiting hours, although *informal* was a completely erroneous way of describing these visits, as everything was done appropriately and triple-chaperoned by their mother, their divorced aunt Edith, and a small army of help. At any rate, there had been no church this morning, because—as their mother had explained on the stair as they approached the parlor—they were going to have to have a very serious talk.

They were now situated in that prison of a room—that was how it seemed to Diana, anyway, when she was forced to sit there for hours and act ladylike—amidst an embarrassment of riches. The floors were crowded with Persian carpets and the walls with gold-framed oil canvases of all sizes, depicting, among other things, the stern faces of their ancient relatives. Above the wainscoting, the walls were covered with embossed olive-colored leather, which ended only at the carved mahogany of the ceiling. The moldings were filigreed with gold, and the fireplace, with its marble mantel, was large enough to crawl into, as Diana and Elizabeth had often done when they were children, and which the younger Miss Holland sometimes still imagined doing during particularly boring visiting hours. Everywhere she looked, there was something delicate or silky or rare that Diana was at constant risk of staining or scuffing.

There were plenty of places to sit, settees and chaises in a jumble of styles were arranged across the floor, but the room had never been comfortable since her father died. He had always said that there was humor in everything, and had tempered Mrs. Holland's formal hostessing style with sotto voce sarcasms. Diana wasn't sure if Sunday afternoons had ever been fun, but they had been at least bearable then. Since her coming out, Elizabeth had assumed her role with extreme seriousness, while Diana developed the habit of retreating to the Turkish corner, where dozens of striped and tasseled pillows were heaped on the floor. She was there now, curled up with the Hollands' oversize Persian cats, Lillie Langtry and Desdemona. Diana had always known it was her father she took after, temperamentally. They were the romantics, while her mother and Elizabeth remained aloof and practical.

"What is it, Mother?" Elizabeth asked, arranging herself on her usual settee, underneath the great portrait of their father wearing his top hat and finest black suit, a little wild about the eyebrows and looking miffed as usual by the world's stupidity. Diana wished he were still there in person to watch over them. Then he would give Elizabeth one of his looks, and she would feel foolish for reigning over Sunday visits with such insufferable imperiousness. "What did you want to talk to us about?" Elizabeth went on, folding her hands in her lap just so.

Diana thought she saw a streak of fear pass through her older sister's face, but then she was composed again. Their mother stood and moved to the fireplace, her slight frame looking especially severe in her heavy black high-collared dress. Her hair was pulled back tightly under her widow's cap. She stood looking into the fireplace, where a few unlit logs lay in wait. Aunt Edith waved Claire, who had been serving tea, out of the room.

"First, I want to tell you how pleased I was to see your glowing reviews in the press. They were absolutely full of your beauty, Elizabeth, and that will be very . . ." Mrs. Holland paused ominously until Claire disappeared behind the parlor's pocket doors. ". . . *useful* to us in a difficult time."

"What do you mean?" Elizabeth asked, her smile turning brittle.

Mrs. Holland turned to look at them, her gaze piercing even from across the parlor. "It is imperative that what I am about to tell you does not become known."

"Oh, everything gets known eventually," Diana put in sagaciously. She found her mother's theatrics vaguely ridiculous, though she couldn't deny her growing curiosity. What did she have to be so terribly grave about?

"Not things about families like ours," Aunt Edith offered from her seat at the little malachite-topped card table. Diana had spent all summer in Saratoga with her, during which time her aunt had often commented on how alike they were in looks and desires. Aunt Edith's marriage had been short and difficult, and it was true that the extent of Duke Guillermo de Garza's debauchery had never really gotten out. But it seemed to Diana that her aunt had bought this discretion by living a decade or more in boredom.

"Mother, what is it?" Elizabeth went on, ignoring her sister. "When father died, *that* was a difficult time."

Diana moved her eyes away from her sister, who was using the soft voice that implied sadness, and sighed. She missed her father every day, but it was a tragedy he would have wanted them to feel and then move on from. Edward Holland would not have wanted them to wallow for the rest of their lives in sanctimonious grief.

"But now Diana and I are back," Elizabeth continued

in her normal, brighter voice, "and determined to enjoy the season. We are ready to get on with things."

"That's just it." Mrs. Holland moved to a fan-backed chair near Elizabeth and rested her arm on its ormolu edges. "Not all of the consequences of your father's death were immediately obvious. It seems getting on will be much more difficult than you think. We shall have to keep a minimal staff, and I'm afraid there will be no more tutor. Elizabeth, you will oversee your sister's studies. You see, girls . . ." She paused and touched the center of her forehead lightly.

Diana was now fully at attention. She sensed that something thrillingly dramatic was about to be announced, and she pushed herself up from the pillows so that she could really hear it. Elizabeth's hands were still in the same position, and she kept her face low, so that no one could see her features.

"I barely understand it myself," their mother went on, her voice growing almost impatient, "though Brennan has explained it to me so many times. It seems that when your father died, he left a tangle of debt and a paucity of . . . of *money*. We are still Hollands, of course, of the Holland line—that means something." She rolled her eyes up to the ceiling and made a curious noise from her throat as though she might cry. "But we are not well off," she added finally. "Not anymore."

Elizabeth brought her hand to her mouth. And though Diana could see her mother's great distress, and was well aware that her sister was having the entirely appropriate reaction to this news, she could not help but clasp her hands together. "We're poor," she breathed excitedly as three sets of horrified eyes fixed on her.

"*Diana, please,*" her mother hissed. She turned to her younger daughter with a look of horror.

"Oh, I know, I know," Diana said cheerfully. She couldn't believe such a romantic thing was happening to her. She felt like she was at the edge of a great precipice and that no matter what she did next, her life would be like floating through air. She felt positively *free*. "No more jewels, no more shipments from the Paris milliner . . . But I am going to wear it like a badge of honor. It will be so much *fun*! We'll be like tarnished princesses in a Balzac novel, like—"

"Diana!" Mrs. Holland interrupted her.

"But we could really be anything now! Hoboes or train robbers, and we could go to Cuba or France or . . ." Diana finally stopped speaking when she noticed that her sister's mouth was moving without producing words.

Mrs. Holland looked at Diana grimly and then turned to her older daughter. "Now, Elizabeth, you can see why everything, absolutely *everything* depends on you. On you and what you are able to accomplish by the end of the season. I was hoping—"

Mrs. Holland was interrupted by Claire, who was sliding open the parlor's heavy pocket doors. She stood with her hands clasped in front of her and her eyes on the floor. "Pardon me, Mrs. Holland," Claire enunciated carefully. "You have a visitor. Mr. Teddy Cutting has left his card in the foyer and would like to know if you are at home."

Mrs. Holland took a deep breath, forced an almost frightening smile, and told her to send him in. A flurry of activity followed, as the Holland women attempted the appearance of normalcy, and then they welcomed their first Sunday visitor with a touch of extra hostessing zeal.

Diana was not the sort of girl who wore powders or rouge. She liked her emotions to play themselves out on her skin, and she could not now hide, even in her remote corner of the room, how ridiculous she thought this all was. She had been dying for something to do with her afternoon—nay, her *life*—and now that she was blessed with the saintly shroud of poverty, maybe she would be able to find it. The rest of her family was block-headedly acting as though everything were the same, as though they were still as rich as anybody who might stop by, but Diana's mind was already busy with the possibilities.

"Miss Holland, I can barely begin to tell you how pleased I am that you are back in town. I have never seen anything so lovely as you as a shepherdess at the Richmond Hayes ball," Teddy Cutting, now situated at the other side of the room on the peacock-colored settee next to Elizabeth, was saying. She smiled demurely and lifted one of her hands to bat the compliment away before neatly reclasping them in her lap. "Ivory is an excellent color on you, though so is sky blue." Elizabeth was, in fact, wearing a high-collared dress of white-and-blue seersucker, but to the male eye it probably looked sky blue enough. Diana thought her sister looked like a cinched doll.

"Teddy, you must tell me, are you going yachting this week?" Elizabeth asked, making the very appropriate move of deflecting the conversation back to her visitor. She was putting on a good show, but the strain of the abbreviated family discussion was evident in her voice. Diana glanced up from her exile in the corner and noted the absurdity of this back-and-forth.

"Oh, Teddy," Diana mimicked, throwing up her hands in faux ecstasy. "You must tell me if you're going yachting this week." She shook her head mirthlessly and added a loud *ha* for effect. They could pretend all they wanted, Diana thought. The rules of decorum by which the wealthy lived and died no longer applied to her. Of course she knew she didn't fully comprehend her mother's announcement as of yet, but she couldn't help but feel like her life—her real life—was going to begin any moment now.

Teddy and Liz turned to Diana as though they had just remembered that she existed. "Mother?" Elizabeth asked pointedly. "Doesn't Diana have somewhere else to be?"

Mrs. Holland let her gin rummy hand fall flat on the little card table where she and Aunt Edith had been playing.

"Diana, you have been acting strange all afternoon. Perhaps you are feeling out of sorts and should go upstairs."

"I never get sick, as everybody knows." Diana turned a page of her book, making a sharp sound as she did. "And really, talking about yachting was boring enough before. Is there really any point when we can no longer afford it?"

There was a moment of shocked silence, and Diana thought she saw Teddy begin to fidget uncomfortably. Elizabeth hung her head, and Mrs. Holland's mouth puckered with rage. *"Diana,"* she said. "You mustn't talk so. Our guest might misunderstand you." Louisa turned in Teddy's direction. "What she meant, of course, is that we can no longer afford to talk of yachting *emotionally*. Mr. Holland loved the sport so."

Diana rolled her eyes at this newest lie. She sank back into the cushions even as her mother and sister and aunt assumed stricken facial expressions. Her father had never given a damn about yachts.

"Of course. Well, I am going yachting," Teddy said, good-naturedly moving on from the awkward moment. "We go whenever we can, Henry and I—"

"How is Henry?" Mrs. Holland interjected. She had picked up her rummy hand again, and kept her eyes fixed on it as she spoke.

"Oh, Henry is Henry, which is why everyone wants to talk to him and nobody ever can." Teddy laughed, and that put an end to the subject. He stayed for another fifteen minutes—bringing his visit to the socially acceptable time of precisely one half hour—and then he gave his compliments to Mrs. Holland for having such lovely daughters and for serving such refreshing iced tea, and he went on with his rounds.

Diana was not sorry to see him go. This was the nuisance of all things appropriate, that the gentlemen visited the ladies, requiring the ladies to stay put. This meant that a lady, or whatever Diana should be calling herself now, had no control over who visited who when. And while Teddy Cutting was perfectly pleasant, he had always seemed to Diana—ever since they were children—nothing more than nice.

"Diana! How could you?" Diana looked up from her reverie to see her mother, standing with fists clenched and face hung with anger. "How could you expose your family that way?" she yelled. "Do you understand what could happen? *Do you?*"

"Really, what's the point?" Diana replied heatedly. "Everyone will know soon enough when you stop paying the dressmaker and the florist and the bills begin piling—"

"Silence!" her mother screeched. Diana looked around her, but found no sympathy. Her aunt laid a hand over her mouth. Claire, who had been standing at the door, would not meet Diana's eye. "You are an outrageous, despicable girl, Diana, and you will go to your room this instant. You will read your Bible. You will remember that you were born to obey your parents." She paused and looked down, and Diana thought she saw a tear glisten in her mother's eye. "Your parent."

Diana couldn't believe the stubbornness of her mother's denial and felt her stomach souring. "I mean, if you're going to punish me for telling the truth about our situation—"

This time Mrs. Holland stopped her with a look more exacting and stern than even her harshest words.

Claire came forward from the wall to escort Diana away. Her titian eyebrows were knit together and pleading. Diana sighed loudly, threw her book on the mahogany floor, and stormed toward the hallway with Claire close behind her.

"Elizabeth, thank God I can depend on you," Mrs. Holland was saying, exasperated, behind her. "The salvation of this family lies with you and you alone."

Diana heard these words as she reached the doorway, and for the first time realized what it was her mother was asking of Elizabeth. Do not marry for money, Mrs. Holland had often said in happier times, just marry where money *is*. She'd said it lightly before, but Diana knew that her mother's intentions were different now.

She could not help a glance back, as she passed into the hall, to see her sister sitting silent and frozen, as though she were part of a still-life painting. Diana's throat choked in rage at the sight of Elizabeth, so passive and seemingly made of stone. It was difficult to imagine that they were sisters at all.

Nine

For my Lizzie, who always
manages to be such a good girl,
on the occasion of her debut.

—EH, 1897

ELIZABETH TRIED TO STOP HERSELF FROM PLAYING with the engraved white-gold bracelet her father had given her as a coming-out present. It dawned on her that she was going to have to snap out of it and start acting more . . . *Elizabeth-like*. She was fidgety and vacant and her thoughts roamed from her father to her mother to Will and then back again. Nothing seemed real to her at this hour. *She* did not even feel real. Particularly unreal was the figure of Henry Schoonmaker preparing to enter the Holland parlor, which she vaguely recognized upon raising her eyes to the open pocket doors.

"Mrs. Holland, Miss Holland." He nodded in the direction of the card table.

"Mr. Schoonmaker," they replied. Mrs. Holland beamed. Elizabeth realized, looking at him, that though he was so very talked about, and though their families were linked by history and class, she had not actually spoken with Henry in years. He was a catch—everyone said so—but that was just an abstraction. She hadn't thought of him as an actual person until he entered the door.

"Miss Elizabeth," he said. She managed to stand and smile at her mother and then at Henry Schoonmaker, who was holding his bowler very properly. She wouldn't have thought a person like him would hold his hat that way, which was perhaps why she kept staring at it vacantly even when he began to twist it nervously back and forth. She had just discerned that Henry was the sort of person to have his initials, HWS, embroidered in gold on the pale blue ribbon that lined the inside brim of his hat, when Claire took it from his hands and announced that she would be putting it in the cloakroom for safekeeping.

His eyes ranged about the room and then fell on her. Elizabeth felt embarrassment at his very look and tried to convince herself that the famous Henry Schoonmaker, whom Agnes lusted for, whom Penelope had danced with, whose father owned some sizable percentage of Manhattan, did not know her secret. Her *secrets*: that her family was poor, that she was in love with a servant, and that she was a selfish girl likely to ruin her family even more than they were already ruined. "That is a very becoming dress," he said in Elizabeth's direction.

"Thank you, Mr. Schoonmaker," she replied, meeting his eyes and then looking quickly away. Here was the bachelor all the debutantes of New York desired, and she supposed she should have been thrilled he had come to visit with her. He was indeed handsome and crisply dressed, which was everything she was supposed to want. She was surprised at herself for being so little drawn to it now. All she could think was that, if she and her family were sent to debtors' prison, he would probably laugh—he seemed like the kind to find comedy in others' misfortune.

"Won't you sit down, Mr. Schoonmaker?" Edith said with an amused expression on her face.

Henry sat on the edge of the chair that his friend Teddy had recently been sitting on. Light fell through the tall parlor windows into the lush, quiet room, which Elizabeth felt suddenly, surprisingly, proud of. It felt like the signature of her family—these neat pieces arranged so perfectly and thoughtfully for company. The embossed leather panels over the mahogany wainscoting, which her father had chosen himself when he inherited the house from his parents. The exuberant curves of the old-fashioned gasoliers. The wall crammed with picture frames. Everything so soft and perfectly aged and rich. She looked over at the card table and noticed her aunt Edith tipping her head to her mother.

"What a sullen little pair," she whispered. Elizabeth realized with an unpleasant jolt of humiliation what her aunt was mumbling about, and that her words were audible from across the room.

Elizabeth turned to Henry, her heart thumping with embarrassment, but he hadn't seemed to have heard. He was examining his cuff links, which were also gold and also engraved with his initials. She might have thought about what a negative sign of his character this was, but she was too busy looking back at her aunt and trying to determine whether she was going to keep on muttering mortifying things. Elizabeth decided she couldn't take the chance and stood.

"Mr. Schoonmaker, it looks like a lovely day and I confess I haven't been out all morning. Would you like to take a walk around the park?" Elizabeth saw Claire blushing out of the corner of her eye and realized she was supposed to have waited to be asked. Her thoughts were so scattered that her manners were failing her, but that of course was not a thing she could explain to Henry. "I meant, if you . . ."

But Henry had already stood and extended his arm to her. "All right, then."

Outside, the day was bright and cooler than she had imagined. A fall-like breeze swept up from the East River and cleansed the air. Elizabeth felt her shoulders relax a little as she took in the leafy smell and the rich blue of the sky. Gramercy was a wonderful repose just off a noisy, dirty stretch of Broadway, hush with the gentility protected for generations by the Holland family and their ilk. Elizabeth tried to tell herself that that age wasn't lost, that it had not been replaced by an era of craven excess to which she did not belong. Inside the vast iron gates of the park, nannies were chasing children still wearing patent leather shoes and bows from church. Carriages circled the square, the horses' hooves clicking against the street. Her grandparents had bought one of the lots around the park when there was nothing built up this far north on Manhattan, and her father had grown up in No. 17. This was the Hollands' little corner of the world; it was unbearable to her that it might not always be.

But that was just more selfishness, she reminded herself. She looked at the elegant wrought iron, those stately brown town houses facing one another across the park, all that healthful shade, and her heart began to drop as she imagined her poor mother brought low. A whole future spread out in her mind, of small, dirty rooms haunted by the mocking laughter of her former peers. The family legacy would be dashed, of course, and here she was, helpless to stop any of it, keeping her posture straight and exchanging platitudes with a well-brought-up boy who would no doubt prefer to be out chasing the skirts of her more *giving* European counterparts.

Still, she walked along with Henry, saying one or two things about the quality of air and sunshine that particular day. She repeated her tale of the rough transatlantic crossing, which did not seem to interest him. They moved at a slow, indifferent pace around the park. They strolled along the west side, past No. 4, the house built by James Harper, the well-known publisher. There were two iron mayor's lamps in front, which had been installed there when, during a second career in politics, he had held that office. They turned onto the north side, and then Henry stopped and turned to her. "My father has planned a dinner party."

"Oh? How lovely," Elizabeth replied. Henry began walking again, his arm linked with Elizabeth's. She realized that she was holding her elbow tensed against Henry's so that they barely touched.

"Yes, I'm sure Mrs. Schoonmaker will see that it is."

"I hear that Mrs. Schoonmaker always throws lovely dinner parties," Elizabeth said, even though Mrs. Schoonmaker was a girl barely older than Elizabeth herself, with half the talent for domestic oversight. "They always get such nice write-ups, at any rate. I wish I could attend, but I'm sure it is a very exclusive list," she added.

Henry emitted a mirthless chuckle and gave the wrought-iron fence a knock with his fist as they glided by it. Elizabeth waited for him to say something more, and when he didn't, she felt herself growing angry. If he had come to visit her, why was he being so cruelly silent? And of course he had no way of knowing that her family was in crisis, but it *was*, and really, hadn't the thought entered his mind that she had better things to do than walk around silently with a boy who clearly wanted to be elsewhere? She was reminded of some vague impression from her childhood, of the Schoonmaker boy who was two years older than she and always smirking and who didn't seem to care about anything.

"I guess you know what the dinner is for," Henry said, giving Elizabeth a cold stare.

She shook her head petulantly. It occurred to her that Henry might be drunk. She glanced around her, as though for a familiar face to agree that all of this was very strange, and very rude. But there were only children and nannies calling to one another. Everybody she knew was hidden behind closed doors, and whatever happened next, she would have to deal with it herself. "No, I don't know what the dinner party is for."

"The dinner party," he said, pronouncing the words with derision, and rolling his dark eyes at the sky, "is for our *engagement*."

"You mean . . . the engagement of you to . . . *me*?"

"Yes," Henry replied with moderate sarcasm. "The much-lauded engagement of Miss Elizabeth Holland to Mr. Henry Schoonmaker."

And then she felt like the ground beneath her was crumbling away. She was hit by the nausea and light-headedness of looking down from a very great height. As she tried to keep herself upright, she couldn't help but picture Will kneeling, so loving and hopeful, in the simple, mote-filled morning light. What a contrast he was to cold, stiff Henry, whose flatly handsome face was staring at her now.

"Oh," Elizabeth said—slowly, and stupidly, it seemed to her. "I . . . had no idea that was what the party was for."

"Yes, well, it is, and so I suppose I should tell you that I would be very honored if you would be my wife." Henry's lips curled around the word *wife*, as though he were unsure of the pronunciation.

"Oh," Elizabeth said again. She tried to regain her breath—she wondered, briefly, if she would ever be able to speak again. She saw a whole other life laid out for her, every day more alien than the next. There would be a ceremony. She would have to promise things before God. There would be sleeping in the same bed as Henry Schoonmaker, and waking up with him. And someday, she supposed, though she found it hard to imagine, there would be little children that were half her and half Schoonmaker.

Only that morning Elizabeth had fantasized about marrying Will. Will, whom she knew and loved. She tried to think what it would mean to Will, but the image she could not banish from her mind was that of her mother's face when she delivered the news that she would not be able to marry one of the wealthiest young men in Manhattan, because she was in love with the coachman.

Elizabeth closed her eyes for a brief moment, imagining the consequences of accepting Henry's proposal—if she could call it that. She was shocked by what she saw: her life as a Schoonmaker looked quite ... *grand*. She pictured her mother's face, which had as of late been so scrunched with worry and gray with sleeplessness, uncreased and glowing with pride. Diana's cheeks flushed as always and free of grime. She saw herself doing what was easy and natural to her—being gracious and admired and well dressed. In this future, her family was wearing clothes no one could laugh at. Elizabeth looked down, surprised by the sudden, peculiar feeling growing from the pit of her stomach and spreading across her breastbone. It wasn't happiness, but it was something like relief.

"How very ..." Elizabeth stumbled over her words, not knowing what form they might take until they came tumbling out of her lips. "How very ... very, very kind of you, Mr. Schoonmaker." She forced her face to contort into something resembling a smile. It became easier as the seconds passed, for out of all her warring emotions, a sense of gratitude seemed to be winning the match. "Thank you."

Then Henry, taking that as a yes, which it was, picked up Elizabeth's arm and walked her back to the house. For a minute she thought she saw Will, crossing in front of the house, and nearly panicked. She remembered how carelessly she had declared Henry Schoonmaker a cad the night before, and felt ashamed of having her arm linked with his now, while their relationship progressed recklessly from one minute to the next. Then she realized it was just one of the Parker Fishes' coachmen out on an errand, and was thankful for the first time in her life not to catch an unexpected glimpse of the man she loved. Of course she would have to tell him, but not now. Not yet.

"Mr. Schoonmaker," she said, as they crossed Twentieth Street. "Do you think we could keep this a secret . . . until the dinner party I mean? Just so everything doesn't go topsy-turvy at once?"

He nodded in agreement, as though he liked the idea, and then they proceeded up the stairs. She tried to let as little of her body touch his as possible, and promised herself she would tell Will soon. Tomorrow.

"And you can call me Henry," he said flatly as they paused on the enclosed iron porch. "We *are* engaged."

She was unable to smile at this. She was too busy wondering if Will might still love her when she was a Mrs. Schoonmaker.

Ten

It is well known that a man, when wooing a lady to be his wife, must first win over the females she most confides in—her friends, of course, and her sister, if she has one.

—MAEVE DE JONG, *LOVE AND OTHER FOLLIES OF THE GREAT FAMILIES OF OLD NEW YORK*

*T*HE HOUSE HAD GROWN SILENT. THERE SEEMED TO be nothing happening—not even in the kitchen, where dinner should certainly have been being prepared. Diana moved through the house on light feet, humming a tune in ragtime to herself, listening for some sign of life. It occurred to her that perhaps Mrs. Faber, having got wind of the disastrous state of the Holland finances, might've packed up the staff and run off—to join the circus, maybe, or to open a brothel in San Francisco. It seemed inconceivable that, set free in this way, the housekeeper would still want the company of dull old Mr. Faber. Diana crept through the back servants' hall without meeting a soul and into the cloakroom, which was at the end of a long foyer. She felt like she was seeing everything anew. She was poor; she had nothing, and thus, she realized with delight, she had nothing to lose.

She looked at the fur coats and velvet evening wraps hanging along the walls and realized they would have to go. She glanced behind the door for her French lieutenant's coat—*that* she would find a way to save—but instead saw a foreign hat. She plucked it from the wall and placed it on her head. It would have been far too large for her except for the fact of her curls, which added enough volume that it fit almost perfectly. Diana turned to the cloakroom mirror and decided that she looked sort of bohemian when she put on the right accessories. Then she peeked out of the cloakroom door and into the long hallway and saw the figure of a man in a black coat, his back turned toward her.

Diana slipped silently down the hall in his direction. When she was a few feet from him, he must have heard her because he turned. His features were set with a look of exasperation. It took her a moment to fit the man's name and face together, though she knew them both. The face was aristocratic and stretched with an air of entitlement, the shifting of a pronounced jaw, the roving of worldly dark eyes.

"Oh . . . I know you," she said, and then smiled, because she was surprised at herself for thinking that he was actually delicious-looking even though everyone else thought so, too. "You're Henry Schoonmaker."

"Yes," he said, glancing at her head, and then meeting her eyes again.

"Do you like my hat?" she asked, touching the brim and watching him. She had heard all about the wild young Schoonmaker while she was in Saratoga. Even Aunt Edith

had gossiped about him. Apparently, he raced those dangerous four-in-hand carriages and drove motorcars and moved
restlessly from place to place and girl to girl. It had sounded to
Diana like he lived the sort of far-ranging life she would lead
if only the world would let her.

"I do like the hat, although I would question your use
of the word *my*," Henry said sharply. Then he winked, which
made Diana even more aware of her heart's rapid tempo.

"What are you going to do?" she asked, putting a hand
on her hip and lifting her chin proudly. "Call the police on me
for trying on your hat?"

Henry's mouth opened with a rejoinder, but he was cut
off by the sound of approaching footsteps within the parlor,
which reminded Diana that despite the quiet, there were still
people all over the house, listening and breathing and thinking in rules. And according to the rules, she was not at all
where she was supposed to be.

Diana was about to slip quickly away when she looked at
Henry and decided that she wasn't done with him. She grabbed
his hand and pulled him into the parlor on the east side of the
house. The lesser parlor, her mother called it, because it was
where they kept the lesser art. It used to be the ballroom, back
when their father was alive and they still gave entertainments
that involved dancing, but it had been rechristened sometime
last spring. All the nice things had been moved to the parlor

where they received guests, leaving this room with a vaguely shabby appearance. Diana took a mental note of the fade on the upholstery so that she could give her nightly diary entry a touch of ambience. When they were on the other side of the oak door, she reluctantly let go of his hand. She looked up at the great canvases above, with their dark, roiling seas. They seemed to Diana like an approximation of her own feelings at the moment.

"What are you doing in my house, Henry Schoon- maker?" she whispered. Diana could hear her sister in the hall. She was using her stuck-up, authoritative voice, asking Claire how she could possibly have misplaced Mr. Schoon- maker's hat.

"I'm not entirely sure that's your business," Henry told her.

She frowned at his answer. It was possible, though unlikely, that he had come to see Elizabeth. Perhaps he had taken that bit about her beauty in the papers for the adver- tisement it was. Or, Diana wondered, perhaps he had caught a glimpse of the younger Holland sister over the summer and his curiosity had been building ever since. *That* would be something. And then it occurred to her that he was likely here, and looking so serious, because her family owed his fam- ily money, which was dreary, but—she had to admit—more realistic. Noting again the worn cushions, Diana realized that she was now in a rather vulnerable position facing someone as wealthy as a Schoonmaker. Then she realized something else: He was admiring her with his eyes.

"The famous Henry Schoonmaker," she said, bravely holding his gaze. "The one who can't sit still and breaks hearts all over the place. Well, that's what they say, isn't it?"

"Why do you girls always love gossip so much?" he asked in reply. She was close enough to smell him. He smelled like hair pomade and cigarettes and just slightly of women's perfume, or so it seemed at that moment. She looked up at his amused face, and he whispered, "Do you think all the stories about me are true?"

"If the stories are true, then you are a very interesting person." She smiled, tucking her lower lip under her teeth.

"Well, I deny them all categorically." He shrugged before continuing: "Except the one about me liking pretty girls, which is more or less true. But how old are you, anyway? You can't have been out in society very long at all. Look at you, you've probably never even been kissed, and you're—"

"I have too been kissed," she interrupted, the way a child would. She felt her cheeks flush, but was too thrilled at being right where she was to really mind.

"Not very well, I'd bet," Henry replied with an arch of his eyebrow.

Out in the hall, Claire was reporting to Elizabeth that Mr. Schoonmaker's hat was indeed quite gone, and then

Elizabeth was expressing her displeasure at the poor quality of service in the household.

Diana looked around at the taxidermy buck heads on the wall and the old heavy furniture. There was a great tin vase full of cabbage roses that were wilting with neglect, their petals browning and falling to the floor. The curtains were drawn, which seemed somehow appropriate. She returned her eyes to the lank figure of Henry Schoonmaker, very real before her, and felt a lovely kind of pain shoot through her chest. There were so many things he knew that she didn't. She could tell by the way he stood that he was older than she was and he had done things she could never do. She wanted to take him upstairs and lock the door and make him tell her everything.

"Truly kissed?" he asked, lowering his eyebrow, which somehow implied even greater skepticism. He leaned closer, his breath warm on her ear as he reached for the hat. For a moment, everything was still. His body was so close to hers that she felt they were already touching. And then, as he gently took the hat from her curls, he turned his face just enough to brush his lips across hers. Her chest rose and fell. The touch of his mouth had been electric.

He was looking intently into her eyes, the corner of his mouth resisting a full smile, and then he leaned in again, bringing his mouth flush against hers. That was it, Diana thought. That was how this was supposed to feel. It was supposed to

go all the way down to your toes and make them dance, just a little bit.

Henry drew his lips away and winked at her, his eyes lively and knowing. Then he put his hat back on his head and stepped into the hall without another word.

"Sweet ladies, it seems I got lost on the way from the cloakroom to the door," Diana heard him say. There was laughter in his voice and she knew that even though he was speaking to Claire and Elizabeth, he was sharing a secret joke with her. "Good afternoon."

"Good afternoon," Diana heard a miffed Elizabeth say. Then the door sounded and he must have been gone. Diana, still listening from inside the lesser parlor, was consumed by the thought of what she had just done. *I just kissed Henry Schoonmaker,* she thought, repeating it over and over in her head. *I just kissed Henry Schoonmaker.*

It was later, after Diana had successfully tiptoed back to her room undetected, that the mysterious package arrived. Claire stood there demanding to know what it was, and Diana had been tempted to open it immediately. She and her maid had often whispered secrets about boys, and traded fantasies to each other that involved ocean liners and heirs to the thrones of small European countries. But something about this was too real to share, so she apologized to Claire and hugged her and asked to be alone.

She listened for Claire's footsteps away from the door and then shimmied the round gold-embossed box top open. Nestled inside the charcoal-colored velvet lining was a very familiar hat, and a note:

Keep it. It looked so good on you

I can't stand the sight of myself

in it anymore . . . nor the thought

of the context in which I shall

have to get to know you better.

—HS

She read his note maybe two hundred times trying to make sense of it. *The thought of the context in which I shall have to get to know you better?* What could that possibly *mean*? Then she put the hat on her head and felt dangerously in love with someone she hardly knew.

Eleven

The first stab of love is like a sunset,

a blaze of color—oranges, pearly pinks,

vibrant purples....

—FROM THE DIARY OF DIANA HOLLAND,
SEPTEMBER 17, 1899

*D*IANA DID NOT TAKE THE HAT OFF UNTIL SEVERAL hours later, when she heard a soft knock on the door. Then she scrambled up from her idle writing position, pulled the hat from her head, and dropped the card inside it, quickly shoving both items under the bed and out of sight. The anemic *rat-tat-tat* on her door repeated itself, and she tucked her diary—whose pages recalled the secret meeting that was inspiring all those dramatic bursts of color—beneath her pillow.

"Who's there?" she hollered, not bothering to disguise the annoyance in her voice.

The face of her older sister, with its pristine complexion, nudged beyond the door. Her eyes were as wide and blank as when Diana had last seen her in the parlor. The sisters hadn't spoken since, but that was no surprise. They hadn't really spoken—at least about anything important—in years.

"May I come in?" she asked gently.

"I suppose," Diana replied, rolling back to the position

she had happily assumed before the interruption, belly down and face toward her pillow. Her diary had been propped against it so that she could write, and now the same pillow was covering that precious compendium of her thoughts. She felt the need to shield it physically from any potential prying on her sister's part, especially since her sister seemed like such a stranger these days.

Over the past two years, Diana had become used to sisterly betrayals. She had watched Elizabeth grow ever more proper and remote, and where once there had been closeness, now there was a low-lying resentment. The interruption of her sacred diary-writing time felt like a mild affront amongst a host of other, more serious offenses.

"I have something important to tell you," Elizabeth said, her voice timid. The balance of the bed shifted as she perched herself on the far corner of the white chenille bedspread.

"Oh?" Diana rolled her eyes in the direction of the pillow, for what was important to her sister these days was most often irrelevant to her. And anyway, her thoughts had already turned back to whether Henry Schoonmaker had had many lovers and what exactly his chest would look like with Diana's head rested against it. She was thinking that it was perhaps fortuitous that her family had chosen just this moment to become poor. Maybe that was the thing that would make her stand out from all the other girls who whispered about him, causing her to glow with a certain compromised luster. She had almost ceased listening to Elizabeth, so enchanting were her musings about Henry, when she thought she heard her sister say his name.

"What?" Diana said, pushing herself up on her elbow and turning to look at Elizabeth.

"Henry, Henry Schoonmaker? He came by this afternoon to propose marriage to me, and now we are engaged. I am to be married, Di—the family is going to be all right."

Diana squinted her eyes and choked back a laugh. She was about to ask Elizabeth to repeat herself—for surely she had misheard, and mixed up the man in her thoughts with this boring engagement story—when her sister took her hand.

"I know it is all very sudden, but you see they have more money than practically anybody, and Henry is the oldest—the only—son," Elizabeth explained, sounding as though she were trying to convince herself as much as her sister.

"He asked . . . *you?*" Diana said. Her lower lip dropped and her eyes widened in shock. She instinctively pulled her hand back to her chest. Elizabeth looked down, and Diana paused for a few moments to absorb this rancid information. The delicious memory of Henry Schoonmaker teasing her in the dark and dusty unused parlor had been snatched away from her. She wanted it back. "But you don't even *like* him," she went on.

"Perhaps in time . . ." Elizabeth kept her eyes down on her hands, where she was fidgeting with her cuticles. "He is very handsome, and, well, you know everybody says what a catch he is."

Diana let out an indignant noise and rolled her eyes to the ceiling. The injustice was searing. It was so like the world to handle her this way, when *something* was finally about to happen. But her anger was growing, and she was now prepared to turn some of it on the man who was, apparently, her sister's fiancé.

"Diana, why are you being sullen? This is good news."

"Because you don't love him," Diana replied bitterly. *And he doesn't love you,* she added in her thoughts. She might have gone on to say the man Elizabeth was planning on marrying was the worst sort of weasel, and that he had kissed the little sister of his betrothed what must have been mere moments after his proposal, but she did not. With all the novels Diana read, she should have known that villains often come with pretty faces. She had made a classic romantic's error, mistaking that one beautiful moment when Henry's lips touched her own for love, but she was going to keep that ugly secret to herself. She had earned it; it was her own. She closed her eyes and said, "Well . . . congratulations, then."

Elizabeth smiled blankly and clasped her hands together. Diana had always found this a stupid gesture, and she found it particularly stupid now. "The Schoonmaker family has a very good reputation, and Henry is awfully polite and . . ." Elizabeth trailed off as if she could not think of a single other nice thing to say about him. She bit her lip then, and Diana thought she saw the glistening of tears in her eyes. "Oh . . ." she said as she covered her face with her hands.

It seemed pathetic that Elizabeth would be overjoyed to the point of tears by the sudden appearance of a fiancé with means, especially since she clearly didn't think much of him either. Diana responded with a mocking guttural noise and then went back to looking at her pillow.

"Anyway." Elizabeth recovered herself, brushing away the moisture from her eyes. "It will be good for mother, and for everyone really, to have a wedding. Flowers and dresses and everything fine and good. Everything new and custom-made . . ."

Diana sneaked a look back at her sister, and saw that her fair eyebrows had floated upward as she went on about all the pure, ivory, wedding-related things she was going to have. It was as though she'd spent the afternoon trapped in some underground sewer and had only now emerged, starving for any sign of cleanliness. In fact, she had spent the afternoon in the Hollands' sumptuous parlor, and upon learning of their family's financial decline had gone straight out and gotten herself engaged to the first wealthy man she could find.

Diana couldn't believe Elizabeth's idiocy, imagining a white wedding with that slippery bastard Henry Schoonmaker, who had apparently entered their home that afternoon with the intention of finding himself a wife *and* a mistress. How very convenient for him. Diana wondered if he hadn't come to repossess some of their furniture as well.

"And Di?" Elizabeth asked, but went on without waiting for Diana to respond. "Penelope and I made a promise to each other, when we were thirteen, that we would be each other's maids of honor. I hope you understand. But you'll be one of my bridesmaids, won't you?"

A mirthless smile crept across Diana's face. She couldn't help but appreciate, in a cynical sort of way, this ironic twist—being asked to participate in the ceremony for a union she felt completely disdainful of.

"Fine," Diana replied in a resigned, world-weary tone. Once her sister was gone, she could begin the diary writing again, and this time in more maudlin hues. Elizabeth emitted a small humming sound of pleasure, and then Diana felt herself being taken up in her sister's weak embrace.

"Oh, and Diana, don't tell anybody, all right? *Promise* you won't tell anybody."

"I promise." Diana shrugged. Her sister's doings didn't seem like a very interesting topic, and she hardly knew whom she'd tell, anyway.

"Good." Elizabeth lowered her eyes. "I just don't want this all to start happening too soon. . . ."

Nor would that wolfish Henry Schoonmaker, thought Diana. He could doubtless use the extra few months to kiss all the Holland cousins and perhaps one or two of their maids as well.

"Of course," Diana finally answered her sister. "Your secret affair is safe with me."

And though she had been searching for words that might cut her sister, just a little bit, Diana couldn't help but be surprised by the look of shock that crossed her sister's face. It was just a joke—why couldn't her sister take even the littlest joke?

Twelve

If the young Miss Penelope Hayes does not receive a marriage proposal from Henry Schoonmaker soon, then it will not come as a surprise to her alone. They say she was seen turning on all her charm for both young Schoonmaker and his father at her ball last night, which can of course mean only one thing: An engagement is in the works. . . .

—FROM THE SOCIETY PAGE OF THE *NEW-YORK NEWS OF THE WORLD GAZETTE*, SUNDAY, SEPTEMBER 17, 1899

THERE WAS A STRANGE AND SUBDUED MOOD HANGING over the Holland household, but Lina didn't care to think much of it. Her mistress, sitting in front of her at the shiny mahogany dressing table in her bedroom, was perfectly quiet and erect. Elizabeth stared impassively at her own reflection and never once let her gaze rise to meet the eyes of her childhood friend. It was only the second day of her return, and Lina was once again nothing but a maid.

It was still difficult to believe that Elizabeth—that perfect American girl, so celebrated for her lily-whiteness, so seemingly pure and helpless—would soon be sneaking toward the carriage house to do forbidden things with one of *them*. One of *us*, Lina corrected herself. She kept the silver comb going slowly over each pale strand, and pitied herself for the fact that the girl whose hair she arranged was her rival in love.

"All right," Elizabeth said impatiently. "You may braid it now."

Lina looked at Elizabeth in the mirror, and anger flashed in her eyes. A long moment passed, and before she could think about how to react, there was a knock on the door.

Elizabeth remained immobile, except for raising her chin ever so slightly. "Yes?" she called.

The door opened, and Lina twisted around to see her sister. She wore a black dress like the one Lina wore, and her red hair was pulled back from her face. A laundry basket was propped against her hip.

"You're not done yet?" Claire asked, looking from Lina to Elizabeth.

"Oh, Claire, I'm glad you're here. Would you mind braiding my hair?" Elizabeth asked, fixing her eyes on the reflection in the oval mirror. Lina drew her hands back from Elizabeth and stepped away to make room for her sister. Claire bent wearily to put down her basket, then advanced across the rich carpet, giving her sister an admonishing look as she did.

Lina hated Elizabeth for making her feel this way, and looked on in quiet anger as Claire quickly and skillfully separated her hair and wove it together into a tight, neat braid down her back. When she was finished, she stepped back and said, "Is there anything else?"

"That is all, but let your sister practice a little with your hair. She seems to have forgotten a few things during my absence."

Lina stood, stung and silent. She was reminded of those painful feelings from her early adolescence, when Elizabeth the aloof perfectionist first began to emerge. It wasn't until Elizabeth turned sixteen that Lina became her personal maid, but it was watching her friend's transformation into a fashionable society girl while she remained plain old Lina that hurt the most.

"Of course," she heard Claire say, before nodding and walking to the mahogany sleigh bed where Lina had laid Elizabeth's dress. She scooped it up carefully and put it on top of her basket, and then grabbed her sister's hand. Lina wanted to snatch it away and demand that Claire not patronize her, but she was too cowardly to speak out. "Good night, Miss Holland," Claire called as she pulled Lina out the door.

"Good night," Elizabeth said, and Claire widened her eyes at her sister warningly.

"Good night, miss," Lina mumbled in a grudging tone.

When the door had shut behind them, Claire dropped her sister's hand. She proceeded down the hallway, which, like the rest of the house, was decorated with low-lit paintings of a Manhattan of farms and hills and of the people who had settled it. Both the Holland sisters' rooms were on the west side of the house, on the second floor, far enough from the master suite—Lina now realized—that one could come or go down the servants' stairs without ever being noticed. Diana's room faced south, and Elizabeth's north onto the street. After a few moments, Lina followed Claire up the narrow wooden staircase, with the ceiling so low that they had to bend their heads, to the third and then the fourth floor.

The garret room that the Broud sisters shared with the other young female servants was impenetrably dark. They still used candles for light, and so when the sun went down, the room seemed to go on forever—miles and miles of rich black space. Lina listened as her sister stepped across the bare boards and fumbled for a candle. She waited in silence to be chastised, and longed to be far, far away. In a few moments the room came into dim view.

"I wish you wouldn't give Miss Elizabeth cause for complaint," Claire said as she lit a second and third candle. She stepped across the creaking floor to the brass bed that they shared. "Say something, Lina. Don't go into one of your silent moods on me."

Lina went to the simple dressing table, where the flickering candles sat, and picked up a few rusted bobby pins— hand-me-downs from the Misses Holland—with which she pinned back several errant hairs. She looked at herself in the cracked mirror, turning her face to the side to examine her profile. She couldn't explain to Claire her burning sense of injustice, her need to change everything about her life. "I'm sorry I didn't help you with the laundry today," she said instead.

Claire sighed, glancing at the basket of clean laundry next to their bed. "That's not what I'm talking about. Now, are you going to share what is so wrong?"

Lina hadn't told her anything about Will, or last night's episode, but her older sister had long been sensitive to her moods and was used to covering for her when she slacked off. This always gave Lina a vague, itching sense of guilt. But what was guilt compared to the furious brew of humiliation and unrequited desires she had been drinking since last night?

"It's a good job, Liney, with a good family," Claire went on, when Lina didn't answer. She shook her head, and her copper bun moved in a slow, disappointed arc. "I don't know why you are always stirring up trouble."

Lina looked into her reflection. She felt, with her over-size feet, and her dull hair, and her total lack of fashionable things, like the lowest of underdogs. But this was an age of remarkable reversals, she tried to remind herself. One read about them every day. Fortunes could be made overnight, and diligence and inventiveness could transform a girl's looks. Lina had always believed that there might be a beautiful girl lurking underneath her plainness.

"I'm just not used to having Miss Elizabeth back," she replied at last. Even saying her name made Lina's stomach curdle a little. It reminded her of how proud Elizabeth's gestures were these days, her voice dripping with fake goodness. Every singsong of that voice reminded Lina of how outmatched she was. "It was all so much more manageable when she was gone," she added defensively.

"I shouldn't have to remind you that there aren't many lines of work for girls like us." Claire shook her head with a touch of extra vigor. She was working even now, Lina realized, folding the fine pillowcases that the Holland girls rested their pretty heads on. "And if we lose this job, well ... we won't be ladies' maids in New York again. You and Miss Elizabeth used to be so close. Of course it can't be like that now ... but if you ..."

Lina couldn't possibly comment on that, so she went to her sister's side and took the pillowcase she was folding from her hands impatiently. Claire turned her drawn and lightly freckled face to her sister. Her eyes were questioning.

"Oh, go and sit. You've been on your feet all day." Lina punctuated her speech with a little jut of her head, and then continued in a softer tone: "Let me do some folding for once."

Claire snorted and went around to the other side of the bed. She propped her head up against the headboard and crossed her ankles. For a few moments she kept her eyes on her sister, watching her almost skeptically as she folded. "Careful with the embroidered things," she said as Lina shook out an ornately embellished shirtwaist.

"I am, I *am*," Lina replied, smoothing her hand over the

intricate embroidery. "Now would you please relax? Maybe you could read from the columns to me."

Lina usually teased Claire about her favorite pastime—reading about the lives of the fashionable and rich—but she smiled at her sister now to assure her there would be no heckling about what a mind-numbing diversion it all was. Claire reached enthusiastically for the folded *News of the World Gazette*, and began to skim the report from Newport in search of the doings of New York society ladies on holiday.

Lina continued to fold as Claire started reading, in a fake upper-class accent. She nodded along as though she were listening carefully, though in truth she could not put away her misery. She could not stop searching her brain for some way to show Will that he had no business with uppity Elizabeth Holland.

She hadn't come up with a thing, when she heard her sister exclaim: "Henry Schoonmaker—that's the young man who came to visit Miss Elizabeth today."

"What?" Lina looked up from her laundry and her thoughts and tried to look like she was at all interested in this Henry Schoonmaker.

"It says right here that Miss Elizabeth's friend Penelope Hayes is rumored to be an item with Henry Schoonmaker. He was the young man who came over this afternoon, and oh, Lina, did you see him?" Claire's eyes were bright with disbelief at the few degrees that separated them from such good fortune. "He was so good-looking, it was almost unfair. And Miss Penelope is going to marry him!" Lina was amazed that Claire could be thrilled for a girl who was always so rude to them, but she resisted saying so. "Though I wonder," Claire added, as a musing afterthought, "why he would have been with Miss Elizabeth this afternoon, then?"

"Maybe he wanted advice on how to propose?" Lina suggested, folding a pair of Miss Diana's plain cotton bloomers into a neat square.

"Yes, maybe . . ." Claire shrugged and went on reading the latest news of the most charmed New Yorkers.

Lina offered her sister a smile, which she was too engrossed in fantastical gossip items to notice, and so she went on folding the Misses Holland's underthings and listening to the comforting sound of her sister's voice.

She soon found her mind wandering back to Penelope Hayes with her translucent skin and fancy dresses and bejeweled hands and aloof manner. You can always tell the rich by their skin, her mother used to say. She pictured Elizabeth's fine porcelain complexion, which was so even and free of flaws, and felt again how excluded she was from the light and fizzy world.

Lina couldn't help thinking that if she were a lady like Miss Hayes or Miss Elizabeth, then Will would never have asked her to leave the carriage house that night. Or any night.

Thirteen

I've always believed in savoring the moments. In the end, they are the only things we'll have. I hope that I have imparted this belief to my children, though it is so hard to tell when they are still stubbornly becoming themselves.

—FROM THE DIARY OF EDWARD HOLLAND, DECEMBER 1898

*I*T WAS WELL PAST TWO, AND EVERY CORNER OF THE Holland house was dark. Elizabeth took the servants' stairs one by one, mindful not to let them creak. Only that morning her mother had cautioned her to be especially careful of appearances, and so she heeded the warning even as she crept toward the carriage house. She held a candle in a brass holder in front of her to better see her way.

She stood in the hay, letting her eyes adjust. It was a little lighter in the carriage house, because Will's window was high and let in some starlight. Elizabeth moved toward the ladder and reminded herself why she had come. Already it was tomorrow, and tomorrow was the day she had promised herself she would tell Will.

She put her slippered feet on one rung after the other, bringing herself slowly up to the loft. She paused there to admire Will, illuminated by her candle's flickering light. It was a scene in warm browns and flesh tones and blacks. Will must have kicked his red quilt off in his sleep, because she could see that he was curled like a baby on the bed, without a blanket to cover him.

Elizabeth moved across the floor, ever careful of the old, creaky wood planks. She set her candle down on the milk crate beside his bed and paused to look at him—the solid curve of his shoulders, the closed lids of his big, pretty eyes. The idea of hurting him was so awful to her that she couldn't even begin to think about it. She lay down beside him, pressing herself against his body. He was relaxed in sleep, and his chest was soft, moving slowly up and down with his breathing. She looked at his face closely and tried to commit it to memory, in case she never saw him this intimately again.

Suddenly a taut wakefulness came back into his limbs, and he pulled her into an embrace. She almost cried out in surprise, but a smile broke out across his face and she laughed instead—a quiet, happy laugh. She felt his hand move to the nape of her neck, where he ran his fingers through her hair. He cradled her head, and she felt the outside world fade as she came alive to what was right in front of her.

"I can't believe you're here again already," he whispered.

"I couldn't sleep," she answered, keeping her eyes on him. His irises rolled back and forth as though he were searching her.

"How lucky for me."

She wanted to kiss him, but she didn't want to break

their gaze even for a second. His hand moved from her neck down her spine and rested again at the small of her back. The way Will was looking at her made her feel like she had lain in the sun for a whole afternoon. For the first time all day she felt her lungs swell with air and her heart with happiness. She tried to remind herself, with a stern internal shake of a finger, that they had no kind of future. But as she gazed into the pure blue of his eyes, they confirmed what she had known about him more than half her life: that she could trust him with anything.

"You must really have missed me," he went on.

"Who are you again?" She only managed to hold her straight face for a moment, however, before she broke out in ringing laughter.

He laughed back, grabbing her around the waist and rolling her over him and then pinning her to the mattress. He hovered above her with a broad smile on his face. She tried to sit up, but he grabbed her by the wrists and held her down. She shrieked with laughter, and then he bent down and quieted her with a kiss.

Sweet as it was, she couldn't help feeling like a liar, and Will was the one person she never wanted to lie to. She pulled her face back gently and gave him a serious look. It would be cruel of her to wait, she told herself. It would only aggravate Will's pain when the inevitable came out.

"What is it?" he asked.

She closed her mouth and opened it again, and then took a deep breath for courage. "Henry—" she began.

"Schoonmaker?" Will laughed, cutting her off and skewing his smile sideways as he did. "You're not going to tease me about that again, are you? I saw him leaving the house this afternoon, and you don't have to worry. I won't harangue you with my jealousies anymore."

He kissed her gently. She felt a tightness in her throat and wished that she could make this moment go on forever.

When he pulled away, he was smiling and there was light playing in his eyes. "I think everything is going to be all right," he whispered after a long silence.

Elizabeth brought her lips back together in a kind of smile, and wondered if he could see how sad it was. "Everything is going to be all right," she repeated in a voice that sounded almost convincing to herself.

Tomorrow—she would tell him tomorrow. All she wanted was one last night when they weren't angry or heartbroken about the way things had to be. Tomorrow, she repeated to herself. How much harm could be done saving the awful news for one more day?

When he pulled her nightgown over her head, she tried to tell herself not to think about how far her family had fallen, and how vulnerable they all were. She tried not to think of her responsibilities to them. Or how it was going to be just as impossible to tell Will tomorrow. Or the tomorrow after that. She told herself to concentrate on the way he was kissing her neck just under her chin, so that she could remember forever how it used to be.

Fourteen

A young man held very much in esteem by the ladies who populate the matrimonial market, and who hails from the house of Schoonmaker, was seen yesterday afternoon at Tiffany & Co. on Union Square. My sources in the engagement ring department tell me he left with a diamond solitaire of uncommon size and clarity worth upwards of one thousand dollars. . . .

—FROM *CITÉ CHATTER*, FRIDAY, SEPTEMBER 22, 1899

*P*ENELOPE HAYES SMILED TIGHTLY AT THE LITTLE English maid who was waiting in the Hayes vestibule to help her with her black mink wrap. The wrap was new, like her dress, which was ivory satin overlaid with black velvet in an art nouveau design—*very* modern. She had never seen this girl before, with her small eager eyes and not altogether neat hair, and concluded that she must be one of the new hires. There were so many new servants these days, what with the size of the new house, it made one fear for the sanctity of one's correspondence. Penelope tried to express this in the irritated way she removed the thick cream card from the shiny silver tray that the maid held aloft for her.

"Mr. Isaac Phillips Buck has arrived to escort you," the girl said with exaggerated formality. Penelope and Buck were intimate enough friends that he hardly needed to present his card anymore, but he could never resist little flourishes like that.

"Thank you," Penelope replied, hurrying down the grand

white marble steps of her family home. She looked back once and realized her mistake. The girl was nearly foaming with joy after the kind words from her mistress. Penelope tried to put her annoyance away—it wasn't good for her complexion, and she was going to a dinner party at Henry Schoonmaker's, where she always wanted to look her best—and turned to see Buck waiting. He was facing the avenue, cigarette smoke wafting back over his shiny top hat.

"What were you looking at?" she asked, and he turned to take her hand. She leaned forward to kiss him on either cheek.

"Oh, you know, just the notables." Buck gave a little sniff and began walking his favorite socialite down the steps. The evening was warm and a little hazy, and indeed the best carriages were passing one another at a spectator's pace on the street. "None of them looked half so good as you."

The Hayeses' driver was waiting with one of the family's four black polished phaetons. Buck helped her up, and then he followed and gave the driver a nod. A girl more mindful of decorum would never have taken an open carriage to an evening dinner party, but Penelope could not at that moment have felt more delighted with herself just as she was. She settled herself into the plush red velvet seat and unclasped her fur wrap so that it fell behind her. She wanted to feel the night air, even though moral minds would doubtless criticize her for such a public display of bare shoulders.

As the horses began their relaxed trot south, Buck reached into his jacket and removed a piece of newspaper.

"I thought this might be of interest," he said casually, though he could not stop his moist lips from curling up in a very pleased sort of smile.

"Oh?" Penelope said as she unfolded it. Her eyes darted across the article, becoming wide and bright as her gaze settled on the words *Tiffany & Co.*, *diamond*, and *one thousand dollars*. She batted her eyelashes, heavy with mascara, and gave a modest little shrug of her shoulders, though modesty was a characteristic she had never really practiced or admired. She turned her face to the east so that oncoming traffic would see her face from the best angle, and enjoyed the short ride down the broad avenue. Henry had said she would know soon enough, and for once he had used the phrase accurately. This felt soon even for an impatient girl like Penelope.

The horses trotted along as the Schoonmaker residence came into view. It took up half a block of Fifth Avenue at Thirty-eighth Street, and though the building was younger than Henry, it was beginning to look dated, with its mansard roof and steep front steps. She and Henry would have a new mansion, of course; perhaps Daddy would build them one as a wedding present. The phaeton came to a stop, and Buck climbed—almost delicately for a man of his size—down to the street so that he could assist Penelope. She saw the carriages of several other guests loitering at the curb, the coachmen leaning against them and smoking as they began their long wait. She recognized the Hollands' coachman among them, leaning against their old brougham with a folded paper—he had big, brutish shoulders, and his name was something Penelope could not recall. Elizabeth had once mentioned in passing that they had been friends as children, and Penelope couldn't help but smirk to herself at how quaint it was down in Gramercy Park, with all their old traditions and their curious penchant for getting muddy with the staff. Here on Fifth, the ladies and gentlemen ascended the limestone steps in pairs, toward the brightly lit doorway, and did not pay the coachmen any mind.

"I may be very late, Thom," she said without meeting her driver's eyes. She focused instead on her elbow-length white gloves, taking care to smooth out any possible wrinkles. She already looked perfect, however, and she knew it.

"I will be here for you when you are ready, Miss Hayes," Thom replied.

She rested on Buck's arm as they ascended to the entryway. One of the Schoonmakers' butlers took her wrap and ushered her into the receiving line, where she found young Isabelle Schoonmaker already red-cheeked from the exertion of so many greetings. She was wearing a shimmering turquoise Worth gown that fanned behind her and cinched her up at the middle so that she tilted forward like the eager, bosomy figurehead of a ship's prow.

"Oh, *Penelope*," she gushed, teetering forward to kiss the younger girl on each cheek. "I am sorry your parents and brother couldn't be here."

"Isabelle," Penelope replied, returning the double kisses. Her parents were dining with the Astors, which was not something one turned down, and her older brother, Grayson, was abroad, overseeing the family's interests in London. "Don't worry about me. I do very well with Buck here."

"I know you do." Isabelle took her hand and pumped it, just as the Richard Amorys, who had been married three years and had remained just as dull together as they had been singly, were coming in. "We'll have to save fun for later," Isabelle whispered under her breath, and then one of the Schoonmaker servants—whose velvet livery was emblazoned with the Schoonmaker crest—appeared and guided her through the halls, to a reception room of deep red walls and fizzing champagne flutes.

"I am going to go see if they need any pointers in the kitchen." The warm light played on the soft skin of Buck's face. "Go do what you do best," he told her with a quick wink.

She paused in the doorway for maximum effect, letting the intricately detailed yards of her ivory-and-black dress spill across the oak floor. As usual, she could feel the muted, almost covetous approval of the people around her, but tried to maintain an aloof turn of the chin. The only person she really wanted to see was Henry, but instead of feeling his large warm hand on her waist, she felt the petite grip of a cold palm on her arm. She turned and saw Elizabeth, who was wearing a washed-out shade again, looking very much like a stiff mixture of milk and water.

"Penelope," Elizabeth breathed, smiling in her moderate way. Her blond bangs curled neatly at the top of her round forehead, and around her throat was nothing more than a simple gold cross. "I have been meaning to call all week. I was so sorry we didn't get to talk more at your ball, but it's been incredibly busy, and—"

"Don't worry about me," Penelope said, for the second time that evening, lacing her arm through Elizabeth's. Elizabeth let her hand rest over Penelope's and smiled warmly. They glided through the low-lit room of ghostly statues and overflowing, potted ferns at a pace ideal for any admiring eyes. As they moved, Penelope noted with a proprietary interest the coffered ceilings and the fine woodwork of the wainscoting. "I've been so busy myself, I hardly noticed. But I *am* glad to see you now." She looked at Elizabeth and cocked a carefully painted brow. "There's news."

"The crush," Elizabeth replied excitedly. Her eyes widened

in anticipation. "I have been thinking of you and your crush all week."

"Always thinking of others," Penelope said, sounding only slightly sharper than she'd meant to. "But before I tell you anything, we must properly toast you." She noticed Elizabeth start but went on. "It feels like you were away forever. My news and your return certainly call for champagne," she said, feeling generous enough to include Elizabeth's homecoming in her celebratory moment.

"Oh, yes." Elizabeth made a subtle gesture at one of the Schoonmaker servants, and soon they were both holding wide-mouthed, gilt-edged glasses of bubbly liquid. They clinked them and sipped. Penelope felt the warm fizzing in her head and a deep satisfaction that Elizabeth was on the verge of being very impressed by her. The elder Holland sister could be a goody-goody sometimes, but Penelope had known her to be fun as well, and of course she had exquisite taste in friends.

"So," Penelope began, threading an arm around Elizabeth's petite, satiny waist. Before she could begin the story of Henry, however, she noticed a handsome man, all in white sporting clothes, who didn't look remotely like any boy she had ever met. He had almond-shaped eyes and skin the color of café crème. "Who is that?" she whispered to Elizabeth.

"Oh!" Elizabeth leaned in to Penelope's ear. "That's

Prince Ranjitsinhji, from India. He's the captain of a team of cricketers, they say, and he's here to play with the younger men in the Union Club."

"Is he really a prince?" Penelope asked.

"Nobody knows for sure," Isabelle Schoonmaker whispered in her girlish tone as she arrived unexpectedly at Penelope's side. "His father was the Fadi of Nawanagar, who, so they say, experimented somewhat extravagantly in matrimony. . . ."

Penelope and Elizabeth giggled into their gloved hands, as Isabelle gave them a merry wink. Penelope was about to ask more questions about the prince, when she noticed the curious figure of Diana Holland, in a pale peach and Belgian lace concoction that was topped off with enormous gigot sleeves. It was very clearly a dress that had been chosen for her, either by her sister or her mother. She was standing by herself and fidgeting, looking resentful and careless and quite possibly like an escapee from an insane asylum. Penelope leaned in close to the blond wisps at Elizabeth's ear, and said, "What is your sister doing?"

Elizabeth's whole body flinched, but she ignored the comment. "Isabelle," she said nervously instead, leaning forward to address Henry's stepmother. "Everything is just *so* lovely. Such a high quality of people. But I do hope we're not causing you to be a poor hostess."

Penelope nodded in agreement, as though to her that would be the worst thing in the world.

"No, no . . . but I should be good and talk to everyone. I'll be back," she said, her eyes already darting about the room. "Thank you, my doves, for being so understanding."

When Isabelle was gone—she landed with the cricket-playing prince, where she began giggling at a high pitch—Penelope turned to Elizabeth and raised an eyebrow. "Well? Does your sister have a nervous disorder, or what?"

"Oh, no, no, no. *You* know Diana. She'll do anything to appear eccentric. But more important . . ." This time it was Elizabeth guiding Penelope through the roomful of trilling guests and into the adjacent picture gallery, where there were only two people, a man and a woman of their parents' age, thoroughly engrossed in a portrait of Mamie Stuyvesant Fish in her box at the opera. Elizabeth turned so that they walked away from the couple. "You must stop stalling and tell me the news. I have been waiting *all week* to hear about your mystery fellow."

"Well," Penelope went on conspiratorially, "he is very tall and handsome."

"Of course."

"He belongs to all the clubs, and he goes to all the parties."

"Yes . . ." Elizabeth smiled at her with bright, inquisitive eyes. The girls had stopped their slow little walk about the room and gazed through the embellished arch separating the gallery from the reception room, to where thirty or so guests appeared to have had a few too many drinks before the dinner.

"He's been making eyes at me for quite some time." Penelope tried to rid her voice of pride, but failed. "And at our little party last week we danced, and then this morning, there was an item about him in one of the papers. Oh, Elizabeth, he was seen purchasing a *ring*."

There was a peal of laughter, and then Penelope saw Henry, on the far wall, with a golden drink in his hand and his mouth curled sardonically. He was wearing black tails and his hair was slicked back to perfection. He was telling some kind of joke to a group of handsome but lesser young men.

"Yes . . ." Elizabeth urged her on, excitedly.

Without taking her eyes off him, Penelope announced with not a little delight: "Henry Schoonmaker."

Elizabeth's arm went slack, and Penelope wondered if she were simply dying of jealousy. Well, good. That was the idea. From the other room she heard the loud tapping of a knife against crystal. Through the arch of the doorway the big elder Schoonmaker was calling attention to himself.

"Penelope, I have to—" Elizabeth whispered.

"Shhh, I'll tell you everything later," she replied in a low tone as she took Elizabeth's arm back warmly and pulled her friend closer toward the reception room. She couldn't help but notice how stiff Elizabeth was, and was a touch surprised that she wasn't able to hide her competitive side better. Isabelle, who was smiling almost giddily, moved through the clutch of dinner guests and took her husband's side. She looked small beside him, especially with his chest puffed up so much. "I have been told that dinner is ready to be served," he began in a booming voice. "But before we go in, I have some news that I particularly want to share with you."

The room murmured at this and leaned in toward the great man. Penelope tried to catch Henry's eye across the room, but his gaze was fixed determinedly on his drink.

"As you all know, I have long been dedicated to this city, to making it great and good, to making it a lasting haven for the kings of our time. I have done so through industry and enterprise, growing this great city as the hub of a great nation. But I am no longer satisfied by what I can do in private business. I have decided to join the selfless ranks of men who have given their names, their hours, their very lives, to the people. I have decided to run for the office of mayor of New York City. . . ."

The room erupted with cheers. Penelope stifled a yawn and looked at Elizabeth for confirmation that this was *not* an announcement worth cheering over. Her friend's face was frozen, however, her polite expression fixed on that blowhard of a future father-in-law. Penelope decided it would be wise if she listened politely also.

"Thank you, thank you. It will be another year we will all have to wait, of course, but I count on your support when November of the year nineteen hundred rolls around." Penelope's eyes drifted away from old Schoonmaker and across the foaming skirts and ermine-trimmed dresses of the guests, who were drinking their champagne and trying not to look bored by the speechifying. Her gaze had fixed upward on the gold leaf doorframe that she was standing beneath, when the speech took an interesting turn. "And I have another announcement to make, this one of a more personal, but no less joyous, nature. Henry . . . my son, my *only* son, who has so rapidly become a man capable of following in my footsteps, recently came to me with the news every father waits for. He came to me, and he said, 'Father, I am in love.'"

Penelope's chest filled with airy delight. This was indeed very soon—almost sudden. After so many months of secret trysts, the idea of Henry confessing his love for her to his father felt gigantic and rewarding. It was inevitable, of course, but to have her desires so publicly granted was remarkable—if a bit presumptuous. Not that she minded, that was just the kind of spontaneous confidence she loved about Henry. She allowed herself a wide, prideful smile and clung tighter to Elizabeth's arm.

"He said, 'Father, I want you to be the first to know that

I have asked for the hand of Miss Elizabeth Holland, and that she has accepted.'"

The crowd let out an appreciative *Ahhhh!* but Penelope couldn't breathe, much less say anything. As all the faces in the crowd fanned in their direction, Penelope's smile disappeared and her full, red lower lip fell. Her mouth went dry. She felt like she had been kicked in the head by a horse, like all the names for things had been mixed up in her brain. A feeling of doom, turning quickly to rage, was galloping through her stomach.

She dropped Elizabeth's arm as though it might poison her, and then watched as her friend stepped forward to bask in the glow of all those ridiculous congratulatory smiles. Elizabeth looked back at Penelope with an apologetic grimace. She turned again just as a familiar-looking man, with a neat mustache and an officious clerklike mien, broke away from the crowd to approach her. After a moment Penelope realized that he was familiar because he had helped her on several of her visits to Tiffany, and here he was now, shepherding the precious cargo to its rightful owner. She watched with horrified curiosity as he took a little velvet box from his pocket. He popped it open, and the sight of the huge, light-catching gem threw Penelope's whole body into revolt. She backed into the picture gallery, where she found herself grasping at things. She felt wood, and then some kind of silver bowl, and the soft leaves of a fern. She knocked the plant aside. Her insides were furious, roiling, and then she couldn't stop herself. She vomited into the silver planter.

It was little consolation that most of the guests were in the other room and didn't see her. Surely they all heard. In seconds, Buck was at her side, whispering that he would get her out of there before any more damage was done. There was a commotion, and Penelope could hear the voice of Isabelle Schoonmaker above the din. She was telling Elizabeth that Henry was ready to take her in to dinner, and that she should go, now, before people started to talk.

Penelope peeked around the substantial shield that was Buck's middle section, and realized that she wasn't even going to be able to give her onetime friend a hateful parting glare. The hostess was already rushing Elizabeth's pale green figure from the room where all of Penelope's perfect plans had been so swiftly snuffed out.

Newly engaged couples will always find ways to flirt with one another, but it is imperative to the health and well-being of society that they not be encouraged to do so in public. They should not be seen traveling alone through the city, especially not to the theater, and at dinner pains should be taken so that they are not seated beside one another. They will only tickle and tease each other, and that is not to be endured.

—MRS. L. A. M. BRECKINRIDGE, *THE LAWS OF BEING IN WELL-MANNERED CIRCLES*

ENRY'S ONE CONSOLATION WAS THAT ETIQUETTE was very clear on the rules of seating at dinner parties, and so he was not forced to actually speak with his future wife during the droning six courses that were meant to celebrate their engagement. He did hazard a look or two, across the long table, at Elizabeth Holland, who was looking radiant and beautiful, though regrettably pristine to his eyes, and whose left hand was now lit up with the pride of Tiffany. Henry stared at the rock, which was so large that it overwhelmed her finger, until he knew he was being rude. He knew because his betrothed executed a delicate cough. It just didn't look like a piece of jewelry that had anything to do with him. He caught the tail of a passing waiter and asked for another drink.

His father did seem pleased, however, and distracted enough by the room of congratulators and sycophants. Apparently, it hadn't registered with him that Henry was keeping himself relatively pleasant by keeping himself quite drunk. The old man sat at the head of the table projecting grandiloquent pronouncements down half its length. At Father's right sat Isabelle. Henry was between her and his younger sister, Prudie, who fancied herself an intellectual and so wore black muslin and spoke to no one. On the other side of the onyx-topped table, Mrs. Holland took the seat directly to old Schoonmaker's left, with some fellow named Brennan on her other side. Next to him—and directly across from Henry—was Elizabeth, who was quietly rearranging the lobster salad on her plate.

Two chairs to Elizabeth's left was her younger sister, Diana, who shone with the otherworldly beauty of a girl he could not possibly attain. She did not sit still the way she was supposed to, the way her sister did. She gesticulated and laughed and pouted and generally made the dress she was sewn into and the room she was inhabiting look ridiculous and constraining. The light of her eyes—which were angry one moment and joyous the next—made the gold service arranged across the table look, by comparison, like a heap of junk. The bank of white mums on the table behind her seemed stuffy as a background for someone so alive. He pictured her in his top hat and smiled privately. Kissing her in the first hour of his engagement to her sister was—according to any logic he might employ—the furthest he was ever going to get. He tried to catch her eye, but she was remarkably adept at looking everywhere but at him.

"Have you read *The Awakening*?" she was asking that cricket player from the Punjab, or wherever it was, who was seated between her and her sister.

The supposed prince shook his head but continued to watch her attentively.

"They say it is too scandalous to ever be published again, but it is a work of genius."

"I am very impressed by all this reading you seem to do." The prince leaned toward her in a familiar way that made Henry want to stand up and swat him. "When I was living in England, it seemed to me that none of the ladies read a thing."

"Oh, yes, well, I find myself unconventional everywhere," Diana replied with the same shiny eyes that Henry had seen last Sunday.

Henry looked down in front of him and happily noted the full glass of Scotch, which had appeared like magic. Having witnessed the inevitable humiliation of Penelope, become officially engaged to her best friend, and found his attractions diverted to his fiancée's little sister, he had settled on drinking as the only safe course of action. He turned to his right and leaned across Prudie to where his friend Teddy was seated. He raised his drink. "Cheers, and thank God you're here to see me through this."

Teddy looked away from the girl on his other side—she

was a Holland cousin or something, Henry couldn't remember, and reasonably good-looking. "Cheers," Teddy replied, raising his glass. "Here's to my lucky friend. You don't deserve her."

"What does that mean?" Henry said loudly.

"Nothing, never mind." Teddy laughed. "Drink up, and stop looking so morose, would you?"

Henry rolled his eyes and refocused on the drink. He didn't think it was unreasonable, this suffocated feeling. A part of him wished Elizabeth might evaporate into thin air, or better, that he would. He was trying very hard not to think about the fun that was being had in other, less elegant parts of the city. Instead he focused on the perversely shiny red globe grapes that occupied the center of the table in great heaps.

"So, Miss Diana," Isabelle, next to him, trilled to the girl across the table. "Have you and Miss Holland discussed colors for the wedding? You know, mauve is very fashionable for bridesmaids' dresses nowadays. In my wedding—"

"Mauve is a made-up color," Diana snapped. A few brunette tendrils unfurled around her neck as if to punctuate her disapproval.

"Oh no," Elizabeth broke in. "It is a very lovely color. Although," and here her voice lowered, as though she had noticed a bit of food on somebody's chin, "it is already very much in use."

"Oh, I know what you mean, dear. But really, the sight of seven of your closest friends in that divine shade . . ."

Henry raised his eyes and tried to catch Diana's. They were dark, and smudged with makeup, and full of feeling. All around the table, there was movement—the servants passing in the shadows of the room, the young people clapping their hands and squealing, the older guests ordering second helpings of terrapin—but Henry held his gaze steady. He could tell that Diana found the whole wedding conversation as lackluster as he did, and all of a sudden he didn't care what sort of party was going on without him. All he wanted out of the entire evening was some acknowledgment of their mutual disgust.

Her eyes roamed over the ceiling and the plates, but finally he wore her down. At last she settled her gaze on him, and for a long moment he managed to hold her stare. Then she emitted a miniature gasp, as though someone had called her a cruel name. She shoved herself away from the table and hurried from the room.

"May I take your plate, sir?"

Henry looked up, startled, at one of the hired waiters. "Oh, yes," he said, watching the half-eaten gold platter of salmon in cream sauce disappear behind him. His father was still engaging in a cross-table discussion at maximum volume about the price of steel. Isabelle and Elizabeth were debating the merits of periwinkle and lavender. Mrs. Holland was staring happily at Elizabeth's engagement ring, and Prudie was muttering something into her glass of claret. A cellist played softly in the corner. Henry took his drink firmly in hand and slipped out of his chair without letting it make a noise.

He stepped into the hall and headed in the direction in which he heard footsteps falling. A figure in a peach-colored dress was hurrying away from him. She disappeared around the corner, but the sight proved irresistible. He followed at what he hoped was a nimble pace, trying his best not to spill any of the drink in his hand.

She took another turn down the long corridor, and Henry followed in thoughtless pursuit. All of a sudden, he had stumbled down a short flight of stairs and into the conservatory, spilling a bit of his drink as he went. Twenty feet ahead of him, the girl to whom his attraction was growing by the second had come to a halt. One of her great, puffed sleeves had slipped, revealing a bare shoulder, and she turned her head, with its precarious pile of curls, upward, as though she was taking in the silent majesty of the place: the arched glass ceiling, the loamy air, the profusion of greenery. He stood still and watched as she took three deep breaths and then bent to put her face close to a big blue hydrangea.

"Lovely, aren't they? You see why my family never has to send out for fresh-cut flowers. . . ." Henry leaned rakishly against the doorway and took a sip of Scotch. "But you know, they don't smell."

Diana turned her face, but not her body. "Oh . . . you. Yes, I know they don't smell." She looked back at the hydrangea and shrugged. "I suppose you want your hat back."

"No, that was for you to keep. It looks much better on you than—"

"Yes, you said that already," Diana cut him off bitterly. "Very cute."

"Why are you being so sullen with me, Miss Diana?" Henry smiled out of the corner of his mouth as he employed a much-used tone and tack. "Didn't you want me to follow you? Why else would you have run out like that?"

"I ran out because I couldn't bear you *leering* at me anymore!" Diana's brown eyes turned a wrathful shade. She let go of the flower and looked around her. "There is only one good thing about you, Mr. Schoonmaker," she went on in a calmer voice, "and I'm afraid that is your greenhouse. But I have to be going now."

She stepped toward the door, and Henry, who was unused to women wanting to escape his company, blocked her way. The anger returned to her eyes when she saw that he was not going to let her pass, but it had the effect of making her look even lovelier. "Do you wish this greenhouse were going to be yours, instead of Elizabeth's?" he asked with a hint of amusement.

"Oh, please." Diana pushed past him, and Henry, who had no intention of really trapping her, gave in easily. He did feel, as she moved forcefully against him and through the doorway, a little bit of the warmth of her body and a few rapid heartbeats. "It makes me sick to even *hear* that. I am not your little windup toy, Hen—"

Before she could finish speaking, or even get fully past Henry, she caught her slipper against his leg and stumbled forward. She steadied herself against the wall, short of falling, and turned angrily. The great volume of her skirt swerved around with her.

"Are you all right, Miss Di?" Henry could not help laughing a little.

Diana pulled up at the lap of her skirt with angry, fisted hands and turned on Henry without acknowledging his concern. "I have never and will never be jealous of my sister with all of her conventional desires and accomplishments. They disgust me, frankly. And now *you* disgust me, too."

She moved back down the hall at a jaunty, almost masculine gait—a style of walking that he had not seen practiced by the other young ladies of New York. Before Henry could even decide whether he wanted to stop her, she was gone.

He took a sip of his drink, sighed, and laughed a little at himself for getting into another ridiculous situation. After a safe pause, Henry reached the doorway to the dining room, where dessert was already being served. He felt a rush of relief that no one seemed to have found his absence remarkable, but it quickly turned to disappointment. The scene before him—all those heavily made-up faces gorging themselves on food, all that shrill laughter coming in the wake of the same tired old jokes—was so pitifully boring. There was only one pair of bright eyes at the table, and they were back to studiously avoiding his.

When he retook his seat, nodding politely at Elizabeth and her mother, he could not shake the feeling that he was, as Diana had declared in her furious little voice, disgusting.

Sixteen

At an intimate dinner party given this past Friday by Mr. William S. Schoonmaker, an announcement was made of the engagement of his son Henry to the beautiful Elizabeth Holland and a ring presented worth upwards of one thousand dollars. Although many in society will be surprised by this match, I quickly came to see the good: They are both children of the best families, and will surely bring the elegance, style, and spirit of their class to the union. A wedding date will soon be announced. . . .

—FROM THE "GAMESOME GALLANT" COLUMN IN THE *NEW YORK IMPERIAL*, SUNDAY, SEPTEMBER 24, 1899

"WHAT ARE YOU DOING?"

Lina turned from the casement window in Edith Holland's third-floor bedroom and showed her sister her most innocent expression. "Oh, I was changing the sheets . . . and it was such a pretty morning, I guess I got distracted looking outside."

She had in fact chosen that chore at that time because she knew that Will had gone out on an errand for Mrs. Holland, and she wanted to watch him when he returned. She was so anticipating this small pleasure that she couldn't help but linger, looking down on the street, in the hope that she might still catch a glimpse.

Claire came to her side and put her arm around Lina's waist. "You've been so good and helpful these last few days, love. I want you to know I do appreciate it."

Lina shrugged as though it all came easily to her. She had worked harder that week than she had since the winter, but mostly because when she was working she didn't have to think about Will being in love with Elizabeth. She thought about how her arms hurt and her head ached and the stupidity of all her menial tasks, so that she could feel angry rather than brokenhearted.

"I know it's hard for you," Claire said in her gentle, mothering voice. "You are so much more restless than I am. But I hope you're beginning to see that if we're good, we will find the lives we deserve."

Lina rested her head against her sister's shoulder. She thought this was a somewhat deluded worldview, but she wouldn't say so. That would only hurt her sister's feelings, and Lina had never really wanted to do that.

"We'll find real love, too," Claire went on softly. "Just like Miss Liz."

"What?" Lina said, jerking her head to look at her sister. She felt a renewed ache in her heart, until she realized that Claire was not talking about Will. Her eyes were shining with some wondrous news, and to Claire, Miss Elizabeth falling in love with the coachman would not be a romantic story. It would be a tragedy. "What are you talking about?" she whispered.

"Miss Elizabeth and Henry Schoonmaker, of course. I just read about it now." Claire moved away impishly and threw herself down in the brocaded armchair by the window. "I guess he wasn't in love with Miss Hayes, after all. Do you want to hear?"

"Yes," Lina replied with quiet urgency. "What does it say?"

Claire smiled and shifted in the chair. She pulled the much-folded broadsheet from the pocket of her apron and slowly ran her finger down its face. "Ah! Here it is: 'At an intimate dinner party given this past Friday . . .'"

Lina listened intently as her sister read the announcement. Just as Claire was repeating the ridiculous and unimaginable cost of the engagement ring, Lina heard the sound of the carriage house door slamming shut.

"I'll be right back," she said with blunt intensity.

Claire's face fell. "Where are you going?"

"I . . . the pillow cases, the embroidered ones . . . I left them soaking and they'll be half-ruined. . . ." Lina was already halfway to the door. She turned and grabbed the paper out of her sister's hands. "Can I take this? I'll bring it right back!" she called behind her.

Already she was flying down the stairs. The helpless self-loathing she had been feeling all week had been replaced, suddenly, by the certainty that she could sway events in her favor. She would tell Will that Elizabeth was engaged, and then she would be perfectly positioned to offer herself as a replacement. Soon she was in the kitchen, which smelled of broiling tripe. This was a familiar smell from her early childhood, when the Brouds had lived in their own small apartment, but she had never known the Hollands to consume something so common. The cook was nowhere to be seen, and one of the kitchen girls was working a pile of potatoes. Lina might have offered an explanation as to why she was hurrying to the carriage house at this time of the day, but the girl—Colleen was her name—barely looked up from her task.

As soon as she saw Will, sitting on a wooden folding chair, his whole body bent around a book, she began speaking. "Have you read the *Imperial*?" Her words were toppling over themselves. "Elizabeth has been lying to you!"

Will looked up at her nervously. His eyes were wide and blank; he seemed to be trying to think what to do next. "I . . . Do you mean Miss Holland?"

"Yes . . . Miss *Holland*," Lina spat. "And I saw her leaving your room very early in the morning, so don't think I don't know what's between you."

Will shifted in his chair, his large shoulders rounding awkwardly. He kept his eyes to the ground as he replied. "I don't know what you're talking about, Liney, but I can tell you with absolute honesty that there is nothing between Miss Holland and myself. It is very dangerous for you to say things like that, and I wish I could make you stop."

"Will, listen to me. I'm your *friend*." Lina knew she must look ugly now, with her lips set and her eyes large and agitated. But she couldn't help it. What she was trying to convey to Will had to be conveyed. "It doesn't matter what you tell me, anyway. Lie to me, if you want. But I think you'll want to know that your Miss Holland is *engaged*."

Will pushed his back into the rickety chair, and his eyes roamed across the floor. He still wouldn't look at Lina, but after a few moments of forming silent words, he managed to say: "How do you know?"

"I read it in the paper, like everybody else. And before you say it's just a rumor, you should know that it's to that man who came by the other afternoon—you saw him, Mr. Henry Schoonmaker." She paused and raised the paper in her hand. She continued in a softer voice, "You can read it yourself if you like."

Will stood suddenly, his chair skidding over and clattering against the hay-covered ground. He walked several yards and then stopped with his hand resting against a post. He faced away from her, but she could see the rigid anguish in his stance and wondered if she had underestimated his feelings for Elizabeth. Across the thick-smelling room, the Hollands' horses breathed and shifted quietly in their stalls. Will's head shook back and forth, and he pushed his hair behind his ear. Lina was almost sorry she had had to tell him, but only almost.

"What does it say?" His voice was ragged and breathless.

She paused and looked down at the paper before reading the item aloud. When she was done she added softly: "It doesn't seem made up to me, Will."

Will drew back his arm and smashed his fist into the post. Like all the wood in the stable, it was rough and splintered easily. He hit it again and again, with such fury that Lina feared what he would do to himself next. Pieces of the post flew into the air. He hit it a fifth, and then a final time, and when he turned to Lina, she could see the blood bursting from his knuckles, and the bits of wood that it was washing out. Finally, he raised his eyes to hers.

The hurt in his face was clear, and she couldn't help but move toward him, lifting up the chair as she went and forcing him to sit down on it. "Here," she said. "Just sit."

She looked around for things to clean the wound and found what she needed. She grabbed the basinful of water, the one Will used when he cleaned the horses, and doused his hand. Then she took the bloodied fist, and with her fingers— long and nimble from stitching—she pulled out the big, obvious splinters. She used the white cotton petticoat under her skirt to stanch the blood, and then continued like this: plucking the rough bits of wood, stopping the blood with her skirt. When his knuckles were clean of splinters, she ripped a long section of fabric from the bottom of her petticoat and wrapped it around his hand. It looked a little puffy and amateurish, but at least her bandage seemed to be soaking up the blood.

She put the folded paper on the floor by his feet.

Without looking at him, she climbed the ladder to his little loft, where she knew he kept his whiskey. The early-afternoon light filtered in over the old chest of drawers and his books and his piles of clothes. She found the glass bottle, half full of brown liquid, stashed in one of his drawers, and carried it back down with her.

When she reached Will again, she offered him the bottle but he shook it off. His thick lips still trembled slightly from whatever emotion was coursing through him, and the paper was resting on his knee. He must have read it again.

"I'm sorry," was all Lina could think to say. She was stunned silent by his reaction. She had certainly underestimated whatever it was between Will and Elizabeth, and though she had hoped this would be the perfect time to confess her love to him, his grave expression made that seem impossible now.

Will looked at her with damp eyes. His lashes were dark and clumped, and his mouth was twisted up. She offered him the bottle again, and this time he took a long pull. "No, I'm glad you told me," he said as he passed the whiskey back to her.

She took a sip and felt the burning against her lips and the warm drop of the whiskey into her belly. She watched Will shake his head in disbelief. Eventually, his eyes turned to her again. "Thank you for telling me, Liney," he said. "Just stay with me for a while longer, okay?"

She smiled at him, feeling dizzy with joy. There was nothing so good as Will needing her. If they could just spend a few hours like that, she felt, she wouldn't have to tell him anything.

"Of course I'll stay with you," she said as she took his hand, the one he hadn't smashed up, and squeezed it. "I'll stay as long as you want me."

Seventeen

Are you sure this isn't why

you've been avoiding me?

—Will

ELIZABETH HAD MANAGED NOT TO LEAVE HER ROOM all morning, and she was beginning to prefer the solitude. How close she had come to losing this luxury, a room of her own—how close she had come to having to share with her sister and perhaps her mother as well—was not lost on her. But every time Will entered her thoughts, she felt tortured by the fact that she had not yet told him. She could not bear lying to him and she could not bear to confess, so she avoided him altogether. She had tried to delay the inevitable by writing him a quick note, on her personal stationery, letting him know that it had been difficult to visit him and that she would come as soon as she could. She had left it on his chest of drawers while he was out on an errand three days ago, and had yet to receive a reply.

But the Hollands were always ready to receive visitors on Sunday, and she knew that she would have to emerge from her safe retreat soon. Her ladies' maid was a silent and strange presence as of late, which Elizabeth resisted telling her mother because they had been close as children and because she did occasionally miss Lina and the way things had been then. So she arranged her hair by herself, in a neat chignon, and dressed in a white shirtwaist and a starched Dutch blue skirt. She could not think of putting on any jewelry—the diamond on her left ring finger that she had kept turned to the palm side of her hand since Friday night added quite enough weight, all by itself.

Every inch of her body felt stiff and defensive—rigid with the thought of Henry Schoonmaker, with the inevitability of her marriage to him. What a careless person he was proving to be. She knew already, from his drunken behavior at the dinner party on Friday night, that their life together would be an unnatural one, full of silent differences and alien nights. She could not even think of Will—she was forcing herself not to. If she thought about him for even an instant, she might begin to melt; her whole self might just drain away. And what would become of her family then?

When she was ready to face the world, she pulled back her bedroom door. She paused at the sight of a gray scrap of newspaper falling to the ground. It was folded into a small neat square, and had been wedged into the bronze handle of her bedroom door. She knew immediately that this was Will's reply, and so it was with trepidation that she bent to pick up the society page recounting of her engagement. Scrawled at the bottom, in Will's handwriting, was an indictment veiled as a question: *Are you sure this isn't why you've been avoiding me?*

The soft skin of Elizabeth's cheeks burned as she read the note. Her stomach dropped and her heart began to beat at a frightful pace. She tucked the piece of paper in her pocket and tried to do the same with the emotion that it raised in her. But she could not stop the trembling of her chin, that familiar dryness in the back of her throat. She looked around, half-expecting to see Will waiting at the end of the hall, and then she hurried down the servants' stairs in search of him.

When she was halfway down the narrow passage, the door from the kitchen opened, and she saw Claire take a few steps upward. The girl stopped when she saw Elizabeth.

"Miss Holland! What are you doing here?"

"Oh." Elizabeth wavered on the stair. It took her several seconds to think of something to say. "I was just on my way to check on dinner, before joining my family for visiting hours."

Claire backed up to allow for Elizabeth to descend. "Oh, you don't have to do that," she said as she reached up and took her mistress's arm. "I will do it. You must go do your hostess duties. Now especially, because . . ." She broke off and shrugged. Elizabeth noticed the blush on Claire's cheek and knew that she had been about to say something about the engagement, but must have remembered her place. Claire escorted her to the hall and drew back the parlor's pocket doors for her to enter.

When Elizabeth stepped across the threshold, she saw her sister in her usual position: curled in the Turkish corner, with a volume of poems. Claire had dressed her quasi-respectfully in a dress of soft rose-brown seersucker, and it spilled over the pillows, calling attention to Diana despite all the treasures in that room.

"Oh, Elizabeth," her mother said. Elizabeth turned and saw Mother looking—in the armor of her fitted, embroidered, long-sleeved black dress—quite fierce. She was sitting on a high-backed chair near the fireplace, which was not lit. "Mr. Schoonmaker—Henry, that is—has just sent up his card. I insisted that he have tea, but it seems that what he really wants is to take you for a ride in Central Park. Isn't that right, Claire?"

Elizabeth turned slowly to look at Claire, who was still hovering in the hall.

"Oh—yes, that's *exactly* what he said," she gushed. Elizabeth saw Diana's eyes dart up over the pages of her book, before she hid her face behind it again. "He is waiting outside," Claire went on, her voice growing more confident as she assumed her role. "And he appears *most* impatient. He won't even come in."

"Very good," Mrs. Holland said.

Elizabeth stood still in the doorway, not sure whether to come in or go out. She watched her mother draw herself up, her stature and imperiousness growing in a matter of seconds. Elizabeth found herself craving some word of encouragement, but she had been trained as a child not to pull at skirts or go begging for affection, so she stayed put. "Since I must be here to receive," said her mother, "and since your aunt Edith is not feeling very well—poor thing, I think she is still recovering from the heavy food that Isabelle De Ford, I mean, Isabelle *Schoonmaker*, serves—Will is going to have to go as your chaperone. He is getting the horses ready even as we—"

"No!" Elizabeth's hands flew to cover her cheeks at the very thought of Will and Henry coming face-to-face. Her ears were full of noise, and every inch of her skin felt coated in a fine, cold sweat.

"What is the matter with you?" Mrs. Holland snapped. She turned her chin up at Elizabeth and set her hands firmly on the arms of her chair.

"I—" Elizabeth tried, but could not think of a reason not to go for a carriage ride on a perfectly lovely, late September day. She fingered Will's note in her pocket and thought how wretched it was going to be to see him. "It's just that I—"

"Just that you what? Really, Elizabeth, I raised you better than this. Your fiancé is waiting. Do not just stand there making yourself unworthy of him."

"But I . . ." Elizabeth stammered. She saw the way her mother was looking at her and knew that she had no choice but to go. So she grasped out for the one thing that would give her strength. "I mean, since we are supposed to be very careful of appearances, maybe Diana could come with me?"

"No!" was the swift answer from Diana's corner.

"But Diana, please?" Elizabeth said, resisting the instinct to stamp her foot.

Diana pushed herself up against the pillows and sighed in exasperation. "I'm not going to go on some long, boring excursion just because you're afraid of your own fiancé."

"Diana, you really are being ridiculous," her mother said coldly. "Go with your sister before you make yourself utterly useless to me."

"It's not that I'm afraid of him," Elizabeth said quietly. She looked up and saw that her sister was already standing up. She wore a wounded expression, and Elizabeth realized that her sister was going to accompany her, if only because she now felt wounded by their mother. "So you'll come."

"Yes, I'll come," Diana said darkly as she pulled at her dress, which had become twisted from lying down amongst all those pillows. "But don't go thinking I'll speak to anyone."

"Girls," their mother interjected, "you must both stop being strange—it is unattractive. And don't forgot your hats. It would be absolutely the end for me if you two came down with freckles at a time like this."

Diana gave her mother a big, obviously fake smile and

charged across the parlor. Elizabeth followed her into the hall, where she could see, through the glass pane in the oak front door, Henry waiting on the porch. He was wearing creaseless, tight-fitting black trousers and a high hat pushed back on his head. He was facing away, toward the little gated park. Elizabeth turned back to her sister, who was slouching and glaring. Even so, Elizabeth was glad she did not have to face Henry and Will by herself. She tried to give Diana a smile to show her gratitude, but found that smiling was, under the current circumstances, very difficult for her.

Claire appeared from the cloakroom with two wide straw hats. She put Diana's on first, tying the thick white grosgrain bow under her chin, and then helped Elizabeth with hers. "Thank you, Claire." Elizabeth's voice quavered a touch as the maid tightened the bow. "And would you start a fire in the parlor before our return? I find it so strangely cold in there."

Outside they were greeted by the clarity of a fine September day, the smell of cooking fires somewhere not far off, and the great expanse of blue sky, interrupted here or there by small puffs of cloud and crowded only occasionally by a building that rose over six stories high. Elizabeth felt almost heartened by the perfection of the weather, but that was before she saw Henry begin a slow turn, and before she heard the sound of the Hollands' four black horses coming around the front. She was suddenly glad of her hat, which tipped forward to accommodate her bun in back, and so shielded her eyes. The only thing that kept her from fainting, right there on her own steps, was the fact that she couldn't see the way Will was look-ing at her.

"Miss Elizabeth," Henry said stiffly. Elizabeth extended her hand, and Henry leaned forward and kissed it. "Miss Diana, you won't be joining us, will you?"

There was a pause, and Elizabeth hazarded a look to her right, under the safe shadow of her hat, to see what Diana was up to. "Well, I didn't *want* to," Diana replied rudely. "But it would pain me to be left out of a ride through Central Park on a day like today. Sometimes, fresh air and a natural setting are the only things that make living at all worthwhile."

"Lucky me, two for one."

Elizabeth thought she detected irony in Henry's voice and disliked it. She took Diana's arm for support, and they walked down to the street.

"May I help you up, Miss Holland?" Will offered with false formality.

"I've got it," Henry said to Will. She wished for some way to sign to Will that she didn't want Henry or his help, but then she felt Henry's hand on her waist, and her whole body being lifted up into the carriage. She tried to calm her heart as she took the padded red leather backseat of the landau.

The balance of the carriage shifted as Henry sat down beside her, and Diana across from them. Then she heard a crack of a whip and the horses bolted into action. They were being pulled forward, and not at a leisurely speed. Elizabeth grasped the iron armrest with one hand and the brim of her hat with the other. She kept her head down, examining the straw weave that was shielding her eyes, and the rich blue of her skirt that stood up stiffly all around her. She listened to the heady traffic sounds—the streetcars, the shouting from the crowds—as they turned and went up Lexington Avenue, and tried not to think about what was going through Will's mind.

"Why not take Fifth?" Henry called up to Will. "Ladies like that route, you know. That's where they really get to show their dresses off."

Diana snorted, but there was no sound from the driver's seat.

"Hey, driver," Henry said. "Fifth Avenue?"

"Don't you read the papers?" Will replied in a voice quiet but intense.

"Sometimes." Henry laughed. "But I try not to pay much attention."

"Well, if you'd paid attention to the papers this morning, you would know that Fifth is a madhouse because of the preparations for the parade this weekend for the admiral returning from the Philippines. Admiral Dewey? He won the battle in Manila Bay?" Will laughed a sarcastic laugh. "You probably didn't even know there's a war on."

Elizabeth kept her smile private under her hat as she listened to Henry's embarrassed reply: "I did. I knew there was a war on. Lexington is fine."

It was only once they were in the park that she managed to look up. She lifted the brim slightly with her hand and raised her eyes so that she could see Diana, who was staring petulantly into the distance. She didn't know what she had been anticipating—perhaps that if she dared look at Will, he would immediately begin loud accusations—but she saw only the silent rebuke of his back. He was wearing the same worn blue shirt as always, with the sleeves rolled up, and his shoulders were thrown back in defiance. Elizabeth glanced quickly at Henry, whose arrogant face was pointing somewhere off into the leafy wilds of the park. She shifted her gaze back to Will and wished she could know what he was feeling.

The landau shook mightily as they went up and down the little hills of the park at a speed that caused several of the parasol-wielding ladies walking amongst the elms to turn and look. Elizabeth wished Diana and Henry were gone, just for a moment. She would touch Will's arm, and he would know to slow down and relax. He would know that she loved him.

These were the thoughts in her head, and so she did not at first register what Henry was saying.

"Miss Diana, I assume you will be standing by your sister at the altar?"

This caused an immediate wave of discomfort through Elizabeth's body. The mention of an actual wedding was awful to her. It must have been to Will, too, because he cracked his whip again, which sent the horses dashing up a small stone bridge.

"No. Apparently, she and Penelope Hayes made a promise to each other as lasses of thirteen," Diana said crossly. "But I don't really care for that sort of thing anyway."

As the horses hurtled down the bridge and picked up speed, Diana was forced to grab her seat to keep from falling out. She shrieked and moved her other hand from her hat to the railing.

Henry looked over in Will's direction angrily. "What is your coachman doing?" he hissed at Elizabeth. "This hardly seems a pace suitable for women."

Will clearly heard this comment, for he jerked at the reins and brought the horses swerving off the road and onto the lawn where, after a few breathless moments, they finally came to a halt. The landau jumped when they did stop, and Diana only managed to stop herself from bouncing out of the carriage by catching Henry's outstretched arm.

"What the hell, man? She could have been killed," Henry said, righting Diana and leaping to his feet.

"I'm fine, *really*," Diana replied dryly.

The rough motion had loosened the ribbon of her hat, however, and at just that moment a breeze picked up and sent it flying off her head and across the lawn. The wind whipped at her hair as well, bringing a heavy gust of curls up and then down around her shoulders.

"Oh, my hat!" Diana cried, pushing the hair back from her face and pointing in the direction it had blown.

Elizabeth stood up and saw the hat cartwheeling across the grass. Henry, who just a moment before had seemed ready to fight Will, jumped down from the carriage and went running after it. "Hold on, I'll get it!" he yelled, taking his own hat off as he dashed away.

"No, you won't!" Diana cried, and before Elizabeth could stop her, she had jumped down to the grass. Diana pulled back her skirt and ran after Henry through a field of green dotted with men in straw boaters, picnicking with their wasp-waisted sweethearts. The men and women taking their leisure in the park that day obviously found the sight of a Schoonmaker and a Holland dashing after a runaway hat amusing. Elizabeth didn't have time to feel embarrassed, however. Will had jumped down from the driver's seat and was leading the horses back to the road.

Elizabeth turned and climbed down, being careful not to get caught in the moving wheels, and came around to Will just as he reached the road. When he turned to look at her, she was surprised to see not unspeakable rage, but a calm and determined expression. Then she noticed the great, sloppy bandage wrapped around his hand.

"What happened?" she asked, reaching for it without thinking.

Will shook his head and held the hand away from her. He blinked with the sun in his blue eyes. The light brought out a few red glints in his usually dark hair. He seemed to know already what he was going to say.

"You don't want that," he said in a low, controlled voice.

Elizabeth looked behind her. The weekend crowds didn't seem to be paying attention, but she'd never spoken to Will this way in public, and it caused her lungs to swell with fright. "I'm sorry, Will," she said with feeling, "I am so sorry that—"

"Don't be sorry," he said, bringing his face closer to hers.

"But you've got to understand, it's my family, we're—"

"I don't want to hear about your family. I'm leaving, Elizabeth. I'm sure you have your reasons, but if you stay here and marry that man, you will be sorry. I still want you to be my wife, Lizzie, and that can't happen here. It could happen out West. That's where I'm going." He looked down but kept his hand on the strap to lead the horses. After a pause he took in a breath and brought his gaze back to hers. "I want you to come with me."

Elizabeth brought her hands to her face. She couldn't bear to look at Will, whose pale blue eyes were wide with the desire to convince her. An abject misery was constricting her throat and bringing a sting to her eyes, so she kept them hidden. She wasn't sure quite what would happen to her if she looked right at him, but the feelings of helplessness and sorrow were already overwhelming. So she stood still and blind, in the middle of Central Park, with her palms pressed firmly against her eyes.

Eighteen

Don't go looking for boys in the dark
They will say pretty things then
leave you with scars.
Do go looking for boys in the park
For that is where the true gentlemen are.

— *A SEAMSTRESS'S VERSES*, 1898

"WAIT!" DIANA YELLED AS SHE DARTED OVER RED-and-white gingham tablecloths that had been spread on the ground, and nimbly avoided a dumbstruck child not quick enough to get out of her way. Her feet were moving faster than her thoughts, but she was taken by the sudden conviction that nothing was quite so important as Henry not touching her hat. "I don't need your help!" she shouted after him.

He slowed at the sound of her voice. The way Henry had spoken to their coachman was still fresh in her mind, and galling—Will had been with their family forever, and his rebellious streak had long endeared him to Diana. She was finally gaining on Henry when she heard the shrill, nasal voice of a female bystander saying, "So *that's* how the Hollands rear their girls these days."

She looked back briefly, with a dismissive look, and then continued her chase. By the time she reached Henry, she was panting, and the wind had gotten through her dress. She brought her arms up around herself to keep warm. She took a final few strides to reach his side and said, as coldly as possible, "Thank you, but I don't need your help."

He gave her the rakish smile that she was now fancying herself already immune to. "All right, Miss Diana," he said. "If you insist, then I won't help."

Diana looked back across the field to where their carriage stood on the path, just beyond the stone bridge. Her sister and Will were out of sight. She turned back to look for her hat, which had landed in the blue-green waters of the pond. The white ribbon that had fastened it to her head was floating away. She sighed impatiently, pulled back her skirts, and took a tentative step toward the muddy edge.

"Now, Diana . . ." She turned back to look at Henry. He wasn't laughing at her or leering, but he was staring at the hem of her dress, already slightly muddied by the water at the pond's edge. "I wouldn't want to push on where I'm not wanted . . . but if you'd prefer that I get that hat . . ."

She looked at him, and then at the gaggle of children who had collected several feet behind them. When she turned back around, she saw that her hat was floating farther away. She felt curiously on display out in the middle of the field, and unsure what to do. She looked at Henry, and he raised his eyebrows in gentle amusement. "Would you like me to get it?"

"Well . . ." Diana looked at him crossly. "I suppose . . ."

Henry smiled at her and put both hands on her hips. The touch of his hands softened her urgency and made her wonder why on earth it had seemed so important that he not retrieve her hat. He stepped on his heels to quickly shuck off his shoes and socks, and then turned and waded in to his knees, his fitted black pants growing wet and sticking to his legs.

"Aha!" Henry cried, nabbing the hat with a splash. Just then a fleet of ducks came over to examine him, and one of them took the floating white ribbon in its beak. "The ribbon, however . . . I'm afraid it has a new keeper," he added, pointing to the brown-and-gray duck swimming away.

"But how will I tie the hat without the ribbon?" she yelled, crossing her hands over her chest and twisting up her face. "If I get freckles, I don't know what my mother will do to you."

Henry looked at the duck and grimaced. Diana, realizing that he really was considering fighting it for the ribbon, couldn't help but giggle into her hand. He looked up at her when he heard her laughter.

"I was *joking*!" she called.

He gave the ribbon a concerned parting glance, and then he lifted one knee after the other and brought himself out of the pond. The gathered children broke out in giggles at his bedraggled appearance, and Diana couldn't help but give him a few hearty claps. She was finding it increasingly difficult to feel taken advantage of by a barefoot man whose expensively tailored trousers were now ruined by mud.

"Here is your hat," he said, with a touch of put-on formality. "But it's sopping, and I would be happy to go on holding it for you. If that's all right, of course."

"Thank you." She bent her head in a kind of nod.

They paused at the edge of the pond, the wind whipping at Diana's rose-brown skirt. He was watching her and she smiled at him, faintly at first and then wider. The moment lasted a few seconds longer than it should have, and then Henry said, "We ought to go back," ending it.

"Yes," Diana said. "I suppose we should."

She watched him slip his shoes back on and wished she could think of something more to say to let him know she wasn't angry anymore. But then he gave her a barely perceptible wink and she knew she didn't have to.

Nineteen

Every family with daughters old enough to marry must be concerned about the costs of a wedding, which, according to tradition, they must shoulder alone. When a girl from high society decides to wed, the costs of course can be astronomical, and many wealthy fathers-of-the-bride have left such happy events feeling like paupers.

— MRS. HAMILTON W. BREEDFELT, *COLLECTED COLUMNS ON RAISING YOUNG LADIES OF CHARACTER*, 1899

ELIZABETH HEARD THE PEALING LAUGHTER OF HER younger sister and opened her eyes. She moved her hands from her face to the shiny, coarse side of the horse. Diana was walking back in their direction with her skirt hiked up, and Henry was a few paces behind her, carrying the wide-brimmed yellow hat. In the distance, the wind was tilting the trees toward the south; everything had a whipped brightness to it. "They're coming back," she whispered.

Will shook his head, very slowly, once left, once right, and fixed his wide, clear eyes on her. "I'm leaving on Friday, last train from Grand Central Station. I'm going to see what the harbor looks like on the other side. You can come with me, or you can stay here forever. . . ."

Elizabeth wanted to press her body into Will's; she wanted to put her mouth on his mouth. She wanted to find the words that would make him stay, and say them clearly and forcefully. But she couldn't. New York was all around her. So she did what she was supposed to do. She ducked around the horse and took several steps forward on the grass, waving her arms above her head.

"You got it!" she cried, as though the retrieval of the hat were some triumph of her own.

Diana's mood seemed to have changed entirely. She looked at Henry and laughed. "Poor Henry practically had to dive into the water to get it!" she called back. "But the ribbon was lost! It's going to make a duck's nest somewhere."

Elizabeth could feel Will watching her, but still she went on playing the part of Miss Holland. She walked forward, her leather boots sinking into the soft earth, her ears chilled slightly by the breeze. When she reached her fiancé, he took her arm and led her back to the landau. She let him help her up, and then she let the wide brim of her hat fall over her eyes again. The horses began to move, pulling the carriage into motion. Only then did Elizabeth allow a few silent tears to roll down her cheeks under the safe shade of her hat.

Elizabeth pulled her hat back from her head as she walked through the door of the Hollands' home. A few strands of hair stuck in the straw weave, but she didn't have time to fix them. She shoved the loose hair back with her hands as she passed the hat to Claire, who was standing patiently in the low-lit entryway.

"Where is Mrs. Holland?" Elizabeth stepped forward and peeked into the parlor through the pocket doors. Her movements were frenetic, as though if she slowed down for even a second, her chances of making everything right would disappear entirely. The room was empty of people, though. Apparently, both her mother and aunt had given up on any potential visitors. "Claire, where is my mother?"

Elizabeth turned to see that Diana had put her arms around Claire and rested her head against her chest. The elder of the Broud sisters had always had that mothering quality about her, even when she was a girl. Claire looked a little embarrassed and offered the elder Holland sister a crooked smile. "I haven't seen her," she said quietly.

"What's the matter?" Elizabeth said to Diana. "I'm sorry I insisted that you come, if you're still upset about that."

She watched as Diana slowly turned her head. She was wearing a melancholy face that Elizabeth hardly had the time to interpret.

"No, I'm glad I came," Diana said. Her voice had grown low and portentous, though Elizabeth couldn't imagine why. She didn't really need to know why, either. What she needed was for Diana to disappear, just as she so often did, so that Elizabeth could find their mother.

"Perhaps you should lie down for a while?" Elizabeth tried to keep her voice even and suggestive.

"Perhaps." Diana let go of Claire and moved toward the stairs, her limbs drooping as though she didn't have enough energy to keep them up properly.

When she was gone, Elizabeth turned to Claire. She ran a finger along her right eyebrow, took a breath, and prepared to ask her question a third time.

"I don't know," Claire said before Elizabeth managed any words. Her eyes were wide. "I haven't seen her. I'll go look on the third floor."

"Thank you," Elizabeth replied. Since talking with Will in the park, her sense of urgency had only grown. All she could think was that the fiction of her relationship with Henry was unsustainable, and that she must tell her mother immediately. If only she could stop this charade, stop playing the perfect miss, then she would be able to show her mother how it had to be. Perhaps their financial state was not in such ruin that she must marry immediately. Perhaps there was some other way, in these modern times, that her family might recover their wealth. Perhaps there was some way she could be with Will.

Claire took the stairs at a near run, and Elizabeth moved to check the parlor again. That was when she saw the painting in the gold-leaf frame, facing the wall on the foyer floor. She half turned to ask Claire what it was doing there, but the maid was already gone. Elizabeth pulled the painting away from the wall so she could see which one it was. She recognized it immediately—it was the Vermeer that had hung in her bedroom for nearly ten years.

The painting had been one of her father's favorites—he had bought it from a Paris art dealer while Mrs. Holland was pregnant for the first time. Several of the big art collectors, the ones who had traded making millions off steel to spending it on old master works, had expressed interest in the little piece, but Elizabeth had begged him not to sell it. It depicted two girls, one fair-haired and one dark, reading a book at a wooden table by a window. The blonde was on the left side, closer to the window, and her hair glittered like spun gold. They were turning the pages of the book, and the light illuminated the pale perfection of their skin.

Elizabeth ran her hand along the gold frame, where a piece of paper was affixed to the corner. The name she saw—Mr. Broussard—was not a familiar one. Even though the painting was hers, she felt like she'd been rummaging in someone else's things.

Elizabeth hurried up the familiar narrow back stairs and peeked in on her mother's bedroom, which looked as though no one had set foot there in a long time.

"Miss Liz . . ."

Elizabeth pulled shut the door to her mother's bedroom and saw that Claire had come up behind her. "Yes?" She wished she knew why she felt embarrassed for poking around her own house.

"Mrs. Holland is downstairs."

"Thank you, Claire." Elizabeth turned and this time took the main staircase, which was carpeted in a rich Persian runner. She was about halfway down, and practically mouthing that she could not marry Henry Schoonmaker, when she saw the man in their foyer. He was bent in front of her Vermeer, and he was looking through an ornate magnifying glass at the top right corner. That was where the signature was, just above the jug of wine. Elizabeth wanted to shout at him that he couldn't touch her things, but some instinct, perhaps her habitual sense of politesse, kept her silent.

"We do not have fakes in this house, Mr. Broussard," Mrs. Holland announced coldly, stepping closer to him.

The man, who was dressed in black and whose long hair was tucked under his collar, turned his head to assess the speaker. He stared at her for several rude seconds and then went back to examining Vermeer's brushstrokes. When he was satisfied, he pulled a cloth from his satchel and wrapped up the painting. He stood, put his hand into his coat, and produced an envelope.

"Here it is," he said brusquely.

Elizabeth watched as her mother cracked the envelope and looked inside. Seeing her painting in the hands of a stranger produced a heavy sadness in her, which began to grow into a kind of helpless anger.

"It's all in there," the man went on impatiently.

"I'm sure it is," Mrs. Holland said. "But I would hate to have to trouble you to come back if anything were amiss."

The man waited until Mrs. Holland gave him the nod, and then he shook her hand and went out into the street. The door came back into its frame with a bang that seemed to cause the whole house to shudder. Elizabeth hesitated on the stair as her mother watched the man go, her black-swathed body framed by the light coming in through the glass pane of the door. Then she sighed and turned sharply. She managed a few steps before she saw Elizabeth, standing halfway to the second floor.

"What are you doing there?"

After watching her mother sell off one of her family's most prized possessions, Elizabeth wondered if she would ever be able to look at her the same way again. The woman below no longer looked like a fearsome arbiter of society. She appeared small and frail and pitiable. She appeared old.

"I was just looking for you . . . to ask you something . . ." Elizabeth managed to say.

"Well, what, then?"

Elizabeth felt as though her heart had frozen over. All her grand emotions, her sense of self-importance, her need to show Will her loyalty and make him stay had drained away. Her family wasn't just poor; they were desperate. She had only one choice, and that was to marry Henry. She wasn't going to have another opportunity like that. "I just wanted to ask if you would like claret with dinner?"

There was a long, silent moment in which Mrs. Holland kept a watchful gaze on her daughter. She blinked once and then said, "No, my dear. We had better save that in case the Schoonmakers come for dinner some night."

Elizabeth nodded feebly. There was nothing else to say, and so she turned away from her mother and went, with leaden feet and a sore heart, to find Mrs. Faber. She would tell her not to bother decanting any wine for their meal that night, or any other night, until she was a Mrs. Schoonmaker.

Twenty

TRANSATLANTIC CABLE MESSAGE

THE WESTERN UNION TELEGRAPH COMPANY

TO: *Penelope Hayes*

ARRIVED AT: *New York, NY*

1:25 p.m., Tuesday, September 26, 1899

Dear Penelope—

Reports of your dinner party episode have reached me even in London. I have been meaning to send you a real letter, and will do so. In the meantime, remember that we were born of the same blood. Be fierce, little sister, or the world will handle you fiercely. <u>No more public vomiting.</u>

—Grayson L. Hayes

ENELOPE HAYES GRIPPED HER BOSTON TERRIER, Robber, as she read the telegram. She peered across the grand drawing room, with its matching blue-and-white silk-upholstered pieces from the Louis XV period and its polished black walnut floor, to where her mother was sitting with Webster Youngham, the architect. Mother wanted it known that the Hayeses were commissioning him again, this time to build a "cottage" in Newport, the kind that came with fifty-six rooms and marble floors throughout. This was not the sort of news one kept to oneself, so she was going on in marathon-style in the hope that he would be forced to stay and thus seen by as many visitors to the Hayeses' as possible.

Penelope examined her mother, Evelyn Archer Hayes, who was wearing a dress of a lavender shade that she was really much too old for, and that cinched her girth unpleasantly. Penelope promised herself that she would never get half that big. Then she stood, letting Robber fall and skitter across the floor, and walked over to one of the floor-to-ceiling ormolu-encrusted mirrors that filled the spaces between Old Master paintings, to look at a more visually appealing subject.

"Penelope, watch that animal on my floor," her mother called from the sofa where she was lounging.

Penelope rolled her eyes at herself in the mirror, and then puckered her lips to assess their fullness. "You know his nails are clipped," she replied. Mrs. Hayes had always been annoying, but ever since Penelope had discovered the engagement of her Future Husband and her Former Best Friend, she found every swallow or breath her mother took to be a personal affront to her sensibility. She listened for rotund Mrs. Hayes to go back to her yapping, and then crumpled the telegram and dropped it into a silver vase bursting with yellow roses. She wished her big brother was in New York to defend her, but a reprimanding telegram from abroad made her feel precisely the opposite of protected.

Penelope's dark hair rose in a dramatic pompadour up from her forehead, and was collected in a small bun at the nape. Grand curlicues and frizzy ringlets were the fashion for girls her age, but Penelope knew perfectly well what suited her already dramatic face. She checked her eyebrows and rubbed the soft skin over her cheekbones so that it took on some color. She was happily examining the sea-foam-blue acres of her dress when the enormous arched pocket doors were pulled open by one of the maids.

Her mother gestured at the maid as though she knew the visitor was for her, but the maid nodded politely and proceeded to Penelope. Of *course*.

"Miss Holland has just presented her card," she said.

Penelope exhaled sharply at the sound of that name she hated, and went back to looking at herself in the mirror. She crumpled the card and thought for a moment. She would have liked nothing more than to give Elizabeth the full brunt of her cold shoulder, but that would only result in a rather pedestrian, unfulfilling revenge. Be fierce, she reminded herself. "Miss Holland can visit with me if she must."

"Very good," the maid said as she backed out of the mahogany-framed doorway.

Penelope looked around the room and took great satisfaction in the fact that it was better than the room the Hollands received in, and also in the fact that her mother was there but distracted by the architect. That would prevent her, in any event, from slapping Elizabeth across her stupid blond head. The dress Penelope had on was exceedingly flattering, she reminded herself—the elaborate bodice, the mandarin collar with the keyhole opening at the chest—and it was embellished all over with tiny waves, embroidered in real gold thread. She went over to where Robber was curled, in a gold trough that was lined with aubergine velvet, scooped him out, and walked moodily across the floor with her small creature snuggled against her chest.

She listened to the housekeeper's formal announcement of the visitor, which included a loud and grand enunciation of that incredibly distasteful name: *Miss Elizabeth Holland*. It brought the delicate hair at the nape of her neck to standing. Penelope kept her face down, close to Robber's black head, and listened to Elizabeth walk, on timid little feet, across the Hayeses' precious polished floor. When Elizabeth was close enough that Penelope could hear her nervous breathing, she looked up and met her eyes.

"Penelope . . ." Elizabeth's brow creased and her mouth quivered around the name.

Penelope stared back at Elizabeth, who was wearing a dress of camel-colored silk, for a healthy interval before she even thought about saying anything. "What? You came this far uptown, and you still can't think of anything to say?"

"No, I . . . I have so *many* things to say. I feel awful about the other night, and—"

"It's really pathetic," Penelope interrupted then, "that you would have to compete with me in this way." She looked past her former friend and saw that her mother was overjoyed to be greeting Ava Astor, daughter-in-law of the great Mrs. Astor, who was apparently her new best friend.

The whites grew around Elizabeth's hazel eyes. "No, no, it's not like that at all. I had no idea that you were so in love with Henry Schoonmaker. You never told me. Penelope, you've got to believe me, I am so, *so* sorry about everything."

Penelope snorted and pretended to look everywhere but at Elizabeth. She could not help a few good sideways glances at the enormous diamond on her left hand. "You don't know him like I do. Believe me, it's not going to be all lovey-dovey for you."

"Penelope." Elizabeth reached for a hand that her friend quickly snatched away. "I can't explain right now, but you have to believe me that I didn't pursue Henry, and that when he proposed to me—I swear, someday I will explain *everything*—I had to accept."

Penelope examined her friend's pleading face, her eyes welling to the brink of tears, and realized that Elizabeth didn't even *want* to marry Henry Schoonmaker. It didn't make any real sense to Penelope, as she herself had been physically ill for five days now with the thought of losing him. But it was perfectly clear that Elizabeth had not the tiniest inclination to gloat. She seemed, in fact, to be unhappy. And she was definitely sleep-deprived and not looking her best. These were consolations of a kind.

Penelope gave Elizabeth a softer look and began to walk slowly along the edge of the room so that her friend had to scurry along behind. "You humiliated me," she said in a low, hurt tone.

"I know, Penny, but I didn't _mean_ to."

"They were all laughing at me, you know." She sniffed as though she were more hurt than she was angry. "It was the severity of the shock. _Such_ a shock you gave me!"

"I know. I cannot even begin to tell you how sorry—"

"And you just said _nothing_. You just _stood_ there. You listened to my story, and you might have warned me, but you said absolutely nothing."

Elizabeth began to fidget with the embroidered edge of her camel-colored bolero. "I was speechless, Penelope, really or I would have—" She broke off, which was a happy thing for Penelope, as her voice had reached an almost whining pitch.

"Can you imagine what that silence must have felt like?" Penelope tried to look more wounded than exasperated.

Elizabeth looked down again and bit her lip. "No, I cannot." Her eyes shifted, and she seemed to realize that all her fidgeting might soon damage her jacket. She clasped her hands together and went on, attempting brightness: "But just think, _you_ will be able to meet and flirt with so many different men, while I will be married young and then for forever. You can still change your mind in love, again and again and again!"

"True," Penelope said guardedly. She let her elbow float up and waited for Elizabeth to take it. They walked slowly past the great canvases and into the smaller adjoining navy-and-white toile-wallpapered sitting room, where Mother and Mr. Youngham and Ava Astor would not be able to watch them. Penelope took a breath and tried to ease into some kind of niceness. "Anyway, Liz, I couldn't be mad at you for long. I'm just glad that you'll be the one who gets him and not one of those other stupid girls."

Elizabeth seemed momentarily taken aback by the mean sentiment, but then recovered her voice. "Thank you for being understanding. Thank you so very, very much."

Penelope tried to return Elizabeth's gratitude with a smile that might conceivably be read as warm. A little color was coming back into Elizabeth's cheeks, and indeed she looked enormously relieved. But her guilt was still fluttering inside her—Penelope could see it, and she was ready to take full advantage. They took a seat on a little cranberry-colored velvet settee, with Robber squeezed between them.

"I've been so miserable thinking I might have hurt your feelings. It would be terrible if, now that one of us is engaged, we wouldn't be able to make good on our promise to be each other's maid of honor." Elizabeth smiled, almost shyly now, her eyes moving slowly up from the dog's black eyes to his owner's blue ones.

Penelope smiled back, widely and unabashed. She forced herself to take Elizabeth's hand—looking again at the ring as she did—and gave it a little pressure. There wasn't going to be any wedding, of course, not if Penelope got her way. And she was beginning to see that the closer she kept Elizabeth, the easier it was going to be to muck everything up.

"You really still want me to be your maid of honor?" she almost whispered.

"Of course, who else could I possibly—?"

"Diana? I mean, she's your sister; won't she be hurt?"

Elizabeth looked pained by the mention of her sister, and Penelope had the happy realization that Elizabeth was sacrificing Diana in favor of her. She couldn't help but laugh at a thought, and had to sputter out the name that went with it: "Agnes Jones?"

Elizabeth looked almost shocked by this suggestion, and then her face broke and she, too, was laughing at the hilarity of the idea. The tension between them seemed to evaporate. "That would be such a disaster," Elizabeth managed, wiping away a giddy tear.

"Or Prudie? I mean—"

"Penelope, you're the only one I can count on."

"All right. Fine." She batted an eyelash and took both of Elizabeth's hands. "It's done."

"And there's an event—on Friday night—the one for Admiral Dewey at the Waldorf-Astoria. That's the first public event that Henry and I will attend, as a couple. Will you be there with me, as my maid of honor?"

"Of course." Penelope tried not to smile too broadly. Already, she was being let in where she could do the most harm.

"I need a new dress for the occasion, of course, and I'm going to my final fitting at Lord and Taylor's on Thursday." Elizabeth's cheeks were flushed with the relief of making plans now. "Come with me, and we can get something for you, too."

"All right. But really, that's not the dress you should be focusing on. You'll wear white to the wedding, of course. But who will make your wedding dress? It will have to have quite a long train, and—"

"Oh yes," Elizabeth interrupted, and before she knew what was happening, Penelope was listening to her friend go on about ivory versus ecru, and all the varieties of pink flowers, about whom she should ask to be the other bridesmaids, and what Penelope really thought of the ring, anyway.

Grayson Hayes's little sister did not vomit in public again, though she did feel like it. Watching the bright eyes of Elizabeth Holland as she imagined out loud the garments of a very large, very rich wedding party brought Penelope's anger back acutely. But despite the gales of bitterness that would have ruined the complexion of a weaker-willed girl, Penelope Hayes kept on smiling. A smiling friend was a true friend, she reminded herself, and that was how she had to appear—for now, anyway.

Twenty One

With the early arrival of Admiral Dewey's fleet in the New York harbor yesterday, and the frenzied preparations for the two parades—one by sea on Friday, and one by land on Saturday—it would seem that the city will finally have something to talk about besides the engagement of society scions Mr. Henry Schoonmaker and Miss Elizabeth Holland.

—FROM THE *NEW YORK TIMES* EDITORIAL PAGE,
WEDNESDAY, SEPTEMBER 27, 1899

"COME ON, RINGMASTER!" CRIED TEDDY CUTTING, shaking his fist in the air.

"Move, you old nag!" Henry added in a somewhat less generous tone. He was sitting beside his friend in the steep and rickety wooden grandstand seats at Morris Park, drinking Pabst from bottles with blue ribbons on them, eating salted peanuts, and generally acting like a man several notches down in class. The racetrack in the Bronx was much prettier from his family's box, but on this particular day Henry was avoiding the judgmental specter of his father, and the Schoonmaker box was a show of opulence intended to make its visitors evermindful of its owner's worldly accomplishments. Henry's worldly goal at the moment was drinking enough beer to be happy and forgetful. "Mooooove!" he cried, in the direction of a mahogany blur of thoroughbred.

Teddy tipped his brown derby back on his head, so that tufts of blond hair emerged from under his hat, and clapped his hands together rowdily as their horse approached the finish line. Ringmaster, with the little red-and-white-clothed jockey on his back, was in second, but as he approached the finish line, he was overtaken. Teddy clapped his hands once in frustration when he saw that his horse had come in fourth. "Well, there goes another twenty bucks," he said, tossing his racing card under their seats.

"Oh, come on," Henry replied, moving his black straw boater to a jauntier angle and leaning his elbows on the seat behind him. "It's not all about money."

"Says you." Teddy smiled good-naturedly. "So who's our money on next? La Infanta?"

"Why don't we just bet on all the horses next time, and then we won't have to worry about losing. I for one am just glad that we're out of the city, and away from all that madness."

Teddy raised both of his fair eyebrows in Henry's direction and took a long sip of his beer. Henry ignored the skeptical look and turned up the collar of his tweed jacket. Morris Park, where the Belmont Stakes were run, was situated in a far corner of the Bronx, a borough that still did not feel like part of New York City. It had been annexed on January 1 of that year, along with Brooklyn and Queens, but it still looked sleepy and rural and felt very far away from the rumbling grid of Manhattan, which was currently being taken over by revelers and patriots. The city was busy preparing the fireworks and streams of confetti to welcome home those who had triumphed in battle.

"I meant the celebration," Henry said, trying to dispel his friend's accusatory look with a serious expression. "Our yacht is going to be in the water parade, of course."

"Ah, yes." Teddy did not appear convinced. Nor did he appear particularly troubled by the lie either. He looked into his beer. "The hero of the South Pacific."

"The Philippines," Henry went on in a far-off voice. He had been reading the papers carefully, ever since the Hollands' coachman had accused him of being ignorant. "What a lot of trouble for such a distant country. The war in Cuba—*that* was a war I might have gotten behind."

"Yes, we all would have enlisted, if only we'd had the time."

"Are you making fun?"

Teddy shrugged. "If you don't want to admit what you're running away from, I'm certainly not going to force you."

Henry sighed and crossed his arms over his chest. Teddy lit a cigarette, which filled the air around them with sweet-smelling smoke. "I live for days like these," Henry said, casting his eyes at the handsome horses, shiny and groomed, being led out to the track.

"Yes, I know, and it's so awful when we're all dressed up and the ladies are fawning on you and the champagne comes in magnums and the plate is made of gold. You just *hate* that."

"That's not what I meant."

"Well?" Teddy exhaled in exasperation. "What seems to be the problem?"

Henry looked at his friend warily, pausing a few moments to find the words. "I'm just not sure about this engagement. Now that actual wedding clothes are being discussed, I'm getting sort of skittish. Details like that make the whole thing feel, I don't know, *real* somehow. I mean, imagine hosting lunches with the Mrs. on a day like today, instead of taking in the horses with you. Instead of doing whatever I pleased."

"But will you think of that, when you have such a pretty Mrs.?"

Henry tried not to frown, but failed. He tried to think of his fiancée as a woman he was attracted to, but the same stiff girl kept souring his thoughts, the one who, on their carriage ride through Central Park, had flinched at his every word. She'd been barely able to look at him, and seemed, especially next to the exuberant sister, with her pink cheeks and carelessness, like a cold fish. "Everyone says she is very pretty," Henry agreed bitterly.

"*I* say she is very pretty. In fact, I'd say that was understating the situation."

"Then *you* marry her," Henry replied.

"I would." Teddy laughed. "But she is already engaged,

I'm afraid. Now, would you care to bet her hand in marriage on the next race?"

"What a scandal that would be. 'Society Boys Horse Trade with Their Brides.' And you know how the papers recount every blow of my nose."

"I wasn't serious, man." Teddy clapped his hand on Henry's shoulder and gave it a little shake.

"I know." Henry looked at his hands, with their long, unblemished fingers. They were hands that had never seen a day of work. "I'm just not sure she's right. I mean, Elizabeth is so shy and polite, and you know very well that I am neither."

"Well," Teddy said, draining his beer and tossing the bottle under the seats, "she is definitely not the lady version of you, if that's what you're worried about."

"No, she is not."

"But she has taste and manners."

Henry rolled his eyes.

"And she will be impeccable in all the areas one marries for. She will host good entertainments, oversee a perfect household, she will give you handsome children, and she will not complain about any of it. You, meanwhile, will sit back and enjoy, and nobody will think twice about you discreetly living your private life on the side, with the same friendships with the same girls and new ones, too. None of your passions last, no matter who it is. So really, Elizabeth is just as good, and probably much better, than anyone you'd likely exchange vows with at any other time." Teddy seemed to think he had put an end to the discussion and he motioned for a passing boy, with a wooden ice chest full of Pabst, to stop by. When Teddy had paid for both of their beers, he handed one to Henry and knocked it gently with his own. "Cheers, my friend. I think you have made an excellent choice."

Henry drank, but continued to look dourly out at the race. It had begun sometime during their discussion, and was now swiftly and loudly reaching its denouement. "Maybe marriage just isn't what I want," he said finally.

Teddy gave a wan smile to that and looked out at the horses, who were coming breakneck around the bend. The men in the crowd were on their feet and whooping, hoping with their whole bodies that the speed of one filly would change their lives. "Well, then, what *do* you want?" Teddy asked, exasperation breaking through his tone.

The horses crossed the finish line, and Henry realized that it had been the last race of the day. Most of the crowd were ripping up their cards or cursing or shuffling away, gazes focused on their feet as they headed back to their dingy little lives. One ruddy-faced man, however, was jumping up and down and pumping his fists in the air. "I'm made!" he cried. "I'm made!"

Henry turned away from the gauche display. His friend

was looking at him as though he might not have heard properly. But Henry had heard, and the question—what *did* he want?—was marching around in his head.

But when he closed his eyes, all he could see was Diana Holland running across the grass, pulling her skirt back to reveal her lovely white calves and yelling at him. Her voice was full of heat and mischief, telling him that he had better not let the ribbon of her hat escape, or her mother would have his neck for letting her get so freckled in the sun.

Henry knew exactly what he wanted; it was just that he had no earthly idea how to get it.

Twenty Two

The whole city is waiting expectantly to see Miss Elizabeth Holland and her fiancé, Mr. Schoonmaker, in public for the first time, tomorrow night at the Waldorf-Astoria, where a party is to be given in honor of Admiral Dewey. I am sure I am not the only one anxiously anticipating the romantic vision of our premier bachelor escorting his chosen one.

—FROM THE "GAMESOME GALLANT" COLUMN IN THE *NEW YORK IMPERIAL*, THURSDAY, SEPTEMBER 28, 1899

$\mathcal{D}$IANA WAS ALMOST DOZING OFF IN THE STUFFY private room where her sister was being outfitted for tomorrow's first public appearance with Henry, when she heard that magical name she had been waiting for all afternoon.

"So . . . is Henry being romantic with you?"

It was Penelope who had asked the question, with a somewhat put-on nonchalance. She was wearing a black chiffon shirtwaist with puffed sleeves and a fawn-colored skirt with black silk trim. She had directed the question at Elizabeth, who was standing on a wood block in the middle of one of the private dressmaker's rooms at Lord & Taylor, but it was Diana whose heart fluttered at the mention of Henry's name. Elizabeth, who was encircled not only by the dressmaker, Mr. Carroll, but also by an attentive Penelope and a small fleet of shopgirls, did not appear interested in the question. She stared ahead vacantly and shrugged.

"No . . ." she said slowly. "But tomorrow night is the first night we will appear as a couple, so perhaps he is waiting till then."

"Yes, he is probably just being shy until he is sure of himself with you," Penelope replied quickly. She seemed to have recovered from her public vomiting of the week before, Diana noted. But of course, girls of their set were like moths to the light when it came to a wedding, as evidenced by Penelope's constant presence beside the bustling dressmaker.

Mr. Carroll was not a tall man, and he wore measuring tapes draped around his neck. Even though he was in his early thirties, he was already nearly bald, and he moved with a decided grace. Elizabeth stood with quiet entitlement at the center of the frenzy, even though he had been perfecting the fit of her dress for nearly an hour, marking various points to be taken in. It was a modest dress in theory, covering clavicle and wrists in Belgian lace, but every alteration seemed to bring the cloth closer to her skin. It was constructed of the palest pink silk, and its skirt was gathered in ripples and waves that cascaded downward toward the floor. The neckline was adorned with tiny freshwater pearls set in gold, hundreds of them clustered together. Diana had heard her mother exclaiming over these pearls that morning—they were a gift from Mrs. Schoonmaker, apparently.

Diana watched from one of the soft plum-colored velvet couches as Penelope pointed out an uneven cut to the dressmaker. The whole of the department store—located on Broadway at the very top of what they called Ladies' Mile, a stretch of luxury shops to rival any in the world—smelled of musk, which wafted up from the lower floors, where gloves, brooches, and bonnets were sold. Every surface seemed to be covered with mirrors, so that at any moment a young girl could be pleased by the sight of her own reflection from a new and surprising angle. Diana usually enjoyed visits to the department store, if only because they were staffed mostly by handsome young men. But today she felt already weary of the image of her sister reflected so many times over, illuminated by glittering chandelier light. She could see only a tiny bit of herself in the mirror, a background face in the grand tableau of Elizabeth's fitting.

Beside Diana was their chaperone, Aunt Edith, who was nodding off. She was wearing a maroon dress, and her neck was covered by a cream scarf, which she claimed would protect her from catarrh. Every ten minutes or so, a salesgirl would reappear with some new treasure to show them— feathered caps and leather opera gloves and bracelets inlaid with mother-of-pearl, all resting in pale pink tissue paper— and occasionally with the glasses of champagne they provided for choice customers.

"And have you chosen a wedding date?" Penelope went on, her blue eyes wide with a peculiar curiosity.

"Oh, yes . . . sometime in winter, perhaps, or spring."

Diana took one of the champagne flutes from the sales-girl and sipped. This was odd, her sister being so vague, but she wasn't about to make a point of it. If she had, she might also have pointed out that Penelope, who had little natural curiosity about other people, was being unusually inquisitive. In Diana's experience, Penelope's favored conversational topic was the subject of herself.

"That is soon," Penelope said. "Maybe you should ask Buckie to help? With the wedding planning, I mean. He is very good at what he does, you know. . . ."

"You think so?" Elizabeth stared vacantly at herself in the mirror. "All right, then. But could you ask him? You know him so much better than I do."

Diana slouched back, her head against the dark blue wallpaper, and waited for her turn to be dressed. There was something going on between Elizabeth and her friend—perhaps Penelope was jealous that Elizabeth was first to be engaged?—but Diana was having trouble following it. Ordinarily she couldn't have cared less, but today she found herself eavesdropping, listening for any mention of Henry. Henry, in any context, was interesting to her again.

Earlier, when they were lunching at the Palm Garden at the Waldorf, Elizabeth had been making a big deal about how much it meant to her that Penelope was going to be her maid of honor, and how beautiful the wedding would be, and on and on and on. When Penelope had gone to sneak a cigarette in the ladies' lounge, away from Aunt Edith's prying eyes, Elizabeth had whispered to Diana that she was sorry that she could not have two maids of honor.

"I really *had* to ask Penelope—you'll forgive me, won't you?" she'd said. "After all, we did make a promise to each other."

"I already told you that I don't care," had been Diana's perfectly audible reply. "Penelope is probably a better candidate for official flower holder at a loveless wedding, anyway."

Elizabeth had drawn back quickly at that comment, although Diana hadn't meant for it to be cruel. It was just a statement of fact. But Elizabeth had been acting withdrawn ever since—moody, even—and that was not a face she wore in public, ever.

"But you have been seeing him?" Penelope prodded. She was extremely close to Elizabeth, almost uncomfortably so, and checking the lace detailing at her throat.

"Oh, yes. We went for a ride in the park, on . . . when was it, Di?"

"On Sunday," Diana replied with authority. She didn't even have to think which *he* Penelope was referring to. "He was very gallant," she added thoughtlessly.

"Oh, was he?" said Penelope, moving her fingers to the pearls near Elizabeth's heart, but turning her eyes on Diana.

"He was nice enough," Elizabeth put in. "He rescued Diana's runaway hat."

"Oh," Penelope said, and returned to examining the dress.

Diana had replayed that afternoon in Central Park many times since, and found herself watching it in her mind again now. The blur of green and gingham as they ran over the lawn, Henry comically heroic as he waded into the murky water. The subtlety of his smile and the knowing way he looked at her.

"Have you ever taken a train in the western direction out of Grand Central?"

Diana looked up from her daydreams to see her sister, still somewhat vacant in the eyes and asking a totally illogical question. The room—with its patterned blue wallpaper and opulent rug—came back into focus as Diana considered why her sister would ask something so strange.

"No, not unless you count Newport, which is due north, I believe," Penelope declared. Diana watched her in the mirror as she bent to examine the ruffles of Elizabeth's skirt.

Elizabeth lengthened her neck, and her seven or so reflected images turned their chins up contemplatively. "How many trains do you think leave from Grand Central, in the direction of California, every day?"

"Why would you want to know a thing like that?" Penelope replied flatly, without looking up from the hem of her friend's dress.

Elizabeth's gaze drifted down to the yards and yards of pale pink satin spilling out around her. "Just that the world is so big now, I suppose. Don't you think about that sometimes?"

"No," came Penelope's quick response. She stood, her arms across her chest, and leaned against one of the mirrors so that she was looking right at Elizabeth. "Outside of New York and Newport, what do you need? Newport was so much fun last summer, by the way. It was truly the best summer of my life." Then she added, in a purposeful tone: "Henry was there."

"No, he wasn't," Diana put in. "At least, not for all of it. He was in Saratoga for some of the season, too . . . at least, I remember there being reports of him." The two older girls were giving Diana a perplexed look, and so she continued in a quieter tone. "Wasn't he, Aunt Edith? Don't you remember everyone saying that William Schoonmaker's son had come to town?"

Aunt Edith, whose head was tipped backward and whose eyes were mostly closed, made a snoring sound. "What?" she said, coming awake for a moment. "Not bustles . . ." she went on dreamily, even as her eyes returned to resting. "Those were all the rage when I was a girl, but no more, no more . . ."

There were muted giggles all around the room, quiet enough not to wake Aunt Edith, and then Mr. Carroll brought them back to the business of the day.

"All right, my gorgeous gal, I am done with you," he singsonged. Elizabeth gave him her old winning smile and allowed him to help her down from the block. Mr. Carroll had long been a favorite of the Holland sisters, and they visited him often at his own shop, as well as at the work-room he kept at Lord & Taylor so that clients like them-selves could get the first pick of fabrics. "Penelope, m'lady, you're up next."

Elizabeth and Penelope linked arms and moved in the direction of the little room where Elizabeth could take off her new dress and Penelope could put on her new one. Diana was slouching indulgently and she was sorry, she realized—looking at the backs of their heads—that they were leaving even for a minute. Surely there would be talk of Henry she would miss, and Henry talk—no matter how banal—made her breath quicken.

"Oh, excuse me, mademoiselle," said a salesgirl in a simple black shirt and white skirt. She was carrying a long, thin, white box. "I have a package from Henry Schoonmaker—"

"Oh," Elizabeth said, stepping forward and turning a little pink in the cheeks.

"—for Miss Diana Holland."

"Oh!" Penelope exclaimed, turning sharply in Diana's direction.

The salesgirl advanced toward Diana, who was still

lounging on the sofa, and handed her the box. Then she stepped backward, hovering expectantly.

"Why would Henry be sending presents to *you*?" Penelope's voice was sharp, and her plush lips were hanging open expectantly.

Diana stared down at the clean lines of the box. She could hardly believe she was holding something from Henry, especially in front of other people. She was almost afraid of what was inside, as though her secret thoughts about Henry were enclosed, ready to be revealed the moment she lifted the top. But Diana was not easily frightened, or so she reminded herself.

"Go on," Elizabeth said. She had drawn herself up the way their mother might have, and was watching Diana irritably. "Open it up."

Diana gave a little exhale and lifted open the lid. Inside was a pretty but really very ordinary ribbon of light blue silk, decorated with little ships, sewn in navy and yellow thread. Diana tried not to look disappointed as she held it up for Penelope and Elizabeth to see.

"Oh, a ribbon," Elizabeth said flatly. "To replace the one on your hat."

"A little girl's gift, for our little Di," Penelope added, smiling in a smug sort of way. "How adorable. You see, Henry *is* being sweet with you, Elizabeth, by sending trinkets to your little sister."

Several witty rebuttals clamored in Diana's brain, but Penelope and Elizabeth had already turned and were heading for the changing room, and the girl who had delivered the ribbon was on her way back to work, looking somewhat let down by what she'd witnessed in the Hollands' private room.

Looking at the ribbon, Diana couldn't help feeling foolish. Penelope was right—that was what stung. It was the kind of gift you gave a child to shut her up. And maybe that was what Henry was trying to do. She pulled at the ribbon angrily, its whole length unfolding from the box, and as she did, a small, intricately folded piece of paper fell to the ground.

Diana raised her eyes and checked the activity of the others in the room. Aunt Edith was still snoring lightly, and Mr. Carroll was moving busily about, mumbling to himself and oblivious. Diana reached down and picked up the paper.

It's the craziest thing,

but I cannot stop thinking about you.

—HS

Her heart paused its relentless thumping as she read, and a thrill crept through the whole of her body. It was almost as good as a real and sudden kiss.

Twenty Three

A society lady's personal maid is usually paid in a month what a shopgirl makes in a week, and is expected to react with glee when offered hand-me-down frocks and other once-costly items that her mistress no longer cares for. It is outrageous that, on the eve of the twentieth century, such disparities should still exist.

—FROM THE EDITORIAL PAGE OF THE *NEW YORK IMPERIAL*,
FRIDAY, SEPTEMBER 29, 1899

*L*INA HOVERED IN THE FOYER OF THE HOLLAND house, hoping for something to happen. Maybe Will would sneak up behind her and whisper in her ear how much he appreciated the gentle nursing of his wounds. But if she'd put away her hopes for a moment, she might have admitted to herself that Will wasn't paying her very much attention at all these days. Since that Sunday afternoon when she'd bandaged his hand, he had seemed completely absorbed in his own private thoughts. His mind was still stuck on Elizabeth, she knew, and Lina was beginning to get the sinking feeling that she should have told him how she felt that day in the carriage house when she'd had her chance.

Outside, the whole city had been thrown into the activity of the parade. Of course, she herself was stuck behind the oak door of her employer's home, looking out through the beveled glass. She wished she could be there in the crowd, eating freshly popped corn at Will's side. Or better yet, on one of those big yachts that the fancy types went all over the world on. What a thing that would be, to feel the ocean air against her face, to be able to go anywhere and see anything.

Supposedly there were soldiers all over the city. She had read in *Harper's Weekly* that tomorrow, thirty thousand of them would march through the city, from Grant's Tomb to the Battery, as part of the parade. She tried to glimpse some of those hordes of uniformed men through the glass, but all she saw was her sister hurrying up the sidewalk. She was with one of the lithe Lord & Taylor boys—they hired only attractive salesmen, the better to lure soft-headed female shoppers—and they were carrying two gigantic, unwieldy dress boxes.

Lina opened the door and decided that the salesman, though certainly worth looking at, wasn't nearly so handsome as Will. "Do you need help?" she called.

Her sister's face was red with exertion, but the Lord & Taylor boy gave her an effortless smile. He couldn't have been much older than Claire, and his face had fair stubble scattered across it.

"We've almost got it," Claire said as she puffed up the stairs, onto the enclosed iron filigreed porch. They managed to get the oblong boxes in through the door, and placed them on the polished oak table by the entryway. Claire sighed and smiled at the salesman who had helped her. "Well, thank you . . ."

He shrugged indifferently, and stared at the red-haired maid with lazy confidence. His eyes were hazel and unflinching.

It was clear that he thought his profession put him several rungs above the Broud sisters. Lina noticed her sister blushing and was embarrassed for her. It was perfectly obvious that the boy's stalling had nothing to do with his interest in them. When the awkwardness had become excruciating, he said, "The payment . . . ?"

"Oh!" Claire gasped, her cheeks turning an unflattering eggplant color. She looked at Lina helplessly. "Well, we don't . . . but I'm sure if you . . ."

He nodded carelessly, then reached into his pocket and removed a bill of sale. "If you could give this to Mrs. Holland, then. And Mr. Carroll told me to remind her that there are a number of unpaid bills."

"I see," Claire said softly as she took the paper. "I will tell her."

"Please do," he said. There was an unpleasant irony in his voice. Then he lifted the brim of his hat and began a slow swagger down the stairs and back toward Broadway. Just before she turned and followed her sister back inside, she saw the Lord & Taylor boy turn and shoot her a wide grin.

"He was handsome," Claire whispered excitedly as they lifted the oversize boxes and carried them up the back stairs. Lina tried to make an affirmative noise, but she only felt bad for her sister for being attracted to men like that. They were hired for their ability to flirt with ladies on shopping trips, not with ladies' maids running errands. But Claire was always more or less living in a fantasy world, and Lina supposed it was better not to disturb it.

"I can't wait to see them," Claire said as they came into Elizabeth's room. They laid the dress boxes on Elizabeth's broad sleigh bed, and Claire removed the top. She pushed aside the tissue paper and unfolded the ornamented, pale pink gown from its resting place. "Isn't it beautiful?" she whispered, almost to herself. The light of the dress seemed to reflect back on her face, illuminating it.

"Yes," Lina admitted grudgingly. It *was* beautiful, and though she was loath to be interested in such things, she could not help picturing herself in it, just for a moment.

"She's going to wear it tonight, when she's in public with Schoonmaker for the first time. She'll look perfect, don't you think?"

Lina grunted. The thought of Elizabeth's perfect appearance gave her no pleasure. It caused her pain, in fact, reminding her as it did that she would never be done up in jewels and silks, that all the tricks with which Elizabeth caught Will's attention were off-limits to her.

"Did you see Miss Liz's ring, Lina? What a thing it is." Claire laid the dress down across the bed. She examined its clusters of gold and pearl embellishments.

"I saw it." Lina looked away from the intricate folds and ruffles and wondered what Will's face would be like if he saw her in that dress. She'd always thought that pink silk would be lovely against her skin, but she had never had the chance to find out. "It's enormous."

"The papers say it cost one thousand dollars. Can you imagine? One *thousand* dollars!"

Lina shook her head disgustedly. "No, I can't. It's immoral is what it is. I mean, just think how long it would take us to make that kind of money."

"Well, we each make twelve dollars a month, so that's . . ." Claire rolled her eyes up to the coved ceiling and seemed to be calculating it. She shrugged when she lost count and said, "I don't know, but a long time, that's for sure."

"We'd get there in something under a *decade*, you ninny. Think what we could do with that kind of money, where we could go. *Anywhere*, really. We could make our own decisions, and get out of these groveling, mind-numbing jobs." By *we* Lina had meant Will and her, and she could feel a smile creeping onto her face at the very idea. "I mean, if we had that ring, and we sold it—"

"Don't talk that way!" Claire's dreamy voice had been replaced by a sharp, slightly frightened one. "It's wrong to be gossiping like this."

Lina couldn't help an affectionate laugh. "But you *love* gossip."

"Not about the Hollands," Claire said in a final tone. She

drew her hand across the dress, smoothing out its wrinkles. Then she picked it up and hung it from the black-and-gold paneled screen that Elizabeth dressed behind. She lingered by the dress, staring at it affectionately.

Lina gave her a moment, and then said, "That was odd downstairs, don't you think?"

"What was?" Claire turned innocently to look at her sister.

"The bit about the unpaid bills."

Claire's eyes darted toward the door nervously and then settled on her sister. She gave her a worried look and said, "Can I tell you something?"

"Of course," Lina said in a low, confidential voice.

"I think they're having some money . . . *trouble*."

"Who?" Lina asked, taking a step closer to her sister across the deeply shaded oriental carpet.

"The Hollands." Claire looked around her, as though she might suddenly find one of their mistresses in the room. "It's just that, I've seen that man, Mr. Broussard . . . the one who sold off some of Mr. Holland's collection when he died? He's been here, I've seen him several times, and he's left with . . . things." Claire bit her lip, as though she was coming to the most painful part. "And not just the out-of-fashion things."

"But the Hollands couldn't be . . ." Lina paused to consider the possibility that the Hollands, with all their fancy things and ridiculous rules and uppity attitudes, could want for money.

Although she had come, in the last few days, to entertain many bad thoughts about her mistress, the idea that her employers might not be rich was shocking. It turned her whole world on its head. It meant that the ways she spent her hours, and the subservience with which her sister carried herself, were absurd.

"And the other day," Claire whispered, "I think I heard something. It was when Mr. Cutting was here, and Miss Diana said—"

They were both startled from their hushed conversation by the scraping of the door against the floor, and the sight of Elizabeth coming into the room. "Oh!" she said, clearly surprised by the sight of her two maids in her bedroom.

"Miss Elizabeth," Claire gasped. She moved away from her sister and tried to put on a big smile. "I just brought the dresses back from Lord and Taylor, and we were making sure everything was all right with them."

"Thank you," Elizabeth said slowly. She looked back and forth at the two Broud girls. Perhaps she was wondering why both of them needed to be there, Lina thought as she shifted under Elizabeth's suspicious gaze. For a moment, Lina felt something like pity for her mistress—she was probably poor, and it would be especially hard for her to get used to a life without gowns, because she was accustomed to it. But then Lina reminded herself of all that Elizabeth had taken from her, and she subtly squared her shoulders.

"And I must say, your dress is exquisite," Claire went on

in a high, silly, overly enthusiastic voice that made her younger sister wince. "You will look truly, unbelievably beautiful in it."

This seemed to satisfy Elizabeth. "Thank you, Claire, that is very sweet of you to say."

She turned her gaze back on Lina, and for a long moment they stared at each other. Lina tried to give her a smile, but her mistress did not return the expression. Once upon a time she had looked up to Elizabeth, but that time felt very far away. Now it seemed like every day she was learning dirty little secrets about her former friend. That perfect image she tried so hard to maintain was cracked all over.

Lina let the smile fade from her face, but she did not budge from the spot in the middle of her mistress's room. She knew what society girls did with dirty little secrets. They collected them and used them to their own social advantage. Well, Lina had ambitions, too, and she could play that game just as well. Sitting around feeling sorry for herself and bemoaning the injustice of her life as a ladies' maid wasn't going to get her anything; she could see that now.

Lina would play her game, and sooner or later, Will would realize how duplicitous Elizabeth was. Then he would be able to see Lina with new eyes—not as a maid—but as a lady worthy of his affections.

Twenty Four

Elizabeth,

I apologize, for the water-parade festivities have turned out to be somewhat more time-consuming than I had anticipated. I'm afraid I cannot escort you to the party, but I will meet you in the Lobby, at eight thirty, and we will make our entrance then.

Regards,

H. Schoonmaker

"So tonight's the night?"

Elizabeth gazed at her reflection in the oval mirror over her dressing table and considered the question. Her face was white with powder, except for her cheekbones, which were colored with blush, and her mouth, which was full red. Her hair was done up in elaborate curls and laced through with little freshwater pearls. These were among the few words Lina had said to her all day, or maybe even all week. She pursed her lips, considering her answer. "How do you mean?"

"Oh, with the young Mr. Schoonmaker, of course," Lina said, with a familiarity that struck Elizabeth as out of character—at least in recent times. "The first night you are a couple," she added, with another wrenching pull of Elizabeth's corset strings.

"Henry?" she asked as her maid yanked her waist even narrower. The mention of Henry was surprising, because all she had been thinking about for days was Will's threat to leave. For her, tonight had hardly a thing to do with Henry. It was the night that Will was leaving. "What time is it, Lina?" she asked, thinking again of the trains and whether Will was already aboard.

"Eight o'clock, Miss Holland," Lina answered quickly.

She could feel her heart sinking. Will had told her clearly what he was going to do, and now he was gone. Of course he was gone. It was eight o'clock, and surely the last train from Grand Central had already departed.

Lina pulled at Elizabeth's corset again, and Elizabeth gasped for breath.

"Will Mr. Schoonmaker be escorting you this evening?" Lina asked as she threaded Elizabeth's corset strings through its last grommet holes.

"We are meeting at the hotel, as Henry has been caught up on the *Elysian*," Elizabeth answered automatically. The sloppily written note had arrived an hour ago, delivered by a servant who had had to row to shore on a dinghy, through the chaos currently thronging the East River. Although she had known from her mother's face that she was supposed to be upset by this setback, she had had trouble having any feeling about it at all. "That's what the Schoonmaker yacht is called," she added, in the same bland tone. "It was in the water parade for Admiral Dewey."

"Oh." Lina gave a final, cinching pull, which caused a sharp pain in Elizabeth's torso. As she stood in front of the mirror, waiting for Lina to begin putting on her dress, a cheer went up from the street. Even in the usually quiet blocks around the park, the sounds of a city in mass celebration were rising up with the evening air. There were the distant fireworks and shouts from revelers on nearby Broadway, the clopping of horse-drawn traffic, and everywhere the footfalls of soldiers in large groups. To Elizabeth, every disturbance sounded like the departure of a train.

"Just the soldiers, miss," Lina said as she returned with the dress. There was something about Lina's prying kindness that irked Elizabeth.

"When did you get so chatty?" she muttered.

"Pardon, I just—"

"I'm sorry, Lina," Elizabeth said quickly. She tried to smile a little bit at her maid, and reminded herself that Lina had once been close with Will, too. She must still feel some affection for him now. Elizabeth recalled the awkward, adoring way that Lina had always acted around Will, back when they were all friends, a little trio, in the days before everything became complicated, in the days before Elizabeth realized how deep her feelings for Will went. It occurred to her suddenly that Lina might already know that he was gone—that she, too, might be saddened by his absence. "That was a cruel thing for me to say, and I didn't mean it. I guess I must be a little nervous about coming out with Henry."

Lina made a little bowing motion with her head, and then returned to her usual surly silence as she helped Elizabeth into the dress. It fit perfectly, the dramatic pearl-embellished neckline highlighting her small waist. As Lina secured it on her, Elizabeth couldn't help but think that if she had been braver, if she had done what Will asked her to, she would never have worn dresses like this again. For a moment she hated silk and pearls and gold detail, and even herself, for being bought so easily. Of course, the reasons for accepting Henry's proposal were many and varied, but at that self-loathing moment it seemed to her that she had allowed herself to be bought for the price of one custom-made gown. She would have burst into tears, but she couldn't in front of Lina, who was slipping on Elizabeth's high-heeled slippers.

"Are you ready?" Diana stepped through the mahogany doorframe. She was wearing a simpler dress than Elizabeth's, with short sleeves and a sweetheart neckline and a big lavender skirt that swayed behind her. A wide black sash marked her little waist, and it made her look much less sloppy than usual. Elizabeth knew that it had been remade from an old dress—the Holland family could barely afford one new frock—but she looked bright and pretty, and Elizabeth found some small amount of joy in this. At least one of them might yet be happy.

"Yes, almost." Elizabeth managed to stand despite her

body being so heavy with regret. She checked her bangs in the mirror and then tried to smile as she took her little sister's arm and accompanied her through the halls to the first floor. She would have thanked Lina, or acknowledged her in some way, but her thoughts were so focused on Will's leaving that she could not think of the words.

When the sisters arrived in the foyer, they saw their mother waiting for them. She was wearing her widow's black, and she looked relieved by the handsome appearance of her two daughters. Even Diana's warm cheeks were full of some kind of happy anticipation, and Elizabeth wondered at herself for being so miserable when she was doing something that brought her family such relief. She managed a nod, doing her best to seem in a normal state of mind as well, and then Mrs. Faber appeared to help them into their evening wraps.

When they were properly attired for the evening, they turned and made their slow way out the great oak door. Elizabeth's throat was tight and she looked out at the street, with all its commotion, and felt overwhelmed and scattered. Then her eyes fell on the Holland brougham, hitched to the Hollands' four black horses. She saw the figure in the driver's seat and blinked twice to be sure.

There was Will, right there before her. He did not look happy—how could he be?—but neither did he look sad or anxious. He looked calm, and his pale blue eyes were fixed on

Elizabeth in so casual a way that she was sure she began to blush. She thought she might float away with joy.

There was a long moment when she forgot what she was supposed to do that night. Her mother and sister did not seem to have noticed that Elizabeth had stopped in her tracks. They were moving forward, descending the seven brownstone steps and waiting for Will to help them up into the carriage. She took a step toward the carriage, wishing she could touch him, just to be sure she wasn't imagining his presence.

He was wearing a short wool jacket with the collar turned up, black trousers over the usual scuffed brown boots, and a derby, which was something he only ever did at night. Although he didn't look at her as he helped her up, she could feel his hands on her waist, and was comforted by his familiar touch. Then she was inside the carriage and the horses were pulling them in the direction of the Waldorf.

"There's a smile," her mother said.

"Oh." Elizabeth instinctively put her fingers to her cheeks. "I'm just relieved is all. Relieved we're on our way."

"Yes. It's a shame, of course, that Henry is meeting you there, and not at our house—"

Elizabeth could not help but continue smiling dumbly, no matter what her mother was saying. She felt as light as air, flying forward through the city, with just a touch of the frenzy reaching her through the windows of the carriage.

"But it is just as well, I suppose. The important thing is that you enter the ballroom together."

"Yes," Elizabeth said brightly. She would have replied brightly to almost anything her mother said right then. Will had not left her. He would come to understand that she was doing what she had to for her family. They could never be together exactly, but they would never be so very far apart, either. She would find a way to see him whenever she could, and maybe he could learn to love her even when she was a Mrs. Schoonmaker.

Despite the heavy traffic of the evening, they soon arrived at the corner of Fifth Avenue and Thirty-fourth. Elizabeth continued smiling, and waited for Will to come around and open the door. Outside, all of New York seemed to be on the streets, clamoring in the direction of the Waldorf-Astoria. The hotel rose fifteen or so stories into the sky and winked from every turret and gable, from each of the countless windows ablaze in the night. Carriages crowded the street down the whole block.

After her mother and sister had alighted, Elizabeth took Will's hand and let him help her down. When her feet touched the ground, she loosened her grip, but he did not. He held on tight, and as she turned, she saw him bend and kiss her hand. The warmth of his lips spread through her whole body. Will raised his eyes to hers. She looked into them, that light, determined color, at his beautifully crooked nose, and below that at the full lips that she had kissed so many times. They were mouthing something, she realized. Will was silently telling her, in front of the Waldorf-Astoria and everybody, that he loved her.

"Will," Mrs. Holland barked. Elizabeth, petrified, drew back her hand. Then she heard with relief her mother's run-of-the-mill instructions—Will was to bring the horses back now, as the Schoonmakers were providing their return transportation—and knew that his dangerous gesture had not been seen. She felt emboldened enough to give him a shy smile, to tell him in her own subtle way how relieved she was that he had stayed. Then she turned and followed her family into the hotel.

"Isn't the weather perfection?" Elizabeth turned to see a corpulent woman in a dress of heavy gold brocade. She didn't recognize her, and decided she must have been one of those mining millionaires from out West who seemed to arrive in New York in greater numbers every day. "Dewey weather, that's what I call it," the woman added with an apple-cheeked smile.

"Yes, it is very nice." Elizabeth realized only after she had spoken how pleasant the air really was—moist and just cool enough. For the first time all week, she felt like she was going to be all right. "Have a good evening!" she called to the woman as Diana took her hand and pulled her into the grand and glittering lobby.

They were moving quickly down a long corridor with walls covered by amber marble and mirrors and a mosaic floor. Party-hoppers lounged on the plush velvet chairs that lined the walls, laughing and shouting and people-watching. The place was full of movement, and Elizabeth began to see why the papers referred to it as Peacock Alley.

"He's not here," Mrs. Holland announced hotly.

"Who?" Elizabeth said. She could see that her mother was irritated, but she could not stop smiling yet. She was still too caught up in happy thoughts about Will.

"Well, Henry, of course. They are all saying he is still on the yacht." Elizabeth watched as her mother crossed her arms. She seemed almost to be huffing, so distraught was she by the loss of this public demonstration of her daughter's engagement.

Penelope came up behind her, then, looking beautiful in her persimmon-colored dress with the low neck and shimmering beaded detail. The dress hugged her hips and fishtailed at the back, and her skin glowed in a very particular way. "Yes, some of the guests from the *Elysian* have already returned to shore," she reported. "And it seems Henry got caught up."

"Oh well," Elizabeth said gaily. "He will be here soon enough. It's no reason not to enjoy the party." She reached for Penelope's hand and gave her friend a warm kiss on either cheek. It was good to have Penelope back—she had the kind of spirit that would not suffer when there was a party to go to.

Mrs. Holland turned sharply and headed toward the enormous ballroom of the Waldorf-Astoria. Elizabeth looked at the bright faces of her friend and sister, and shrugged. "Somebody should tell Mother that *she's* not marrying Henry Schoonmaker."

Penelope laughed, and Diana giggled, and then the three girls linked arms and walked into that glittering grand fete, as happy together as they would ever be.

Twenty
Five

There are so many parties being given, so many festivities planned, that it seems certain that one man will be much talked about but seen not nearly enough. That would be the man who licked the Spanish in the Pacific: Admiral of the Navy, George Dewey.

—FROM THE FIRST PAGE OF THE *NEW YORK IMPERIAL*,
FRIDAY, SEPTEMBER 29, 1899

$\mathcal{S}$ ITTING IN THE BALLROOM OF THE WALDORF-ASTORIA hotel felt to Diana like being buried in the most heavily ornamented mausoleum ever constructed. The walls and ceilings and even the floors seemed to glow a divine shade of yellow, as the profusion of mirrors reflected every bright thing in the room. Light blazed down from the forty-foot ceilings, casting the faces of the guests in warm, sparkling hues. There were all the usual people—the sons and daughters of old New York families mixing with the new millionaires, in black tails and skirts of tulle and spangled satin—and the naval men, with their epaulettes and swords, too. With every passing day, Diana thought, she was seeing more of the world.

"Did you see Agnes?" Penelope was saying to Elizabeth now. The three girls were sitting on one of the plush sofas that lined the walls, fanning themselves with real lace fans and resting between dance partners. Their skirts—lavender, pink, and red—spilled across the floor. Every time the door opened from the hall, they looked to see if it was Henry who was coming in, but none of them seemed particularly bothered that it never was. Diana had been able to think of nothing else since receiving his note yesterday afternoon, of course, but Henry's arrival would only mean watching him dance with her sister for hours on end.

"Agnes really is in dire need of a new dress," Elizabeth replied in a low voice, bringing Diana back from her thoughts of Henry.

"And dancing with a soldier! She would make a good soldier's wife, I suppose."

"Oh, hush . . . let's not be mean." Elizabeth's voice fell to a whisper. She was embarrassed, but Diana could hear the amusement in her voice, too. Sometimes it seemed like her sister had two personalities, warring with each other over whether to be cunning or good.

"I would marry a soldier," Diana put in merrily. The words immediately produced an image in her mind of Henry in uniform, looking very straight and clean and handsome. "Then I could go anywhere in the world."

"But Di, you already *can* go anywhere in the world," Penelope said.

Diana remembered her comment of the other day, about Newport and New York and not needing anyplace else, and decided that Penelope's idea of what constituted the world was very far from her own. She kept her mouth shut and leaned back into the overstuffed velvet cushions of the sofa. In front of them couples moved across the shiny floor, keeping one eye on their partners and the other on the constant ebb and flow of guests.

"Did you see your neighbor Brody Fish?" Penelope went on, above the din. "He's gotten better-looking, I think."

"Yes," Elizabeth agreed. "There's something broader about the shoulders with him, isn't there?"

"Well, someday, when you're a matron and very bored by everything, perhaps you can have a little fling on the side with him."

Elizabeth put her gloved hands over her pink cheeks. This was the response Diana would have expected of her sister, of course—prudish and proudly shocked—but she couldn't help but pity her for the deepening red shade of her face. Diana reached out and squeezed her sister's hand. "Liz, we all know how very, very moral you are, and we don't think any less of you because you think Brody Parker Fish has nice shoulders." She paused and looked out at all the men, young and old, in their tailored suits, and thought how merely adequate they all looked compared to the boy in her thoughts. "*I* think so, too," Diana offered.

"It's just that I would never . . ." Elizabeth trailed off, before changing the subject. "What do you think our mothers are talking about?"

The three girls turned and saw the dour faces of Mrs. Holland and Mrs. Hayes. They were seated across the room, on a golden crushed-velvet couch of their own, watching the crowd and leaning back occasionally to whisper to each other. Diana could remember a time when her mother wouldn't so much as call on Mrs. Hayes, despite her husband's entirely neutral feelings for Penelope's father, but those days were past, apparently. Even their mother could not afford to be snotty anymore, Diana thought happily, as a group of dancers waltzed in front of the older women.

"The Misses Holland, Miss Hayes . . ." Diana looked up to see Teddy Cutting, in black pants and tails, making a little bow. His blond hair was slicked to the side, and there was a touch of sunburn on his nose.

"Teddy," Elizabeth said warmly.

"Hello, Mr. Cutting." Penelope gave him a remote smile.

Teddy went down the line kissing each of the girls' hands. Diana looked past him, through the scrum of bodies. Her mother had bade farewell to Mrs. Hayes and was moving along the wall with her chin raised. Diana was watching to see whom she was walking toward when she heard their male visitor say, "I'll be wanting to dance with all of you, of course. But perhaps tonight, if you'll allow me, I will begin with the youngest. Diana, may I?"

Diana looked up, startled. Though Teddy was one of her sister's friends, and so generally around, he had always seemed too taken with Elizabeth to notice her existence. It felt somehow odd that he was smiling at her now and offering his hand. She took it, noting out of the corner of her eye that her mother was now speaking with a large, familiar-looking man.

"No sign of Henry?" Teddy asked as they moved onto the dance floor. Diana tried not to smile at the mere mention of the name, but then she noticed that Teddy was looking back in the direction of Elizabeth and Penelope, anyway. She suddenly wondered if there wasn't a reason he was asking her in particular. Perhaps Henry had even mentioned her name. Everyone knew that he had been friends with Teddy since forever, after all, and it seemed likely that if he were going to talk about her with anybody, it would be with the man she was dancing with right now.

"Not a one."

Teddy's hands were barely touching her, and she couldn't help but wonder if he might somehow think of her as Henry's girl. Teddy might even like that—then he might still have a chance with Elizabeth, whom he had always obviously desired.

Diana tried to concentrate on her steps—she was not so polished a dancer as her sister, but she seemed to be following along well enough. As they moved, she got a better view of her mother and realized that it was William Schoonmaker to whom she was talking. He was bowing his head in a confidential way, but his face had taken on a hue that suggested some sort of rage. She was wondering what it must be like for Henry, to have a father like that, when Teddy spoke again.

"Elizabeth seems all right, though."

"Oh." Diana paused and tried not to give Teddy a pitying look, though it was sort of pathetic how enamored of her sister he remained. They turned and then Diana could see, over Teddy's shoulder, that Elizabeth's face was lit up with laughter. She and Penelope were holding hands and shielding their open mouths with their lace fans. "Yes, actually," she said. "She seems entirely happier not to have Henry around."

She had meant it as a joke, and Teddy laughed. But as soon as the words escaped her mouth, she realized they were true. How curious, she thought, peeking back at her sister, that the perfect girl with the perfect-catch fiancé was relieved not to be with him.

"We were on the yacht together this afternoon. I should have made him come with me," Teddy was saying. "When I left, Henry was still there with that Buck fellow—who is apparently now one of the groomsmen." Teddy shook his head in disbelief. "And Buck assured me he would see to it that Henry arrived here on time. But now I see he hasn't."

Diana looked at her partner, whose concerned features were flattered by the golden light, and wondered why he was so worried about his friend, anyway. Certainly Henry could take care of himself. They had done a turn around the floor, and she could again see Henry's father over the black coat-covered shoulders of the men and the elaborate hairpieces of the ladies.

"Well, I see someone who isn't so pleased with his not being here on time," she said, jutting her chin in the direction of her mother and Mr. Schoonmaker, who was still speaking into her mother's ear and gesticulating with his hands. He seemed to be demonstrating some plan with the movements of his broad fists. Teddy looked and shook his head sadly.

"I wouldn't want to say anything bad about Buck, but he seemed intent on making us all have *too* good a time." Teddy exhaled audibly, and as they stepped lightly around, he looked out of the corner of his eye at Elizabeth again. "And by us, I mean Henry."

Diana found herself involuntarily smiling again at the mention of Henry's name. Teddy was saying it an awful lot, which seemed like more evidence that he might know of their flirtation. The music swelled and then all of a sudden stopped. She and Teddy came to a halt and turned toward the door along with the rest of the guests in the crowded room. Loud cheers of "Bravo!" suddenly erupted into the cavernous space.

Diana stood on her toes and peeked around the bodies in front of her until she got a glimpse of the man who had just entered. He was of average height and had a drooping gray mustache, and wore a handsome dark blue uniform with tassels and gigantic brass buttons, and a long, slender sword attached to his belt. He raised his hand and smiled at the shouts of "Admiral" and "Hooray!"

"So that is the hero of the Pacific?" Teddy said as he joined in the clapping. Several of the guests in front of them had taken out small American flags and were waving them about in the air.

Diana began to clap, too. The whole crowd was on its feet, applauding the admiral of the Navy. William Schoonmaker nodded to her mother and then moved to a spot just behind and to the right of the admiral. The color of his face had not mellowed, but he did smile as he began waving at the crowd, as though he, too, were some sort of military hero.

Diana smiled as well, but not because she was in the presence of military greatness. She smiled because the man who had just arrived was not Henry. He might have come and danced all night with her sister, but she felt sure, as she threw her hands together and called out in celebration, that he was out in the dark somewhere, thinking of her instead.

Twenty Six

Dear P,

Just dropped the boy-o off at home, as planned. He was merrily blotto all afternoon, and is now nursing some well-deserved black coffee.

Your humble servant,

JPB

ENELOPE HAD DONE IT DOZENS OF TIMES BEFORE.
She pulled her black wool cape around her and let
the hood fall down over her eyes. Then she slipped around back
of the Schoonmaker residence and let herself in through one of
the servants' entrances. She moved through the familiar back
arteries of the house, lifting her skirts as she went, quietly and
cautiously, to the room where she knew she would find Henry. It
was well past midnight, and she had already had a full evening of
dancing and being talked about. She was not in the least tired.

Determination was coursing through her instead. She
felt alive with the trespass, and beautiful, and a tad hateful.
Elizabeth had been her usual self all night, smiling quietly
through her humiliation. Henry had never shown, of course.
He had gotten caught up with all the sparkling wine that Buck
had arranged to be poured into his glass throughout the day.
Everything had gone just as Penelope had planned it: Henry
had spent the day drunk and then drunker on his yacht. He
had grown happy and then rowdy, and he had forgotten all

about his pesky obligations to his new fiancée. It had unfolded exactly as she'd hoped it would, except that Elizabeth had been graceful and lovable even in defeat.

Penelope would have enjoyed tearing Elizabeth's blond hair out of her pretty head. She would have liked to rip that expensive pink skirt to shreds. But Penelope was not playing for quick victories; she was playing to win. And she could not win by attacking the sweetheart of Old New York. So she moved invisibly through the third-floor hall, looked back once to make sure that she had not been seen, and entered the study that adjoined Henry's room.

"Henry," she whispered as the carved oak door closed behind her. Henry was lying across the deep brown leather couch in the center of the room. His eyes drooped, and a lit cigarette rested between his lips. *"Henry,"* she said again, a little louder this time. Slowly, he reached up and plucked the cigarette from his mouth and then turned to her.

"Oh," he said, his dark brow rising slightly. He was as burned by the sun and the drink as a real sailor, but he was still excruciatingly handsome.

"You look like a prole, Henry."

He looked down at himself, at his white dress shirt unlinked at the cuffs, and his light blue trousers rumpled by his day on the river, but ignored the comment. He replied flatly: "How was the party?"

"You mean the party you never showed up to?" Penelope let her hood fall back now, but her smile was subtle enough that Henry might not have noted it.

"Yes, that one." Henry lifted the cigarette back to his lips.

Penelope pulled off a long white glove and began idly swinging it back and forth. "Say, wasn't that the party where you were supposed to make some kind of entrance with Elizabeth?"

Henry exhaled a white puff of smoke. "I'd rather not, Penelope."

"But don't you think it's meaningful, Henry? That somehow you forgot to attend the opening night of your own engagement? Her mother was furious, you should know."

"Was she?" Henry said softly.

"You know, there was a time," Penelope said, crossing the parquet floor and taking a seat on the leather couch near Henry's feet, "when you would have found that *funny*."

Henry didn't answer. He took a drag of his cigarette and stared past Penelope's shoulder. She reached for his cigarette case, which rested on his stomach, and lit one.

"Henry." She paused for a few thoughtful drags, drawing her knees up so that her skirt overflowed onto the couch. Her voice grew soft now that she was close to him. "Why didn't you tell me, Henry? Why did it have to be such a mean surprise?"

"Well, Penny . . ." Henry pushed the crown of his head back into the leather couch cushion and looked up at the fresco on the ceiling, which depicted a happy garden party in the new, loose style. "I did try to tell you, actually. Perhaps if you weren't in the habit of burning my letters, you would know that."

This was an unhappy realization for Penelope, that Henry was capable of breaking things off with her in a note. Her pride smarted as she remembered what they had done while that card burned. She was beginning to feel that she might lose control of the situation altogether. "I had no idea I was so . . . *nothing* to you."

"It's not like that." Henry took a last drag of his cigarette and put it out in the cut-glass ashtray on the ground. "I didn't mean for it all to be so awful for you. But you're going to have to believe that this is what I have to do."

Penelope stood up sharply, so that her glistening reddish-orange train came hurrying along behind her. There was a strange echo to his words that she disliked. She walked in the direction of the bookshelf, with all its unread books, and spat, "That's exactly what Elizabeth said to me."

"Really?" Henry pushed himself up on his elbows and followed Penelope with a curious gaze.

"Yes. Now *really*, what's going on here? You don't love her, I know you don't. She's a mannered little priss, and if you don't know it yet, you will soon." Penelope turned quickly and moved across the room. She landed at Henry's side, her hand on his, her legs folded beneath her on the floor. "Henry, you are in love with *me*. Can't you see I'm the only one who can keep up with you? Who else could possibly—?"

The darkness around Henry's eyes had taken on a far-off quality. Penelope stared at him, her mouth agape, wondering what else she could say. She had just put it as clearly as she knew how. The logic was obvious.

He lifted his hand away from hers suddenly and stood up. His hair, which was usually so perfectly pomaded into place, was comically mussed. A black bunch of it stood up in back.

Penelope stiffened. "Where are you going?"

"My dear Penny," Henry replied. He appeared to have to concentrate on balancing for a moment. When he had collected himself, he went about tucking in his shirt and combing his hair with his fingers. With a few gestures, he was again the dashing figure she was so proud to be seen dancing with, even if he was wearing day clothes at night. "I'm afraid you're going to have to excuse me. I have an errand to run."

"An errand? At this time of night?" Penelope pushed herself against the couch and put on a petulant expression. "And after I went to all this trouble to visit you."

Henry went over to the desk, where an elaborate samovar

sat. He poured coffee into a small silver cup and drank from it. Then he turned back to Penelope, lifted and dropped his shoulders, and let his gaze linger on her for a minute. The light in his eyes danced. "You know, I don't feel drunk at all anymore. And I was in a real state earlier."

"I know," Penelope said bitterly. She had had nothing but Vichy water all day, so as to better fit into her dress, and she was feeling awfully empty all of a sudden. "I arranged it."

"Really." Henry took a final sip of the coffee and then put the cup back down. "That doesn't surprise me, I guess. Oh well."

"Oh *well*? Henry, I'm here. I am right here." She raised her eyebrows and tried to give him the same flirtatious look she had given him so many times before. "What else do you need?"

Henry crossed over to the couch, where Penelope was still lounging on the intricate parquet-wood floor, and kissed her airily on either cheek. "I don't think you'd really understand."

Penelope looked up at him, her great blue eyes narrowed to angry red slits.

Henry returned her expression with an almost careless smile. "You know how to find your way out, don't you? I'm sorry I can't escort you myself, but right now I have to go make my amends to the Holland family."

Penelope sat on the floor in a pile of red silk, still unable to grasp what she was hearing, as Henry plucked a straw boater from the post of a chair. His step was light as he exited the room, and he did not pause to look behind him. Watching that slender, slightly rumpled figure walking out the door, Penelope felt, for perhaps the first time, humiliation tinged with the worst kind of loneliness.

Twenty Seven

A lady must retain always her composure. Even in a rainstorm, she must appear joyous and dry. When she loses her composure, then the respect of her peers and her staff will follow in short order.

—*VAN KAMP'S GUIDE TO HOUSEKEEPING FOR LADIES OF HIGH SOCIETY*, 1899 EDITION

ELIZABETH HAD LEFT HER PATIENCE SOMEWHERE in the riotous streets of Manhattan. All the time it would take—to wash her face and take off all the layers of dress—would have driven her insane. As soon as she knew her mother was in bed, she took the familiar back-of-the-house route, custom-made petal-pink dress and all.

Henry had never arrived at the ball, so Elizabeth could still feel the touch of Will's mouth on her hand, unsullied by any potential encounter with her sham fiancé. They had ridden home in a Schoonmaker carriage—Henry's father, sweaty and clearly irritated by his son's no-show, had insisted—but even that couldn't change the direction of her thoughts. She had gazed out its window at the explosions in the sky, and counted the blocks until she was home.

All night she had been thinking of Will. Even when she was dancing, moving gracefully through those golden hours with a smile for Brody Parker Fish or Teddy Cutting, she was counting the hours until she could be with him again.

They were in love; they would find a way. Elizabeth felt dizzy and light with the possibilities. She was almost mouthing the words to herself as she crossed the empty kitchen and went hurtling down the wooden steps into a darkened stable.

"Will?" she whispered into the darkness. She kicked off her slippers and hurried toward where she knew the ladder to be. The old floorboards were soft against her feet, the hay sharp and ticklish. She pulled herself up the ladder with her hands and darted across the loft. "Will?" she said again. "Will, are you there?"

She fell to her knees on the bed, feeling the mattress in front of her. It was bare—the blankets and even the sheets were gone. She pushed herself up and climbed backward down the ladder. Then she went running across the floor to the far side of the stable, between the stalls where the horses were kept.

"Will?" she called. "Will, are you there? Will?"

She could remember one previous time when she had come to visit Will and had been unable to find him. It was before her father died, when nothing seemed very consequential. She had tiptoed through the stalls, giggling and whispering his name, until she found him, standing against one of the wooden posts that separated the individual stables. His eyes had been half shut, and he had been drifting off into one of those dreams set on the other coast. He was almost sleeping standing up, the way the horses did. When she woke him by saying his name, he told her that Jumper, Elizabeth's favorite thorough-bred, had fallen ill. Will had been sleeping by her side. That night, they had stayed up together till dawn, cooing to her.

But tonight there was no sign of a coachman sleeping amongst his charges. She ran back and forth, whispering his name, but there were only the black-lake eyes of the horses staring at her blankly over the Dutch doors of their stalls, and the sweet, grassy smell of the hay as her bare feet fell upon it. She turned, and turned again, bewildered by his absence. She had been so looking forward to seeing him all night. It was inconceivable that he wasn't there, feeling exactly the same thing.

Elizabeth took a few breaths and went back up to Will's loft. She was afraid of the oil lamp, because of all the hay and because she had never had to light one herself, but her eyes were adjusting without it. The naked mattress stared back at her plaintively. The wooden milk crates that he had once used as bookshelves were empty, and she knew without looking that the chest of drawers, a shabby piece that had been her father's as a child, was now empty of his clothes. She went back to the edge of the loft and sank down to the place where Will had always waited for her.

Her hair was coming undone, and she pulled at strands until the pearls that had adorned them all night began to come loose and roll across the warped wooden floor behind her. The image of Will in front of the hotel was so fresh for her, it might have happened seconds ago. He had been looking at her with such intention, and she had taken it as confirmation of his love. He had taken her hand and kissed it, and she had taken this as a recklessly romantic gesture. She replayed the memory, like some jerky motion picture, and with a water-logged heart she began to understand what Will had been doing. He had been trying to say good-bye.

She pulled her hair back from her face and felt her throat begin to close. The tears were coming, sobs racking her whole body. She bent forward and let them soak her skirt, quietly saying Will's name again and again. She must have been going on like this for some time, when the voice broke in.

"What have you got to cry about?"

All of Elizabeth froze. "Excuse me?" She was too frightened to look up just yet and see who had caught her in her secret life.

"Your dress does look a wee bit ruined. Does that explain the tears?"

Elizabeth's eyes rose slowly. There was Lina, her arms crossed against her chest, standing at the entryway where Elizabeth always paused when she was coming to visit Will. Lina was wearing that same ugly black dress, which fell, unflatteringly, to just above her ankle, and she was tapping her left foot.

"No," Elizabeth replied. She sat up straight and steadied her voice. "Not the dress."

"Well, what then? Is it Will?" Lina shook her head disgustedly, and added ironically, "*Your* Will?"

"What?" The skin around Elizabeth's eyes tightened as she stared down at her maid. She was reminded of Lina as a child, crying because she felt excluded from Will and Elizabeth's games. There was that same hurt look in her eyes, although she seemed more erratic and somehow frightening now. Elizabeth brought her legs up to the loft floor and scrambled to climb down the ladder. As she went, her skirt caught on the rough wood. She looked up only when she heard a ripping sound and saw that a heap of pink silk was caught at the top of the ladder, but she kept going. At that moment she could not have cared less about anything.

She landed on the ground with purpose and turned to Lina just as she was saying, "You never deserved him."

Elizabeth wasn't sure whether to argue with Lina or find some way to convince her not to tell anyone about the secret between her and Will. They stared at each other for a long moment. As the fierce beating of her heart slowed a little, she noticed the pained cast of Lina's features. She was trying to be cruel to Elizabeth, but she too was clearly devastated by Will's disappearance.

"You don't know anything," Elizabeth said in a firm,

quiet voice. She could feel her cool returning. "And you most certainly are not where you are supposed to be."

Lina's smirk was constant. "And where would that be, miss? Up in your room, helping you off with your gown? Makes my job awful hard, having no mistress to serve."

"That's exactly where you are supposed to be. And don't forget, you serve at my pleasure. You are an *employee* of my family."

Elizabeth drew in her breath and propped a hand against her hip. She stared at Lina, with her nose darkened by freckles, and her big bony shoulders. She lifted a fair eyebrow and said, in as authoritative a tone as she could manage, "You must be such a disappointment to your poor sister. It is for *her* sake that I am not going to fire you."

Elizabeth let her arm fall back to her side disgustedly. She pulled her torn skirt away from her feet with one hand and let the other one swing as she walked past Lina and toward the kitchen door. She paused with one foot on the first step and turned her head in Lina's direction. "That's why I'm not going to fire you *yet*."

Lina stared back, her eyes narrow with hatred, but said nothing. Elizabeth tipped her head upward slightly and let the moment unfurl. The knowledge that Will was gone, one person lost in a vast country, was gnawing at her from the inside. But she kept herself from crying as she moved slowly and proudly away from her maid, and up those worn steps for the final time.

Dear Elizabeth,

It looks like you won't be going
with me. I am trying not to feel
too brokenhearted, though, and am
leaving with the hope that you will
soon be following me. I am going to
California, and I can only pray that
I will one day see you there. Or if
you've changed your heart already,
meet me at Grand Central. The last
train leaves at eleven o'clock.

Your faithful,
Will Keller

*L*INA FOUND THE NOTE IN THE TOP DRAWER OF WILL'S dresser, tucked into the pocket of a navy coat. She lit the oil lamp on the chest, cranking the canvas wick and touching it gently with a match. The letter was written on a torn piece of thick cream paper, the kind that Elizabeth used for all her correspondence.

She ran her fingers along its gold edges, and thought how difficult it must have been for Will to resist Elizabeth. She must have seemed very rare to him, a possessor of magic objects, which was how she used to seem to her personal maid, too. But now Lina was catching glimpses of a new Elizabeth. She was a girl who had to be put together, hair and face, who preened alone in her own rich bedroom. She was a mirage.

Lina turned the note in her hand, her face growing hot and furious as she thought about the things her onetime friend had just said to her. Her words had been brutal and her haughtiness disgusting. As long as she thought about Elizabeth she stayed angry, but then the memory of her mistress faded and the reality of Will's absence began to set in. Lina lay back on his mattress, stretching her long arms over her head, and tried to think him back into the room. This only made her growing sadness worse. The only boy she'd ever imagined herself loving was gone. And she had never so much as kissed him.

She put the heels of her palms against her eyes to keep from crying, and when that instinct passed, she brought herself back up. The worst of it was, he had left without even considering Lina—but perhaps it was not too late for that. She went to the dresser and removed the navy coat. It was the kind of coat that sailors wore and she had seen it on Will in winters past, when he was shoveling snow or bringing blankets out to the horses. He must have left it for Elizabeth, in case she decided to follow him into the night—that was the kind of boy he was—but Elizabeth had overlooked it. Lina put the coat on and slipped the note back into its pocket. She collected the little pearls from the floor that she had laced into Elizabeth's hair earlier in the night, and then took the small side door onto the street.

The night was balmy and Lexington Avenue was still full of people. They had been celebrating the return of their war hero all day, and they continued to celebrate now, charging through the streets with flags, leaning on one another in happy fatigue. No one noticed Lina as she walked quickly, pulling Will's coat around her body. She hardly needed it, but it smelled like him—like hay and soap—so she kept it on.

She walked the more than twenty blocks to Grand Central without letting her feet bother her. The delicate Elizabeths of the world would not understand, of course—walking like this in the middle of the night would frighten them or tire them out or destroy their reputations. But to Lina, it felt dignified and good. When she saw the great building, with its imposing classical façade, turreted towers, and oval-shaped windows, she broke into a run.

Inside, the terminal was almost empty. There were a few people, covered in light blankets and napping in the long wooden seats. Lina hadn't thought to look at a clock in a long time, but it seemed much later here than on the street. She hurried across the waiting area, her low heels clicking lightly against the marble, until she reached the ticket counter. The attendant was asleep, and she had to knock on the glass to wake him. When he finally heard her, he pushed the black cap away from his eyes and leaned forward. Lina gave him her most hopeful face. He was young, probably not much older than she was. He looked like he might sympathize with her mission.

"Yes, ma'am," he said, focusing his sleepy eyes on her.

"I want to know . . ." Lina began, and then stopped herself. It occurred to her for the first time that she might look a bit crazed, that she was carrying no luggage and hardly wearing the proper clothes for travel. "Could you tell me," she began, trying to make her voice sound confident, "was there a young man who came through here tonight? He would have been going west? Maybe to California?"

"A young man?" The ticket counter attendant repeated slowly, a faint smile spreading across his face. "What kind of a young man?"

"About your age, I guess." Lina felt a little breathless and she didn't know why the attendant seemed so amused by everything. "He would have been traveling alone."

"A young man traveling alone? And why would you be trying to find out where he was going so late at night?"

"That's none of your business." Lina pulled the coat around her and tried to look as entitled as possible. She wanted to do what Elizabeth would have done in the same situation, and so she turned her chin upward and to the side. "Well," she went on, "are you going to help me, or are you just going to stand there?"

"I would like to help you," the attendant drawled, his eyes sparkling at Lina. She couldn't imagine why, but he seemed to be looking her over with a certain interest. "But I work for the New York, New Haven, and Hartford Railroad. If your fellow was going to California, he would have been taking the New York Central."

"Oh," Lina replied in a smaller voice. She must have looked a little sad and confused, because the attendant pointed across the huge waiting room.

"Their operation is in the next hall over, right through that doorway there."

Lina nodded in thanks, then turned and began to run in the direction he had pointed.

"If you can't find him, come back and pay me a visit . . ." he called after her. Lina paused to have a look back and caught a wink from the attendant. She couldn't be sure, because she had never been flirted with before, but she thought perhaps the railroad attendant was doing just that. This seemed like a good sign. She managed a smile, and then resumed her hurried pace across the marble floor.

At the New York Central ticketing booth, she found an older man who was fully awake and completely indifferent to any charms she might possess. He wore muttonchops, which did nothing to disguise a large, shiny face.

"He was tall, you say?" the New York Central man replied.

"Yes, tall, with very light blue eyes and a handsome face. He wouldn't have had much with him, and he would have been traveling alone."

"We get plenty who fit that description." The man paused to rearrange some papers, as Lina looked on urgently. "But not so many late of a Friday night. I know who you're talking about, and he left on the eleven o'clock train to Chicago. If you say he's heading to California, I'd imagine he'd transfer there for another train, take him all the way to Oakland."

"What time is it?" Lina said, her heart sinking. She knew from the way he was speaking that the eleven o'clock was long gone.

"It's ten to two."

"When is the next train to Chicago?" she asked, pressing her callused fingers against the marble counter.

"Not until morning, young lady. Seven o'clock is the next Chicago-bound train."

Lina thought about going back to the Hollands' and facing Elizabeth again. "I'd like a one-way ticket to Chicago."

The attendant gave her a skeptical look. "All right. How much money do you have?"

Lina's eyes fell to the ground. She felt in her pockets— maybe Will had left train fare for Elizabeth there? But there was nothing, of course. He would never have left money behind, when Elizabeth had so much. "I don't have any," she said pathetically.

"Well!" the attendant said loudly. "Come back when you do."

Lina turned away from his window and walked back between those churchlike rows of seats. They seemed to go on forever, and she considered for a moment settling into one. Perhaps she would be swept up by the social reformers, and sent to a house for loose women. That would be a fittingly awful end to her evening, and anything seemed preferable to facing Elizabeth again.

All the locomotives were asleep under their glass dome, and beyond them to the east was the shantytown of Dutch Hill, where the new Irish squatted. A girl like her might go in and then never come out again. Will—gorgeous, perfect Will—had made sure that he had the means to escape the Hollands, but Lina could go only as far as her feet would carry her. She walked swiftly and without looking at anyone as she left the station.

When she emerged back on the street, she found the noise and lights almost shocking. There were cheers with every exploding spray of color in the night sky. Up above her, the universe was expansive and incandescent, but it seemed to Lina to be mocking her, reminding her that while it was large and glittering, her own world was small, unforgiving, and inescapable. She hated her job and herself, but most of all she hated Elizabeth. It was Elizabeth who had ruined everything, before Lina even had so much as a chance to win Will.

Tonight she had been too tired and too poor to get out, but as she looked at the New York sky, so big and so full of eruptions, she knew that there had to be a way.

Twenty Nine

There are those old-fashioned mothers who believe that windows should be always closed to prevent corrupting agents from entering their daughters' bedrooms. We take a more modern approach: fresh air in moderation is healthful for young girls, and on seasonal nights the windows of their bedrooms may be left open.

—*VAN KAMP'S GUIDE TO HOUSEKEEPING FOR LADIES OF HIGH SOCIETY*, 1899 EDITION

*T*HE FIREWORKS WERE STILL ECHOING OFF THE brick façades of New York, although it seemed to Diana that the loud merrymaking had finally taken itself somewhere farther downtown. She looked at her own reflection and saw the round, black pupils and dark, generous lashes of a girl whose mind was full of deliciously wrong thoughts. Diana could not have felt any more adored if he had actually been there with her. Henry's failure to attend his public debut with Elizabeth felt like a long, charged glance from across a room full of people, or a dangerously delivered secret love letter. And of course, she'd already experienced both.

Diana pulled the little plush footstool that she was sitting on closer to the full-length mirror with the gilt edges, and brushed those few, determined curls back from her forehead where they belonged. It had been at least an hour since Claire had helped her off with her dress, washed and rubbed her feet, and put her hair up for the night. But Diana wasn't tired. She felt energetic and a little silly. She liked the sight of herself in the long white chemise, which was loose and a little see-through around her small, round breasts. She gave herself a pout and examined the skin of her neck. "It's really not a crazy thing at all," she whispered to her own reflection, "that you can't stop thinking about me, Henry Schoonmaker."

"I can't say I disagree with you."

Diana nearly fell off her stool, scrambling upward and instinctively putting her arms across her chest. She was speechless with embarrassment. She turned slowly to the window, which faced the gardens behind all the houses on their block, and saw a slightly disheveled version of the man she had been thinking about all night.

"What are you doing here?" she whispered, taking a step toward the long double windows, which she had left open just a crack to let some of the cool night air in. He was standing outside, on the narrow wrought-iron balcony, wearing blue trousers that were rolled above the ankle and a white dress shirt that was crumpled and a little dirty. He was looking at her with amusement and a little something else, which Diana would have liked to think was desire. The big, elegant line of his jaw was turned at a three-quarter angle, and contained evidence of a smile being barely suppressed. "I mean, how did you even get here?" she went on, when it seemed that he might go on staring and never say anything in reply.

"I took an alley off of Nineteenth Street, hopped the

Van Dorans' fence, and then hopped yours. From there it was a quick climb up the trellis." Henry gave a little flourish with his hand and bent in her direction. "And here I am."

Diana bit her lip, feeling self-conscious about the appearance of her bedroom for the first time ever. The light pink silk that covered the headboard of her square little bed, the piles of books on the worktable, the old bearskin rug that covered the floorboards near the fireplace—it all seemed very old-fashioned and very girly at once.

"I was thinking about you all night," she told him shyly. Henry was wedged between the wood and glass of the window and the iron railing of the balcony. She realized that his face had been browned by the sun.

"I wish I could say the same." She opened her mouth but then Henry winked, before she could misunderstand his words. "I was drunk from two till ten, at least. But once I got some good black coffee, I can safely say that the only thing I could think of was you."

"Truly?" Diana's mouth spread upward into a full, guile-less smile, and her cheeks warmed with color.

"Yes, I—"

"Di?" came a muffled voice from the other side of the bedroom door.

Henry instinctively ducked. Diana thought first of her mother, and then of Claire, standing in the hall. Her heart raced. She looked at Henry, her eyebrows moving together in fear and disappointment. She ached to touch him. She wanted to pop the buttons off his white shirt one by one and then drag him down onto the rug. Henry bent his head and looked at the door, and then back at her. He was trying to ask her something with his eyes.

"Di?" the voice said again. "Can I come in? I—"

Henry lifted his hands up, asking her what he should do, and she raised her arms above her head, waving them at him ridiculously. *Go!* she mouthed. He turned quickly, still with the gentle smile on his face, and prepared to do as she'd told him to. She heard an ominous creaking from the trellis, and then something like wood beginning to splinter, but she didn't dare go to look. The door from the bedroom was being pushed open.

"Di?" Elizabeth said timidly as she peeked her head around the door.

"Oh!" Diana gasped, turning to look at her sister, whose dress was torn and wet, and whose hair was falling down as though she had been caught in a gale.

"Is that all you're wearing? You'll catch cold; you should close the window—" They both turned in the direction of the backyard when they heard a crashing noise, a rustling, and something like a cry of pain. "What in the world?"

"Just the people from the parade, I'm sure," Diana said

quickly and assuredly, moving to close and lock the windows before her sister did. She tried but failed to see what Henry was doing down below. "Are you all right? Your dress—" She pointed to her sister's enormous pink skirts, which looked like they had recently been used to clean the kitchen floor.

"Oh, I . . . I tripped going down the stairs. I was going to get some water, and my skirt must have snagged, and—"

"Have you been crying?" Diana interrupted. Her sister's eyes were puffy and angry-looking.

"No. I mean, maybe a little." Elizabeth looked almost shyly at her sister. "It's just that . . ." she trailed off, but she kept looking at Diana in an almost vulnerable way.

Diana stared back, unsure what exactly Elizabeth was trying to say. After all, she had seemed so content to be abandoned by Henry earlier. Evidently, the embarrassment had set in. And so the anxiety of being caught with Henry faded, and even Diana's annoyance at having the precious moment interrupted. She was almost concerned about her sister. She was almost sorry for what she wanted.

"Yes, it's only that . . ." Elizabeth sighed, as though she couldn't find the words to match what she was feeling, and let her shoulders drop. She put her hands over her face like she might start crying again. "Do you remember that Vermeer painting that father gave me?"

Diana rolled her eyes. "He gave the Vermeer to *me*." She

remembered the story of the painting very clearly. Her father had bought it from a Paris art dealer while Mrs. Holland was pregnant for the second time, and he had always intended for it to hang in his second child's room. But then Elizabeth had impressed everyone with her understanding of its composition, and so Father decided that the painting would hang in Elizabeth's room until Diana was sixteen. But by the time she turned sixteen, her father was dead and no one was willing to discuss the placement of pictures. "But then you insisted on having it in your room," she added, with a touch of bitterness.

"Oh," Elizabeth said, in an off-key voice that assured her younger sister that she didn't remember it that way at all. Diana shrugged—she hardly needed to win fights like this one when there were handsome men engaged to her sister making late-night visits to her window. Elizabeth took a big, teary breath. "I guess it doesn't matter now. But I just wanted to . . . I mean, if it would be all right . . ." Elizabeth's shoulders sank and she put her hands over her face.

"You can sleep in here if you want." Diana went to her sister. She wrapped her arms around Elizabeth and pressed her close.

As she helped Elizabeth out of her dress, she tried not to think about Henry and those few, brilliant moments when he'd stood at her window. She knew she should just be glad that they hadn't been discovered, especially now that she saw how clearly distraught her sister was by everything.

But even as they lay down to sleep side by side for the first time since they were children, Diana couldn't help but hope for another little glimpse of the one bachelor in all of New York she could not have.

Thirty

One of the many parties given last evening in celebration of Admiral Dewey's return to our shores—the fete in the Waldorf-Astoria ballroom—was also expected to welcome the recently betrothed couple of Mr. Henry Schoonmaker and Miss Elizabeth Holland. While Miss Holland attended, looking exquisite as always, Mr. Schoonmaker never arrived, leading certain cynics to wonder if his passions have turned elsewhere so quickly.

—FROM THE "GAMESOME GALLANT" COLUMN IN THE *NEW YORK IMPERIAL*, SATURDAY, SEPTEMBER 30, 1899

ENRY WAS AWAKENED BY THE ROUGH SWATTING of a broadsheet against his face. He reached down and felt his torso; he had slept in his clothes, and not on his bed, either. The inside of his mouth was chalky. His arms felt raw, as though they had been scratched at by a herd of feral cats in the night. He touched his forearms and felt cuts, bubbled over by new scabs. All of this dawned unkindly on Henry, who had been dreaming of Diana Holland's soft white skin.

"Henry . . . open your goddamn eyes," came the low, angry voice of his father. William Schoonmaker spoke in a nasal, irritated tone even in his carefree moments, and this did not seem to be one of those. "Do you want some orange juice?"

Henry cracked one eye and then the other. The looming form of his father came unpleasantly into focus. "Do you have orange juice?" Henry asked meekly.

"*No.*"

He was fully awake now, and he knew where he was. The little room where he was sitting, under the long shadow of his father, was the same room where he had laid down for a short rest last night, in order to recover from the epic party on the yacht. It was his own study, adjacent to his bedroom, a good, dark room to nurse a headache in. Though apparently that was no longer on the agenda.

Henry looked from the sneering face of his father to the pale maid who hovered behind him. She was wearing a black dress with white cuffs and a white collar, and she was holding a tray with a cut-glass pitcher full of a liquid that certainly had the appearance of orange juice. Henry opened and closed his pasty mouth, and then looked back at his father.

"Don't give him any, Hilda." Henry's father took a few steps forward and clasped his hands behind his back. "Now, Henry, I see that you are in quite a state, and it seems possible to me that you don't remember last night with perfect clarity. I have done some research, however, and I am here to help you remember. *Hilda* and I are here to help you remember."

Henry looked back at the maid. She had been with his family for some time, and she had kept his secrets before. She wouldn't meet his eyes now, however. Her skin was an unhappy pallor, and her eyes were fixed on her tray. Henry looked longingly at the orange juice, and then turned his eyes to his father, whose great frame was clothed in a three-piece suit of metallic brown-gray fabric. It was the kind of costume that impressed mid-level railroad employees and servant girls. Henry tried to give his father a look that showed it did not impress him.

"Go on, Hilda," his father was saying. "Tell Henry what you told me."

The girl paused as long as she could, which was long enough to make both herself and Henry wretchedly uncomfortable, and then said, "I saw a young lady leaving quite late last night. She wore a beaded gown of a reddish color, and she made quite a noise when she left. The dress looked new, sir, and quite expensive."

Henry's whole body went slack. He remembered Penelope's coming there in her dramatic dress. He rested his forehead against his fist and listened as his father issued a swift, firm dismissal to Hilda. He could barely watch as Hilda gave a reverential nod, and turned for the hall, taking with her the sloshing pitcher of sweet orange juice that might have soothed his parched throat.

"I didn't think she'd need to hear this next bit, Henry." The elder Schoonmaker crossed his arms across his chest. "Do you remember how you got home?"

"No, sir," Henry croaked.

"A hackney dropped you off," Mr. Schoonmaker spat. "You had bruises on the left side of your body, and cuts consistent with an unfortunate meeting with a rosebush. Any of this sounding familiar?"

Henry shook his head. "I was drunk," he said, trying to sound both ashamed and firm in this belief. He remembered the rosebush incident very clearly, of course, but he knew that sneaking to the bedroom window of his fiancée's little sister wasn't something he wanted to explain to his father. Sometimes, Henry reflected, being taken for a perpetual drunk was sort of convenient.

"Henry, I am not a fool. I know very well you were drunk. Now, would you like to tell the story or should I?"

"You seem bent on it," Henry answered bitterly.

"Read it yourself." His father's head snapped back in obvious disgust as he threw the newspaper in Henry's direction. It made a rustling noise as it soared through the air and hit him on the forehead. Henry picked it up dutifully, avoiding eye contact with his father, who was, in any event, walking furiously back and forth across the elegant parquet floor. The paper was folded to the item in question, from that overwrought gossip column in the *Imperial*. It had been circled in red ink.

"Well, that's unfortunate," Henry said, when he had read it. Despite his ironic tone, he did in fact mean this. The picture of him as a drunk dandy about town was starting to bore even him. But more pressing at the moment was how very desperately in need of something to drink he was. If only he could get some liquid to his dry mouth, he might be able to handle this deteriorating situation.

"I should say so," his father replied in a voice that matched, if not bettered, Henry's sarcasm. Henry watched as his father slowed his pacing and walked toward the casement windows that overlooked Fifth Avenue, his arms stilled behind his back. He lowered his voice, which made it no less menacing. "Would you like to know where *I* was last night, Henry?"

The son kept his eyes on his father, and said nothing. He knew the answer would be forced on him sooner or later. Sooner, likely.

"I was at the Waldorf with the governor and Admiral Dewey himself. You know they say he may run for president? It was a tremendous political opportunity. Not that I expect that to mean anything to a wreck like yourself."

Henry shifted on the couch. He tried to smooth his shirt with his hands and look indeed a little less like a wreck. His father turned back from the window and glowered at him again.

"I was expecting—all the city was expecting—to see you and your lovely fiancée acting like a couple at the Waldorf. Can you imagine the disappointment felt by all when you *neglected to show up*? It was an evening when the entirety of New York's gossip-seeking class was out looking for color. And you gave it to them. You have proved yourself a liability yet again, Henry."

The older man rocked on his heels with a look of regret,

and Henry, still parched and deeply uncomfortable, could think of nothing to say that might make his father view him as something less than a disappointment. He watched as his father collected himself, and then went on in the usual, irritable, businesslike tone.

"Here's what we're going to do, Henry. Your little escapade last night made the engagement look like a sham, which some people surely take it as already. But the sham-engagement story won't stick if we overwhelm them with an even *bigger* story."

Henry, who had always made a dashing figure in the papers without really trying, looked up at his father with what he hoped was not a thoroughly confused expression. His father came walking slowly toward him. Henry contemplated the great red face, with its unfortunate contrast to the slicked, black hair, and wondered if he would ever make the old man happy. "A bigger story?" he repeated mechanically.

"Ah, you follow. How nice. Yes, an even bigger story. You go make nice with the Hollands tomorrow. I will send Isabelle to talk to Mrs. Holland this evening—an advance guard, if you will. It's perfect, really. And it only took from the time I woke up till breakfast for me to come up with it."

Henry had been trying to appear attentive, but he was getting an increasingly sick and nervous feeling in his stomach. "So . . . what is this idea?"

William Schoonmaker turned his animated eyes on his son. He smiled, spreading his dark mustache across his face. "We're moving the wedding up. The greatest wedding of the nineteenth century, that's what they'll call it in the papers. People will like that."

"You're talking about *my* wedding? To . . . Elizabeth?" Henry asked. His face had gone cold, and he could not get his mouth to shut. "Moving it up to what date?"

Henry watched as his father pulled his gold watch from his pocket. He was smiling, clearly amused by his own stunt, confident in his genius. He was enjoying this, it seemed, making Henry as uncomfortable as possible.

"If you prefer to be disinherited, I would oblige. . . ." Henry's father paused to give him a pointed look. "I'd rather not, but I will if it comes down to it."

"No, sir, I wouldn't prefer that." Henry lowered his eyes so that he wouldn't have to feel the full brunt of his cowardice. "I mean, I'd rather you didn't."

"Well then, Henry, my boy, if you don't have any other plans next Sunday—that will be the eighth of October—we'll make you a married man."

Henry watched as his father's mouth spread into an almost gruesome grin and knew that, despite his misery, he had finally run out of time.

Thirty One

A certain young bride-to-be is said to be looking a little brokenhearted after her fiancé's less-than-amorous showing during the celebrations of the Dewey holiday.

—FROM THE SOCIETY PAGE OF THE *NEW-YORK NEWS OF THE WORLD GAZETTE*, SUNDAY, OCTOBER 1, 1899

*T*WO DAYS OF PARADES AND PARTIES HAD DEPLETED New York, and on Sunday a collective hangover kept her citizenry docile and indoors. Elizabeth could feel the lull without even looking out the window of her family's drawing room. Even those principled types that dropped by for tea and idle chatter during the Hollands' Sunday visiting hours were looking a little glassy-eyed. Elizabeth had not read the papers, but if she had, she probably wouldn't have had the strength to deny that she was looking a little brokenhearted. It was a relief, though a thin one, that the world already knew her official excuse.

Apparently, it had not occurred to her childhood friend Agnes Jones, however, that nobody wanted to talk about the parade anymore.

"And the aerial regatta was *too* divine," Agnes was saying, her hands folded over her tartan skirt. "Who even knew that there was such a thing in this city as a kite expert, or that they could do a thing like that with what are really just elaborate toys. . . ."

Elizabeth smiled faintly at her, and wished that Aunt Edith, who was sitting by the fire and pretending to be disgusted by that Friday's *Cité Chatter*, would join in and carry part of the conversation. Agnes's eyes were bright and delighted with her own conversation, and her chestnut hair was tucked back, with a few squiggles loose at the ears. This did nothing for her overripe chin, which Elizabeth might have found a gentle way to communicate to her if only she had had the strength.

"And all the little ships covered in lights! I had never seen anything like it." Agnes paused and lowered her eyes, in a show of considering whether she should say what she was thinking or not. "So . . . are you very angry about Henry's not showing on Friday night?"

"Oh," Elizabeth said slowly, her eyes moving from the window back to Agnes. She'd found herself staring at the window often that afternoon, hoping for the appearance of an unexpected figure. "Not very, thank you for asking. . . ."

"Not very is better than very," Agnes said enthusiastically.

Elizabeth exhaled in an anemic show of agreement. She didn't know how Agnes had grown into such tactlessness. Elizabeth had always taken in friends, no matter how rough they were. This was the Christian thing to do, she told herself, and you never knew where a true friend might be hiding. Just look at Penelope. Despite her rough manners when they first became acquainted, she had proved herself such a loyal friend, agreeing to be Elizabeth's maid of honor even though Elizabeth was being so wretched to her by marrying her crush.

Agnes brought Elizabeth out of her thoughts by taking a noisy slurp of tea. "You will have to do something really spectacular to get attention if you're having the wedding this season. I've heard of three engagements this weekend alone. Martin Westervelt proposed to Jenny Thurlow. . . ."

Elizabeth tried to stay alert as Agnes gave her the matrimonial report. It was no wonder that Diana was avoiding visitors in her room, reading ridiculous novels and talking to herself. Only two nights ago Elizabeth had heard her carrying on a whole conversation in her room when nobody was around. She really did have to finish her studies with a tutor, Elizabeth thought, or she was going to end up completely wild. This was some consolation to Elizabeth—at least her inertia would benefit the family. At least she wouldn't have to worry about her younger sister ending up like . . . Agnes.

Mostly, though, Elizabeth felt overwhelmed and numbed by the loss of Will. Her appetite was gone entirely.

"And Jenny just looks so happy, Lizzie, you would cry if you saw how happy she was. . . ."

Elizabeth nodded vaguely, thinking that Agnes was probably correct in that regard. But news of her peers becoming engaged through the normal flirtations and anxieties and parental blessings gave her no pleasure. It just made her think of Will, and how strong and right he was, while she walked around in a fog of her own creation, dishonestly calling what was hardly an acquaintance the beginning of marital love.

"Miss Elizabeth?"

Elizabeth focused her eyes on the hall door, where Claire stood waiting. Elizabeth looked around the room and realized that Claire had been calling to her for several moments already. This always happened when Elizabeth's thoughts drifted to Will—she looked up and a whole room was gawking at her.

"Yes, Claire?" Elizabeth straightened in her bergère chair, instinctively putting her hands over the armrests, where the gold leaf was chipping away.

"Mr. Schoonmaker has just sent up his card."

"Oh!" Agnes winked in Elizabeth's direction. "I'll be going then."

"Thank you for paying me the visit," Elizabeth said, managing a little smile at her old friend.

Agnes bent to kiss her on the cheek, and when she pulled back, she said, "Look a little happy, for goodness' sake. Your fiancé is here to see you."

Elizabeth's face fell—she couldn't help it—and then she watched with relief as Agnes left the drawing room.

"You can show Mr. Schoonmaker in, Claire." Elizabeth

watched the red-haired maid bow her head deferentially, and was reminded how horrid Lina had been on Friday night. "And Claire, don't think you have to do everything around here. Your sister is perfectly capable of making tea and fetching coats."

Claire blushed slightly and nodded, before backing into the hall.

Elizabeth checked the little buttons of her burgundy blouse and brought her knees together under her long ivory linen skirt. When she looked up she saw Henry in the doorway. He was wearing a dark gray cutaway jacket and matching slacks, and he was actually looking at her somewhat earnestly, which Elizabeth found new and discomforting. His straight brows were drawn together, and the creases on his flat, handsome face were deeper and more obvious, even from across the room.

He bowed his head in her direction, and she returned the gesture. Then he walked across the room, took her hand, and kissed it.

"Won't you sit?" she asked him.

"Thank you." He gave a quick glance about the room before taking the matching chair beside hers. She wondered if he was assessing the embossed, olive leather over the wainscoting as old-fashioned, or if he thought of the crowded gold picture frames and the layered Persian carpets on the floor as clutter.

"Would you like some tea?"

"Yes, tea would be wonderful." His answer sounded stiff

to her, but then she had to admit that she wasn't being particularly warm either.

Elizabeth wondered if Henry kept looking over his shoulder because of Aunt Edith, who was seated near the large marble mantel. She might have found a way to whisper that Edith wasn't paying any attention if she had thought he might have anything remotely interesting to tell her. But she did not.

"Miss Holland, I just wanted to tell you that I am very sorry about Friday night."

"Oh no, that's quite all right—"

"It isn't." Henry's voice was mechanical, but there was something in his face that suggested genuine remorse. "It was awful of me to stand you up like that, and even if I didn't hurt your feelings, I am sure it has been an embarrassment."

"A little," Elizabeth acknowledged as she moved her gaze to her hands.

"But I don't want you to think I am nervous about marrying you," Henry said slowly, as though he were having trouble finding the words.

"No?" Elizabeth's eyebrows raised involuntarily.

"No, not at all. In fact, I—oh, thank you." Elizabeth watched as Lina appeared over Henry's shoulder and began to pour him a cup of tea. She was wearing a face of quiet servitude, but even in benign form the sight of her brought back the anger Elizabeth had felt Friday night. "No cream, thank you," he said, and then took the little blue porcelain cup with the hand-painted gold rim.

"Miss Elizabeth?" Lina asked.

"Yes, please, with sugar and lemon," Elizabeth replied in a businesslike tone. "Mr. Schoonmaker—you were saying?"

"I was saying that, well . . ." Henry paused, frowned, and then let his gaze meander again across the many objects in the room. Elizabeth leaned forward as she waited for him to continue. Eventually, his eyes came back to her—he seemed almost surprised to find himself looking into her eyes—and then he continued in a halting voice. "I wouldn't want you . . . thinking that I was getting cold feet. And, well, the fact of the matter is I really am eager for us to be . . . married. And—*anyway*—what would you think about moving the wedding up?"

"Up?" Elizabeth said, barely comprehending. The idea of marrying Henry Schoonmaker at all was incomprehensible; that it could come any sooner was beyond her powers of imagination. But then an image darted through her mind— her mother sleeping blissfully for the first time in months. Elizabeth had nothing left to do but please others, anyway. She was trying to form a response when she was distracted by Lina's clumsiness as she moved forward with the tea.

"Yes, to next Sunday. I understand my stepmother has already discussed it with your mother. The logistics, I mean. . . ." Henry shifted uncomfortably in his seat before going on. "The advantage is that that way, everybody would be so surprised and—" He suddenly broke off, moving uselessly toward Elizabeth. "Careful!"

Elizabeth was already in a state of surprise and confusion when the boiling hot water hit her thigh. She cried out and pulled the soaked skirt away from her leg to stop the burning. She looked up slowly, her eyes falling first on the dainty gold-rimmed teacup dangling from Lina's finger, and then on Lina's smirking face.

"Oops," Lina said flatly.

Before she could think what she was doing, Elizabeth grabbed the teacup off Lina's finger and clutched it protectively in her hands. "I loathe your incompetence," she said in a low, hateful voice that must have come from some very remote corner of herself. It was like no speaking voice she had ever uttered. "Get out of my house."

"It was an accident," Lina explained, in an even tone.

Henry was looking at the ground, and Aunt Edith was staring at Elizabeth, shocked by her outburst. Claire appeared in the doorway, her eyes wide with fright. Elizabeth didn't care what anybody thought. "It was not. You are a sloppy girl and a liar and I will not have you in my family's house. Claire, I am sorry, but she leaves within the hour."

Lina stood still in the middle of the room, giving

Elizabeth a hateful glare. "It was an accident," she repeated unconvincingly.

"Thank you for your commentary," Elizabeth said. Her voice was crisp and even now. She could feel the brown stain of the tea spreading across the light fabric of her skirt, but she refused to look at it. "You're still fired. Mr. Schoonmaker, I am so sorry you had to witness this unpleasant scene. Please pretend it never happened. If you'll excuse me, I am going to my room to collect myself."

Elizabeth picked up her skirt and walked quickly across the room to the far hall door. She could feel the tears coming already, but willed them back for a few moments. The fact that Lina had been there to witness anything between her and Henry, much less wedding talk, made her feel both furious and ashamed. She sniffed and turned back to see Henry, Lina, Claire, and Edith all frozen in their positions.

"Thank you for coming by, Henry," she said quietly from the doorway, "though I am sensing that I may in fact need to lie down for some time, to compose myself. Perhaps Miss Diana will do to entertain Mr. Schoonmaker for the rest of his visit?"

Henry's face, which had previously been drawn downward by concern and discomfort, brightened considerably. There was a healthy shade coming back into his cheeks. "You should by all means get your rest."

Elizabeth had taken another step through the parlor's doorway when she remembered that she had not responded to Henry's proposal. She felt no new warmth toward him, but still—if she had to marry him—it might as well be done quickly, and in a manner that satisfied the most parties.

"Mr. Schoonmaker," she said, as she set another foot into the hallway, "I believe having the wedding next Sunday is an excellent idea."

Without waiting for his response, Elizabeth made her way toward the main stair. Perhaps now she could put an end to all this agony and wondering and get on with the long haul that would be the rest of her life without Will.

Thirty Two

A maid of honor to any young bride must be always poking around—seeking information about her friend from the groom-to-be, her family, and even the staff. The bride does not of course want to seem to be always asking for things. But if her maid of honor asks the right questions of the right people, then she will be able to serve her friend exceptionally well, meeting every one of her needs and desires as they arise.

—L. A. M. BRECKINRIDGE, *THE LAWS OF BEING IN WELL-MANNERED CIRCLES*

*T*HE RESENTMENT AND RAGE THAT LINA FELT FOR her mistress had been a long time in the making, but her dismissal from the Holland house, when it came, came quickly. There was Claire, staring at her in a frightened, quiet way as she handed her the small suitcase that had belonged to their mother and a paper bag of tea sandwiches that she had hastily prepared. Her face was full of concern, yet Lina could barely bring herself to say anything. She gave her sister a nod and then she stepped onto the enclosed iron porch. Soon she was walking away from practically the only home she had ever known.

The sidewalk was beneath her, but she could scarcely feel it. She pulled Will's coat tighter and kept moving without any idea what her direction should be. She was so suddenly untethered from everything. That was when she heard the sound of wheels and horses' hooves against the street and then a voice she recognized.

"Excuse me."

Lina stopped and turned slowly to see who might want to stop her on the street. She stood, silent and blinking, for a long moment before she grasped that it was Elizabeth's friend, Penelope Hayes, who seemed to want to speak to Lina. She was perched high on one of those two-seater carriages with the dramatically large wheels, and looking down with a decided interest. "Are you all right?"

"Not really," Lina replied eventually. Penelope was wearing a long skirt of wool houndstooth, and a tight-fitting, bell-sleeved jacket of the same cloth. A little matching hat was pinned into her hair. None of this made Lina feel any better about her black dress, her worn boots, or the oversize man's coat she was wearing. "It's been a god-awful day, if you want to know."

Penelope leaned forward and rested her chin on a fist covered in gray suede. She continued to look down with heavily lashed eyes on Lina from the perch of her shiny phaeton. "I'm sorry to hear that."

Lina felt that she was being watched intently, as though she were a canary in a cage, which was all the more bizarre because Penelope Hayes had never looked her in the face before.

"Thank you, Miss Hayes." Lina moved her small scuffed suitcase from one hand to the other, trying to remember everything about the gossip item her sister had read aloud about the impending proposal to Penelope by Henry. How could this haughty girl have taken the news of his engagement to Elizabeth? Her heart was thumping, and it took a few moments to voice the question she had formulated in her mind. "Is it true that you were so hot about Henry Schoonmaker?"

"Who says that?" Penelope answered sharply. She seemed a little shocked to be talked to in this way by a servant—but Lina wasn't a servant anymore.

"I guess I read it somewhere," Lina replied, casting a quick glance back at No. 17. There was no evidence of anybody watching them. "I'm sorry if I—"

"Where are you going?" Penelope interrupted. She made a motion with her hand that seemed to imply that she had forgiven Lina her impudence.

"I suppose I don't know." Lina sucked in her breath and moved her hand to her face, where she brushed back a few strands of hair. There was no point in hiding it, she decided. "I've just been fired."

"That's *horrible*," Penelope said. She left her mouth open, so that it formed a shocked *O*—it seemed to Lina that she was trying awfully hard to seem concerned. "What will you do?"

Lina, who was still wondering how Penelope felt about the young man now sitting in the Hollands' parlor, gave an indifferent shrug. "I don't know."

"Well, why don't you get in?" Penelope smiled wide and gestured to the coachman, who had been sitting quietly all this time. "I was on my way to the Hollands'—I'm Elizabeth's maid of honor, you know—but if they're being so nasty they can certainly wait. We'll take you wherever you want to go."

Lina pretended to consider a moment, and then took the outstretched hand of the driver and let herself be pulled up. She sat on the padded white leather seat beside Penelope and listened as she instructed the driver to go. "I'm Lina," she said, as she put her suitcase down between them. Gramercy Park South began rolling away underneath them. Already Lina felt that she didn't live there anymore.

"I remember," Penelope told her.

Lina paused and considered this almost certain lie. The person she was trained to be would have nodded and been thankful, but she had just been forced out of her old life. The person she would be in her next life was finding her way one second at a time. "Why are you being nice to me?"

Penelope smiled faintly at this and then peered over her shoulder at their new surroundings. They had passed out of that charmed parallelogram between Sixth and Third Avenues, below Fifty-ninth Street and above Fourteenth, where society lived. They were now in the territory of the working poor, with their herds of children and prematurely aged faces. The avenue was clotted by traffic and darkened by the shadows of the elevated train tracks. The shouts of deliverymen and shopkeepers were periodically overwhelmed by the rumbling of one of the stuffed El cars, passing on the steel girders above. So this was where they were going—a part of town where Penelope would not be afraid of being seen with the Hollands' fired maid. Looking around her, Lina couldn't help but feel something like distaste. She wanted Penelope to know that this wasn't where she belonged either.

"So whatever did you do to the Hollands?" Penelope asked, turning her face back in the direction of her guest. They were very close, and Lina couldn't help but notice the clarity of her skin. It was just as she had imagined it would be.

"Nothing . . ." Lina paused and told herself to choose her words wisely. "There was an incident with a cup of tea, which ended poorly. . . . And I think they always wanted me to be just a mindless worker, the way my sister, Claire, is. Not that she's mindless, exactly . . ." Lina brought her hands together, rubbing the dry skin of one with the other. "But I just never saw myself being a maid forever."

"That all?" Penelope prodded. She brought herself even closer to Lina and smiled.

"The real reason is . . ." Lina went on slowly, "I think I may have been fired for knowing *too much*." It was now Lina's turn to hold Penelope's gaze, and she paused, letting the phrase hang in the air. She remembered hearing Penelope mock Elizabeth for her goodness on more than one occasion, took a deep breath, and resolved to go on. "It was humiliating really, having to serve her. . . ." As soon as the words were out of her mouth she wanted to take them back. Lina lowered her eyes and then brought them quickly back up. "I mean *them*. I'm glad to be gone. Really I am."

"You know . . ." Penelope pursed her lips. She seemed to be considering which words to use as well. The carriage swerved to avoid a ragpicker in the road, and both girls took hold of the railing while keeping their eyes on each other. "I think," she enunciated carefully, "we may dislike the same person."

Lina felt a surge of relief. So she had not misread the situation after all.

"Do you mean that we might *hate* the same member of the Holland family?" Lina's voice became forceful, but still broke a little as she enunciated the word *hate*. Her body swayed with the movement of the carriage.

"Yes." Penelope's mouth flickered at the corners. "That's exactly what I meant."

Lina slouched backward and returned to examining the roughness of her hands. She was amazed by how quickly she had arrived at a way out of her problems, but she didn't want to go too fast and ruin it. "I think I understand what you're saying," she answered cautiously. "And I think that what I know would be of interest to you. But, as you can see, I am completely adrift. I would need some kind of . . . gesture. To feel right about telling."

"Of course." Penelope reached over and took Lina's rough hand in her own soft gloved one. Lina had touched many fine objects at the Hollands', of course, but she was taken aback by the utter smoothness of Penelope's suede-covered palm. "But give me a hint first."

Lina had been keeping the secret to herself for so long, she couldn't help blurting out the truth. "Elizabeth is not a virgin."

Penelope turned her face sideways and squinted at Lina. She emitted a small, throaty laugh and shook her head. "We're talking about Elizabeth *Holland* here, yes?"

"I have proof." Lina reached into the pocket of her coat and pulled out Will's note. She passed it to Penelope, who turned it over and examined the watermark until she was satisfied that it was Elizabeth's.

Penelope read it twice and then said, incredulously, "Who is Will Keller?"

Lina's lips parted and she bounced slightly with the carriage as it went over a patch of particularly uneven cobblestone. "He's the Hollands'—*was* the Hollands' coachman."

Penelope bit her lip and emitted an amused sound from the back of her throat. "You must be joking."

"Not joking." Lina shook her head firmly and thought how much better it would have been for her if it had all been some gag. "I've seen her, going into his room late at night, and leaving in the morning. And there were many nights when I would go to help her undress, and she would just be gone."

"Since *when?*" Penelope held her skeptical tone, but there was a new light in her eyes. It was obvious how giddy she was to be receiving this news.

"I don't know when it started, but I am sure it was a while ago. It was going on until very recently. I'm sure it was still going on until Friday evening when Will left in the night."

Penelope settled back against the comfortable leather of her carriage. "Lizzie never fails to impress me." Penelope paused. "Though that really must have killed her—usually she's the one who likes to play hard to get." She drew her red lips back from her teeth, which Lina was unsurprised to see were perfectly straight and white. "In love with a poor boy!" she went on in the same mystified tone. "No offense intended."

"None taken." Lina paused and coughed into her hand. She wondered if it was true, what Penelope had said about Elizabeth playing hard to get, and if that really was how she'd kept Will's attention all this time. After all, he never would have been able to possess her. Perhaps that was the allure. "And that's not all I know about the Holland family."

"Oh, really? What else do you have for me?" Penelope leaned forward, her eyes positively gleaming with excitement.

Lina shook her head. "First I've got to know what it's worth to you."

"Oh, I can assure you, you will be well compensated. I am

going to take you to a little hotel I know of on Twenty-sixth Street—clean, anonymous—and get you a room for tonight. Tomorrow I will come meet you, and in exchange for this letter, I will give you . . ." Penelope paused and drew back a little as though she were assessing her new acquaintance.

"One thousand dollars," Lina replied in as firm a voice as she could manage. Her price sounded magical when she said it out loud. It was the price of a Tiffany ring, of countless ball gowns, of carriages. It was more than enough to go to Will—it was enough to get him back in far grander fashion.

Penelope was silent as they hurtled down the avenue, which was considerably more jammed and smelly than Fifth, and louder, too, because of the trains rumbling above them. Lina worried, momentarily, that she had asked for far too much, that she had already given up the desired information without any insurance that she would be paid for it. But then Penelope shrugged and gave her a reckless smile.

"That's a lot of money," she said. "What would you say to five hundred?"

"Thank you, Miss Hayes." Lina's shoulders relaxed, and she felt relief warming her bones. A thousand had been an unimaginable sum, but five hundred seemed to her equally outlandish. She would get a chance to make everything right after all. "Thank you so very much."

"This has been fortunate all around." Her new friend

gave her a slow, purposeful wink.

"Yes, it has." Some instinct made Lina lean forward and pluck the piece of cardstock on which Will had written his last thoughts to Elizabeth out of Penelope's hand. "All the same, I'm going to keep this until tomorrow. And of course, in time, perhaps there will be other things that I can tell you. For the right price."

Penelope looked saddened not to have the piece of paper in her hand anymore, but she nodded her grudging assent. "Then I will deliver your fee personally. You see, I am going to need that letter tomorrow."

Lina did of course wonder why she wanted the letter so quickly—and what she planned to do with it—but her mind was too alive with what she would do with this profound sum of money. The girl she used to be would have used it to go chasing after Will, while he remained ever fixated on the elusive Elizabeth Holland. But this was Lina's chance to make herself new, and she wasn't going to repeat any of her old mistakes. She was going to make herself into something even brighter and more shining than Elizabeth Holland—the kind of lady Will would notice, and then be unable to ever look away from.

Thirty Three

If a certain dashing bachelor whom we all know and love does not exit his engagement soon, and reveal some new paramour, there are those of us who will have placed losing bets.

—FROM THE SOCIETY PAGE OF THE *NEW-YORK NEWS OF THE WORLD GAZETTE*, SUNDAY, OCTOBER 1, 1899

IANA WATCHED AS HER AUNT EDITH TURNED down the hall and began to descend the main stairs, the white appliqué of her skirt trailing behind her. Diana pushed at her hair and practiced breathing with her stomach sucked in and her shoulders thrown back. She was wearing the same seersucker she had been wearing last Sunday when Henry had come to visit, which hadn't seemed like a bad idea when she'd still been planning to stay in her room with her Amélie Rives novel all day. There was nothing to be done about it now, of course. Her aunt wasn't likely to sympathize with her needing to put on a smarter dress for her sister's fiancé.

When she entered the drawing room Henry stood up quickly, and almost awkwardly.

"Miss Diana," he said, bowing his head and suppressing a smile.

She walked across the floor, wishing that Edith could be gone for just one minute—what she could do with that minute!—and took the chair next to Henry's. From this position, her aunt could see the right side of her profile, although Diana could not see her. This was the seat Elizabeth had only recently occupied—she could tell by the damp and tea-stained armrest. She set her lips together, but still they twitched, threatening to curve into a full-blown smile. She raised her eyes slowly until they met Henry's. There was a nervous cast to his features, and she knew that he knew that they were being watched.

She folded her hands in her lap and took on a high, lady-like voice: "The weather has been very fine, Mr. Schoonmaker, but I fear it may turn."

"You're right, quite right," Henry replied, mimicking her tone of extreme and dull gentility. "As I was coming in, I got a touch of cold breeze, and found it *most* foreboding."

"Oh, *dear*." Diana punctuated her statement with a wink.

Henry crossed a leg and fidgeted with a button on his vest. He was wearing a dove-colored suit, and it made the darkness of his eyes and hair look especially arresting. She watched the minute workings of his cheekbones as he tried not to give away the joke.

"And did you enjoy all the festivities on Friday evening, Mr. Schoonmaker?" She watched as the left corner of his mouth flexed upward, and hoped that the phrase *Friday evening* resonated the same way it did in her own mind. "I heard you were quite busy . . . on the *Elysian*."

"Yes . . ." he said slowly. "I did enjoy that evening most, out of all the festivities of the last week. It started out dull, but later that night became particularly . . . *revealing*."

Diana could feel her blush spread across her collarbone. She desperately wanted to come up with some clever reply, but all she could think of was her nearly naked self, being watched by Henry in the window. She stammered for a minute, and then heard herself say the first thing that came into her head. "And what brings you to our house today?"

The playfulness left Henry's face, and Diana immediately regretted her lack of cleverness. With all the novels she had read, surely she could have come up with some witty remark. She had half formed one in her mind, when she heard her aunt say, "Oh, it is for a very good reason. *Tell* her, Mr. Schoonmaker."

Diana looked up and batted a stray curl off her forehead. "What?" she said, in an inadvertently high, childlike tone.

Henry studied her for a moment and worked his jaw back and forth. "Perhaps you should tell her," he called to Edith, with forced lightness. Diana noticed for the first time that there was a bruise on his left cheek. So he had fallen hard from the trellis.

"No, Mr. Schoonmaker. You should."

Henry paused and shifted uncomfortably in his seat. His gaze went all around the room, and then back to Diana. It felt to her as though the temperature had suddenly dropped.

She was staring at Henry so intensely, waiting to hear what Aunt Edith was prodding him to say, that she felt she might get a sudden attack of headache. "Your sister and I . . . we've decided—Elizabeth and I—to move the wedding date . . . up."

"The wedding date?" Diana lowered her eyes quickly. A date implied an actual wedding, and Diana realized that until that moment she hadn't really believed in any of it. Henry and Elizabeth were merely engaged, and not very ecstatically at that, and she supposed she'd thought things would progress in that way forever. "But why?" she asked, her voice losing itself in the back of her throat.

Henry's dark eyes glanced quickly at Edith, and then back to Diana. He held her gaze for a long moment and nothing was said. She understood. The fun was over, and she had to put a stop to this ridiculous dreaming.

"Yes, it is wonderful," Henry went on, as though he had explained everything and Diana had already congratulated him. His voice projected across the room. It was a bit much, really, but then Diana had never been one to disguise her feelings. She could well enough imagine what she looked like at just that moment. "In fact," Henry continued, "I should be going now. There is so much to be done, if the wedding is indeed to happen in only a week's time. I must go tell Isabelle that Elizabeth has agreed to be married next Sunday. She will put it all in motion."

Diana looked up and saw that Henry was already standing. His eyebrows reached sweetly together even as he looked carefully in Aunt Edith's direction. Then he moved so that his body blocked her view. He bent very suddenly, and Diana felt his breath and then his lips against her neck.

He stood to leave and said, in a loud and formal manner, "Good afternoon, Miss Diana," but the brief, ticklish touch of his mouth on her skin had begun a series of pleasurable little tremors, which were now radiating through her body.

She sat very still and listened as Henry said good-bye to her aunt. He left quickly, and then she was alone with her aunt in the room where all their big moments—joyous or woeful or heart-lancing—were supposed to occur.

Diana slouched into her chair and looked at the empty space where Henry had been. That was when she noticed the small volume of Whitman that must have fallen from his pocket during his visit. She reached forward and snatched it up, and turned immediately to her favorite passage. She liked the idea of finding it in Henry's copy. But she never got as far as reading any verse, because that's when his bookmark fell into her lap. There, in what was now the familiar scrawl of Henry Schoonmaker, was a message that had been inked just for her.

I have been wanting to show you

the hyacinth in my family greenhouse.

Will you come have a look soon?

I have no plans on Tuesday,

after nine o'clock.

Diana glanced up at Aunt Edith, to see if she was watching, and then around her family's drawing room. The many antiques and heirlooms and objets d'art appeared small and dull in the late-afternoon light. But the beating of her blood and the fast tick of her heart and the glowing spot on her neck where Henry's mouth had been—these were all bright and shining. Diana felt she was beginning to understand why, in all those novels she read, the headiest loves were the loves that couldn't be.

Thirty Four

Monday, October 2, 1899

Dear Penelope,

Exciting news. We've decided to move the wedding up—to next Sunday! I absolutely must pick out the fabric for our dresses today, or they will never be ready in time. Will you meet me at Lord & Taylor at one o'clock?

Affectionately,

Elizabeth

*A*S SHE ALWAYS DID ON ANY REALLY IMPORTANT day, Penelope Hayes wore red. It was the deep shade of American Beauty roses, and the sleeves of her matching bolero were elaborately embroidered in the same crimson. She had ordered the dress from Paris for the fall season, and was now especially glad that she had. She painted a violent streak of color across the fabric department in Lord & Taylor as she followed Elizabeth through the great piled bolts of sumptuous white muslins and silks and laces. Elizabeth was wearing a very pale blue, so she might have almost blended in with all those bridal hues, except that her dress was made out of ordinary cotton eyelet.

"There's really nothing." Elizabeth sighed, turning back to Penelope and wrinkling her small nose. "If only we had time to go to Paris."

"We'll find something perfect." Penelope watched Elizabeth's narrow back bend to examine some Alençon lace, and practiced her coldest stare while no one was looking. It was remarkable to her that this slight, finicky girl had all along been harboring a secret passion—for someone who lived in a stable, no less. Penelope still found it astonishing, and really sort of fascinating, that Elizabeth Holland, who never spoke out of turn, had desires, too. Under other circumstances she would have liked to have her old friend tell her the whole, sordid story. But it was too late for that. "You've just got nerves, that's all," she went on, mustering a bit more counterfeit kindness. "That's why nothing looks good enough to you right now."

"You're probably right," Elizabeth replied absently. She stood and ran her fingers along a bone-colored mousseline de soie. "This is going to be the most hideous wedding party ever."

"Hush, it's all going to be divine, even better than you could imagine. But Liz, how *are* you managing without your maid, during a week as mad as this one?" Penelope moved close to Elizabeth and drew her fingers across the unbelievable intricacies of the fabric.

"Did I tell you about that?" Elizabeth paused, and for a moment Penelope worried that in her eagerness to seem nice she had shown her hand too soon. But her friend's thoughts were evidently too scattered for her to pick up on such subtleties. "It might have been a disaster, but Mrs. Schoonmaker has lent me two of hers for the week. And really, that girl I had, Lina, was totally unsuitable. I should have fired her long ago."

Penelope edged closer, letting her shoulder graze Elizabeth's. Lina really had proved to be a canny girl, commanding such impressive sums for her information. Of course, if it had come to it, Penelope would have parted with twice as much in exchange for that outrageous secret. She had gotten the five hundred out of her father easily, by claiming that she wanted to donate it to an organization that was building an orphanage in the Sixth Ward. And then, just to put Lina back in her place a little bit, she had set her up in a little hotel on a street that was known for its brothels. "This is very pretty," she said.

"Yes. You're right. Mr. Carroll!" Elizabeth called out to the dressmaker, who had been scurrying around the fourth-floor fabrics department, pulling various things he thought would be of interest to the Holland-Schoonmaker wedding party. The entire prospect had thrown him into a tizzy, and Penelope had been wondering whether he or Elizabeth had the worse case of nerves. He scuttled over now.

"Yes, m'lady?" he asked, holding firmly to the measuring tape around his throat and leaning forward eagerly.

"What do you think about this one?" she asked, running her hand over a matte white silk. "Perhaps with that ivory point de gaze you showed me earlier?"

"I think it would be bee-*yoo*-ti-ful," he replied with a flourish of his small hands.

"Can you pull this then, while I continue to look?"

"Yes, m'lady." Mr. Carroll collected the bolt and went off, and Elizabeth turned down the next row. Outside, a cloud moved out of the way of the sun, and a beam of light fell through the high, arched windows and across the almost factory-like room, with its row upon row of cloth and simple wooden floorboards.

Penelope cleared her throat. "Liz," she said, "can I ask you something?"

Elizabeth looked up and gave her a gentle smile. "Of course."

"Are you . . . nervous?"

"About what part?"

Penelope made a show of looking around them and averting her eyes. "You know . . . the *wedding night* part."

Elizabeth covered her face with a delicate hand, but Penelope could see perfectly well that she wasn't blushing. She almost liked her more, now that she knew Elizabeth was not so hideously, boringly perfect. "Not really," she said.

"Don't you think it might hurt?" Penelope gave Elizabeth a girlish nudge.

"No," Elizabeth replied with a shrug. Then she quickly

added: "I don't know why, I just, that's not the part that I'm afraid of. It's strange, I suppose—"

"Not *that* strange." Penelope met Elizabeth's eyes, and put away the sweet persona she had worn that afternoon. "Not strange at all, really."

She watched the blood rise in her rival's cheeks. Her pupils grew large and black, and for a long moment the girls did nothing but face each other, their pretty lashes flickering over watchful eyes.

"It's just that I wasn't *thinking* about that part," Elizabeth replied defensively.

"No. Why would you have to?" Penelope asked, her voice dropping to a cold whisper. "When you're already doing that part with a member of the *staff*."

Elizabeth's lower lip dropped. "I don't know what you're talking about," she whispered. A cloud moved in front of the sun again, now, and the whole room took on a dark hush.

Penelope rolled her eyes. "If you want to waste an hour on false denials, that's fine with me. But I know for a fact that you have been spending nights with one William Keller, coachman." Penelope couldn't hold back a little smile. It was fun, this putting Elizabeth in her place. "And I have proof."

"What kind of proof?" Elizabeth asked in the same slow, stunned voice.

"A letter. From him to you. Sweetly enough, he left it on

the night he skipped town." Penelope gave a careless flour-ish of her hand. "It's an entreaty for you to follow, which you obviously didn't heed."

"Will left me a letter?" Elizabeth's smooth forehead creased poignantly as she thought this through.

"Oh, yes. Forgive me. *Will*."

Elizabeth was virtually shaking with this news, and her eyes were damp. She folded her lips together so that they disappeared, and clasped her hands. "Penny, you can't tell anybody about this."

"Oh, really?" She gave Elizabeth a little fake pouting look. "Why can't I again?"

"You're still angry about Henry . . ." Elizabeth said slowly.

"Oh, that doesn't even *begin* to describe it. But yes, Liz, my dear friend, I am still angry. Henry was mine. We were *gorgeous* together. And then some perversity of fate mucked it up. I don't know how that happened. But now I know how I can undo it. I am going to *ruin* you, Liz." Penelope gave Elizabeth a small, malicious smile. "But really, darling. *You* did all the work. I'm just going to let your nasty little pigeon out of the coop."

Elizabeth's gaze fell once again to the slightly scuffed wood floor, and she continued to work her hands together. The natu-ral light in the room caught her pale hair, giving her a look of angelic distress that did nothing to soften Penelope's stance. She tucked her lower lip under her pearly teeth and met Penelope's eyes. "Penny . . ." she whispered. "Nobody likes a mess."

"*I* do."

"Yes, I know." Elizabeth spoke in quiet, pointed words. "That's why you're you . . . and I'm me. But if you set about to ruin me, nobody is going to end up liking you any more than they do now."

"Nobody has to know that I was the one—"

"And when you charge in and try to marry the former fiancé of the fallen favorite? Oh, Penny. Don't be *stupid*." Elizabeth took a forceful step forward, and for a moment Penelope glimpsed the hot-blooded creature that lived inside that perfect lady's cool skin. "Penny?" she went on. Her voice was still confident, though the thing she wanted and the extent of her desire were plain across her face. "Can I see the letter?"

Penelope threw back her head and exhaled impatiently. She reached inside her jacket, drew out the letter, and waved it at Elizabeth long enough for her to recognize her own stationery. "You can have it for keeps if you do what I say."

Then she turned sharply to show Elizabeth her red-sheathed back. She listened as Elizabeth took a timorous step in her direction. "What do you want me to do?"

"Meet me at my house on Wednesday morning—at ten o'clock—and I will try to think of a way for you not to marry Henry without the total ruin of your reputation."

"But I—"

"Liz," Penelope broke in, still facing away from her. She ran a hand over several bolts of gold- and silver-embroidered silks, and then looked over her slim shoulder at her friend, whose eyes were large and petrified in muted fear and fury. "You really don't have much of a choice."

A light sheen of sweat had broken out on Penelope's forehead, and her stomach had a sour turn to it. It was time to go. She drew her crimson skirt away from her feet and began marching for the elevator. She didn't bother looking back. She knew that Elizabeth would be waiting for her on Wednesday morning, wearing that same desperate face.

As she reached the end of the ivory and ecru row, she set her hand on a worktable and called back, "Oh, and Liz?" She turned and met Elizabeth's doe eyes with what she fully intended to be an intimidating stare. "Choose your own damn dress."

Thirty Five

A word about colors: Reds, scarlets, and cerises are to be chosen with great care, especially by young women who are concerned about the impression they will make.

—*LADIES' STYLE MONTHLY*, SEPTEMBER 1899

THE AFTERNOON OF HER FIRST FULL DAY OF FREEDOM, Lina was pleasantly overwhelmed by all the fine, varied things she might do with herself. She stepped out of her hotel on Twenty-sixth Street and headed toward Sixth Avenue, full of anticipation for what her brand-new life held. Now that she was possessed of such a life-altering sum of money, she hardly wanted to go on avoiding eye contact with her betters or please people besides herself. She wanted everything she did to be very grand.

She had spent most of the morning giving Penelope Hayes little details about Elizabeth and Will, embellishing where she thought it might make her new benefactress happy, although she had withheld her belief that the Hollands were poor now. Lina was becoming ever more mindful of how girls like Penelope wielded secrets, and now that she saw how valuable that piece of information might be, she wanted to keep it to herself a little longer.

In exchange for the information about Elizabeth and

Will, Penelope had given her some old clothing and jewelry. The dresses seemed like last year's fashion already, but Lina could hardly complain. The plain black maid's dress was in her past. She spent a good hour trying on her new clothes, eventually settling on a red dress with a Swiss dot pattern. Penelope had said that it was one of her favorites, but that everyone had already seen her in it last spring. The shoes that Penelope had given her, however, were entirely too small, and Lina was forced to resort to the old scuffed boots that she used to wear while running errands for the Hollands.

Lina glanced at her reflection in the window of a florist's storefront on the corner of Twenty-sixth and Sixth and admired her silhouette in the red dress. It was very tailored and had been made for a different shape of girl, but still it looked good enough. Her upturned, freckle-splattered nose and her full lips were not what society called beautiful, of course, but she lifted up her chin and knew that she was pretty in a way. It was vindicating to see her skills for hair arrangement and beauty turned on herself.

Lina told herself that someday when Claire saw her little sister's name in the society pages, above the name of Elizabeth Holland, then her angry dismissal from the Hollands' home would seem fortuitous. Will would see her name, too, of course. She delighted in imagining how surprised he would be when he saw how high old Liney had risen. He would come looking for her, his eyes shining with admiration, and tell her how much he had missed her. It was the Elizabeth Holland way to win a heart: Never go chasing after, always play hard to get. That was what Penelope had said.

Lina smiled at the reflection that seemed to be changing from moment to moment before continuing east on the street, passing the bonbon shops and tailors with their striped awnings, getting closer and closer to the old neighborhood as she went. Soon she was on Fifth walking south. She was in Elizabeth's territory again, only a few blocks from the Hollands' town house, but her former life as a servant girl seemed a world away. As she walked along the little park in Madison Square she saw the Dewey Arch, which had been so recently constructed for the parade, and its colonnade. Behind her, the tower of Madison Square Garden rose above the hazy treetops—she knew that Will had once or twice gone to sporting events there. Then she looked across the thoroughfare and saw the Fifth Avenue Hotel, which was one of the old places the Misses Holland used to go with their aunt to have afternoon tea. That's what ladies did with themselves when there was nothing else to do, Lina remembered. She looked up at the white marble edifice, rising six stories up from the street with all of its little hooded windows, and considered it a sign.

Lina smoothed out the wrinkles of her red dress. The avenue was crowded with horse-drawn carriages and trolleys and pedestrians in bowlers and waistcoats. She was on her way to have a simple tea, yet it felt like her very own debut. For the first time, she would be waited on instead of the other way around. She wondered briefly if she might even see Elizabeth there, perhaps on a break from one of her fittings at Lord & Taylor, which was, after all, only three blocks away. How shocked Elizabeth would be to discover she was no longer Lina Broud, ladies' maid. She was Lina Broud—Carolina Broud—with five hundred dollars in her purse and her whole future ahead of her.

Lina darted out into traffic with her skirt pulled safely away from the filth in the street. She walked past the collection of carriages and bellboys that loitered at the entrance, and into the lobby. Her eyes darted across the deep carpets, and she breathed in the rich aroma of coffee and fresh-cut flowers, which she recognized from the few times she had been brought here before on some errand for the Hollands. She had even once caught a glimpse of the glass and gilt case in the tea room, where all the layered, colorful pastries were on display. She took a step in the direction of that room and saw one of the hotel clerks darting in her direction.

"Good afternoon, Miss—" he began, but stopped himself suddenly. He looked from her dress to her feet and then to her face. Lina, who a moment before had been so full of excitement, was suddenly overwhelmed by self-consciousness. "Are you a guest of the hotel?"

"No," Lina admitted a little sadly. "I'm staying in the West Side Inn, on Twenty-sixth Street. . . ." She trailed off when she noticed that the man was again looking at her feet. She looked down—her dress was still pulled up the way she had carried it to cross the street, and so her old scuffed boots were completely on display. The clerk made a motion to one of the other clerks, who was wearing the same burgundy uniform, and then the second man approached.

She looked around her and realized that the other ladies strolling through the lobby were accompanied by chaperones or their own servants. She wondered at herself for thinking she could pass, so easily and so soon, for a society girl. The first clerk was looking at her and whispering to the second, who shot another distasteful look at her shoes.

"Excuse me," the second clerk said. "Are you meeting someone here?"

"No," she replied miserably.

"Then we are going to have to ask you to leave," the first said, adding a sneer that was entirely unnecessary, as he had already made Lina feel her place quite acutely.

If she could have made herself disappear forever right then, she would have done it, just to be out of the glare of those two clerks' dismissive faces. Lina backed toward the door and the red dress rustled around her legs as she ran into the street. She was going to follow Broadway, where it crossed

Fifth, carving out a triangle-shaped block. To take Fifth would only be to remind herself how foolish she had been. She was moving so quickly she could hardly see, and so the man's chest was doubly shocking when she smacked into it.

"Pardon me, miss."

Lina recognized the man she had collided with immediately, but it took her a moment to believe that he was actually speaking to her in so polite a tone. It was the Lord & Taylor boy, the one whom Claire had called handsome the other day. The one who was hired to sweet-talk ladies. As she had just been so painfully reminded, she was not a lady at all.

"I'm sorry," she said, lowering her eyes.

"No, I'm sorry," he said sheepishly. He was wearing a light beige collared shirt under a brown silk vest, and his jacket was thrown across his arm. He was better-looking than Lina had thought before, which didn't help the matter of her not having anything to say in the least. Instead she stared stupidly into his hazel eyes. "You probably think it's rude of me to speak to you this way. But you look very familiar. Maybe I've had the pleasure of serving you at Lord and Taylor's department store?"

Lina's smile was instantaneous. There was at least one person in the world who didn't take her for a lowly servant.

"Or maybe I've seen your portrait in the papers?" The Lord & Taylor boy was smiling now, too. He had a long nose and an almost downy layer of hair on his chin, and he was much taller than Lina. "Maybe a mention of you attending a ball?"

She shrugged evasively. After being turned away from the hotel, she felt she had to be very cautious not to misstep. But she couldn't end the moment. Being taken for a lady, and by someone so gracious and handsome, felt too nice to just turn away from.

"Well, you can't be all alone? Are your parents still at the hotel?"

Lina looked back at the white marble building and was glad to see neither of the two clerks who had so recently shunned her. "Oh . . . no. I'm staying here by myself."

"You look so familiar . . ." he said again, turning his head to look at her sideways.

Lina couldn't help but continue to smile her wide, happy smile. "I'm a mystery, I guess."

"Well, would you mind if I thought about it a little more? Over a drink maybe?"

Lina felt herself blushing and wished she could stop.

"Oh, I know it must seem improper, but you wouldn't be the first society girl I've shown other parts of town. And I promise to have you back in one piece."

"It's not that," Lina said, feeling uncomfortable again and at a very great risk of revealing her real identity. "It's that I'm spoken for already," she explained, remembering Will and how this transformation was all for him. Or perhaps not *all* for him, but certainly most of it.

"Oh, that's all right." He smiled rakishly. "It's only for an afternoon, and I promise not to tell anyone about it."

Lina thought of Will again, and wished that he were there courting her instead. But she also wanted this gorgeous moment of being mistaken for a fancy society girl to last a little bit longer.

Once her eyes adjusted to the light, she saw a floor covered by sawdust and walls plastered with newspaper. Barmaids younger than she traversed the floor, going from table to table with mugs of beer. There was a fat female vocalist in the corner singing "Old Folks at Home," which was familiar to Lina from the warblings of her sister. Although it was still afternoon outside, the scene inside the saloon made her feel like she'd stepped into the middle of the night.

"Pretty different from Fifth Avenue, isn't it?" her Lord & Taylor boy asked.

Lina nodded, although she was suddenly worried that she had made a mistake. She had become aware of the fact that she hadn't eaten all day, and was feeling a little light-headed. More important, all the money that Penelope had given her was tucked into the silk purse under her arm, and here she was perched on a bar stool in the Bowery, which was famous for its groggeries, pawnbrokers, brothels, and dangerous characters. "What did you say your name was?"

"Tristan Wrigley." His light-colored hair grew back a little wild from his head, and when he smiled at her it was with an energy that she couldn't quite put her finger on. "And yours?"

"Carolina Broud," she answered. She liked the way her full name sounded aloud, and smiled to herself. She only wished she had thought to expand her surname as well, so that she could claim to be *Carolina Broudhurst*, or *Carolina Broudwell*.

"You'll forgive me if I keep staring at you." Tristan motioned to the barkeep, and before long two mugs of dark beer appeared before them, with froth spilling over their rims and onto the unfinished wood of the bar. "It's just that I'm sure we've met before, but I don't recall the name Carolina Broud. . . ."

"Well, I haven't been out so very long." She took a gulp of the beer and wasn't sure if she liked it. She had never had beer—only occasional sips of Will's whiskey—and it tasted like something gone bad. But she remembered one of the kitchen girls telling her that when there was no food to be had, a stout and a smoke was almost as good. So she took another pull and said, "I must look like a lot of girls."

"Not a bit." He gave her the smile again—it wasn't like

any smile Lina had been the recipient of. It gave her a warm, pleasant feeling, and also a little stab of guilt. "You're a mighty pretty girl, Miss Broud."

"Don't get any ideas, Mr. Wrigley," she warned him. "I told you I'm spoken for. He's seeking his fortune out West, but that doesn't mean that—"

"Oh, I get it," Tristan replied lightly. He winked at her, and she thought she saw something almost Will-like in his eyes. "Your fellow doesn't have enough money to make your folks happy, so he's gone out to make some pennies and then win your hand with them."

Lina was flattered by the little story he had just told her, and wished it were true. She blushed, and he seemed to take this as his cue to change the subject.

"So, I bet you've never seen anything like this before." Tristan turned on his stool and surveyed the long room, with its low tin ceiling. "See over there, the fellow in the plug hat?"

Lina followed his gaze and saw a medium-size man with a mashed nose and close-set eyes. He was sitting at a table, surrounded by women who struck Lina as almost as well dressed as she. "The ugly one?"

Tristan snorted. "That's Kid Jack Gallagher. Killed a man in a bare-knuckled match only two weeks ago. It was a long fight, and his opponent was unbeaten. Well, before that, of course."

"If he's a murderer, why are all the pretty ladies fawning over him?" Lina looked at the women fluttering around him.

"Those aren't pretty ladies. Those are whores. And they're fawning because he has prize money to burn."

"Oh."

Lina watched as Tristan lifted his mug and threw his head back. Slowly, all the beer disappeared from the glass. He looked at Lina with half-wild eyes. "You want to try that?"

Lina smiled. She'd always liked a challenge. She threw her head back and drained the beer in several chugs. She was sputtering when she came back up, but the beer was gone.

Tristan motioned again to the bartender. "Have another," he said when they arrived.

"All right, then," Lina replied, looking down into her second beer. She was beginning to feel very light-headed indeed, but she was finding Tristan's impression of her as a society girl gone bad to be completely irresistible. And anyway, she couldn't go home to be by herself just yet. Not to that room on Twenty-sixth Street with the ancient wallpaper and the air-shaft view. "If you insist."

As the hours passed she made up little stories about herself, although she was careful to keep them vague and minimal, and he listened in rapt attention. Three more beers came and went, and then she found herself drooping forward off her stool.

"Hey," Tristan said gently, as he pushed her upright. "Careful."

"Thank you." She giggled and burped into her hand, and then gave the man next to her a grateful, sloppy smile.

"You know, Christian," she said. She squinted her eyes at him and wondered if that name sounded a little wrong. "I like you. Not as much as my Will—I could never love anybody but him—but I've enjoyed talking with you."

He took her hand and kissed it. "I think I've finally figured out who you are. You're friends with Adelaide Wetmore, and you came in with her to look at brooches two weeks ago."

She giggled and shook her head.

"One of Commodore Vanderbilt's granddaughters, perhaps?"

Lina raised her eyebrows at this suggestion, and then had to shake her head no again.

"Then perhaps I recognize you because you're in the Schoonmaker-Holland wedding party?" Lina felt her smile disappear from her face. "That's it, isn't it? You're one of Elizabeth Holland's friends?"

"The *Hollands*," she said hatefully. "They're awful. Especially Elizabeth."

"Really? She always seemed so well mannered when I saw her in the store."

Lina nodded disgustedly. She reminded herself that if

it weren't for Elizabeth sneaking around and tricking Will into falling in love with her, he'd be in love with *Lina* right now instead. "That's the way she seems in public. But everyone who knows her knows that she's nasty as can be." Lina paused and decided that she was rambling unwisely. Then she remembered how the very man she was sitting next to had demanded payment of her former employers. "I'm far richer than they are now anyway."

"Really?" Tristan said, lowering his mug slowly to the bar. "The Hollands are such an old family, though."

"Oh *yes*," Lina said proudly. She knew that she was going on really foolishly, but she couldn't help herself. "I could buy and sell them."

"Oh, really," Tristan said lightly. "And what would you do with them when they belonged to you?"

"I would make them scrub my floor and mend my stockings, and then I'd send them out to find me lilies in a very particular shade." Lina couldn't stop herself. She was enjoying this fantasy too much.

"Sounds like an awful lot of work for Holland girls." Tristan's eyes were full of mischief.

"Oh, you've never met them. Awful family. Real princesses. Elizabeth especially." Lina paused to slurp her beer. "I wish she'd never lived."

"I could make that happen." Tristan leaned forward

confidentially. "I know you look at me, in my tailored suit and my fine way of talking, and think I'm probably out of my element with the Kid Jack Gallaghers here. But if you want a little problem like Elizabeth Holland gone . . ." He trailed off, raising a blond eyebrow.

Lina dropped her mug to the bar heavily. She was suddenly discomfited by this bend in the conversation. But then she looked at Tristan—serious now but so light before—and realized he must be joking.

She put her hands over her face and giggled. She felt terrible laughing at a thing like that, but there *was* something funny about the idea of Elizabeth being done away with by one of the men who used to deliver her dresses. And anyway, it was just an elaborate story. "It would serve her right," she added when her giggles had quieted down.

"Cheers to that, Carolina." Tristan raised his eyebrows and clinked his mug against hers.

Pretty soon everything began to feel warm and fuzzy; the faces in the room grew long and distorted, the warblings of the vocalist grew louder, and clinking glasses with Tristan Wrigley was the last thing Lina could recall.

Thirty Six

My dear Lizzie,

At this stage of life, I've begun
to worry what will happen to you
when I am gone. Remember
always to be true—as true and honest
as the girl I know.

With love,

Your Father

ELIZABETH WOKE EARLY ON TUESDAY AND COULD not fall back to sleep, although she was grateful to have slept at all. The night had been restless and full of ghosts. She didn't have the energy to choose a new outfit, so she put on the same dress she had worn the day before, the eyelet with the square neck and ruffles on the three-quarter-length sleeves. When she had finished dressing herself it was still well before breakfast, which she had little interest in anyway, so she went up to the morning room on the third floor. It was the room where the Holland women wrote their letters and stored their correspondence.

The most striking thing about the room, when she entered on that particular morning, was the heap of bridal fabrics from Lord & Taylor, which must have been delivered the previous afternoon. The room was simpler than the rest of the house, with wide dark floorboards and a plain metal frame for the fireplace. The wallpaper was an earthy brown with a velvet leaf pattern over it. The yards of silk muslin and point de gaze caught all the light and seemed almost to glow from the worktable in the center of the room. There was a note from Mr. Carroll, asking her to approve the fabric and informing her that his assistant would be by in the afternoon to pick it up and take it to his shop on Twenty-eighth Street. She didn't have a mind for that, however; what she wanted, more than anything, was to talk to her father.

The letters Edward Holland had sent to his oldest child were kept in several of the small drawers in the great mahogany cabinet. She had received crisp white envelopes embellished with the stamps of Japan and South Africa and Alaska, and she kept them all in dated order, each month's tied together with light blue ribbon. They were full of his quiet observations of foreign peoples and his carefully espoused principles of personal dignity. Her father had traveled a great deal, ostensibly on business, although really he had just wanted to see the world.

Elizabeth opened one of the cabinet drawers and pulled out a stack of letters. Even before he had passed, Elizabeth used to come here sometimes and pick a letter at random, looking for advice or wisdom. She needed that more than ever now, so she closed her eyes and ran the tip of her soft finger along the neatly opened edges of the stiff white envelopes. When she settled on one, she opened her eyes and saw her father's long, slanting script. She pulled open the envelope, and reread the little note, which must have accompanied some gift or other.

"Remember always to be true," she read his words in a whisper. *"As true and honest as the girl I know."*

A creeping shame set in around her chest bone. So this, she knew instantly, was what her father would have said if he were here. She closed her eyes, and thought how little the words *true* and *honest* applied to her now. But perhaps she still had time to change all that.

Elizabeth turned and marched across the hall to the room that once was her father's study, letter in hand. It was now the room where her mother went every morning, to look over their mounting bills and go through the papers as though she would somehow find a way to make them rich again. Elizabeth leaned her face against the door and knocked.

There was no answer. Elizabeth waited a moment and entered on timid feet. She saw her mother, a figure in black, behind the big oak desk with the burgundy leather top that her father once used. Her mother's hair, which was always pinned in a dozen places, if not also covered with a hat, was completely loose. It was the same chestnut color as Diana's, except streaked with white, and it streamed down her shoulders. She glanced up from her letter briefly and wished her daughter a good morning.

"Mother," Elizabeth said as she tiptoed into the room. "I've got to talk to you about this wedding."

Her mother nodded for her to continue, but she kept her eyes on the letter in her hands.

"I have been thinking about what Father had wanted for us, about how he lived his life, and how he expected us to live ours. I was reading through his letters this morning, and I came across one in which he urged me to stay true and honest. And when I think about it, marrying Henry Schoonmaker would make me neither of those things." Elizabeth waited for her mother to say something, but she barely even moved. "I think Father would have wanted me to marry for love," she went on, in a shaky voice. "And though I am deeply flattered by Mr. Schoonmaker's interest in me, and while I am very sensitive to his position in the world, I know I do not love him at all. I don't think I will come to love him either."

Mrs. Holland leaned back in her oak-and-leather chair, but still did not lift her eyes from the piece of paper to look at her daughter. She pressed her lips together, but otherwise remained completely still. Though she had never been a beauty, and had aged considerably since her husband's death, Elizabeth could see the woman who must have so impressed Edward Holland when she was still Louisa Gansevoort. There was a particular authority in her every gesture.

"I suppose I should be happy that our servants are

defecting, since I can no longer support them. Still, it is painful, especially when he was your father's valet."

Elizabeth was so stunned by this allusion to Will that she said the first thing that came into her head. "Mother, what are you reading?"

"It is a letter, child."

"From who?"

"From Snowden Trapp Cairns, your father's guide on his trips to Yukon Territory."

"Oh." Elizabeth had a vague memory of the gentleman from Boston, who had fair hair and nice manners, despite his mountaineering spirit. "Is it very interesting?"

Mrs. Holland finally put down the letter and looked up. Her eyes were dark and calm, and she assessed her daughter with an almost melancholy stare. "It would be very nice if you could marry for love, my child, and perhaps if your father had not gotten himself killed . . ." She paused, and the wrinkled skin around her mouth puckered. "But not now."

"*Killed?*" The word stuck painfully in Elizabeth's throat. All of her conviction drained away to make room for this newest misery. "But Father died in his sleep of a bad heart."

Mrs. Holland threw up her hands. "That was the only way it was possible to tell the story to you girls . . . and to everyone." Her eyes drifted sadly. "Your father was very young for his heart to fail, and Mr. Cairns tells me that there was some highly suspicious trading of claims, ones that your father had invested in around the time of his death. Those people are not gentlemen like the Hollands. Prospectors do not come from good families like ours. They are criminals, usually. And your father was caught up."

Elizabeth thought she might be sick, and refocused all her energy on standing up straight and keeping the rising bile out of her throat.

"It doesn't matter now, my Elizabeth. Your father made some very ill-advised gambles with his inheritance, I am afraid. He may have wanted you to marry for love, but he also would not have wanted his family to be destitute. Is that what you want? For your family to be destitute?"

Elizabeth shook her head in a slow, pained motion. She could feel the tears coming again, and already she felt like she had been crying for days.

"Good, because there is really only one thing to do. Your father would have wanted you to think of your family before yourself, Elizabeth. It is what our kind of people have always done." She lifted her chin now, and her voice rose slightly to make her position clear: "You *must* marry Henry, Elizabeth. You will not be my child if you do not."

Miss Carolina,

It was a pleasure to meet you.

Don't worry, I'll take care of

everything.

I noticed you went out in your

old walking shoes yesterday. I hope

you don't mind that I took the

liberty of getting you a new pair.

Yours,

Tristan Wrigley

WHEN LINA WOKE, SHE FOUND HERSELF IN A COLD sweat. Her head ached and there was a wretched hum behind her eyes. She was in a bed, but it was substantially wider than the one in her hotel. The ceiling was made of bare wood boards, and there was only one narrow, grimy window overlooking a downtown cobblestone street. She tried to recall how she had come to be in this unfamiliar place, but all she could conjure was a dark saloon filled with blurry faces and her own uncontrollable laughter. Soon after that she remembered Tristan, and the scene in the Fifth Avenue Hotel, and the fact that she had walked out into New York yesterday with every cent of her recently acquired fortune.

She clutched her chest, and then bolted out of the bed. She was still wearing Penelope's old bloomers and corset, and found her things piled on the single, unvarnished wooden chair. Her purse rested on her neatly folded red dress—not a single bill had been removed—with a note perched beside it.

She read the first bit with only foggy comprehension—

what was it that he was going to take care of exactly? The part about the shoes was very clear, however. Lina's shame-making boots were gone, and in their place were a pair of shiny black patent-leather lace-up shoes, with low wooden heels. They were as polished and new as anything in the Hollands' closets. For a moment she could concentrate on nothing but them.

She slipped them on and stepped lightly across the room, wearing nothing but her corset and bloomers and her brand-new shoes. She had never had anything that fit so well. She imagined how her future as a society lady would be filled with nothing but custom-made dresses, and elegant slippers, and how there would be a wedding to Will Keller, who would have made his fortune out west by then. For a moment she was filled with delight, but then some logical thinking broke through into her stuffy head, and all of her good feelings began to turn quickly to shame.

She was prancing around a near-stranger's barely furnished room, wearing nothing but her former mistress's former friend's undergarments. Yesterday she had had the chance to be a lady, and instead she had gotten drunk in the wrong part of town and now here she was, waking up in a strange room with a spotty memory of what had gone on the night before. Lina despised herself for having fallen so quickly, and so far, off her intended path.

She threw on her dress, took her purse and the note, and left as quietly as possible. She found her way down a slender tenement staircase and onto the street, all the while wondering how anyone could be so easily duped. Tristan had taken her for a lady, and she was now painfully aware that she was anything but.

Thirty Eight

Apparently, Miss Elizabeth Holland has forgiven her fiancé, Henry Schoonmaker, for his poor showing during the Dewey holiday, for the wedding date is said by many people in the know to have been moved up, to this Sunday, the eighth of October. Owing to the truncated time for preparation, all manner of florists, chefs, and couturiers are said to be working round the clock to pull off the lavish event. The Holland-Schoonmaker nuptials are looking very much as though they will turn out to be the greatest wedding of the nineteenth century.

—FROM THE "GAMESOME GALLANT" COLUMN IN THE
NEW YORK IMPERIAL, TUESDAY, OCTOBER 3, 1899

"'THE GREATEST WEDDING OF THE NINETEENTH century,'" Penelope spat as she walked, at a slow, agitated gait, across the floor of her personal drawing room on the second story of the Hayes mansion. The afternoon was bright and bustling outside. She held Robber close to her chest and kissed his head. "A little bit of hyperbole, don't you think?"

"Definitely a bit too much," Buck put in, between drags of a small fuchsia cigarette. "And you know I am an arbiter of all things a-bit-too-much," he added.

"Oh, please." Penelope punctuated her dismissal of Buck's commentary by rolling her large blue eyes. "The point is, it should be my name in the papers with Henry's, not Liz's. She is just so *infuriating*."

Penelope stomped her foot once and then turned sharply and walked from the west-facing windows to the south-facing ones. Buck crossed one pudgy leg over the other and exhaled. "You know, I am acquainted with that Gallant fellow. Davis

Barnard is his name; he's my mother's second cousin or some-thing. Maybe we could—"

"But it doesn't matter, because I'm not presently engaged to anyone, am I?" Penelope was feeling hot and itchy inside her black dress, and impatient with every little thing. Her instinct was to do some violence to the white-and-gold upholstery that decorated the room, but she had not so lost her head as to want to ruin good brocade. Not yet. She sighed, turned back to Buck, and said in a low voice, "I'm sorry. I didn't mean to be short. It's all so hard. . . . She more or less threatened me, you know."

"Really." Buck inhaled. "How?"

"She said that if I exposed her," Penelope answered, her voice returning quickly to a near shriek, "it would only end up making me look bad. *Me*. As though I were the one acting like a whore in the carriage house!"

Buck lifted his light-colored, sculpted eyebrows. "She's right," he ventured cautiously. "It will be difficult for you to get Henry if you appear at all related to Eliza-beth's fall, or if you seem to benefit from it. Society does not like an opportunist," he added with a slight wag of his finger.

Penelope emitted a wounded guttural noise and widened her eyes at her friend. "I am not an opportunist!" she wailed. Robber squirmed in her arms, but she held him firmly to her.

She strode back toward Buck and threw herself down onto the couch beside him. A few moments of awkward, heated silence passed, and then Penelope went on as coolly as she could manage: "I couldn't stand it if she got him. Do you understand? We need a plan—a perfect plan—to ensure that their engagement is broken immediately."

"We'll come up with one." Buck reached out and scratched Robber's head, and then petted Penelope's slender fingers.

"She's coming tomorrow morning," Penelope huffed. "How are we going to come up with a foolproof plan in less than twenty-four hours?"

"Penny, you know I'm very good with a plan—"

"She's just so perfect at everything!" Penelope interrupted. She stood up and dropped Robber into Buck's lap. "Everyone *thinks* so," she went on, pacing agitatedly across the black walnut. "And meanwhile, behind that act, she was . . . *you know* . . . with the help." Penelope smiled faintly, as a thought occurred to her. "She probably thought she was doing the Christian thing, giving herself to someone who really, really needed it."

Buck's face broke into a sneering little laugh at that. "So, do you think she'll come in the morning?"

"Of course. She must be scared out of her mind. *I* would be." She chuckled mirthlessly as she crossed her arms across her chest and continued to move restlessly across the floor. "You should have seen her face, Buck. She was white as a ghost."

Buck tipped the end of his cigarette into the ashtray that was held three feet off the ground by sculpted, gold-plated nymphs. He rested his chin on his palm contemplatively, and said, "Well . . . that's a good start."

Penelope's jaw tightened and she balled her hands into little fists, which she began to shake in frustration. "Of course it's a good start. It would be better if the next step were outing her as the slut she is. Then everyone would see plainly why she can't be with Henry, and the world would return to its rightful order. But apparently that would make *me* look bad." Penelope let out a little shriek, then collapsed onto the floor and pounded it once with her fist.

Buck stood and lifted her up by her armpits. He gave her a generous smile, his waxy cheeks rising with it, and then said, "You're going to have to calm down. You're never going to win if you can't keep your nerves under control."

"I *know*." She tried to take a few breaths and remind herself how much was in her favor. She leaned heavily on Buck, as they moved to the windows that looked down on Fifth. The avenue's afternoon parade of slow-moving carriages was on display, with passengers who pretended not to be watching one another, and who perhaps looked up now and then to see if they might catch a glimpse of the finest silhouette in the city. Penelope turned the dramatic curve of her back onto the street below. She hated that any one of those gawking masses below might perceive her as weak. "The idea," she went on, "that they would move up the wedding just to thwart me—"

"Well, I'm sure it wasn't *just* to thwart you."

Penelope's eyes flashed at this suggestion. "It is intolerable that I should lose out to Elizabeth!" she screamed. "That a twit from one of those old inbred families would appear to have stolen what everyone—*everyone!*—knew was mine."

"Be calm, my dear," Buck said, rubbing his friend's shoulder. "We can't keep going back and forth. We've got to come up with a plan for tomorrow morning. We have all the right cards. It's just a matter of when we play them.

"And we will," he told her in a sugared, reassuring voice.

Penelope turned her face into Buck's lapel, and let her thoughts wander to the episode in Lord & Taylor, trying to pinpoint her rival's weakness. Instead, she began fixating on Elizabeth's face, with its trembling chin and its eyes all welled up with self-pity.

Penelope could not cool the rage spreading inside of her. She turned quickly away from Buck and took long strides back to the couch where Robber had been lounging.

When she reached him she swept the Boston Terrier up into her arms. He let out a few sharp barks, but still she clung to him. "Whatever it takes, Buckie, we've got to find a way. I cannot bear to lose. I would rather see Elizabeth dead than married to my Henry."

Thirty Nine

If I go, I will remind him of Elizabeth's feelings, and that no matter how prearranged their engagement may be, the potential for her to become very hurt is quite real. Perhaps I will remind him, too, that it is the impossibility of our ever being together that lends such fascination to each of our meetings. That would be very wise, though I am not sure I believe it myself.

—FROM THE DIARY OF DIANA HOLLAND,
TUESDAY, OCTOBER 3, 1899

"SO IT *WAS* NINE AT NIGHT!" DIANA EXCLAIMED AS Henry led her from the side gate, across a gravel drive, and into the greenhouse with its arched glass roof. As the door closed, he turned to her and grinned. She looked into his face and in an instant forgot all the things that she had planned to say.

"I worried you might misunderstand," Henry said, with a playful backward glance. "But I didn't worry that much."

As she followed him to the greenhouse she kept a hand on his note—the bookmark that she had found in his Whitman—which she had brought in the pocket of her cape. She had in fact read it several times on her way over, just to prove to herself that Henry Schoonmaker had asked her to visit, at an hour not suitable to young ladies.

Inside it smelled of dirt and hothouse flowers. It was just as wondrous as it had been on that night a week and a half ago. They walked under giant leaves, past beds of rare blossoms, and at the far end of the building Henry led her through a little door into a small room. The ceiling was glass here as well, though it was low and frosted, and there was a bed covered by a hand-sewn quilt.

"It was the gardener's room," Henry explained. "But then he took up with one of Isabelle's seamstresses, and now they're married, so he lives in the house. He lets me use it sometimes."

Diana wondered for a minute what he meant by *some-times* and also what he meant by *use*. But then the beauty of the room took over and commanded her senses. The air was fresh from all the verdure, and the room was lit with simple yellow lamps. There were no candles or incense or champagne, which were always present in seduction scenes in the serials. "It's lovely here," she told him. It felt both very civilized and remote at once.

"I didn't think you'd come, to be honest. I mean, given that the only good thing about me is my greenhouse," Henry teased her, and Diana was reminded of how different he'd seemed when she had furiously uttered that phrase. "I thought you'd *want* to come, but—"

"But you didn't think I'd find a way? I'm a crafty girl, Henry." She gave him a wink, and he smiled in return. Neither of them could seem to stop smiling. She pushed the hood of her cape back now and waited for him to take it off. He did, after a minute, unbuttoning it at the neck first and then lower down, until she was standing there in the simple dotted navy batiste dress that she had chosen so that, if she were caught, she wouldn't look like she was going anywhere.

"I'm glad you are." He gazed at her appreciatively until she began to blush. He put his fingers to the neckline of the dress, where the little white buttons began. She felt her blood rush to that tender spot.

"I didn't want to be nicely dressed in case of—"

Henry stopped her with a long kiss on the mouth. His arms reached around her and brought her close, so that her body was pressed against his. She was exquisitely aware of the pressure of his palm against her back. The kiss was moist and it had its own rhythm and it lasted and lasted. She feared the flutters it was giving her might be too much for her untried little heart. When he pulled back, she saw that Henry was grinning, but there was a new softness to the curl in his lips.

He took the top button between his fingers and twisted it. Diana felt her chest rise and fall, and then he pushed the button out of its loop. He unbuttoned the next one and the next, all the way down her torso. The bodice of her dress fell around her waist revealing the sheer, ruched chemise below. She pressed her lips together in the hope that that would calm her restless breathing. Henry kept his eyes on her as he pushed the dress off her waist. It fell to her ankles, and she was left standing, in the middle of a greenhouse, in nothing but her underclothes.

She tilted back her head and let a sparkle cross her dewy, dark eyes. "So you lured me here to ruin me?" Her voice seemed to have grown husky in a matter of seconds.

Henry kissed her neck, on the opposite side from where he had yesterday, and then loosened his grip on her. "No, I promise I won't do that," he said. Diana tried not to look disappointed as he fell back on the bed and folded his arms behind his head to make a pillow. He was wearing a pale yellow button-down shirt, and he looked long and slender against the bed. "I lured you here so that you could ask me all those questions you tried to ask me the first time we met. Any question at all, and I swear to answer honestly."

Henry gave her one of those winks that made her heart slow and warm again, and she felt relieved, just a little bit, that she wouldn't have to do that thing she was always thinking about. Not yet, anyway. "Anything?" she asked, sitting down on the bed next to him.

"Anything you want." He reached over to the bedside table, pulled a cigarette from the small gold case there, and lit it.

She took Henry's cigarette from him, dragged on it, and then handed it back. Her eyes wandered up to the ceiling as she exhaled, and glittered when they fell back on him. "All right . . . if it's really *anything* . . . then tell me what you think of me."

Henry chuckled and took a thoughtful drag. "I think

that you are the most naturally lovely girl I have ever seen. When you get that mischievous look about you, I want to know exactly what is going through your head, and then I want to plot something devious with you. I like the funny little way you walk and the way you seem always to be too big for the room you are in." Diana took a deep breath of warm, earthy air to slow her breathing. "To put it succinctly, Miss Diana"—he took her hand and kissed it—"you are more alive than anyone I know."

Diana bit her lower lip and felt the blood rising to her cheeks. "I like this game," she whispered.

"I could go on complimenting you all night, but you'd get bored of it quickly. Ask me another one."

"Have you really broken as many hearts as they say?" Diana was conscious of the strap of her chemise slipping down her white shoulder, but she didn't do anything to stop it.

"I have broken hearts, but not nearly as many as they say."

"Have you ever been in love?"

"Yes," Henry said firmly, looking almost pained. "Once."

"Who was she?"

"Now here is where you must promise not to repeat what I am about to tell you."

Diana took in an excited breath, and then lay down, so that she was on her side facing Henry, her head propped against her fist. "I promise."

"She was a daughter of New York like you, and her maiden name was Paulette Riggs, but when I knew her she was already Lady Deerfield."

"Paulette Riggs! She's nearly *thirty*," Diana couldn't help but exclaim. "And married to a *lord*."

"I know." Henry laughed wistfully. He lifted his hand and maneuvered it deftly under her chemise to the rise of Diana's thigh. "But I was eighteen and she was the most worldly thing I had ever seen. She spent that season in Newport, because her father was ill that year, and Lord Deerfield went off on so many hunting trips that I suppose she got lonely."

"How did it end?"

"Badly." Henry sighed, and let his fingertips press into the flesh of her leg. "She just tired of me after a while, and I of course kept on writing her letters and trying to arrange meetings like a real ass."

"Do you ever miss her?" Diana was a little frightened to know that this woman, who she remembered as having very white skin and very red lips and carrying herself like royalty, had once been Henry's lover. But of course she still wanted to know everything about it.

"Not anymore. Seems like a long time ago, now. She had a way of looking at me, with those moody eyes . . . sort of like you, actually. But no. I stopped missing her a good while ago now."

"And she was the only one you have ever been in love with?"

Henry nodded, and drew his hand back and forth along Diana's thigh.

"How many have you . . . *loved*?" Diana fixed her eyes on him, even through her embarrassment. He seemed to be smiling faintly at her lack of vocabulary.

Henry paused, whether to count or to reconsider his promise to answer anything she wasn't sure. "Five," he said at last.

"Were they all married to English lords?"

"No! Nor were they all well-brought-up girls like you. But I had good times with each of them."

"And who was the last girl to be loved by Henry Schoon-maker?"

Henry shifted, bringing himself up to rest on his elbows and bringing his hand away from her thigh. He met Diana's face, and he worked his lips in agitation.

"You said anything!" she exclaimed, and wondered whose name could give him such pause.

He would not meet Diana's eyes as he pronounced a name she knew quite well. "Penelope Hayes."

"*No . . .*" Diana wasn't sure whether to admonish him or giggle. "She must have been angry about . . ." Diana trailed off, realizing that she wasn't ready to bring up Elizabeth just yet. Henry rolled his eyes and let out an exasperated sigh of agreement. "No wonder she's been acting so bizarre lately. And you . . . you . . . *her*."

Henry grabbed onto Diana's thigh again, this time with a firm grip. She was very close to Henry now, and she could feel the slightest movements of his body.

"She's one to . . . well, she's more savage than I thought she was at first."

"Oh." Diana could feel the conversation growing heavier, and she didn't mind. She wished she had a way to tell him that she liked being serious with him, too. *"Well,"* she said, "I guess I know all about you now."

"But I don't want to be like that anymore." Henry paused and fidgeted with the buttons of his shirt. His voice had grown low and self-reproaching. "Careless, I mean, with people's hearts. I don't want you to think that this was all some kind of game. You told me not to treat you like a toy once. I don't want you to think that I've been playing with you."

"That's why you asked me here?" She pushed herself up farther with her elbow, and kept her shining eyes on him. "To clear that up?"

"Yes. Well, that and . . . When I marry your sister, I can't go on . . ." Henry looked down, and moved his hand along to where her hip sloped into the small of her waist.

Diana nodded. "You have to marry her, don't you?"

"Yes. . . . Well, it's that . . ."

"I understand." Diana had been thinking of her sister's reasons for marrying, and suspected that there must be some similar force driving Henry. "And I don't want to know why." There was a sadness gripping at her, but she felt the need to be the one who said what she was sure they were both thinking. "This will have to be the only time we are together."

He raised his eyes to hers again after a moment and nodded. He reached up and put his hand on the back of her head, bringing her face closer to his. She examined his dark prettiness with intense eyes, so that she could commit it to memory and have it always. Outside, a gust picked up, blowing the trees noisily against the roof—a storm must be coming—but still he held her gaze. Then he kissed her with a hungry intensity that made her want to weep.

"Now, if I promise to leave you as pure and perfect as you are now, will you stay the night with me?"

Diana nodded and gave him a reckless smile, which he returned.

"Excellent, because there is a question or two I want to ask about you."

And with that, she let down what was left of her guard and gave herself over to Henry's knowing gaze and unfailing charm.

Forty

The most important thing for any bride, even if she is gifted with all the loveliness that good family and impeccable upbringing guarantee, is rest. She must be always resting, or nerves will get the better of her, and then on her wedding day she will look like a girl who has already known too much of the world.

—L. A. M. BRECKINRIDGE, *THE LAWS OF BEING IN WELL-MANNERED CIRCLES*

*T*HAT NIGHT ELIZABETH DREAMED SHE WAS IN a faraway part of the country with Will, where there were hills between houses and no one had a favorite Paris dressmaker. Then she dreamed that she was done up in white, with an elaborate and ridiculous point de gaze collar, and Penelope was laughing at her sadistically and throwing poisoned rice in her direction. But mostly she stared at the ceiling and wished that she were not so constantly awake. She had barely slept on Monday night, and now it looked like Tuesday night wasn't going to give her any rest either.

There wasn't even much to think about, because her options were so few and unattractive. She had been raised to please others—please them with her looks, her comportment, and her deeds—but now she could do nothing but be selfish. If she pleased her mother, she would be exposed as a wanton who had betrayed her class. And if she pleased Penelope— who had revealed herself to be the most duplicitous sort of friend, anyway—then she would be cast out from the only home and way of life she had ever known. And if she pleased herself . . . well, it was too late for that.

When she had finally had enough of staring at the ceiling, she pushed herself up and went to her closet. She took out her white kimono and tied it around her small body. The whole day had been spent at the dressmaker's. There was the wedding gown to be made, and the dress for the reception afterward, and so many little things for her trousseau. She had stood up straight and erect all day and listened to herself talked about as though she wasn't in the room.

The worst of it was, she had been alone. She had often imagined herself as a bride when she was young, and in all kinds of settings. As a bride in a simple wedding, with gerbera daisies in her hands; as a bride in a lavish event that got written up in the papers, where she would wear a long train decorated with tiny silk roses that flowed behind her all down the church steps. But she had always imagined that the part about the dress would be fun. In reality, she had spent the whole day playing mannequin for a small fleet of seamstresses petrified of her disapproval. She was left feeling nothing but sore and isolated, and was driven home by Mr. Faber instead of Will, who once upon a time would have been waiting for her with the carriage when she finished such an errand. Of course Penelope hadn't been there. But Diana—there was no reason for Diana not to have come and help her determine whether she looked beautiful or ridiculous—but she had shrugged off the task as well, preferring instead to remain in her room, reading and moping about who knew what.

Elizabeth walked across her bedroom, growing almost angry as she thought about Diana's absence. After all, Elizabeth was sacrificing her own happiness for the sake of her family. She was renouncing her own wishes, so that the Holland women would not fall. And Diana could not even be bothered to take her nose out of her book for one day.

Elizabeth threw open her door and marched down the hall. She raised her fist to knock on Diana's door, but then admonished herself. It wasn't Diana's fault that her older sister had fallen in love with the wrong person, and continued to love him even when she knew it would only lead to trouble. It wasn't her fault that their family was so badly off financially. Elizabeth rested her hand against the door and took a breath. Then she knocked in a gentle, sisterly way.

"Di?" she called. She looked down the hall to where their mother slept, and hoped that she wouldn't come to see what the matter was. Since yesterday morning, Elizabeth had felt a great distance open up between her mother and herself. She had nothing left to say to the old woman. "Di?" Elizabeth called again. When she didn't answer a second time, Elizabeth pushed into the room.

It took her a few moments to realize that the room was

empty. Of Diana, anyway. There were dresses thrown across the bed and floor, and shoes turned at all varieties of angles. Lillie Langtry gave her a hazy look and crossed her paws.

Elizabeth began distractedly looking through the closet and behind the chairs. She checked the high windows onto the balcony—they were jammed closed but unlocked. She was about to go downstairs to see if Diana had gone there to search for a book or a glass of milk, when she noticed a hatbox protruding from under the bed. The gold lid was askew, and Elizabeth saw from across the room a dark brown bowler. It was just like any bowler, but it brought her back instantly to a day two weeks ago when her world began to disintegrate.

She remained transfixed by the hat as she walked across the room. Lillie Langtry gave a little meow, and trotted along beside Elizabeth before walking in a quick circle around the box and flopping down next to it. When Elizabeth picked up the hat the first thing she noticed was the gold embroidery on the pale blue ribbon that ran around the inside of the brim: *HWS*.

She sat down heavily on the chenille bedspread, looking into the hatbox as she did. There were two scraps of paper lying there, against the charcoal velvet. She had to force herself to pick them up and read each of the notes that Henry had written to her sister. They were signed simply *HS*, but she had no doubt to whom the initials referred. She couldn't be sure when he had sent Diana the missive telling her to keep his hat, or the one that indicated he couldn't stop thinking about her. But his intentions were clear, and Diana's absence from her room at that hour spoke well enough for hers.

A cold shock was settling into the muscles of Elizabeth's face. She lay back and brought her knees to her chest, and twirled the bowler on her finger distractedly. Lillie Langtry stood, stretched, walked around Elizabeth, and then settled on the pillow beside her head. Elizabeth put down the hat and sighed. She might have laughed if she had been the kind of girl to find humor in perversity, but this horrible evidence of her sister's corruption was not in the least funny to her.

Elizabeth's mind was seized by a cool fury, as she realized something else: that her predicament with Penelope was at least half Henry's fault. Whatever his involvement with Penelope, it had surely inspired some of her vengeful actions. Now he was no doubt out somewhere in the city seducing naïve little Diana. And after all of that, on a day not so far in the future, he still expected Elizabeth to be his wife.

She got up from the bed as though she had some purpose, but there was nothing to do but gather the clothes strewn about Diana's room. The angry, desperate feeling grew inside her with every passing moment as she put away all the many dresses that her younger sister had considered wearing to her misbegotten tryst.

Forty One

For my True Bride.

"WHAT DOES THAT MEAN?" DIANA SAID, GLOWING with joy as she turned the lapis-encrusted cross with the inscription on the back. She ran her fingers along the letters, longing for a way to be his real bride instead. But she already knew that could not be. Since they had left the greenhouse, every moment with Henry felt imbued with its own rare luster. The sounds of the city on its way to work were just outside their carriage, but they might as well have been coming from across the river.

"My father gave it to my mother before they were married. I've never understood what it meant. I suppose he might have given it to the seventeen-year-old girl he married in the hope that she would always be seventeen." Henry gave a muted, ironic laugh. "But that's not why I'm giving it to you."

"I know," Diana said as she tucked the cross into her bodice.

"It's more understated than all the things he gave her

later; maybe that's why I like it. I don't remember her very well; I was only four when she died. But I think she was that old-fashioned, natural kind of beautiful that doesn't benefit from all the ornament."

Diana took this in. She had learned so much about Henry over the last evening that he practically constituted an entirely new person, and everything he said now seemed a wink to her special knowledge. She leaned forward from her seat in the plain buggy, the one vehicle Henry could possibly have managed to borrow unnoticed from the Schoonmaker carriage house, and around the black folding top. They were paused on Broadway, waiting for the right moment for Diana to slip into the morning crowd and make her way home. She turned her sleepy, adoring eyes back on him and tried to smile as best she could. "It'll be hard watching you marry Liz, Henry. . . ." She had intended something more finalizing and profound, but her throat was constricting so painfully now that she knew she wouldn't be able to say any more.

Henry kissed her below her right eye. Diana took a final look at him before pulling her hood firmly over her face and slipping down to the street. Once her feet touched the ground, she found it easy to move forward and join the hordes on their morning route. All around her, men in bowlers and cheap three-piece suits walked at a swift gait that didn't allow for time to wonder at the darting girl with the hood.

Before long she had found the alley off Nineteenth Street, which led into the Van Dorans' property and then into her own family's. She had risked the trellis the night before, which had been nearly as dangerous as venturing out by herself into the New York night, but today she took the easier route of the hatch door into the basement washing room. From there it was a breathless dash up the servants' stairs and she was on the second floor and very close to the door to her own safe bedroom.

There was nobody there, which was some kind of relief, but the room was altered from when she had left it. All the dresses that she'd pulled out to consider wearing for her evening with Henry had been put away. All her high-heeled slippers, too. And sitting on top of her neatly made bed was the hat that Henry had worn on the day they met. Anxiety began to grip at Diana as she went to the bowler and picked it up. She was frozen in place, immobile with the sad, awful thought of who had been there the night before.

Forty Two

It has become widely acceptable to be late, a new social phenomenon I frown on intensely. A true lady always arrives at precisely the promised hour.

— MRS. HAMILTON W. BREEDFELT, *COLLECTED COLUMNS ON RAISING YOUNG LADIES OF CHARACTER*, 1899

*I*T WAS NINE THIRTY ON WEDNESDAY MORNING, AND Elizabeth found herself stopped on Broadway, in the middle of all the morning bustle, her limbs paralyzed by hopelessness. All the chaos—the horse-drawn delivery carts, the trolleys, the yelling of drivers, the sounds of carriage wheels against the battered pavement, the throngs of pedestrians—ceased to exist in her mind. The scene she had just witnessed was not, after the evidence she'd seen the night before, a surprise, but the emotion it awoke in her was startling.

The hooded figure of her younger sister had already disappeared down Twenty-first Street. The sight of Diana, on a Manhattan corner so early in the morning, had confirmed all of Elizabeth's suspicions. But she remained strangely stuck to her spot, watching the person who had been left behind. He had stepped down from his buggy, and was just standing there on the curb. She couldn't be sure, because she had always been the one doing the running away, but she was nearly certain the forlorn way Henry was looking down Twenty-first

Street wasn't so different from the way that Will must have looked every morning when she turned her back on him and went into the house.

Elizabeth had barely managed to sleep the night before, and still she had risen from bed without the slightest idea how she could subdue Penelope, how she could save Diana, or how she could possibly resign herself to marrying the loathsome Henry Schoonmaker. She had tried to dress herself with some determination, in the same dress of blue-and-white seersucker she had worn the day he had proposed, and because she sensed the weather was about to change, a camel wrap with a hood and flannel lining. Once she was dressed she still hadn't known what to do, and so she had decided to walk, all the way up Fifth Avenue to face Penelope. Every member of the household was employed in some wedding-related task or other, and in the few moments when her opinion was not required she had managed to slip out the door.

Last night she had come to the conclusion that her fiancé was the most licentious man she had ever met. But his appearance now dispelled that belief. She stood there watching him a moment longer, in his simple black suit, with his face overcome by loss, and felt sure that he was not trying to take advantage of Diana. He actually did love her sister, and though she couldn't totally explain it, she had the growing conviction that her sister loved him in return. Elizabeth had been wrong. Her anger had dissolved in seconds.

A high, black coach, with men in work clothes standing up on the back, paused between Henry and Elizabeth, considering how it should enter the fray on the wide thoroughfare. When it had passed and her view opened up again, Henry had turned and was looking in her direction.

Henry lowered his head, but kept his eyes, full of remorse and resignation, looking directly into her own. She could see now that he was not so unlike her—that he was willing to marry for some reason having more to do with family and duty and class than love, but that his heart lay elsewhere. He took off his hat and tipped it gently in her direction. She bent her head slowly in reply, to let him know they understood each other, and then turned away and moved northward into the crowd. She had an appointment for which she could not be late.

Everything was different now, but still as impossible as it had been before. Elizabeth realized with sadness how easy everything would be if she simply did not exist. She no longer needed the forty-block walk to the Hayes mansion to figure out what to do. In an instant she had realized what that single devastating thing was.

Forty Three

We see our sins reflected everywhere: in the pallor of our intimates' faces, in the scratching of tree branches against windows, in the strange movements of everyday objects. These may be messages from God or tricks of the eye, but in neither case are we permitted to ignore them.

—REVEREND NEEDLEHOUSE, *COLLECTED SERMONS*, 1896

$\mathscr{D}$IANA HAD BEEN STANDING STILL IN HER ROOM for well over an hour, wondering what she should do with that hat, when a scream from downstairs broke through her state of shock. A new frost alighted on her heart. When she had left the house the night before, it had seemed impossible that she might get caught—nobody was paying any attention to her doings these days, and besides, her whole evening had seemed like an episode out of time, ending as abruptly as it had begun. But the noise coming from below was most certainly a cry of grief, anger, confusion, or some combination of all three.

Diana looked at the hat, placed just so at the center of her bed. She was trying to think of some story to explain this clear evidence of her misbehavior, when another cry—this one more of a moan—came up from the first floor.

Diana threw Henry's hat under her bed and turned to her closet. The dresses she had taken out the night before were all there. It was too late to change, she told herself, so she quickly checked herself in the mirror. She did not look any different, after her night with Henry, but she felt much older already. Then the moaning started again, and she had no choice but to take the stairs two at a time to face what would surely be an inevitable circle of accusations and confessions.

Diana burst into the drawing room to find Penelope Hayes, her dark hair unusually low and messy, and her red muslin dress dripping onto Louisa Holland's favorite Persian carpet. She was drenched and blubbering, punctuating her nonsense with occasional shrieks.

"Thank God you're here," Aunt Edith said, coming up beside Diana and wrapping her in her arms.

"How could you sleep so long on a day like today?" her mother added as she, too, came over and pressed Diana's head to her breast. "Out of all the tragedies the Hollands have suffered."

"What are you talking about?" Diana whispered. It was the loudest voice she could manage. She looked out from the clot of arms around her, at Penelope, who had all of a sudden quieted down.

"It's almost too much to bear," her mother said.

"It is certainly too much to bear," Aunt Edith seconded.

At that moment Claire came rushing into the room. "I found a policeman on the street," she said hysterically, "and he said he would go to the precinct and summon his superiors. Mrs. Holland, do you need salts?"

"Yes, Claire, please. And water."

The three Holland women moved in a cluster to the nearest settee and sat down together. Diana was by now cognizant of the fact that this had nothing to do with her late-night tryst. Something far worse must have happened. She glanced once more at Penelope, whose expression implied that she had borne witness to a very grave occurrence.

"What's this all about?" Diana managed. Her heart was thumping so loudly now that the rest of her surroundings seemed muted. Both her mother and aunt looked pale and exhausted from crying. They clasped each other's hands across Diana's lap.

"Your sister . . ." Aunt Edith began in a faltering voice.

"She's . . . well, she's gone from us, Diana."

"Gone?" Diana whispered stupidly. "Gone where?" It was only then that she began to take in the details. The hat, placed with such perfectionist zeal at the center of the impeccably made bed. It was a message from Elizabeth. With every passing second, it was becoming more horribly clear. She felt dizzy and sick with herself.

"It happened this morning," Penelope broke in, suddenly regaining her speaking voice. She moved forward assuredly, and situated herself on a small silk hassock in front of Diana and her family. Every sound and color seemed extreme to Diana now, and she was painfully aware of the droplets of water falling from Penelope as they hit the ground. "Elizabeth came by to visit me early this morning. We had planned to go to the dressmaker's together." Penelope spoke carefully, as though she were thinking out each word or trying to keep herself from crying. "She was all nerves about the wedding. I think it was just dawning on her how much there was to be done by Sunday. I thought it might be a good idea to take an early-morning ride by the water to calm her down. I wanted her to able to speak freely, so I tried to drive us myself. I just wanted to reassure her. After all, it will all get done . . . or it *would* have. That's what I told her."

Penelope's speech slowed, and Diana turned her wild eyes toward her mother, expecting her to complete the story. Before she could, Penelope broke in again: "There was a strange man by the waterfront. The horses got spooked, and . . . and . . . I couldn't control them! I couldn't . . . oh . . . oh, oh, oh."

"She was thrown," Mrs. Holland said distractedly. "Into the river. And then Penelope and the carriage were pulled for many blocks before she managed to get control of the horses, and by then there was no sign of Elizabeth anywhere."

"My new phaeton," Penelope continued, more to her hands than anyone else. "It goes so fast and it's set so high!" she explained, and there was something in her voice that reminded Diana of bragging. "I can't even really make sense of what happened. And then the water, when I tried to see if I could find her. It was so cold, so bone-chillingly cold."

Diana was stunned and full of disbelief, but what she had seen upstairs told her that she had to believe. Surely it was Elizabeth who had come into her room and put all the clothes away. And surely she knew where that hat had come from and, put together with Diana's absence last night, what it meant.

"But how could she have been thrown while Penelope remained in the carriage?" Diana asked. She didn't want to ask these questions, but she had to. A nauseating guilt was sweeping through her, and she could feel Henry's cross, underneath her dress, digging at her skin and reminding her of what she'd done. Her sister was dead, and it was her fault. She brought her eyes up to Penelope, who was staring back with what must have been pure shock in her face. "I mean . . ." Diana went on, in a barely audible voice, "you don't think she threw herself, do you? On purpose, I mean."

Diana felt the bodies of her aunt and mother draw back from her own, and a silence descended on the room.

She thought she saw a spark of interest cross Penelope's face, but it disappeared as quickly as it had come and once again Diana saw only a mask of distress.

"We're all a little shaken," Aunt Edith said. "Or you wouldn't say something like that."

"Diana, this is an awful moment, and it is understandable

for you to not quite know what you're saying. You couldn't, or you wouldn't say things like that." Her mother was struggling to keep her voice level, and though her face was unmoving, there was a muddy quality to her eyes that suggested untold grief. "You must go to your room. You must rest. But don't go on saying things like that—you must not—or someone might give them credence."

Diana was grateful that they wanted her to leave the room. She walked to the hall without a backward glance. Her chest was brittle with grief, like it might catch fire or crumble away. The thought of being around people who believed she was innocent was abhorrent to her. Perhaps, in her way, Elizabeth *had* loved Henry. Perhaps she had been so distraught by her sister's secrets that she had wanted to do herself harm. Elizabeth must have felt like the whole world was upside down, and maybe the cold embrace of the Hudson had, in the end, seemed preferable to a world where the Hollands were not wealthy, marriage had nothing to do with love, and her future husband spent the night with her little sister.

Diana entered her room and picked up Henry's hat. The things she had done yesterday had been thoughtless, but their result was horrific and everlasting. She had never really known guilt, and now it was overpowering her. Diana lay down on the crisply made bed, put the hat over her face, and let her whole body be racked by tears.

Forty Four

... And then there is the American princess who met with the waters of the Hudson in an untimely fashion. The mysterious case of Elizabeth Holland is being called an accident, but there are a number of reasons to believe it was the opposite. There are simply too many loose details, including some reports that a man—tall, slender, and well dressed—was witnessed at the river's edge. . . .

—FROM THE "POLICE BLOTTER" COLUMN IN THE *NEW YORK IMPERIAL*, THURSDAY, OCTOBER 5, 1899

ON THURSDAY MORNING, LINA ROUSED HERSELF AND chose a dark-colored skirt and a light-colored shirtwaist. These pieces were not quite so flashy as the red dress she had put on two nights ago, but Lina had had her fill of red for the moment. And anyway, what she was wearing was nice enough to impress her sister without making her feel jealous. During her hurried departure from the Hollands' home, she and Claire had agreed to meet at eleven on Thursday—the one hour when her older sister was reasonably sure she would not be needed by her mistresses—on one of the benches in the park in Union Square. Lina was still feeling a residual shame for her drunken behavior of the other night, and hoped that, when and if she managed to find Will, he wouldn't somehow sense the depths of her depravity. It was some relief that she couldn't remember much of the episode in the saloon.

She did her hair the old way, with a sharp part and a low bun, and then she put on a little tailored jacket. When she realized how late it was getting, she tucked her purse under her arm and scuttled down the stairs.

She hurried through the small lobby, past the single drowsing clerk. Outside she could see the rain was falling heavily. It occurred to her that, given the weather, Claire might not even be able to make it to their meeting. But Lina felt she must go. Her sister would do everything in her power to be there, so she must do the same. And besides, she was harboring a secret hope that Claire would have heard something about Will. Perhaps she knew something that would help Lina find him. As there was no forgotten umbrella upstairs, she swiped the copy of the *Imperial* that was lying at the clerk's desk.

She stepped tentatively onto the one little step down to the street, where she was still protected from the rain by an awning. The sky was an ominous slate color, and the air smelled of all the grime being washed out of crevices and into the street. A few people ran by, shielded under black umbrellas, and those passersby who had not thought to bring such protection were quickly soaked to the bone. She unfolded her paper, propping it open so that she could at least shield her head from the onslaught. A chill set in at the back of her neck when she saw Elizabeth's name.

There it was, on page eleven. Elizabeth Holland had been plunged into the Hudson River and was presumed dead. It would have been less surprising to see a front-page banner headline proclaiming that the end of the world had been scheduled for later that afternoon. Lina had felt so many things for Elizabeth—adoration, envy, jealousy, and fury—it seemed impossible that she might simply . . . *die.* This thought revived something in Lina's memory, but she couldn't quite grasp hold of it. As the news settled into her consciousness, Lina began to feel a little sick and dizzy.

She forced herself to step forward and onto the sidewalk. As she did, she brought the paper up above her head so that it made a kind of tent. The water was into her shoes within seconds. She started off at a run, moving eastward along the street. She only managed to make it a few blocks before her newspaper was entirely soaked, and she had to take cover on a little ledge that led into a flower shop and was sheltered by an awning.

She could see, down the street, the expanse of Fifth Avenue. She was still quite far off from her destination, but she was now very close to the site of her humiliation at the hotel. The rain was pounding the uneven pavement, and there was a crack of thunder somewhere in the distance. Lina looked up, and saw a man across the street, partially obscured from her view by a gigantic black umbrella. She was suddenly reminded of the phrase *tall, slender, and well dressed,* which had appeared in the item about Elizabeth. She was beginning to feel very nervous all of a sudden. She saw the man with the umbrella move forward and cross toward her with long, quick strides.

She wanted to move, but the newspaper in her hands was too sopping to be of any use.

The man was close enough to her now that she could make out a neat, fair stubble on his cheeks and a sculptured nose. Soon he was close enough that she recognized him as someone she had met. He was without a doubt Tristan from Lord & Taylor. She thought back to the evening with him in the saloon and the note he'd left, and she stepped away from him as he approached.

"Remember me?" he said, as he brought his huge umbrella over her head. The raindrops fell against it loudly. Her face was completely wet, and she had to blink back the rain from her sage-colored eyes.

"Yes," she said in a small voice.

"Miss Carolina, whose face I simply can't get out of my head. I see you've read the *Imperial* already," he said, and Lina looked away quickly. The ink from the paper had run and was now all over her fingers. "What do you say we go get breakfast, and I tell you what you've missed?"

Lina nodded. She didn't know what else to do. She was confused and cold and she felt fearful and nauseated. At least she was no longer being soaked by the rain. Tristan tipped his head and gave her a reassuring smile. But she couldn't help but wonder, standing under the protection of a Lord & Taylor umbrella in the drenched streets of New York, what it was she had wrought.

Forty Five

The dramatic loss of one of society's rising stars is made doubly tragic by the fact that Elizabeth Holland was to have wed one of New York's choicest bachelors this very Sunday. All who loved Miss Holland are said to be congregating at the home of her fiancé, Henry Schoonmaker, in a sort of vigil. The father of the ill-fated bridegroom, William Sackhouse Schoonmaker, has tripled the reward offered by Mayor Van Wyck for any information leading to the recovery of Miss Holland's body. There has been much whispering about Miss Penelope Hayes's attendance at these places, she being the last person to have seen Elizabeth alive, as well as a one-time paramour of young Schoonmaker.

—FROM *CITÉ CHATTER*, FRIDAY, OCTOBER 6, 1899

"IT IS SHOCKING, UNCONSCIONABLY SHOCKING, THAT there is no sign of her." Henry's father's voice boomed through the drawing room of their Fifth Avenue home. "The mayor should be ashamed."

Henry winced as his father made the gross connection between Elizabeth's death and Mayor Van Wyck's corruption and incompetence. He had to stand next to the man, however, and nod along. It was too tragic a time for Henry to risk being seen as cavalier, especially not when a reporter from the *New York World* was his father's chosen audience. Not to mention, all of the Schoonmaker and Holland relatives and friends who had crowded into their home, to sob together and wait for any news of Elizabeth.

So Henry stood beside his father, looking slight and pale by comparison, and nodded. "No body," the elder Schoonmaker went on, "not even a piece of clothing floating by the piers. For all we know, she could have been fished out by a tugboat crew and sold into white slavery. Every week, the papers bring stories of that ilk. And I hold the mayor fully responsible. He is just a shill for Tammany—no reason for him to actually *do* something."

"And you, Mr. Schoonmaker," the reporter said, looking toward Henry. "Any thoughts on the rescue effort?"

There was nothing appropriate to say, and so Henry simply lowered his eyes. A moment passed before his father succumbed to the temptation to go on speechifying. Not even the death of his son's fiancée, it seemed, could keep him from turning to the endless, dirty topic of New York politics.

"There's a scandal coming," Henry heard his father say. "Just you watch. He's all tied up with Consolidated Ice, and they've been buying up the competition, you know. Wait till they try and raise the price of ice—and it's only a matter of time before they do, maybe even *doubling* it—the people will call for the mayor's head. But oh, yes—Elizabeth. The reward money Van Wyck's offering for her body is so low it's an insult. And my son, Henry . . ." Henry set his lips together as he felt eyes on him again. "Look at him—he can barely speak, he's so broken up about it."

Henry was already moving away for fear he could no longer hide the disgust he was feeling toward his father. He wandered toward the lavish spread, set up for visitors, of sweet breads, coffee, cider, and a decadent quantity of fresh fruit. The heavy silver had been brought out and arrayed upon a coarse black cloth. Henry reached beyond the pile of black grapes for the cut-glass Scotch decanter, and refreshed his drink. For the last two days he had felt as though he were barely inhabiting his own body. All around him, the machinery of mourning was in motion. The heavy black fabrics in conservative cuts had come out, along with the gravest faces. No one looked at Henry directly. They skirted him at a distance and nodded their sympathy in his general direction. A few of the bolder— or perhaps stupider—of the young unmarried girls covered their mouths with their hands and shot flirtatious glances in his direction. He was too sad to look at any of them. He felt sad for Elizabeth, but also for Diana. He felt sad for the whole, twisted mess. It was impossible to stop thinking of that look that Elizabeth had given him on the corner of Broadway and Twenty-first that Wednesday morning before the world got turned on its head. Her face had been so melancholy, and she had looked at him with such weary intelligence that he felt sure she'd known every bad thing he'd ever done.

"You have my sympathies."

Henry looked and saw the worn, once-handsome face of Carey Lewis Longhorn, the man the papers called the oldest bachelor in New York. He was in his seventies, and was famous for collecting portraits of society beauties. Henry was certain Elizabeth's likeness was in his collection.

"Thank you, sir."

"You'll be all right, young Schoonmaker." The old man turned his sad eyes away. Before leaving he patted Henry on the back and said, "I've always been."

Henry loitered near the refreshment table, and gazed across the parlor to the area of the room that Elizabeth's grieving relatives occupied. They had colonized several plush chairs and two paisley-printed sofas situated under a vast window. The Holland family seemed to have grown. What had always seemed to Henry a family of four was now a family of twenty or more. All of the cousins and aunts and uncles had stepped out of their private orbits, and now stood clannishly around Mrs. Holland and her one remaining daughter. The latter wore a short black veil that covered half of her face, and kept her gaze lowered so that it was entirely impossible to meet her eyes. Outside the rain was falling on Fifth Avenue just as it was everywhere, but Diana sat still and quiet and seemingly oblivious to the storm in the window frame or the storm all around her.

If in the last few weeks Henry had become ever more aware of the need to be a more serious kind of man, the last two days had made him one. The death of a girl from his own set in so illogical a manner alone would have been a cause to stop and reconsider. That it was a girl who he was to have been intimately connected with, and knew so little of, created almost unbearable guilt and anguish. Henry couldn't help but feel that if he had somehow been more respectable all along, none of this would have happened. And still he had to fight himself not to look in Diana's direction too often.

It was a kind of torture, to have her in his house and yet to be kept at such a distance from her. There were so many people crowding the parquet floor between them. She looked almost dainty in her black dress with the long, fitted sleeves, and her erratic curls hidden under her hat. Henry knew that she must be consumed with sisterly grief, and that the night they had spent together, trading secrets and kisses, must now be a corrosive memory to her. He longed to go to her and to know what she was feeling. He wanted to hear her voice assuring him that she did not blame him. That she did not hate him. But there was no way to draw her out from behind the wall of family that enclosed the Holland women, so Henry sighed and turned back to his drink.

"You look like you're in need of a friend." Henry took his eyes off his drink and saw Teddy Cutting. He peeked, and saw that Diana was refusing the food that one of her cousins was insisting she should eat, and then looked back at his friend. Teddy was wearing a black jacket and slacks, and in his lapel the white rose that many of the gentlemen were sporting. It had become the symbol of Elizabeth. Henry was not wearing one, but only because he'd put his coat down somewhere and could not be bothered to find it. No one was about to scold him for wearing only a vest and shirtsleeves and having unkempt hair on a day like today anyway.

"Yes," Henry answered simply. He allowed Teddy to take his arm and lead him through the rooms, thronged with visitors, adjacent to the parlor.

"You look pretty shaken, friend."

"I am."

"We should go out and help. Be active. The men dragging the river can hardly have the spirit we would have. Perhaps we should round up the crew of the *Elysian,* and head out to see what can be done."

"Perhaps," Henry replied moodily. They slowed, in a room none of the other guests had yet reached, and Henry realized that it was the dark red room where his engagement to Elizabeth had been announced. He thought back to how squeamish he had been about the whole idea of Elizabeth Holland then, how the very word *marriage* uttered aloud had made his heart shrink. He remembered thinking that if somehow she were to disappear he would be free, and he despised himself for it now. "I can hardly make myself want to do anything."

"It's so awful. So unbelievably awful." Teddy sighed, and blinked eyes red with sadness and fatigue. "The world seems changed today, don't you think? Do you remember how we talked at the racetrack?" He paused and shook his head with weary astonishment. "And now she's dead."

Henry remembered the things that he had said and could not look at his friend. He was only glad that Teddy had not been witness to the disconsolate expression that Elizabeth had worn on the day she died.

"Now you can go back to avoiding matrimony, and all the girls can go back to trying to bag you. . . ." Teddy attempted to chuckle and then looked at his friend when he did not laugh. "I'm sorry I said that. I didn't mean it. I'm just . . . shocked."

Henry nodded and put his hand on his friend's shoulder to let him know that he understood. He took a sip of his Scotch and sighed. "I keep drinking this stuff, but I can't seem to get drunk," he said quietly. "But thank you for talking to me. Just hearing you say anything is better than being alone in my head."

Teddy nodded. "Anyway, we've got to do something. What do you say we join the rescue effort? It will take your mind off things."

"Yes." Henry used his fingers to get his hair back in place, and then attempted a smile in Teddy's direction. "I'd like to do that. I would. It's just that Elizabeth's sister, Di . . . Diana. I'm worried about her is all, and I wouldn't want to leave without—"

"Without what?" Teddy looked uncomfortable all of a sudden, and the can-do color in his cheeks faded.

"It's just that I keep looking at her." Henry turned back toward the room where all the mourners were collected. There were several rooms in between, but he could see through the series of doorways the windows at the end. He couldn't see Diana at that moment, but he knew she was there amongst all those people. "And I keep wondering what she must be going through. She must be miserable. And I keep thinking how lovely she is, and that maybe in time—"

He broke off when he sensed Teddy's discomfort. Maybe in time, he had wanted to say, he could marry Diana instead. Perhaps that would be the beginning of everyone being happy again.

"Henry," Teddy said. He glanced over his shoulder and then looked back to his friend. "You're experiencing the loss of something that can never be replaced. I can understand that you might want to try. But what you just suggested . . . just don't say that again, to anybody. It's not right."

Teddy turned and began walking back to the main room. Henry, feeling stung and stupid, and wishing more than any- thing that he could turn his desire for Diana back into a secret, followed quickly behind.

"Teddy, I—"

"Henry, it's all right, man," his friend interrupted with a wave. A few seconds later, both their thoughts were broken by the cacophonous wailing that was coming from the great central drawing room. They moved forward slowly and saw, through the series of doorframes that separated them from that central stage of grief, the figure of a dark-haired girl sunken to her knees on the floor. Her black skirt made a cone-like poof about her lower body, and on her head rested a black velvet hat. There was no veil to cover her face, and so it was plain, even at a distance, that the loud crying was coming from Penelope Hayes.

"Let's go down to the water to see what can be done," Teddy said disgustedly.

Henry was revolted. He wished that somehow he could meet Diana's eye for a moment so that he could communicate to her how false he knew all of Penelope's hysterics were. He risked a glance at the Hollands' encampment, and just then Diana, still squeezed between two black-clad matrons, raised her veil and looked at him. Her eyes were sad and resigned, and he knew that she recognized Penelope's falseness, too. A man moved between them, toward Penelope, and for a second, Henry's view of Diana was obscured. When the man had passed, Diana's veil was back down, and Henry could not help but wonder if he would ever be able to gaze directly into her eyes again.

Forty Six

Society is too shocked to speak. Its members are too aggrieved to be seen on Fifth Avenue, or to throw the entertainments they are famous for. And today will mark the lowest day our city has seen in some time, for Miss Elizabeth Holland's funeral will take place at ten o'clock this very morning at the Grace Church.

—FROM THE "GAMESOME GALLANT" COLUMN IN THE *NEW YORK IMPERIAL*, SUNDAY, OCTOBER 8, 1899

*D*IANA HOLLAND HELD STILL AS CLAIRE CAREFULLY brushed and separated her hair for braiding. It was simpler than she usually wore it, but it was going to be covered by a hat, and anyway, it hardly seemed to matter anymore whether she was pretty or not. Her face had grown puffy and then gaunt in a matter of a few days. Over her shoulder, in the mirror, she could see that the milk-colored face of her maid showed almost as much wear from crying as her own. "It will be all right," Diana heard herself saying, although she hardly believed it.

"Oh, Miss Diana," Claire said, wrapping her arms around her mistress and squeezing her. "You poor dear."

Diana smiled faintly and let herself be coddled. "It's just still so hard to believe," she said, once Claire had resumed braiding her hair.

"I know. I know. But today you will lay her to rest before God, and then slowly it will become real."

Diana drew her fingers along the tender skin just

below her eyes, hoping to somehow make it look fresher. She had spent several days now in a prison of grief, surrounded by cousins and uncles and aunts. Their speech was always short and woeful, their food plain and miserly, and they moved between the Schoonmakers', who held a daily reception in the dwindling hope that some information on Elizabeth or her corpse would arrive, and the Hollands' own Gramercy drawing room. She would not have been able to escape the memory of her sister even if she had felt right about doing so.

Diana had done a wretched thing. She had known this on the day of Elizabeth's death, but the knowledge had grown in her, putting down roots and crawling up her spine ever since. She deserved to look plain. She hoped that she did.

"All right, you're ready now," Claire said. She had fixed the hat and veil so that Diana's puffy eyes were obscured. Diana stood and allowed her maid to check all the fastenings on her dress. It was one of the black serge ones she had worn while mourning her father, and it was extremely plain, with no trimming or color anywhere. The waist was corseted, and her torso sloped into its narrow confines.

"I wish you were coming with us."

"I know," Claire said, putting an arm around Diana and walking with her to the door. "But there is the meal to be prepared for later, and who knows how many will come—all of the Hollands surely, and poor Mr. Schoonmaker and his kin, and your cousins on the Gansevoort side, and . . ."

Diana leaned her head against Claire's shoulder, and as they walked down the stairs she continued to list all the things that would have to be done around the house before the funeral was over. It was soothing in a way to listen to this enumeration of ordinary things. When they reached the door to the parlor, Diana smiled and kissed Claire on the cheek and then went in alone. The furniture was draped with dark fabric, and the air was filled with the heavy perfume of the hundred or so bouquets that were crowding into the already densely packed surfaces of the Holland home. Bad weather had come to stay, it seemed, and the light that reached indoors was diffuse and moody.

Several of her relations, in their black outfits, acknowledged her with sympathetic eyes. Diana tried to look appreciative, but she was impatient for the ceremony to be over. The grief she was experiencing was of a most private, self-loathing kind.

"Oh, Di . . . Di!" Diana turned sharply and saw Penelope approaching at a hustler's pace. She looked shockingly beautiful in her black dress with its exquisite lace trimming and richly textured skirt. Her blue eyes were as fresh as after a dance, and her head was adorned with the thickest clump of ostrich feathers that Diana had ever seen. She was suddenly reminded of the word Henry had used to describe her. *Savage*.

"Oh, Di, how can you even stand today?" she gasped as she reached out for Diana's black-gloved hands.

"How can *you*?" Diana's tone was cool, and she drew back as she said the words.

"Well, I can't, of course." Penelope still had the conviction of her performance in her posture, but she had given up the quavering-voice part.

"Oh, yes. Right." Diana tried to keep her voice from rising, but she felt nothing but disgust for Penelope's fraudulent grief. Clearly, she was pleased by the turn of events. Already she was dressing up, in the vain hope that she might attract more attention now that her rival was gone. It was insulting that she should even think she was welcome in the Hollands' home. "Everybody knows how famously aggrieved you are, Penelope," she continued in a low, hateful voice. "We have all seen your tears. Why don't you quiet it down a little, so the rest of us can have some peace?"

"But, Diana," Penelope said, so quietly and intensely that no one else could hear, "I am sure I don't have any idea what you're talking about."

"You're a liar." Diana was glad for her veil. It muffled her voice and disguised the emotions now coloring her cheeks. "You're such an obvious fake," Diana added in a sharp whisper that was loud enough for Aunt Edith, standing only a few feet away, to hear.

Aunt Edith murmured to the Gansevoort cousin she'd been talking to, excusing herself. Within seconds Diana's mother was at her side. Penelope was still there before her, staring with wide, mocking eyes. But Diana's mother took her by the elbow, waved apologetically at Penelope, and pulled her daughter back into the hall. The pocket doors were drawn closed behind them.

Diana listened for her mother's rebuke but felt the sudden sting of a slap. She winced, more from surprise than pain. "What was that for?" she gasped.

"Diana, please, today will you be good? I cannot stand any more incivility. You are all I have. You must learn to uphold this family's name." Her mother's voice was slow and fatigued, and she implored Diana with red-rimmed eyes. Diana saw in a moment that her mother's whole world had come apart and that she could barely hold herself up. "Please do not disappoint me on the day we say good-bye to Elizabeth."

Diana bowed her head at her mother resignedly.

"Thank you. Now go into the lesser parlor, and when you are feeling all right, you will come back and join us for the cortege. You are clearly too agitated to be around people."

Diana wished she could say something reassuring, but she only managed a nod before she entered the room on the other side of the hall. The room she saw was completely changed. The walls were bare, and all the old hand-painted vases, all the trinkets and statues, had disappeared. The paintings that she had looked at, that day when she had first met Henry Schoonmaker, with their turquoise seas and black skies and desperate cases, were gone. There was not even a wilting bouquet left to decorate the room. Her poor mother—she'd sold everything. Diana sat down heavily on one of the old settees, and began to realize that whatever happened next to the Hollands was not going to be romantic at all.

There were footsteps in the hall—the Hollands' guests were leaving. They must have forgotten about her, for no one stopped to tell her it was time. She could hear them proceeding on noisy feet from the hall into the street on their way to the funeral. Penelope was one of them, pretending to be overwhelmed by her misery, the thought of which made Diana draw her hands back into tight fists. She took a deep breath and loosened her hands. She would have rather gone anywhere besides the church, but she couldn't hide from what she'd done.

The cold air touched her as soon as she stepped out of her family home. It was early in the year yet for such a chill, and even the park seemed to have taken on the dolorous quality of a more advanced season. Gazing at the glum day, so overcast it was almost black-and-white, she felt more alone than ever.

Up ahead, there was confusion on the curb. Her relatives and family acquaintances were trying to clamber up into their carriages with some dignity and were having a hard time of it without raising their voices. She looked up and saw that her own family's brougham, with Mr. Faber in the driver's seat, had already pulled away.

It was then that she felt the tug at her elbow. She turned to see that a boy had arrived at her side, as though from out of nowhere. He was the kind of thin that could not have seen food in several days, and his coat was patched all over.

"Are you Miss Diana Holland?" he asked, squinting at her.

Diana nodded cautiously. She could hear the last of the carriages departing, and wondered for a moment if she should chase after them.

"You're sure?"

"Yes," Diana replied indignantly. She noted the pair of horse-drawn hansom cabs loitering down the street, and told herself that they would bear witness if anything were to befall her. "Of course I'm sure."

"Don't look at me that way," the boy said seriously. "I was told that it was very important that I not give it to the wrong person."

"Give what to the wrong person?"

The boy shook his head. "First you have to answer the question."

"What question?" Diana's eyes widened at the absurdity and impudence of this exchange.

"The question about the Vermeer that your father gave to your sister, Elizabeth. . . ."

There was some instinct in Diana so deep that it overrode the gravity of the day and her sinking, guilty spirits. "He gave that painting to *me*!"

The boy narrowed his eyes and assessed her, before breaking out into a grin. "That's just what she said you'd say." Then he reached into his pocket and drew out a letter. It was in a square yellow envelope, and Diana saw her name scrawled across it in handwriting she knew very well indeed. "Where did you get that?" she breathed.

"In Chicago. I got my fare here in exchange for delivering this to you—to the girl who would insist the Vermeer had been hers."

"Thank you," she said softly as she ripped open the envelope, and read with frenzied, darting eyes the letter within.

My dearest Di,

Please forgive me for the scare
I've given you, and know how much
I miss you. What I've done I had

to do, because I am in love with

Will Keller. I've loved him always

and finally realized that marrying

Henry Schoonmaker would mean

a lifetime of regret. You were right

that it would have been a loveless

marriage, and while I hardly know

how I'll find Will, I now know

that I must try.

I am sure this must be very

shocking, and I can only explain

quickly: Penelope assisted in making

it look like I'd had an accident so

I could leave without it causing

a scandal, but she had her own
reasons for being so helpful. Diana,
she wants Henry for herself, and
she seems bent on getting him no
matter the cost.

Di, I know about you and Henry,
and you needn't worry. I'm not
angry, and I understand. But be
wary of Penelope, be discreet, and
don't let anybody find out about any
of this. You're the only one who can
know that I'm alive.

The whistle's blowing, I must
send this off. But be careful, and

remember what I said about

Penelope. I promise more news soon.

With love,

Elizabeth

When Diana finished reading, her headache had evaporated and a warmth was spreading across her chest. So she had been wrong. *Elizabeth* was the romantic sister, the one harboring a great love. *She* was the one who had stepped out of her life for an epic adventure.

Diana looked up at the sodden trees quivering in the breeze and felt reborn. She did not have to go on turning her eyes away from Henry forever. Elizabeth was alive—Diana had not driven her sister to the unspeakable. The world was still lying in wait for her. She gave one more grateful nod toward the boy, who was already wandering in the direction of Broadway. She tried to make herself look like a girl with a funeral to go to, but she couldn't help it. A radiant smile had spread naturally across all of her face. She took a breathless step forward and extended her arm in the air to hail a hansom cab downtown.

Acknowledgments

This book has benefited from the doting attention of many people, and I'd like to gratefully acknowledge them all. Thank you to Sara Shandler, who so gracefully juggles kindness and smarts, and to Josh Bank and Les Morgenstein, who manage to make stuffy conference rooms seem like such very fun places. Thank you to Lanie Davis, Allison Heiny, Andrea C. Uva, and everybody else at Alloy Entertainment. Thank you to all the wonderful people at HarperCollins, especially Farrin Jacobs for wanting to do this book and for her eleventh-hour brilliance. Thank you to Elise Howard, Susan Katz, Kate Jackson, Cristina Gilbert, Alison Donalty, Barb Fitzsimmons, and Ray Shappell. Thank you also to Claudia Gabel and Ben Schrank, who doted early on. Thank you to Ed Weidenfeld. Thank you to Janet Adelman and Bob Osserman. I am also indebted to all of the insanely knowledgeable librarians at the New-York Historical Society. And big thanks to Ben Turner, who bore stoic witness to more than one hair-pulling episode during this process.

Chris Mottalini

ANNA GODBERSEN

was born in Berkeley, California,
and educated at Barnard College.
She currently lives in Brooklyn with
her husband. For LUXE secrets and
gossip, go to www.harperteen.com/
luxebooks and visit Anna online at
www.theluxebooks.com.

For exclusive information on your
favorite authors and artists, visit
www.authortracker.com.

READ ON FOR A PREVIEW OF

THE EXCITING SEQUEL TO

Prologue

I have just been invited to a most secretive, but assuredly most elaborate, celebration in Tuxedo Park sponsored by one of Manhattan's finest families. I have been sworn to secrecy for the time being, but I promise my loyal readers that I will report all when the week is over and the general word is out. . . .

— FROM THE "GAMESOME GALLANT" COLUMN IN THE *NEW YORK IMPERIAL,* SUNDAY, DECEMBER 31, 1899

*I*T HAS BECOME ALMOST REGULAR FOR THE LOWER classes of New York to catch glimpses of our native aristocracy in her city streets, tripping in for breakfast at Sherry's after one of their epic parties, or perhaps racing sleighs in Central Park, that great democratic meeting place. But here in the country it is different. Here the rich do not have to suffer the indignity of being spied upon by a thousand eyes. Here in the snowy hills forty miles northwest of Manhattan, whatever business deal, whatever hustle, whatever random act of violence is being done back in the city, cannot touch them. For they and they alone are allowed in.

In those final, frigid days of the year 1899, the beau monde had escaped the city quietly, in small groups, according to the instructions of their hosts. By the eve of the New Year the last of them had arrived by special train to Tuxedo Park, disembarking at the private club's private station. There had been special trains all afternoon: one bearing orchids, another caviar and game, another cases of Ruinart champagne. And

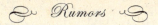

now came Schermerhorns and Schuylers, Vanderbilts and Joneses. They were greeted by coaches newly painted in the Tuxedo colors of green and gold and decorated with commemorative silver bells from Tiffany & Co., and whisked across the freshly fallen snow to the ballroom where the wedding would take place.

Those who had their own self-consciously rustic residences there—one of those shingled cottages, say, with touches of moss and lichen—went off to freshen up. The ladies had brought their historic jewels, diamond-tipped aigrettes for their hair, silk gloves. They had packed their newest and best dresses, although there were several despairing of being seen in gowns they had already been described as wearing over the course of what had been a rather unhappy season. The city's most charmed socialite, Miss Elizabeth Holland, had met with a watery end right in the middle of it, and nobody had felt comfortable acting joyful since. The best people had been sitting around waiting for January, when they might finally escape for cruises in the Mediterranean and other points east. Now, so near New Year's, with a blessed but unexpected fete on the horizon, the mood seemed likely to pick up again. One or two of the women mentioned, in low tones, as they dabbed perfume behind their ears, that the bride was reported to be wearing her mother's dress in the ceremony, which would add a touch of humility to the proceedings. But then, that was a sweet tradition and did not excuse any lack of modishness on the part of the guests.

Already they were being ushered, by liveried footmen, to the ballroom at the club's main building. They were being served hot spiced punch in little cut-crystal cups, and remarking how transformed the ballroom of Tuxedo was.

Down the middle of its famed parquet dance floor was an aisle, delineated with white rose petals, several inches deep. Bridal arches wrapped in chrysanthemums and lilies of the valley dominated the center of the room. As the guests began to file in, they whispered of the exquisiteness of the display and the high caliber of guests who had made sure of attending, even at such short notice, for the invitations had arrived only a few days before by hand delivery. There was Mrs. Astor, behind her dark veil, present despite the ill health that had kept her in for much of the season and prompted rumors that she was ready to abdicate her throne as queen of New York society. She rested on the arm of Harry Lehr, that winning bachelor, so often spoken of for his flare in leading cotillions and issuing bons mots.

There were the William Schoonmakers making their way to the front row, young Mrs. Schoonmaker—she was the second lady to wear that honorific—blowing kisses and adjusting her blond curls and ruby tiara all the way. There were the Frank Cuttings, whose only son, Edward "Teddy"

Cutting, was known to be such good friends with William's son, Henry Schoonmaker, although since mid-December the two had been seen out together only a few times. There were Cornelius "Neily" Vanderbilt III and his wife, née Grace Wilson, who as a debutante was considered too "fast" and had nearly caused her husband to be disinherited. She looked regal now, in lace-trimmed velvet panne, her auburn hair done up in elaborate curls, as much a Vanderbilt as anyone. But for all the well-born people taking their seats there were several who were notably absent. For amongst those hundred or so guests—a far more selective list than the four hundred allowed into old Mrs. Astor's ballroom—there was one great family unrepresented.

This omission was to many strange and, beneath the gentle string music that announced how very soon the ceremony would begin, one or two of the guests whispered about the absence. Meanwhile, the wind whistled around the building. The icicles hanging from the eaves glittered. The last guests to arrive were urged to take their seats, and then a set of groomsmen in black tails—not the shorn dinner jackets that were the namesake of the resort—moved purposefully to their places.

The last of them, Teddy Cutting, cast a glance back to be sure his friend was ready. As the music rose, the crowd nodded approvingly at the sight of Henry Schoonmaker, his dark hair slicked to the side and his handsome face imbued with a new maturity, taking his place at the altar. Was that a touch of nervousness in his famously rakish features? Was it excitement or was it trepidation? Then he, and indeed every set of eyes in the room, looked down the aisle, where the loveliest debutantes of New York, dressed in glacier blue chiffon, began to emerge. They moved in a slow march, one by one, across the little mountain of rose petals toward the front of the ballroom, trying as best they could to put away their girlish smiles.

When the opening strains of Wagner's processional played, the sylphlike bride appeared in the frame of the first flower-laden arch. The beauty of that girl was remarkable even to her family and friends murmuring in their seats. She was dressed in her mother's bridal lace, and a massive bouquet of frothy whites tumbled from her clasped hands. Her emotions were obscured by her ornate veil, but she moved forward to the altar with a steady purpose.

It was just as she took her place across from Henry that the door swung open and a young member of the staff appeared, breathless, and whispered into the ear of the woman stationed at the entrance. A cold rush of air was followed by a quiet gasp and then an almost inaudible murmur. The intermittent whispers that had begun before the ceremony doubled, then tripled, and now created a low hum in the room even as the reverend cleared his throat and began the ceremony. The

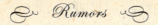

groom's dark eyes roamed across the room. Even the bride stiffened.

The reverend's voice droned insistently on, but the faces of the assembled no longer seemed quite so placid or joyous. A growing discomfort had reached the privileged class even here, where it was warmly ensconced in its winter palace, even on the titillating verge of celebrating the union of two of its brightest members. The eyebrows of the guests were raised; their mouths were open. It was as though, suddenly, the wilds of that city that they'd left behind were not so very far away, after all. Something had happened, and it would forever alter how they remembered the last days of 1899.

One

It has been a dreary few months in New York, given the death of Miss Elizabeth Holland—who was one of society's favorites—and the blizzard that arrived in late November and left the city blanketed for days. But elegant New York has not given up hope for a fine winter season of evenings at the opera and gay cotillions. And our eye has more than once been caught by the newly ladylike comportment of Miss Penelope Hayes, who was the best friend of Miss Holland during her short life. Could Miss Hayes inherit her mantle of impeccable decorum and congeniality?

—FROM _CITÉ CHATTER_, FRIDAY, DECEMBER 15, 1899

"EXCUSE ME, MISS, BUT IS IT REALLY YOU?"

The day was clear and bracingly cold, and as Penelope Hayes turned slowly to her left, where the crowd had massed along the narrow cobblestone street, she exhaled a visible cloud of warm breath. She focused her large lake-blue eyes on the eager face of a girl who could not have been much older than fourteen.

"Why, yes." Penelope drew herself up, willing the full effect of her slim frame, her elegantly ovular face, her incandescent skin. There had been a time when she was known as the pretty daughter of a nouveau riche, but she had recently taken to wearing the pastels and whites preferred by the demurest girls her age—although today, given the state of the streets she was traversing, she had chosen a darker hue. She extended her gloved hand and said, "I am Miss Hayes."

"I work at Weingarten the furriers'," the girl went on shyly. "I've seen you once or twice from the backroom."

"Oh, then I must thank you for your service," Penelope

replied graciously, then quickly added, "Would you like a tur-key?"

Already the procession was moving along ahead of her. The marching band playing noels had crossed onto the next block, and she could hear the voice of Mr. William Schoon-maker through the megaphone wishing the crowds who thronged the sidewalks a joyous season, and reminding them in as subtle a manner as he was able who had paid for their holiday parade. For the parade had been his idea, and he had financed the band and the traveling nativity scene and the holiday fowl, and he had arranged for various society matrons and debutantes to pass them out to the poor. They were the real attraction, Penelope couldn't stop herself from think-ing, as she turned to her loyal friend Isaac Phillips Buck and reached into the large burlap sack he was carrying.

Even through her dogskin gloves and a layer of news-paper wrapping, she could feel the cold squishiness of the bird. She tried not to show any signs of revulsion as she moved forward with the promised Christmas turkey. The girl looked at the package in a blank way and her smile faded.

"Here," Penelope said, trying not to rush her words. She suddenly, desperately needed the girl to take the turkey from her. "For you, for your family. For Christmas. From the Schoonmakers . . . and from *me*."

The girl's whole mouth hung open with joy. "Oh, Miss

Hayes, thank you! From me . . . and . . . and . . . from my family!"
Then she took the weighty bird from Penelope and turned
back to her friends in the crowd. "Look!" she caroled. "This
turkey was given to me especially by Miss Penelope Hayes!"

Her friends gasped at the prized bird and shot shy looks
at the girl in the fitted coat. Already they felt they knew her
from seeing her fantastical name so often in the society pages.
She stood before them as the rightful heir to the place in the
public's heart once held by her best friend, Elizabeth Holland, before Elizabeth's tragic drowning a few months before. Of course, Elizabeth had not drowned, and was in fact
very much alive—a fact Penelope knew quite well, since she
had helped the "virginal" Miss Holland disappear so that she
might more easily be with that member of her family's staff
she'd apparently been enamored with. And so that, more im-
portantly, Penelope could reclaim what was rightfully hers:
the fiancé Elizabeth had left behind. Her ascension was so
nearly complete that already society's most exalted matrons,
as well as its newspaper chroniclers, were whispering how
very much more Elizabeth-like she seemed now.

This was not something Penelope would have previously found flattering—goodness being rather overrated, in
her private opinion—but she had begun to see that it had its
advantages.

Penelope repaid the warm embrace of the girl's adulation

by lingering a moment longer, her eyes beaming and her smile as broad as it had ever been. Then she turned to Buck, who was highly visible in his coat of beaver fur that covered the length of his generous body.

"You've just got to get me out of here," she whispered. "I haven't seen Henry all day, and I'm cold, and if I have to touch another—"

Buck stopped her with a knowing look. "I will take care of everything."

His features were soft, muted by the fleshiness of his face, and his fair eyebrows were sculpted in a way that lent him the appearance of canniness. Penelope looked back up the street in the direction of the elder Schoonmaker's voice and knew that his son, Henry, with his dark eyes and his troublemaker's lilt, must be crossing into new streets along with him. Her heart sank a little. Then she turned back to Buck, who had already formulated a plan.

Buck moved now, as he so often had before, to shield the girl who most benefited from his loyalty. He had not been born rich—though he claimed to be a relation of the famous Buck clan who these days mostly resided in grand old moldering mansions in the Hudson Valley—but was invaluable when it came time to host a party, and as such was often given fine things for free. Penelope pulled the veil of her hat down over her face and followed him into the crowd. Once they had made their way safely through the throng, Buck dropped his cumbersome bag of turkeys and helped Penelope into a waiting brougham.

While Buck said a few words to her driver, she settled into the plush black velvet seat and exhaled. She removed her gloves in one deft motion and then tossed them through the open carriage door. Buck glanced at the slushy puddle into which they fell, and then took a step up and into the seat beside Penelope. As the wheels began to crunch across the rough pavement, he leaned forward and pulled a polished wooden box from underneath the seat.

"Kidskin gloves?" he said. "Or would you prefer silk?"

Penelope examined the slender white fingers of her hands as she rubbed them against each other. Most girls like her, whose fathers were industrialists or bank presidents or heads of their own insurance empires, changed their gloves three or four times a day as they moved from teas to dinner parties to intimate little musicales. But Penelope thought her hands were superior, and so preferred to change gloves ten or eleven times. She never wore the same pair twice, though her recently discovered virtue had inspired her to donate them occasionally. "Kid. It isn't warm outside, and you never know who you'll meet on a drive."

"Indeed," Buck replied as he removed a hand-sewn pair for her. "Especially when *I* am giving the coachman his instructions."

"Thank you." Penelope drew the gloves over her wrists and felt like herself again, which was for her always a good thing.

"They adored you today," Buck went on contemplatively.

"If only it weren't all so unbearable." Penelope let her head rest against the velvet. "I mean really, how many poor people can New York possibly hold? And don't they ever get sick of turkey?" She brought her kid-covered fingertips up to her high, fine cheekbones. "My face hurts from all the smiling."

"It is dull, always keeping up the pretense of being good." Buck paused. "But you were never one to lose sight of a goal," he went on delicately.

"No," Penelope agreed. "And I haven't."

Just then, the carriage came to a stop, and Buck put his hand on the little gold crank to lower the window. Penelope leaned over him and saw that they had come around to the front of the parade and now stood in the intersection look-ing down at the head of the procession. There was William Schoonmaker, both tall and broad in his black cloth suit. Beside him was the second Mrs. Schoonmaker, née Isabelle De Ford, who was still young, and who was currently a vision in furs and lace. They were framed in the canyon of tenement buildings, and they paused at the sight of the carriage in their path. In a moment Henry came up to their side.

Penelope's breath caught at the sight of him. There had

been a time when she saw Henry Schoonmaker almost every day, when they had been intimate with each other and with every secret corner of their families' mansions that permitted behavior not suitable to the maiden daughters of high society. They had done the kinds of things girls like Elizabeth Holland had been famous for not doing—until one day Henry announced that he was engaged to Miss Holland.

She had rarely been near Henry since then, and the sight of him now was like a concentrated dose. He still wore a mourning band on his left arm, which Penelope noticed even as she willed Henry to meet her eyes. She knew he would. And in a few moments, he did. Penelope held his gaze with as much modesty as she could muster, smiled an oblique little smile, and then pulled the veil back down over her face.

"It was a lovely parade, Mr. Schoonmaker!" she called out the window, resting her hand on the half-raised glass.

As she settled back into the velvet carriage seat, she heard Buck tell the driver to move on. But she wasn't thinking about where she was going. She was thinking about Henry and how very soon he would be done mourning Elizabeth. He was standing back there now, she just knew, remembering what kind of girl she was under the virtuous veneer, and all that had passed between them. And this time, it wouldn't be just stolen kisses in back hallways. There would be no secrecy and no humiliation. This time it would be for real.